DOWNLOAD INCOMPLETE

R. M. GAYLER

ISBN: 0986435201
ISBN 13: 9780986435201
Library of Congress Control Number: 2015936702
RAVG Publishing, Park City, UT

To Family

Chapter 1

High in the night sky a light burned, a pinprick pulse of amber hidden in the backdrop of infinite starlight. From the rift of both time and distance, a tiny probe emerged. It mapped the planet's surface and confirmed its destination. The cylindrical device no larger than a grain of common beach sand entered the outer atmosphere of the blue and white planet, maintaining a course to minimize the intense heat of entry and keep the airwaves free to beam a high frequency radio transmission.

Plasma formed around its thin ablation shield but didn't prevent receiving an answer, a greeting of binary digits from the billions of its kind waiting below.

As it dropped, the probe chewed though the summary data. Transporting an embryo of sentient life, the probe contained the data records of eleven failed attempts to incorporate the programming into a suitable recipient. Each attempt ended in death. The evolutionary progression of the dominant intelligent species had been insufficient to facilitate success.

The new data was suggestive, though not conclusive, yet worth the effort.

The probe entered the upper atmosphere, allowing gravity to finish its insertion process even as turbulent winds of the planet's jet stream battered the bioengineered device. Factoring in temperature and hundreds of environmental conditions, it assembled data in preparation for a multitude of possible landing sites. Drifting on the tail end of an atmospheric cold pattern, the probe sorted through billions of terabytes it had received from the enormous response to its signal.

A subroutine pinged. Command complete.

2.417 seconds later, the probe had its answer.

A highway paralleled a chain of desolate mountains rising from high desert sage-brush. One peak in particular jutted higher into the atmosphere than its neighbors. Small streams trickled down the west face to create draws lined with succulent trees, painting squiggles of color on the canvas of blue-tinged sagebrush. The busy artery of transportation gave a high probability of access to the most favorable host.

Conserving its dwindling fuel supply, the probe decelerated on a gentle circular breeze, falling into a canyon nestled in a remote area between the tall mountain and a smaller sister peak to the east. The landscape was thick with vegetation. Skipping across smooth river rock of a dry creek bed, it settled on a dead leaf. A puff of wind sent the tiny device whirling up then falling into a thin gap between the washed stones.

Concealed and secure, it established contact with *actives* within its limited range. It identified itself as an Alpha probe and transmitted two commands. It waited.

Three minutes passed. A small plume of chalky dust erupted from the ground. Resembling a miniature nuclear explosion, the mushroom of probes boiled, popping with tiny sparks of static electricity. The cloud gained volume, growing in exponential increments.

The mission had begun.

⋀

A billboard advertising a McDonald's Happy Meal at exit 185 triggered the memory of a four-year old boy, and Richard Preston's throat tightened. The boy, Andy, sat on the seat of the pickup next to Rich, and pointed at the sign with a chubby little finger, asked for a "hagamer", said he was "firsty". Rich reached for a bottle of water trembling in the cup-holder.

McDonald's remained a sad reminder of his dead son. He squeezed the steering wheel hard as he changed lanes, passing a shiny black diesel pulling a load east on Interstate 80.

There would always be something, even in the middle of fucking nowhere.

Two days ago, Andy's younger brother, Matt, a pimply-faced freshman at the University of Nevada, Reno admitted he was experimenting with Oxycontin pain pills and it frightened Rich enough to drive 375 miles, and give his son a necessary talking to, face to face.

By the time Rich reached the campus, he'd calmed down enough to realize any lecture on the evils of drug use would be ignored. The frat parties, the girls, the recreational drugs, all were a distraction from the grind of college. He let droopy-eyed Matt off with just a serious discussion on the addictive power of the prescription pain medication. He could only hope Matt's experimentation was a hiccup – not unlike his own escapades at Arizona State during the cocaine-laced disco era.

Besides, he'd had enough of trying to force changes on his children.

Damn, Andy.

He stepped on the gas, pushing the blue Ford F150 king cab to pass another truck. He massaged his right temple throbbing from a hangover. The air inside the cab reeked of stale cigarettes and spilled beer. And guilt. He'd spent his last night in Reno almost invisible amid the gamblers and video poker machines inside the noisy Silver Star Hotel and Casino, downing free Budweiser's served by buxom cocktail waitresses until he realized a precious four hundred dollars had disappeared into the insatiable gambling machines.

What the hell! It was almost worth four hundred bucks to put off going home to an empty house in Boise.

Rich pulled off the I-80 and into a busy Flying J truck stop in Winnemucca, Nevada. He rolled up the sleeves of his denim shirt while waiting for a hunter's muddy truck to move from the gas pump.

As his truck fueled, Rich again waited in line to purchase his water and snacks, including a miniature bottle of a five-hour energy drink. The customer ahead of him, a curly-haired hobbit of a man still dressed in summer Bermuda shorts and sandals, insisted on an endless debate with the store manager. Tilting his head back, Rich rolled his eyes and exhaled.

C'mon, Buckwheat. Move it.

He picked up the weekend edition of USA Today. A new superbug flu epidemic, Al-Qaida gaining strength in Whocares-istan, North Korea making noise about nuking the South. Lions, tigers and bears, oh my. Anything to scare people.

The hobbit moved on and Rich tossed the paper back atop the stack. No cash in his pockets, he swiped his MasterCard for the snacks. He shut his eyes thinking of the money he'd lost, and the airfare or gifts it might have purchased for the upcoming holidays.

Yeah right, Christmas died four years ago, in Afghanistan, with Andy.

With the truck idling, Rich tapped a text message to his wife, Cyndi. He checked his Gmail account and sighed. The government jerks wouldn't respond to his emails on Sunday, or any other day for that matter. Unwilling to wait for a response from Cyndi, he pressed the gas pedal and started for home.

"I'm a survivor, a winner, things are gonna change. I can feel it."

He'd been repeating that mantra he'd gotten from Rev. Card's self-help tape for weeks now, but he still wasn't feeling like a winner. He cracked open the driver's window to help blow some of the fog from his head.

Beneath a hazy blue sky, the early afternoon air held a chill from an overnight snowstorm that had dusted the mountain peaks of northern Nevada. Rich settled back, holding the truck's speed at eighty, five miles above the limit on Highway 95. The radio scanned the AM band on an infinite loop, unable to pick up either Hannity or the Rush Limbaugh Show. *Now, what's the problem?* He'd listened to them for five crystal-clear hours on the trip down. Their holier-than-thou rants were sometimes irritating, but it was a small price to pay to hear them eviscerate worthless politicians.

The truck engine revved as it downshifted to climb a steep rise. Farms and ranches dotting the landscape thinned out, and became rare in an ocean of sagebrush. Rich floored the gas pedal to pass a rusty flatbed truck. Off to his right, a cloud of white smoke erupted from the base of a mountain. The radio stopped on a channel awash in static.

A year ago, he'd have guessed the smoke was a sandstorm, the type commonplace around Phoenix, but in the higher elevation… the cloud seemed odd. The cold air flowed noisily into the window. His hand searched blindly for the pain relievers as his attention shifted to the static-filled broadcast of Hannity.

He tore a travel-pack of Advil open and gulped two tablets with the energy drink. His eyes lingered on the $4.99 price tag of the sour drink. Clenching the small bottle, Rich threw it hard, to ricochet off the passenger window. *Fucking banks!* They were the reason he was unemployed and financially shredded. With no chance of finding a job as an electrician in Phoenix, he uprooted Cyndi for a move north to Idaho. He swallowed the last of the bitter liquid, wondering if his decision to move away from family and friends was smart.

Topping the last of a series of rolling hills, Rich squinted at what were now plumes of smoke sliding down the mountain, like God was squeezing the trigger of a fire extinguisher. Rich eased his foot off the gas pedal and sat straight up. The source of the smoke had to be a dark black thunderhead sitting at the base of an arrowhead peak. The translucent gray-white cloud was easily thirty feet high, probably more. The top layer flew parallel to the ground, its leading edge tumbled and rolled as it raced toward the highway at an amazing speed.

Another memory returned and snuggled beside Rich, six-year old Matt holding his arm tight as he read excerpts from Stephen King's novella, *The Mist.* Cyndi warned him that Matt would be terrified, but the story of a grocery store full of helpless shoppers trapped by a heavy fog and menacing monsters was too good. Matt refused to sleep in his own bed for months, and with Cyndi's cold shoulder for warmth, Rich slept inches from a midnight fall to the floor. Patches of fog, low-hanging clouds, or lazy smoke always brought his mistake back to mind.

"What monsters lie within?" Rich lifted his eyebrows in mock horror.

Imitating his own father's ritual, Rich patted the dashboard of the truck with an affectionate hand. He straightened, checked the rearview mirror and geared up to pass a crimson Ford Taurus as soon as the smoke enveloping the highway had cleared. The sedan disappeared inside the haze just as its brake lights flashed red.

Rich switched the headlights to high beam. *I'm a survivor. I'm a winner, things are….*

Dust!

The stuff was dust, not smoke, or even fog. A beehive of chaotic dust particles swirled past the windshield. He closed the window. He'd driven into hundreds of heated dust devils in the Sonoran desert, and he knew a broadside of unusually fierce wind would hammer the truck any second. He gripped the wheel tight and glanced at the sagebrush and tall grass lining the highway, hoping to gauge the wind speed.

What the hell?

The shrubs and grass stood tall and dead calm. The radio volume suddenly increased, static surged from the speakers as if he had passed beneath high voltage transmission lines. The hair on his bare forearms stood at attention.

Hannity and static screamed from the radio.

And then the truck died.

Officer Clayton Crane of the Nevada Highway Patrol sipped sweet vanilla coffee as he waited for the cruiser's gas tank to fill. Life was good. It was a lazy Sunday swing shift. The traffic flowing in and out of Winnemucca's casinos would provide plenty of opportunities to find winners of his citations – and maybe a DUI - a Saturday night party animal could still produce a .08 into the breathalyzer. Keeping the highways safe and making his quota, all with out-of-towners. Yes, life was good.

Crane hummed an almost recognizable tune while stroking the corners of the Charger's ignition device. The high-tech vehicle was a reward for diligent work intercepting the influx of drug couriers. A few more drug busts, and he was looking at first-class travel, training seminars in D.C., and media accolades, at least from the local stations. He'd already been recruited for a new federal grant program aimed at curbing the influx of meth and heroin headed into rural Oregon and Idaho. Heck, maybe he should think about joining the FBI or the DEA, and really get in the game.

Gently setting his coffee in the cup holder, Crane started the car, and admired the mini-computer screens light up with colorful digital readouts, a touchpad of radio frequencies and even Google Earth. He smiled, remembering Captain Kirk and the Enterprise. He giggled to himself as he read 'Place Call' on the satellite radio display. At the end of the shift, he'd use it to call Melina, the rookie 911 dispatcher he'd like to ask out on a date. She'd get a kick out of it.

He exited the parking lot of a convenience store located twenty-two miles north of Winnemucca and gunned the high horsepower engine as he headed north for Oregon. A few citations to keep Captain Whitehead happy and he'd be back to Winnemucca for an early dinner. He figured to make the roundtrip three times in the eight-hour shift.

Topping a hill in Monitor Valley, Crane spied a cloud of smoke crossing the highway a mile away. The smoke sparkled like a giant diamond or was it lightning that had flashed from inside?

He eased off the gas pedal as the momentum of the cloud's movement stalled. The storm halted as if it had hit an invisible barrier. The smoke turned… solid? He blinked twice and checked the rearview mirror.

Dear Lord.

⚊

Bred and bioengineered specifically for the planet Earth, the Alpha probe had issued a high frequency radio burst. *Transmit all visual data. Prepare contact.* Dormant second-generation Beta motes within a 10-meter radius reactivated, replicating themselves until achieving a number sufficient to obey the command.

The Alpha processed the data streaming in, filtering it through a search algorithm predesigned for the mission. The tiny artificial intelligence operated with considerable leeway, but the Designers wanted this particular segment of the mission fulfilled. The search process returned with a positive, and a second signal ordered the dormant probes to accelerate the self-replicating process.

Spinning at super-collider speeds, individual Beta motes gathered the necessary molecules of inert matter - silicon, hydrogen, oxygen - and began to assemble the raw material into a functioning quantum lattice. Like a child's top spinning on its axis, the duplicate of the almond-shaped original disengaged and continued the process. The cloning required .956 seconds. Each new generation contained identical lattice technology, Designer programming, and the intact memory of the original. With an unlimited supply of zero-point energy, the volume of singular motes grew geometrically, a rate unfathomable to the human eye.

The Alpha issued instructions to the growing cloud of Betas; commence 'swarm' programming subroutines. With trillions and trillions of motes replicating each second, the swarm expanded like the smoke of a raging brush fire.

Each particle transmitted sensor data to the Alpha. The semi-aware artificial intelligence sorted and processed the low-resolution "pictures" from each single mote, then combined the data of millions, and transmitted a revised search algorithm.

Crossing U.S. Highway 95, the hive of computerized dust detected approaching metallic objects. One contained the subject, matching its requirements.

The alien computer rebooted, moving to second-tier instructions.

The new 'system' waited on standby.

A

With the sudden deceleration, Rich jerked forward, lurching into the seatbelt strapped across his chest. He felt a surge of adrenaline, unsure what was happening. The dashboard lights went black, the brake pedal and steering wheel stiffened, but he was still rolling and hadn't hit anything. His forearms hurt as his fingers squeezed the hard rubber of the unresponsive steering wheel.

He couldn't see through the weird fog, or dust, or whatever it was.

The adrenaline rush jolted his mind to start working again.

He turned the wheel gently right until the wheels chattered on the highway rumble-strip. The shoulder was wide and he braved the rearview mirror hoping his own funeral wasn't coming with the next vehicle plowing into his truck bed.

Nothing behind him but air as thick as a coastal fog bank. Hard taps on the brake pedal slowed the truck's progress into the gray. Searching for a level plot off the highway, he didn't see the crimson Ford Taurus until he was almost on top of it.

Fighting the steering wheel, Rich aimed for the matted grass tracks to the right of the red sedan with Oregon license plates. The truck bounced down the embankment, mowing down sagebrush before finally coming to a halt. At least he was out of reach of an oncoming semi. He released his foot from the brake pedal and flexed his fingers, already sore from gripping the wheel. A brief moment of relief, and Rich turned the ignition key.

Nothing. Not even the rat-tat-tat clicking sound of a dying battery.

Feeling foolish, he shoved the transmission lever into Park, and twisted the key again. Crap! No radio, no dash lights, nothing.

He hammered the wheel with his palms. "C'mon!"

Broken down in the middle of freaking nowhere. Lady Luck hadn't abandoned him, she had stuck around to laugh and kick sand in his face. Rich checked the side view mirror again waiting for a passing 18-wheeler to rock the truck. No traffic appeared through the few yards of visibility in either direction. Rich opened the door. The air was warm, smelling of ozone and sage.

He began a mental inventory of the emergency gear stowed in a bin on the rear seat. Two middle-aged women with Marge Simpson hairdos exited the red Ford. Rich slammed the door and slapped the dirty hood like a disobedient dog then walked around to the protected passenger side. The women approached, their voices animated with bickering.

Brushing gray dust off his hands, Rich hawked a wad of grit from his throat and spat.

Chapter 2

Millions of Beta probes were sucked into the air vents of vehicles penetrating the system, allowing the Alpha to process waves of updates on the biological life forms contained in each. The biological entity in the fifth vehicle satisfied the conditions for its search formula. With an expanded menu of choices, the rebooted alien operating system issued new commands.

"Search Completed. Initiate containment program."

"Initiate isolation subprogram IP23."

Akin to a fetus kicking the womb, the artificial intelligence nested within the Alpha probe's programming erupted with excitement. Tiny ripples of energy rolled through the system, like invisible waves on an ocean.

A birth was coming.

⚐

"Thanks for stopping!" one of the women said. "Can you help us?"

"Our car just quit!" The other said.

The twin sisters converged on Rich, cigarettes and perfume permeating the thick air. As soon as they came close enough for him to see them clearly, they both stopped, narrowing their eyes with suspicion.

Fuck me, Mildred.

Rich folded his arms across his chest. This kind of appraisal was nothing new. His olive-toned skin browned from decades of exposure to the Arizona sun, and jet-black hair graying at the temples often led people to assume he was Hispanic or Middle Eastern. And it always made a difference, at least for a moment.

He towered above the women and shook his head imperceptibly. "I didn't do it for you, ma'am. My truck quit, too."

"Don't know what happened," the first one said. "The car quit as soon as we hit this crap. Just a couple miles from the house, too."

Rich shrugged. "Then I…, I guess we're in the same boat." He stepped back, checking the road for a car or semi. His standoffishness was palpable and probably a reason he was lonely in Boise.

"Wonder why nobody else is driving by?" the second woman said. "It's Sunday, for God's sake."

The first one put on the rimless eyeglasses hanging around her neck. "This is a strange fog, rare around these parts. But I've seen it before."

"Yeah, it's pretty weird." Rich glanced at each woman, then towards the mountain range where the fog had originated. The ridgeline was clear against the blue sky. Rich swatted at the dust like an unwelcome stench and the particles swirled like fanned smoke.

The first woman pointed down the road. "Looks like help is on its way."

Dulled by the haze, the flashing red lights and emergency strobes grew brighter, and Rich thought he might have caught a break.

"Oh, my heck, aren't we lucky." One woman exclaimed.

"Well, you should've been lucky at poker last night."

"You didn't help throwing that flush away for a longshot."

"That's what JJ says you're supposed to do if ya have four to the royal."

"C'mon, let's go tell him about our car. Maybe he can give us a jump." The first woman shouldered her purse, and pulled her twin by the arm.

Rich shook his head, but was satisfied the distance between him and the two chatterboxes was widening.

"We'll have him call you a tow truck, if you want?" one said over her shoulder.

Rich gave a meager wave, reminding himself they were only trying to be friendly.

Rich blinked. Was the fog parting in front of them? The crap opened up as if cut by a sharp knife, then zipped closed behind them.

Weird.

A sudden grip of claustrophobia made him open the rear door, to retrieve some things before beginning his own walk of shame.

A list began formulating in his head. Call Linda, the dog sitter, make sure she fed Brooke tonight. Call his wife, Cyndi, and maybe the kids. No. One phone call to Cyndi and she could call anyone who still cared. Besides, his stepchildren, Nikki and Noah, probably wouldn't take his call anyway. Rich reached into the front seat for the iPhone, staring aimlessly at it as his thumb stroked the dust off the glass. He would've called Andy first. Andy would have appreciated his predicament. They would've laughed, reminisced about their own two-hour hike out of the White Mountains, abandoning the same truck tilted on two flat tires. The quail hunt a bust, but it was still fun. Andy was non-stop talk, excited that his basic training was finished, but nervous about being deployed to Afghanistan.

Bitter bile tasting of grape energy drink rose in the back of his throat. Rich swallowed hard and squeezed the phone. Three times his call to Cyndi showed 'CALL FAILED' on the screen.

"Great. Pile it on!" Rich said.

Rummaging through a plastic storage bin that had rubbed a nasty red stain on the blue leather seat, Rich inventoried the items he'd packed for an emergency. He had hoped to coax Cyndi into exploring remote sections of Idaho someday, so they had packed one of Matt's old Hurley book bags with emergency matches, a whistle, compass, water purification tablets, and his old Army poncho. None of which would help him now. But the backpack was a convenient way to carry his jacket, water bottle, and phone. Rich's mouth watered remembering the jumbo-sized bag of trail mix Cyndi had stashed in a side pocket. He groaned as he pulled out the empty plastic packaging folded neatly inside and threw the trash next to the empty bag of pretzels.

He threw the pack over his shoulders and adjusted the straps. At least he was wearing his hiking boots instead of the sandals he usually wore on long road trips. A final check and he decided the old 12-gauge double barrel shotgun hidden beneath the overnight bag was on its own. Nobody would give him a lift and he'd look like a hillbilly walking down the side of the highway with a gun slung over his shoulder. He reached over the front seat to grab the half-empty Aquafina bottle and slammed the door shut.

The air around him was soup, an ugly clam chowder, far thicker than it had been when the talkative sisters were here. A rustling came from the gray fog. Rich cocked his ear, then jumped back as a skinny black-eared jackrabbit rushed past him, brushing his pant leg before disappearing beneath the truck. Goosebumps rose on his arms. The two women and their chatter would be welcome now. The strobe lights of the emergency vehicle had disappeared in the gloom, but he was positive it hadn't passed by. The thickening haze played havoc with his internal compass, and he felt unsure of which direction to turn. The fog parted as if a breeze blew, revealing a narrow alley shaded in dull sunlight.

Rich swallowed gritty spit, his throat burned from the bile.

What monsters lie within?

All macabre enjoyment was lost with his first step towards home.

Blocked by a wall of solid dust.

▲

As the cruiser crested the hill, Crane checked his seat belt. The cloud engulfed the highway. A brush fire? Maybe a bored farm boy doing donuts with his tractor in a dusty field. But the westerly flow of smoke had stopped, as if hitting an invisible wall.

He'd seen some bizarro stuff cruising State Route 375, the infamous Alien highway adjacent to Area 51. On the lonely graveyard shift, he'd seen odd formations of light, streaks of fluorescent plasma in an endless night sky. His butt twitched, remembering sitting parked beneath cottonwoods at the turnoff to Hiko, his cup of coffee rippling, then splashing on his leg as if Spielberg's T-Rex was coming. He searched for the source of the vibrating hum but drove away convinced that some machine buried beneath the ground was the cause. He said nothing to avoid the ribbing and cajoling from the snarky veterans.

The cloud was at least thirty feet high, miles in width. Crane switched on the flashing emergency lights and slowed to a crawl. Three vehicles had stopped a few hundred yards short of the enormous cloud.

Why hadn't the desert breeze dispersed the smoky mass?

Passing the first vehicle, two middle-aged women wearing jeans and light winter jackets emerged from the cloud.

Aw, hell, Ladies, just hang a cardboard sign on your back asking a trucker to mow you down.

Rolling past a Subaru Outback, the cruiser's high-tech engine died.

He turned the wheel hard to the right, passing a rust-eaten Dodge truck, and rolled to a stop. The drivers of the stalled vehicles all seemed to open their doors simultaneously. Crane clicked on the police radio's handset. "Base, copy?"

Nothing.

"Base, copy?"

Drivers and passengers of the stalled cars began to drift toward one another. Crane climbed out and eyed the lane where a trucker, driving blind, could emerge at any second. "Get out of the road! Everyone! You're going to get hit!"

"We couldn't see a thing in there." one of the ladies said.

"And the cars don't work in there, either." the other added.

"That doesn't mean a truck ain't coming! Now get over here!" Crane swept his arm for emphasis. "Everyone, move to the passenger side of your vehicles!"

Crane wiped his chin, and took in a big breath. Behind him, a column of cars and trucks was growing, but at least the driver at the front had showed the common sense to stop 200 yards away. He raised both arms, gesturing for the driver to stay put. An 18-wheeler would emerge from that cloud any second, barreling along at 70 mph.

He just knew it.

"Now what's going on with you two?" Crane opened his trunk with a metal key - needing a few moments to find the keyhole - and slipped into a neon orange emergency vest. He inventoried the emergency road kit containing flares and bright orange cones, but his concentration was bombarded by babble from the two women.

"Our car broke down in the dust."

"The other guy's truck did the same thing."

"We weren't speeding, just driving home from the casino."

"You were speeding, Jo."

"How would you know, Miss Asleep in the front seat?"

Crane held up his free hand, his index finger pointing to the sky. He took a deep breath, and issued a loud shush.

"Now you." He pointed at Jo for no particular reason. "What's going on?"

"Well, we were driving home, not speeding mind you. Our turnoff is just past McDermitt, and when we went into that fog, the car just quit. I mean nothing, no lights or anything. I had a heck of a time keeping it-."

"Did you actually pull your car off the road?"

"Well, sure. I don't really…it was too thick. You could hardly see a thing."

"Did you feel the rumble strip?"

"Oh, that's right. Yes, yes I did."

Okay, even with zero visibility they hadn't parked in the middle of the highway. "You mentioned another guy? Where is he?"

"Oh heck. We have no idea. We left him standing by his truck, right in the middle of that… stuff, whatever it-."

Crane closed his eyes for a moment. "Was his truck off the road?"

"Oh my heck, yes. It was practically in the brush."

"You're sure the truck was off the road?"

'Well… I believe so. But you couldn't be sure which was up inside that stuff."

"The guy was definitely not from around here." The other interjected, earning a stern look from Crane.

Although he needed to do ten things all at once, the safety requirements of motorists came first. And that meant verifying that both the two knuckleheaded women and the guy with the truck had actually pulled their vehicles off the highway. Then he could allow the mounting traffic to proceed safely. He would caution them to drive slow and keep their headlights on. After that he could deal with his own car problems with a phone call.

He ordered the women over to a creosote fence post beyond the asphalt, then placed the orange cones at evenly spaced intervals back to the idling vehicles.

"What's going on?"

A tanned farm girl leaned out the door of her idling Chevy truck.

"Please stay in your vehicle, ma'am."

Crane studied the cloud closely as he approached it. The breeze was light, chilly but had no discernible effect on the wisps and tendril edges sprouting from the cloud. The black road ahead completely disappeared. Any hope of a farm kid doing dusty doughnuts faded. This was something much bigger.

An on-coming tractor-trailer roaring through the cloud stuck in the back of his mind, he slowed his pace. The cloud was thickening. No, it was solidifying. Crane blinked. It was smoke, or dust, or fog but couldn't be solid.

He bumped into the soft warm wall and took a quick step backwards.

His heart was thumping. What the hell? He poked his finger into the white wall. Penetrating it a few inches, like pushing a finger into beach sand, the first few inches hot and soft, then then hardness of compacted sand. Electricity bit into his finger and he jerked his arm away.

Or had the sand pushed him out?

And what about the guy with the truck who was still in there?

The vetting of the human candidate was complete and the system had completed a subroutine expunging the other human objects from within its current domain. The surrounding air molecules were analyzed and atmospheric elements native to the planet were allowed to pass through the system's membrane. Scanning the area a thousand meters beyond its perimeter, warnings of additional mechanical devices converging on its location were transmitted to the Alpha.

The operating system executed a subroutine ordering 73,333 trillion Beta motes to produce a low-level electromagnetic pulse. Splitting molecules of hydrogen simultaneously, the Beta probes released charged electrons, creating an intense burst of electromagnetic energy radiating out from the system. The energy, similar to that generated by intense lightning strikes, covered a wide length of the EM spectrum. The surge destroyed delicate electronics, phones circuits, radio equipment and the computer chips contained in the mechanical vehicles approaching the system. The electronics in vehicles ceased functioning.

Preventing physical objects from penetrating the system, the countless Betas intertwined using an advanced form of covalent bonding. Electrons discharged by the electromagnetic pulse no longer belonged to a singular probe, but were shared by the mass of tightly condensed motes. In a more complex molecule than hydrogen, covalent bonding involved the outermost electrons, but the probe Designers extrapolated the concept, using the engineering matrix to enhance mote technology. Tightly bound as a single entity, the system produced an impenetrable sheet of small probes. The resulting connection insured the kinetic energy of bullets, speeding vehicles, or biological probes would find a thickness of motes twenty-nine times greater than the opposing force.

The subject was isolated.

A new menu of options became available, and the next phase began.

CHAPTER 3

Rich stumbled and fought to keep his balance. The toe of his boot had bounced off… solid dust? Tufts of green grass beneath his foot were layered in the gray soot. He shook his head to awaken his brain muddled by alcohol and rattled by caffeine. He kicked the sand again.

"Son of a…?"

The wheat grass, sagebrush, and the red of the truck's taillight were all disappearing, the white stripes of the highway barely distinguishable. Rich reached out and immersed his arm in warm granules, the dust tightened, pushing it back out, as if it were alive.

Rich checked his hand and found it clean. Whatever it was, it didn't stick. He wiped his sweaty brow.

He jabbed the gray substance turning darker in front of his eyes. It returned to its original shape like a soft sponge. He couldn't swallow, his throat was dry and coated in grit.

"Hey!" His voice cracked. "Hey! Hey, ladies! Can you hear me?" The walls seemed to absorb his voice.

He closed his eyes, fear and confusion jockeying for the lead of his racing thoughts. *Wake up! Just wake the hell up!*

He opened his eyes. A seamless gray sheet surrounded him. Except for a narrow tunnel of clean air, leading to a mountain peak shrouded in clouds. Rich made a break for the truck door, and slammed his forehead against the wall, his skin tingling from a sensation of electrified sandpaper.

Not possible. Not possible.

Rich took two tentative steps towards the mountain. The sky was alive, turbulent with puffs of gray.

"No! That's not the way I'm going!"

A quick 180-degree turn back to the truck. The space behind him had vanished, replaced by undulating grey dust filling the void.

Like a mime in a box, Rich tested the walls with his hands, and kicked them with his boots. But these walls were real, all too real.

"Hello? Can anyone hear me? Hey. Hello!"

The sound died as if he were in a coffin.

He wasn't lost. He knew exactly where he was - on a busy highway with traffic and the police a scant fifty feet away. And he couldn't get to them.

Dammit, this wasn't a horror movie - there were no monsters or ghosts hiding in the gloom. This was the desert of Nevada. Only rattlesnakes to be afraid of. And yet, he was terrified. He wasn't even sure he was thinking straight. But he had little choice.

Maybe he could walk towards the mountain and circle back around after finding the edge of the cloud, fog or… whatever the hell this was.

A risk free plan. Maybe fifteen minutes at the most, to find a way out of this crap, then reverse course and back to the highway. The truck couldn't have traveled too far without power. The silence and warm air unnerved him, but there wasn't anything particularly threatening about it. Three deep breaths, and against his own instincts, he began walking.

He weaved his way through thin gaps between the dense sagebrush, probing the walls with his hand, searching for a soft spot or opening. The spongy electrified sensation slowly became his new normal.

Rich hiked up the corridor the dust had left exposed, expecting to step clear of it any second. The myriad of other possibilities – that the dust wouldn't let him go, or close in on him...

He refused to think about that.

Rich pushed through the waist-high sagebrush, and within minutes, his thighs felt raw from their sting. The route dropped him into a dry creek bed scattered with football-sized boulders bleached white with alkaline. Gnarly branches protruded from the gray walls like boney claws.

Crossing the rocks, careful not to snap an ankle in one of the crevices or holes, he began to prefer the sagebrush. At least the ground was flat. Slapping the odd walls, his hands tingled from the electricity. The fifteen minutes was up. He turned around.

Nothing but the gray. It was like he'd never even started.

Disorientated, he faced the mountain again. He sighed and continued hiking.

The fuzzy outline of a jackrabbit, sitting between clumps of sagebrush. He bent down and squinted at the normally skittish animal. It stared back, unblinking, locked in place. He smacked the spongey wall with his hand, felt the electrical charge run up to his elbow, but the rabbit held. He couldn't tell if it was even alive. He resumed his rock hopping.

This had to be some kind of secret military crap. Nevada was the perfect state for it - Area 51, nuke testing, and poor Mr. Rabbit had to call it home.

Thirty minutes of stumbling up the dry creek, the terrain began to level out and the boulders transitioned to smooth river rock, the sagebrush disappeared, replaced by rusty canyon walls disappearing at an easy angle into the gray. Rich reached into the backpack's netting and eyed the water bottle -- a quarter full -- and took three huge swigs.

Since abandoning the truck, the walls stayed a comfortable distance away, a few feet out of reach, but twice Rich stumbled and the electrified walls gave him a nasty jolt as he recovered his balance. The terrain was easier to negotiate, but now his maneuverability was increasingly restricted as the vertical canyon walls painted with alkaline waterfalls inched closer together.

He stopped, a thumping noise, getting louder.

A helicopter. They were looking for him, or maybe others trapped in this crap.

Rich turned one hundred and eighty degrees, resolute in his determination to return to the truck, and found the gray closing in.

⋏

A giant egg was laid across Crane's section of Highway 95, miles in length, maybe miles in diameter.

And impossible! Absolutely, positively impossible!

His hands raw and red from probing the coarse dust, so Crane poked the cloud with an old wooden survey stake, looking for some kind of weakness, even a soft spot, searching for a way to understand what the hell the thing was. His thrusts penetrated the surface a few inches, earning him two painful splinters in his palm but the object's broken granite texture was unmarked. He threw the stick back into the sagebrush. A few minutes of tapping the stuff with a dead flashlight and he realized he wasn't going to learn anything more than what he already knew. It was time to take care of the people he could reach.

He gathered the stranded motorists who had waited patiently watching his futile probing, and herded them back to a growing line of vehicles that disappeared around a curve of the highway. The farm girl leaned against her truck's grill smoking a cigarette. He commandeered her cell phone, relieved it had power, and adequate reception. Crane called his shift supervisor, Mark Tuttle, and tried his best to explain the situation.

After listening to remarks about Crane spending too much time on the Alien Highway, Tuttle promised to advise the Oregon State Police to investigate from the north.

Crane ended the call and stared awestruck at the massive white object. Tuttle's promise of sending four tow-trucks, and additional police backup seemed like throwing buckets of water on a forest fire.

He looked up to locate a helicopter sounding its arrival into the Monitor Valley.

In less than a minute, the throbbing grew thunderous as the KVBT-12 news chopper crested the mountain ridge and dropped into the valley from the west. The thing circled wide over the …the egg, doubtless looking for the best angle for its cameraman. It hovered a mile away then began to move in close.

Crane looked at all the stalled cars nearby. They had been disabled for a reason.

He flipped open the phone and tapped buttons looking for the redial command. He had to tell Tuttle to call the station's dispatcher before…

It was too late. The sound of the chopper's engine sputtered, and the motor cut out. The tail began spinning counter clockwise to the main rotors. The chopper wavered then fell in a downward spiral, slamming head first into the desert floor. The rotor blades sheared off one by one. The choppers dented and bruised body twisted, metal groaning, and settled onto its side, engulfed in a bloom of silt.

Crane stomped his foot. Freaking idiots, looking for a story without thinking about the danger. He found redial.

"What is it now," Tuttle said.

"Don't talk, listen. The KVBT new chopper just drilled into the desert floor a hundred yards from where I'm standing. Whatever this thing is, it's killing anything electronic that comes anywhere near it. Get the word out – no choppers, no planes, no nothing."

He hung up before Tuttle could reply. He grabbed his first aid kit and ran toward the wreckage.

$$\lambda$$

The physical exertion of the hike helped take the edge off the anxiety – it was harder to be scared when you didn't have the energy for it. His thoughts just drifted with the monotony of the next step. Rich thought of Matt, learning to live on his own for the first time. He thought of Cyndi working in Park City, and his own lack of employment – he was going to have to swallow his pride and move to join her. He thought of Cyndi's twins, Nikki and Noah, and their remarkable business success back in Phoenix. He wasn't their biological father, but he'd considered them as his own.

He thought of Andy, and the U.S. Army and their flat refusal to explain the manner of Andy's death in Afghanistan, not even when Senator McCain and Congressman Pastor had pressed the issue.

He thought of his own guilt, and sighed.

He couldn't think about that, not now.

He sat down in his small open area, surrounded by three sides of gray wall and rummaged through the backpack, taking inventory. The pack was a great idea though outfitted with cheap, "I'll never need it" stuff. He pulled out the waterproof match container. Maybe he could build a signal fire? The sound of a helicopter told him a search had to be underway.

Rich pulled out a match, struck it on the strip on the bottom of the container, and held it up against the gray. No combustion, no retreat, even black soot from the flame marked the dust for only a moment before it was absorbed. Matches in hand, he walked another thirty feet down his narrow corridor, gathering small dried branches, leaves and twigs. When he had enough firewood, he assembled the precious twigs into a coned shaped steeple. Rich touched a match to the smallest twigs in the center then smiled as the wood burned with dry intensity. As quickly as the fire flamed it began to burn out, but his confidence was surging. He spied a nice juniper branch just five feet ahead. He jumped to grab the twig, and raced back - into the spongy gray wall.

The meager fire was swallowed by the dust, just like the jackrabbit. The flames were gone, the fire's gray smoke joining the enemy.

Rich bared his teeth. "What are you?" He punched the wall.

His hands trembled as he returned the matchbox. Flinging the pack over his shoulder, it bounced and hit his head. The dust was right up against him, stroking his shoulders at each side as he moved ahead. Stepping back to avoid a small cactus, Rich felt the spongy fog on his shoulder blades, buttocks, and on his heels.

One way only, forward, up a slot canyon of strange gray dust.

The backpack held to his chest in a death grip, the realization hit him like a gunshot at pointblank.

He was being forced.

Funneled.

Like a cow to a slaughterhouse.

Chapter 4

"Let's go, keep moving." Crane waved the driver of an Odyssey minivan to move forward.

The Hispanic driver wasn't listening, neither were his wife, or the three kids crowding the front seat as they craned their necks to see the massive grey cloud riding the highway like a weighted balloon. The woman's mouth was agape, a wad of gum waiting on her tongue.

Crane glanced over his shoulder and heaved a sigh. He slapped the van's hood with his palm. "Move it. *Andale.*"

The task of redirecting hundreds of cars, trucks, trailers, motorcycles and semi's jamming the northbound traffic lane was daunting. It had taken ninety minutes for backup to arrive, but somehow he seemed to be the one in charge. The Nevada Highway Patrol had blocked any incoming traffic at Pole Line Road, a mile north of Winnemucca and Oregon state police had effectively shut down US 95 at the community of McDermitt at the state line. Isolated feeder routes used by ranch trucks and farmers needing access to the highway were quickly intercepted by patrol cars and diverted. It was now safe to turn traffic around and clear the congestion.

The whole situation was like Disneyland on steroids. Drivers abandoned their cars to stare at the huge apparition. Friends of city council members and police chiefs were allowed through the blockades, as were media vehicles. Gawkers stood everywhere. Everyone wanted to be a part of ... whatever it was. He couldn't say he blamed them, but it wasn't making his life easier.

And no one knew what the thing was, how could anyone know if the thing was dangerous.

Crane pointed a finger at two college age girls walking up the highway shoulder towards the cloud, their phones held out to snap pictures.

"Any closer young ladies and you'll be buying new phones." He'd placed three cones across the road as a demarcation point, where all electronics seemed to die.

They looked at him, and whispered, and giggled, and kept going.

Crane's attention shifted to a utility van from KNBC-3 news in Winnemucca. He watched the van sideswipe a stalled car and pause near two ambulances waiting to transport the helicopter crash victims. The van continued, angling into a flat area Crane was using to turn around the troublesome 18 wheel semis. The van's door slid open and two men jumped out. One was readying equipment, the other primping in the side mirror.

"Out. Now!" Crane yelled.

The driver approached with open palms, "Look, we need a staging area. This is national news, and people have a right-"

"Get that van out of here."

Camera lights fired up, annoyingly bright even in the afternoon sunlight. The reporter rushed by, the cameraman in his wake.

Crane shook his head, and let the warning about electronics die on his lips. Let them figure it out for themselves.

He tapped the roof of a black Lexus. "Keep it moving."

⅄

Rich's heart pounded with an increasing sense of claustrophobia.

His mantra popped into his head, and he repeated in a loud voice. "I'm a survivor. I'm a winner, things are going to change… and fuck this."

He ran hard, sidestepping the largest rocks, bouncing off the stinging walls like a pinball, the water bottle sloshing in his backpack. An ancient cottonwood blocked his way ten yards ahead, its broad umbrella canopy decapitated by the gray ceiling. Clear on the other side, had to be. Had to be! Sucking in air and grit, he'd slip past the tree trunk on its right. Over his shoulder the gray fog closed in, zipping shut in his wake. He sprinted harder as the tree disappeared, closing the last window of hope. Rich spat grit collecting on his tongue, lowered his head and rammed into the gloom. He sank into shallow sand, the skin on his face and arms tingled with vibrating electricity. A shockwave ran down his spine, into his hips and paralyzed his legs.

Adrenaline surged into his nervous system, but the fight or flight hormones were useless. His fingers were pried open by dust swelling in his hand. The backpack fell silent to the ground. His body convulsed as it was submerged in a bath of warm sand. His eyelids blinked furiously, watching in horror as the grayish white particles merged, forming an impenetrable barrier. A semi-solid tomb.

His mouth filled with hot sand. He resisted the involuntary spasms of choking. He said a final goodbye to his family, one he'd practiced for years, comforted that his wife Cyndi would be better off with him dead. No more pain, or anger, or bitterness in her life. He regretted not being able to tell his children not to worry, that death was painless, and colorless, and lonely. Was Andy's death so easy? Tears clouded his vision. He gagged as a lump of sand slithered down his throat. Would Andy be there to greet him in the afterlife, could he finally get the answers to questions he'd spent years searching for?

Rich's eyelids ceased blinking, pressed shut by the weight of a limitless dust.

Isolation and immobilization complete.

The Alpha probe rotated thirty-eight degrees. Using fuel stored in its propulsion module, it fired its thrusters. Almost weightless, it rose into the ocean of computerized granules. Like worker ants to the queen's arrival, the Betas parted, opening a tiny tunnel for the Alpha to reach the man's face. Insufficient fuel reserves to make it into the optical nerve, the probe entered the man's left nostril. Using the last of its fuel, it burned through nasal membranes to follow a route encoded in the integration subprogram. Using the telemetry provided by the millions of Betas the man had swallowed or inhaled, the Alpha monitored the man's irregular heartbeat, shallow respiration, noted bodily fluids at substandard but not dangerous levels, and catalogued his decoded DNA.

With a map of the human's anatomy stored in memory, it traveled with the man's oxygen supply system, through veins and capillaries, passing through the ventricles of the heart, into the carotid artery and up to the brain. The probe scanned for distinct electrical signatures of certain brain neurons. With short bursts of thrust, the probe entered the jugular, veered into a narrow vein, and extended barbed landing nodules that clamped it in place in the soft tissue.

Spider-web lines uncoiled from the probe's body, disseminating into the pliable gray matter. The insertion module was complete.

A communication subroutine executed. Intercepting a single neural pathway, the probe followed the impulse, analyzed its terminus and released the pathway. A second pathway was searched. Each unique impulse was treated identically, and at an increasing speed. The mapping process continued as the artificial intelligence began to extrapolate, interpret and learn from Rich's memories.

The Alpha's programming did not include changing the candidate's physical health, at least not at this time. Currently, it was concerned with establishing a seamless means of communication with the operating system. The frontal lobe of the candidate's brain was an optimal location for insuring efficient data transmission.

The probe's download routine executed.

The transmission of the massive amount of scientific data, star mapping, chemical and molecular physics and a communication program required to complete the Designers' mission began. The transfer process required 1.23 rotations of the planet's surface in relation to its sun.

Eleven thousand years ago, the Designers' first candidate died during the process.

To avoid the same failure, the Alpha's subroutines were rewritten, though not tested.

⚔

His breathing was difficult, his short raspy breaths sucked in mostly gritty soot. But Rich didn't feel as if he was suffocating. Whatever the dust was doing to him, it wasn't killing him.

A shrill noise began to resonate in his head, like a MRI machine had switched on. He shuddered. The tones reverberated intermittently, randomly, but they weren't coming from his ears. Something tickled deep inside his head, an itch that couldn't be scratched.

What was happening to him?

Rich flexed his arms, and tried to wiggle his fingers loose, wanting to tear out the biting insect burrowing deeper into the center of his brain. His cocoon constricted, tightening its grip.

Pictures began flashing; mathematical formulas, wooly mammoths, giant planets, tornados, insects, brilliant star clusters, strange symbols. With no symmetry or organized order to the images his rational thoughts began to drift and join the procession. He concentrated but was unable to hold any one image for more than a microsecond. Was this life flashing before his eyes. But it didn't look anything like his life.

So whose life was it?

Rich clung to the question for a fleeting moment, then lost consciousness.

Cyndi Preston was bone tired and stretched out on the twin bed in what she called her Ann Frank bedroom. She pulled her shoulder-length chestnut hair free from its ponytail, rolled over and began to scroll through the *Park Record's* online-classified section for rental homes. There was nothing affordable this late in the season.

The weekends spent alone were getting harder. Rich refused to leave Boise, Nikki and Noah were home in Phoenix, and Matt was now in Reno. But she had a job, and one she truly enjoyed.

Cyndi was eight inches shorter and four years older than Rich, a beautiful dark complexion, and an athletic figure could still attract a man's attention.

At least Rich had picked a good time for his impromptu visit with Matt, but he refused to tell her exactly what prompted it. Her flight scheduled to Boise wasn't until the following weekend, so Cyndi spent the day searching for late fall flowers or wildlife to photograph in the fertile Provo River bottomland. The droves of fly-fishermen had made the effort even more difficult.

A hot shower intended to wake her up only made her wearier. Cozy in cotton pajamas, Cyndi began downloading her photos onto her Mac, discarding most, flagging others to share with Rich or the kids.

As she ate an apple and soaked up the sunny afternoon, Cyndi had made up her mind, to settle the chaotic living conditions eroding her marriage and family. Rich wasn't having any luck finding work in Boise so he'd just have to pack up and move again. Boise was okay, the people were friendly, but their savings account balance was dropping each month. Airfare, food and maintaining a second household was expensive in a ski resort community. Rich would sulk like a child for a few months but the matter was settled. She wielded the power of the only paycheck.

Unable to fight off sleep any longer, she texted Rich. *Please call when you get home.* The hills outside her window bathed in a full moon. Rich had probably turned down some lonely dirt road to explore some nameless new lake or river he would want to fish next spring.

Too weary to look for the television remote, she decided to skip *60 Minutes* and crawled beneath the covers.

▲

By late Sunday evening, the airspace surrounding the alien egg was swarming with eight news helicopters, all respecting a two-mile no-fly zone recommended to the Federal Aviation Administration by the NHP. The object was three miles along its axis, a half-mile wide and thirty-six feet high, reaching over fifty depending on the tendrils of dust undulating up from the surface in a chaotic rhythm. A dark nucleus, like an egg yolk, was buried deep in a shrouded rocky canyon.

And it was now the center of the world's attention.

A small army of police, emergency workers, fire personnel, news trucks and weather experts joined a swelling crowd of onlookers. A road paved in trampled sagebrush, courtesy of three ranch hands using high clearance 4 X 4 trucks connected the bisected highway, a safe distance from the egg. Traffic on the rowdy impromptu road created a genuine plume of dust that drifted into and around the alien monstrosity.

Crane walked alongside Captain Lou Tabot, rehashing the story of the Williams sisters' emergence from the object, his probing of the substance, and the helicopter tragedy that took the life of a female news reporter and sent two others to the hospital. Wasting two hours for the ten-minute drive from Winnemucca, Tabot was fuming when he finally climbed out of his car. He waddled past Crane's useless cruiser and poked the object with his right index finger. Tabot jerked his arm back and rubbed his wrist.

Like a sponge, the small intrusion into the egg returned to its original shape and texture.

"I'll guarantee you this is something the military let loose!" Tabot spat and looked the thing up and down, "Guaranteed!"

"So call em." Crane said. "Let them clean up this mess. This is getting uglier by the minute."

"Oh, I'm sure they're watching the news just like everyone else." Tabot stuck his finger out to touch the cloud again but held back. "And I'm sure at least two governors have called them. Who else got caught in there?"

"The twins said something about some other guy's truck wouldn't start either."

"So this other guy is still inside?"

"I assumed the guy walked out the other side, probably hitched a ride with one of the rerouted vehicles."

"Hard to walk away from a circus like this," Tabot said. "Still, there's not a lot we could do even if he was still inside."

While making the slow crawl up from Winnemucca, Tabot had called Crane and ordered him to maintain a secure perimeter of a thousand meters around the object. Crane had tried his best, but even after reinforcements had arrived, there wasn't much of a perimeter. Tabot's chubby jowls reddened and he put his hands on his hips. Foolhardy hikers pushed through the sagebrush to reach the object, only to stand like statues staring at dead cell phones.

Tabot was deep in thought as they returned to Katy's Ford truck. The smart girl sat on the tailgate selling her twelve-ounce plastic bottles of water for five dollars each. Katy had been heading home with six cases and though not setting any records, the chubby girl was already ripping into case number three intending to raise the price. Tabot picked his cell phone up from the truck's hood and checked his messages. Crane watched Katy jump from the tailgate, her ample bosom bouncing beneath her thin yellow blouse.

He'd memorized her phone number.

Crane arched his eyebrows as Tabot shook his head, ending the call. "That was the governor. CNN is reporting the substance contained in the cloud is radioactive. Fox says there's a possible link to a terrorist plot by Al Qaeda."

"What'd you tell him?"

"The truth. I haven't a clue of what it is." They walked back to Tabot's car parked in the sagebrush, "I'll get you as many men as I can spare. Try to get a real perimeter around this thing. Maybe we can…"

Sergeant Rodriguez jogged up to them, panting for air. "Sir, the media wants a briefing for the latest."

"Latest information?" Tabot looked at the thing. "They know as much as we do."

"Maybe that's what you should tell them." Crane said.

Tabot stared at the top of the egg. "Nah. Let his honor the Governor do it when he gets here."

⚔

Cyndi woke up with her thighs stiff and her calves sore from climbing the Provo River's steep rocky embankments the day before. She reached for her iPhone, expecting to see Rich's text or missed call. Her golden retriever, Brooke, holding her beloved rope toy, smiled back. But no message from Rich.

He could be so inconsiderate.

She looked up Rich's contact info listed under ICE (In Case of Emergency) and dialed. She expected him to pick up with a sleepy voice, but instead listened to his monotone telling the caller to leave a message.

"You never called and thank you very much for worrying me all night." She hung up with a touch. She'd teach the old dog a new lesson.

Showered, and dressed in Monday's mango scrubs, Cyndi heard the phone's ringtone for her brother, Doug, her roommate in the two-bedroom condo.

Putting down the eyeliner she'd been fidgeting with, she thought Rich had better be the one to call next if he wanted to prevent a problem from marring their reunion next weekend. She pushed it from her mind. Rich was going to be stinky enough after her ultimatum.

"Hi."

"Hey, need me to pick you up?" Doug said.

"That would be nice."

A dentist, Doug Abrams, moved to Park City to build a new practice after the Great Recession had put an end to his plans of an early retirement. Weary of the heat in Phoenix, he moved to *'where the money is'* and convinced Cyndi to manage his new start-up. After all, the pair had achieved success with Doug's first practice. Doug's wife and children remained in Phoenix until the new business could generate enough money to secure his large family's relocation to Park City. Flying home each weekend to see his family, Doug didn't usually return until his first appointment each Monday.

"What's the schedule like today?"

"We're pretty booked till 4:00 and then just hygiene after that."

"Good, I can get to the gym early. Hey, what do you think of that crap going on in Nevada?"

"Haven't been watching. What stuff?"

"That's just it, nobody knows, a giant cloud, or egg, or something blocking a highway. It's all over the news, it's the only thing on the news. Helicopter crashed, somebody died, it shuts down electronics that get too close. They don't know what it is. Some channels say its radioactive or terrorist crap, stuff like that. Anyway, I'm heading up the hill and will be there in thirty. Bye." He hung up without pause.

Cyndi dropped the eyeliner, and ran into the bedroom, switching on the old color TV crowded into the closet. The news came up immediately. She sat down on the edge of the bed to watch and listen. A strange cloud of an unknown substance disabled vehicles and electronic devices within 500 yards, according to the continuous crawl beneath the talking heads. Plenty of people willing to talk about it but it became clear they didn't know any more than what the crawl said in two sentences.

A cold chill rose on the skin of her bare arms as she looked closely at a map of Nevada when it came up again. Labeled with a red star, the town of

Winnemucca was the closest population center. A man was presumably still inside an impenetrable object blocking U.S. 95.

Her fingers flew to her lips, she gasped.

Rich drove that highway.

Chapter 5

By Monday morning, the news media had shifted into overdrive, inundating viewers with stories related to the mysterious cloud blocking a highway in rural Nevada. Stories detailing the amount of traffic normally traveling the highway; the economic impact of isolating the surrounding communities; of people who couldn't get home; of people who wouldn't go home; any angle an imaginative producer could conjure.

A massive revolt against the Islamic regime in Egypt was mentioned only on the crawl. North Korea's saber rattling rhetoric accusing the U.S. of releasing a weapon of mass destruction was used as an appetizer for talk show hosts, and paid pundits, and so-called experts to give their varied opinions on what the cloud was, or speculating what it might be, or what authorities should do next.

CBS reported the Geiger counter borrowed from the School of Mining at the University of Nevada at Reno confirmed no signs of radioactivity. CNN's Anderson Cooper was broadcasting live from the site as of Monday afternoon, telling Wolf Blitzer about touching the cloud, the sensations of sticking his fingers in warm sand, and the object pushing them back out, with a measure of electrified enforcement.

An enthusiastic Anderson Cooper fan, Crane had slyly escorted the reporter into the "quarantined" area for the exclusive report.

Citing reliable sources, the 'fair and balanced' Fox News reported that military researchers at Groom Lake Air Base, known as Area 51, just 120 miles south of the cloud site had accidentally released a secret government experiment.

ABC, CBS and NBC News dispatched their marquee anchors, each intending to broadcast their Tuesday night edition live from the site.

The media darlings du jour were Jo and Dot Williams, matronly twins routinely referred to as "cloud survivors". The gregarious women talked to anyone who listened, about a ghostly presence they sensed inside the cloud, their struggle to find a way out, and their narrow escape with their limbs still attached. Asked if they saw anything or anyone in the cloud, they would briefly mention the strange man with bloodshot eyes and dark skin. They quickly dismissed him. "We think he walked back to Winnemucca".

Every news organization assigned a junior producer or intern to locate the Williams sisters' missing *Winnemucca Man* and get his story.

Winnemucca was thriving. Every motel was booked solid, room rates raised to exorbitant levels. The small casinos overflowed with new customers; technicians, producers, equipment handlers, and drivers. The media swarm was not shy in spreading their wealth.

And spending hours of primetime news coverage on something they literally knew nothing about.

⚔

What she'd seen on television was terrifying, mostly because it was so… mysterious. Cyndi dialed Rich every chance she had, still leaving plenty of time for scary scenarios to race through her imagination, one after another, until she settled on her husband being caught up with the mass of people observing the egg. Matt Lauer of **The Today Show** had described phones as being 'fried' by the object's electricity. Hundreds of cell phones rendered useless. Rich's was probably one of them. It would be just like him to stick around. He'd argue with the authorities to the point of arrest if they tried to make him leave.

But he would have contacted her by now.

Her tendency to imagine the worst was nerve wracking. If someone was ten minutes late for a dinner, Cyndi imagined an auto accident. Thirty minutes and they might be dead, struck by lightning.

She called Linda, the dog sitter in Boise, but she hadn't heard from Rich either. Cyndi suffered through Linda's long-winded description of Brooke's evening walk around the small ponds near the house then asked her to keep feeding the dog until she heard back from her or Rich.

Doug texted he had arrived and was waiting in the car. She grabbed a jacket and ran for the door.

She climbed in the Escalade and threw her bag between her feet. "Thanks."

"Sorry I'm late. The airport was a zoo. Flight's delayed and even cancelled 'cause of that egg thing, I might not be able to fly home this weekend, it's gonna get worse."

Cyndi bit her lip but she couldn't hold it in. "I think Rich is the one missing inside that thing."

Doug hit the brakes, "What? They're not even sure there is anyone inside. Everybody walked out."

"He texted me when he was leaving Winnemucca. Now I can't get through to him."

Doug shook his head. "Have you seen the crowd around that thing? Probably having the time of his life, chasing reporters around, trying to get them to investigate Andy."

They arrived at the office building, and she mulled the thought while the underground garage's door lifted. That would be exactly what Rich would do. She sat back. It was comforting to have her younger brother's perspective. He was able to see things more clearly than she did and rein her in.

Cyndi relaxed her grip on the door handle. "That would be like him."

Minutes later, Doug unlocked the front door of the office and Cyndi followed him in and dropped her purse on the desk. She ignored a stack of checks needing to be deposited and headed to Doug's private office, and turned on the television. They were still recycling the same lack of information.

For the rest of the day she stayed busy with phone calls and patients, and she couldn't get back to the television. She found herself short and edgy with the patients - disastrous for a new practice building a client base - she practiced a lot of deep breathing. The happenings in Nevada were a convenient icebreaker for new patients filling out paperwork, and Cyndi listened to the strangers for any new developments.

The whereabouts of the missing Winnemucca Man was never mentioned.

⅄

Not exactly asleep, yet not fully aware, Rich couldn't tell if he was lying down or standing, floating in warm air or submerged in water. Thinking with any clarity was difficult and erratic but at least he wasn't dying. His out-of-control mind streamed pictures like an slide show stuck on fast forward. Math formulas, engineering schematics, unusual sea creatures, geometric domes, buzzing insects, giraffes, velvet-red roses, nebulas, and clusters of galaxies.

The star clusters, those were the most disorienting. He was somehow aware of their size and brilliant colors – and how gravity held them together. Infinitely beautiful, impossible to conceive but they were the only thing he could hold onto as he fell deeper into a black abyss.

⅄

Doug shook his head. "Pretty sure it has to be 24 hours before you can file a missing person's report. You sure Rich isn't still in Reno partying with hookers and co-eds?"

Cyndi glared. Sometimes she wanted to slap him. His flip remarks meant to be funny would anger her. Two months ago, she texted him a perfect photograph of a beautiful red-crested Sandhill crane nesting in a field and he'd texted her back - *Thanksgiving turkey, shoot it.*

She turned her back and left his office. Rich would be irritated when he found out she called the police. Since Andy's death, uniforms were like waving a red cape at a wounded bull. But at this point she didn't care, she had to do something.

Cyndi began twisting a strand of hair above her ear into a tight corkscrew. Did she call the Ada County Sheriff in Boise, where he lived, or the police in Reno where he had been visiting, or the police in Winnemucca where he might be staying?

The staff trickled out, and Doug headed to the gym. Cyndi sat on the edge of her seat and called her daughter, Nikki, needing some emotional support before calling the police. Nikki's business-like voice told her to leave a message.

"Hi, just checking in. No big deal. Call me when you want to catch up." No need to worry her daughter with her unfounded fears.

She called 411 for a connection to the Ada County Sheriff's department and waited on hold for 23 minutes before a female operator finally answered and asked Cyndi the obligatory question,

"When was the last time you spoke to your husband?"

"He texted me about noon yesterday, he was just leaving Winnemucca and heading home."

"You do realize that a lot of people were blocked on 95 yesterday? I think you might want to wait another day to file a report."

Maybe she was right. Maybe Rich was hanging out at the cloud, maybe Rich's phone was toasted by the egg's weird pulse. Cyndi ended the call still twirling her hair. Maybe Rich was right. The police were useless.

Until you needed them.

Biting her cuticles, Cyndi stared aimlessly through the waiting room's wall of glass as the last of the sun faded. She had called Matt earlier, with the hope he'd heard from Rich but he rarely answered, responding only to texts. He was no different from most teenagers, and his friends were paramount. Two months away from graduating high school and he announced his intentions to get as far away from Phoenix as student loans would get him. She hoped he would've stayed close to Nikki and Noah, and the support they could offer.

She tapped out a text on the iPhone - *call me about Dad.*

Cyndi turned her head towards the hallway and the voices of the television news, then tapped a text to her son, Noah. Her phone strummed with the ring-tone set for Matt.

"Hey Matt, how's it going?" Cyndi said.

"What's up with Dad?"

She swallowed, "I haven't heard from him since yesterday. Have you?"

"Nah, just when he left Sunday morning."

"I'm nervous, it's not like him to just disappear and with all that news about Winnemucca I'm not sure what to do."

"Jeez, you know Dad. He was talking about driving up to Alaska and working on a crab boat or something. He's been acting a little sketchy ever since…"

"I know."

Matt sounded tired. "A lot of the people were driving to Winnemucca. Sociology class was almost empty. He probably got caught up in it."

"You're probably right, but I had to check," she said.

Cyndi put an encouraging spin on the conversation, asking about dorm life, roommates, and she told him she'd text when she heard from Rich.

Rich *had* turned moody and resentful after Andy's death, but Matt had seemed to bloom socially, burning candles at both ends, as if he was trying to live two lives at the same time.

Cyndi decided to skip her gym workout and locked the office door. Her old Jeep Cherokee still parked at the condominium, she began the short walk home. She called Nikki again.

Nikki answered immediately.

Cyndi's words came in a torrent.

"Slow down, Mom," Nikki said. "There's no one missing in the cloud. The grandmother twins said the missing man hitched a ride back to Winnemucca."

Cyndi slumped to sit on a concrete curb, and rubbed her forehead.

"Maybe that was him inside," Nikki said. "But he walked out with those ladies. His phone's dead and he's trying to figure out how to get home. You know he's not gonna leave that stupid truck."

Rich did walk out of the cloud, just a few steps behind the two sisters. Nobody saw it. Nikki was right. Rich wouldn't leave his truck. It had been Andy's. It made perfect sense. Mystery solved. Tears streamed down her cheek.

He'd call any minute. His story would fill in all the missing pieces. Cyndi anticipated it. She expected it.

Except he didn't call.

Chapter 6

Rich fell hard onto the rocks, curling his legs into his chest, his mind drowning in a sea of stars. His eyelids fluttered open. A hammer pounded iron inside his head, keeping pace with the beat of his heart, but he had some control over his mind again. His hand rose to shield his eyes from the light. The images in his mind raced at incomprehensible speed and he reached for something, anything to stop them.

Cyndi in a tropical print bikini walking on the beach of Lanai before their wedding, a willow-lined pond at a familiar cabin in Montana, his family posing for a photograph atop a mountain ski resort, Andy in a blue cap and gown at high school graduation – all photo's shuffled as a screensaver on Rich's laptop. He willed the pictures into the painful stream of alien symbols, blue planets, and three-dimensional diagrams, forcing them to take hold until the speed of the unrecognizable pictures slowed.

Rich blinked and focused on a dead leaf inches from his face, concentrating on its ridges, veins, and intricate scalloping along its edges. The musty smell of warm moist earth wafted upwards. The gray floated like heavy fog, but it gave him space. He trembled with the memory of his truck hitting the dust storm, the anxiety of his hike to the tree, the terror of being buried alive.

His throat was parched. His right thumb began to trace the seam of his jeans. He wiggled his toes then other bodily sensations returned. An overwhelming thirst made Rich roll onto his back and stare at a bright sun muted by the dense cloud of dust.

He was alive.

Satisfied with his weak effort, Rich fell into unconsciousness.

A nervous little man escorted three men down a long sterile hallway. With their hair buzzed to military precision, three men dressed in tailored gray business suits slowed to look through tempered panes of glass and examine a busy encapsulated clean room.

"You'll have to follow established protocols," the escort in a white lab coat said.

The men undressed, and hung their garments on stainless steel hangers. With naked assessments completed, each stepped into a shower stall for a ninety-second rinse followed by a drying with powerful exhaust fans.

A short bulldog man said, "Too much to ask for a towel?"

A tall muscular man responded, "You follow the rules. But it's worth the effort, my friend."

They put on fresh, disposable jump suits made of synthetic fiber. Donning hoods and masks, the three moved in unison through a laminar airflow curtain. They stepped into an airlock of negative air pressure.

The narrow clean room glistened in sheets of polished white fiberglass, the joints flawlessly sealed with an impenetrable locking mechanism. Fluorescent lighting hung in an orderly geometric fashion, illuminating three-meter wide stainless steel worktops running the length of the room. The men passed an enclosed room containing computer monitors wired to microscopes operated by workers with heads shrouded in hoods. They glanced up from their work but otherwise ignored the three visitors.

The men stopped at a table supporting a glass storage device with aluminum tubes protruding from both the bottom and top. They stooped and peered into what looked to be an empty aquarium.

"They activated just about the time that cloud in Nevada showed up." The escort said, his voice muffled by a mask. "You can see them better on the monitor over here." He pointed to a flat-screen monitor, black as night though pricked by dabs of starlight.

"Why?" the tallest man asked. "Why now?"

"Don't know yet," the escort said.

"Can they get out?"

"The particles are enclosed within a redundant, miniaturized clean system. Unless the tempered glass breaks, nothing was supposed to escape."

"Supposed?"

"At least fifteen have winked out since that cloud appeared."

"Winked out?"

"Gone. Just disappeared. Not sure how, maybe they self-destructed, maybe combined with another, I don't know.

"Have you been able to decipher how they float?"

"We think it's their lattice design. Catches air aerodynamically. Like a dust mote floating in sunlight, but with some sort of control mechanism. An amazing configuration."

The escort walked over to the flat-screen monitor and pointed, "The active particles haven't been confined for analysis yet. Any method used so far, chemical or mechanical has destroyed their fragile composition. The inactive buggers dissolve with the slightest touch, but I'm sure you knew that, sir."

"Interesting. And they've come alive now?"

"Yes, sir. But not 'alive'. They aren't biological. Spectral analysis reveals the things are active with minute energy signatures. That's what you see on the screen. Like tiny fireflies."

"What kind of energy signature?"

"It's like nothing we've ever seen. But we'll figure it out."

The tall man leading the group looked at the two others, waiting for input.

The bulldog man spoke, "What do you think, David?"

"I don't believe in coincidences. I'll call the Minister, but I'm sure he'll want to proceed as we discussed."

Rich's eyes fluttered, his arm twitched, but the pain of a full bladder woke him. He remembered the nightmare, the fog, and he sat up in the faint morning light.

The blanket of living fog receded from his every movement.

The urge to pee made him stand up and his thirst was powerful. The particles recoiled from his hand reaching for the backpack. Was it afraid of him? His hands were shaky as he pulled the bottle out, unscrewed the cap and guzzled the last inch of water.

"What are you?" he whispered.

In an instant, his brain exploded with images; an ovoid shaped waffle, mathematical formulas, strange syntax and a three-dimensional object labeled with strange words. He dropped the bag and clutched his head.

"Stop!"

The images stopped.

He sucked air in huge gulps. Then the urge that woke him reasserted itself. He unzipped and let go, groaning with relief.

"You'll let me leave, right?" He felt foolish talking to the dust but feeling foolish was the least of his problems.

The dust parted.

He squinted.

Was that the dark blue of his truck miles away? He picked up the backpack, and a wave of dizziness and nausea buckled his legs.

His thoughts drifted to Cyndi and he began scratching the coarse stubble on his cheek. She was going to rip him a new one for wandering off like a small child. But he could explain. Certainly, she would believe him, about the fog forcing him to hike into the hills, and then burying him alive.

Sure. Who could ever doubt a story like that.

His eyes traced the creek bed cutting through the sagebrush.

My truck?

The swarm parted, thrown back as if Moses himself commanded it, revealing the length he had traveled. Three miles at least, maybe five. His thirst burned.

He rummaged through the bag, unable to remember how much water he'd started out with. He pulled the phone from the bottom expecting the device to be useless, and he pressed the power button with trembling hands. He concentrated on Cyndi's picture of the Boise River reflecting a sunset. 10:44, Tuesday, November 11. He'd been out for more than two days. Two dots revealed cell service but the battery symbol was red.

The cool water in the picture was tantalizing. And two days? That explained the foul odor wafting from his armpits and crotch.

Rich laughed, sending pain down his parched throat. His thoughts wandered as he entered the wrong pass code into the phone's lock four times. Colorful icons dazzled his eyes on the fifth attempt. What would he say? The fog was alive? It killed his truck? Water. He needed water. But he couldn't remember. Cyndi would think he found a cocktail waitress and had a good time. Andy would help.

Andy?

He wanted to laugh at the absurdity of his thinking, but his swollen throat screamed 'don't'. He slumped to the dusty river rock, sitting like a guru with no audience. He balled his fists.

Think, man.

He tapped the message icon to find Cyndi. Eyelids fluttering, holding on to consciousness, he tapped in a message. She deserved to know he was alive, at least.

He hit the send button with a shaky finger and watched the progress bar of the text message stop before finishing. The phone dropped from his hand.

Rich fell over, dehydration taking its toll.

Seconds later the phone dinged, message sent.

$$\blacktriangle$$

The Alpha had downloaded a high percentage of the information stored in its memory, filling Rich's grey matter to capacity, with files containing the chemistry, mathematics, physics, and engineering constructs deemed necessary by the Designers to complete the mission. Also implanted, were 16-byte off-line addresses for files containing the planet's development and ecology, gathered by the Betas for decades. Everything the Designers needed to complete their mission.

Every available memory space in the man's brain was used, but the data inserted was unsorted, unorganized and difficult to access. The human candidate's existing memories, relatively small files, were decrypted and cataloged for future input/output. The man's language structure was deciphered, but the process of communication was one sided.

For now.

Rich's brain stored more information than the human race might acquire in a thousand years, perhaps five thousand years.

But Richard Preston didn't know what he knew.

Chapter 7

By Tuesday morning, the media staging ground was buzzing with activity, resembling an anthill of motorized vehicles agitating the desert, creating a cloud of beige dust that often rivaled the greyish-white object of their attention. Film crews jockeyed for different camera angles, using the cloud as a backdrop for their broadcasts. Producers promised rewards to the growing number of forest rangers, BLM hotshots, military observers, and NHP officers in return for their strategic assistance. Journalism interns paraded their unique talents to executives, with hope of furthering their careers. Technicians called for additional power generators, wider bandwidth for satellite uplinks, and more palatable food.

Celebrity reporters demanded side-stories, unique and undiscovered by their competition. The media's air force swelled to twelve helicopters that circled the valley like vultures. Afforded the best view, the pilots christened the object, 'The Egg'.

People who had made physical contact with the mysterious substance were located, interviewed and allowed to contribute their two cents to the stream of conjecture. The darlings of the special group known as 'cloud survivors,' Dot and Jo Williams, overplayed their hand. Telling a story that had become increasingly fraught with danger, punctuated by a daring escape, intending to extend fifteen minutes of fame into thirty. Mainstream news began to back away from the pair.

Police cruisers, fire trucks, forest service vehicles, elongated motor homes, and mobile generator trucks scarred the landscape around the system. Nondescript men and women dressed plainly in denim jeans and work jackets blended into the bustle, observing, taking notes, and documenting people of interest. Others occasionally stopped to talk or listen using wireless earpieces.

Agents with the Department of Homeland Security mingled with their counterparts of the FBI, CIA, NSA and other government agencies. Like dogs marking their territory, the DHS barked the loudest.

After thirty-six hours of non-stop police work, Clayton Crane stood at the open door of an NHP cruiser idling on the shoulder. The radio inside was non-stop chatter. His skin felt filthy with dust, his scent hung in the air. He was finally given a day off to recuperate from the overtime. He thought he might need more. The madhouse was overwhelming.

He climbed into the car and nodded to the driver to go. He scratched his stubble and shook his head. He watched CNN with his morning coffee. The Egg had brought only negatives into the world. The stock market was reeling with wild swings and drops, grocery stores across the West were overrun with frightened shoppers, many stripped clean. The long line of cars waiting at gas stations would only get worse.

He waved to a group of National Guardsmen waiting their turn.

The Egg could go to hell.

⅄

Her hair pulled into a low maintenance ponytail, Cyndi pulled out a long strand and began twisting it into a tight curl around her finger. She feigned a smile to a blonde woman across the checkout counter and continued checking the insurance billing information. Concentrating on the routine task was almost impossible and she hoped the woman would remain quiet.

Patients who came through the front door seemed to feel compelled to discuss Winnemucca's Egg, compelled to give their opinion -- positive it was the governments fault, or it was a new form of terrorism by Al-Qaida, or even Mother Nature taking revenge for humanity's ills.

"It's space aliens," an eight-year old girl had said, hiding behind her mother's leg.

The inane conversation was more than she could stand. She patted her assistant Megan on the arm and moved to the break room where she stared aimlessly at the mess of Chinese food cartons spread over the table.

A familiar chime of a new text broke her malaise. Rich's tone. She rushed back to the front desk and fumbled with the phone.

Egboj

Cyndi hit the call button for ICE and got only Rich's voice mail. She hit redial.

"You reached Rich Preston. Congratulations. Leave a message"

She squeezed the phone hard. His stupid drawl, memorized from seventeen years of marriage, had become insufferable in the last forty-eight hours.

Cyndi dismissed the guilty thought and concentrated on texting.

WHERE ARE YOU!!!!

She hit the send button.

Egbok - Everything's Going to Be Okay - a word texted often in the months following Andy's death. He would drive into the Paradise foothills, usually drunk, and sit to contemplate the value of his own life. No parent should outlive his own child. No father had the right to live if he was responsible for his own son's death. He would text Cyndi the compact acronym to allay her fears but never told her of his dark, morose thoughts.

Rich's phone chimed, chimed again, and again. The incessant ring woke him and he struggled to sit up. He dropped the iPhone back into the pack and staggered to his feet. His thirst was enormous, his thinking muddy.

Keep walking or die. Get to the truck.

A swollen throat made swallowing almost impossible.

Dehydrated. Don't give up …. Keep walking!

His mind wandered with random thoughts, strange images, but his feet didn't move. He looked around, saw nothing but fog.

Dry creek. Hike up. Find the truck.

His thirst became a taskmaster, whipping him forward with hope.

Rich sniggered thinking of Brooke's bright orange Home Depot water bucket.

Gotta feed her. Fill her bucket. Fill it to the brim. She's old, can't get her face down too far. Saliva moistened his dry mouth.

He started again. The uphill climb hurt his thighs.

He would bend over and put his own head into that bucket. Swim in it and drink it dry. Delirious, fixated on the orange bucket, his mouth salivated.

Keep walking. He wandered past the cottonwood but his mind returned to the orange bucket sitting in the garage, surrounded by fluffs of Brooke's hair. He rasped a laugh.

Dog hair bunnies. Everything drinks from the orange bucket of dog water. Gotta sweep up before Cyndi gets home.

An intense amber light blazed in the center of his vision, igniting from the center of the orange bucket. The edges of the fire burned open in an amoeba shape, stretching out from within. Smokeless. It burned the orange plastic away, exposing…the same bucket. He reached for the storage boxes lining the wall behind the bucket of delicious water.

"Keep walking," he muttered.

Rich stepped into his garage, tripped over his own feet, and fell onto the cold hard concrete. And vomited.

He lay on the cold concrete, not wanting to move his head. Brooke poked her cold nose in his face, sniffed and began licking the droplets of bile off his face.

"No," he said in a raspy voice.

Brooke stepped back and hovered above him, wagging her bushy tail.

The hallucinations had won. For the second time in as many days' reality had malfunctioned. He blinked to focus on the orange bucket. The mirage was just inches away, its black lettering foreign. He lifted his head and smelled the water. Strands of Brooke's translucent hair floated on the surface.

Rich dunked his face into the water. The first swallow difficult but he drank hard, fast, and indifferent to the dead leaves floating on the bottom. He jerked his face out of the bucket and gulped in air.

The broken flap on the doggie door, the tennis ball hanging from the garage ceiling, two dusty bags of golf clubs, camping gear stacked in the corner. If this was a mirage, it was a damned good one.

Rich looked back at the dog water, swallowed and shoved his face back into the bucket.

Finally satiated, Rich rolled over onto his back and stared up at the ceiling, afraid to move, afraid something might stop his delicious illusion. Was he home or dying back in the desert? Maybe he'd fallen in the garage, cracked his skull and that whole dust in the desert thing was the hallucination?

He wiped water from his chin. It certainly felt wet.

He sat up. Brooke watching him, lying with sasquatch-sized paws crossed lady-like, her tail slowly sweeping the floor. Rich grunted and rolled onto his side then up to his feet. He stumbled into the kitchen and looked around. He reached for the faucet on the kitchen sink and drank again. The water tasted metallic and the disposal smelled with an unpleasant odor.

He stood at the sink, checking the window curtains, the wooden dinette table, and the furniture in the living room.

He was home.

▲

Jonathan Burdette stared at Cyndi Preston's picture atop the CNN Breaking News banner. Syrian and Italian heritage, no police record, her father a retired Air Force colonel, Mrs. Preston didn't quite fit the profile. But what was typical these days? Chechen brothers bombing the Boston Marathon finish line showed him, again, to expect the unexpected.

Burdette glanced down at the half-inch thick manila folder on his desk. On the other hand, her husband, Richard Joseph Preston, could be the poster child for a homegrown terrorist network.

He checked his watch. Twelve minutes and his team would assemble in the conference room.

Deputy Chief for the Inspector General's office of the Department of Homeland Security, Burdette was a retired Army Captain whose star was on the rise. Though his department conducted oversight of the Secret Service, Coast Guard, FEMA, ICE, and the TSA, Burdette's passion remained in field investigations, specializing in the neutralization of domestic threats.

Burdette glanced at a post-it note stuck to his phone with John Caldwell's phone number scribbled on it. Caldwell's lackadaisical response in maintaining a proper crime scene outside the Winnemucca Egg might be a reason for the ex-Marine Corp Major to retire from the DHS or at least consider another line of work.

He felt two steps behind in the Egg investigation, and it hadn't even started. With an event of this magnitude, time was critical. Time was always critical.

He glanced at his watch again and stood up. An imposing height and a solid two-hundred pounds, he was the youngest Deputy Chief in the department. To hide the premature graying of his hair, he kept it trimmed to no more than three days growth. A mole needlessly removed by an Army dermatologist left an eraser-sized scar on his otherwise unblemished scalp.

He narrowed his eyes and folded his arms. The driver's license photograph of Cyndi Preston appeared behind the CNN reporter again. He guessed it would be seventeen minutes before Richard Preston's picture would pop up next.

The ex-Army Ranger had honed his investigative skills with a tour of duty in Iraq for the military and another for the CIA. The offers from defense contractors, security companies and private sector firms seeking his talents were rejected, and he joined the DHS specifically for the position's oversight capability.

Neesa Becks and Steve Cable hurried to the conference room, each carrying files similar to the one he had just reviewed. He checked his watch then stared at the news. His team would now lead the investigation after Smalley's unit had failed. He ordered every shred of information on these 'cloud survivors.' The missing *Winnemucca Man* was a crock. Preston had crossed his radar before.

Now he landed right in the crosshairs.

Preston was an unemployed electrician, but in no way did he conceive an object able to generate an energy pulse that even the U.S. Military could only duplicate by detonating a nuclear device.

No, Preston was a heartbroken father looking for answers. Or he had been.

Now, maybe he was looking for revenge.

⚔

Rich was home but mindful of the dehydration. You didn't live or hike in the Sonoran Desert without knowing the signs – including hallucinations. The tan leather couches, large screen television, high back bar chairs, the pottery vases Cyndi used as centerpieces for the table…by God, they all looked real. The stack of mail and newspapers Linda had piled on the granite countertop seemed to be the only thing different. His head felt like a bail of cotton had been stuffed inside, but he was home.

He pulled open the smudged white refrigerator door, and bypassing a carton of Cyndi's almond milk, he pulled out jars half-full of jalapeno olives, pickles, sundried tomatoes, anything edible. Rich grabbed a red apple and took a large bite. The pulp was moist and juicy. He moaned as the sweet liquid eased down his raw throat. A handful of processed turkey breast followed, soft and easy to swallow. Rich lunged for the pantry door and ripped open a package of double stuffed Oreo cookies. He pushed two into his mouth, dropping two others onto the hardwood floor. He closed his eyes as they disintegrated into pure bliss. Pulling the tab on the lid of a can of Progresso clam chowder, he began slurping it with his swollen tongue.

He searched his three-bedroom rental as if seeing it for the first time, shoving handfuls of turkey and Oreo's into his mouth. Something would be screwed up, had to be. No way could he be home.

He paused at the array of pictures hung in the hallway. A young Matt kneeled, outfitted in a Green Bay Packer little league football uniform, his toughest sneer cracking a smile. The twins, Nikki and Noah, dressed in silky teal caps and gowns, both beaming perfect teeth. Babies smiling, toddlers laughing, and teenagers playing sports, a progression of his family's lives, and sad reminder of his own.

He ran a finger on the glass over a picture of Andy in his dress blues, proud of the blue striped 3rd Infantry Division patch on his left shoulder.

His mouth was full of turkey but he couldn't swallow.

Brooke followed him, vacuuming up the morsels he dropped.

With his hunger and thirst satiated, Rich's physical exhaustion reasserted itself. He was satisfied that he wasn't hallucinating, yet he wasn't ready to figure out exactly how he arrived home. He picked up the remote control and turned the television to CNN.

The screen filled with an aerial picture of an expansive egg shaped object. Filmed from a distance with a mountain range in the background, the landscape gave the cloud of dust scale. It was huge. The narrative of the reporter eluded him.

He was there. He had lived through all that.

He watched the news, washing down stale cookies with the almond milk. Ignoring the TV voices, Rich began to remember his journey through the sagebrush, the jackrabbit and the cottonwood.

And now he was here. How the hell did he get home?

Images of an amber flame, its edges burning like a sheet of paper, flashed into his mind's eye. Physics equations and foreign symbols paraded into his thoughts. His ocular vision clouded. Rich dropped three Oreos to grab onto the countertop as a wave of vertigo washed over his body.

"Stop!"

The images stopped.

Brooke jammed her head between his legs to reach the cookies. Rich jerked his head around at a familiar name spoken by the television.

"Yesterday afternoon, Cyndi Preston of Boise, Idaho reported her husband, Richard Joseph Preston as a missing person with the Ada County Police Department. He was presumably driving home on highway 95 Sunday afternoon, at about the time the cloud first appeared. Authorities have not yet confirmed that he is indeed the missing Winnemucca Man, but Richard Joseph Preston has been named as a person of interest by the FBI. He is still believed to be in the Winnemucca area, or possibly, still inside this unusual object. Anyone with information concerning the Winnemucca Man is asked to call the FBI at the number on the bottom of your screen.

Now, we turn to Dr. Sanjay Gupta with a report on the possible health effects of a substance some scientists say simply cannot exist…"

Rich choked on a lump of cookie, and he spat into the sink. Person of interest? Like he had all the freaking answers? And Cyndi, oh Lord, right smack in the middle of this bizarre shit. She'll go ballistic.

Rich patted his pockets looking for his phone. But what would he say? His story was too bizarre, even for the National Enquirer.

Rich's legs buckled thinking about how he could've arrived in the garage.

The uninvited images began again.

Chapter 8

Agent Neesa Becks stood on the sidewalk outside a two-story office building housing the Park City Dental Spa. She snapped pictures with her phone then tapped in details of the building's tenants, and layout, noting each possible exit. The office windows allowed a panoramic view of the artificially turfed ski jumps constructed for the 2002 Winter Olympic Games. A potential high-profile target. Working for a man like Burdette, she could ill afford to miss any details.

Assigned to watch Cyndi Preston, Neesa had prepped for the plum assignment by calling the spa to schedule an appointment, and she was lucky enough to get an opening due to a cancellation. Two news vans from nearby Salt Lake City stations had staked their claims across Ute Boulevard. The reporters and camera operators gathered outside the Human Bean coffee shop were geared up and waiting for their opportunity. Neesa had no doubt she would see a live report broadcast from her location during the evening telecast.

A striking, beautiful woman of African/ European heritage, Neesa had graduated from UCLA magna cum laude, with a degree in political science. But her classwork in the Iranian language, Farsi, was her ticket to a job. Recruited fresh out of college by the DHS with a generous salary, full benefits, and forgiveness of huge student loans, she spent six years learning Agency methods and systems until fortune smiled when a large clumsy man skidded into an elevator with her just as the doors closed. He crowded her in the small box as it lifted, elbowing the stack of files she carried, causing a few to fall to the carpet. The man ignored her. She glared at him then dropped to her knees to pick up the mess.

Then the man said, *"Ma3aless."* Oh well, in badly accented Farsi.

Neesa spat her answer in the same Farsi dialect.

"Pig."

The man ignored her and stepped off the elevator at the next stop.

Three days later, she learned of her reassignment to the Inspector General's office, where she met her new boss, Jonathan Burdette. Neesa straightened her posture, lifted her chin and extended her hand to the rude man she had confronted in the elevator.

Neesa and two DHS agents landed at Salt Lake City airport in a G5 jet chartered for quick insertions. Given her dark skin tone, Neesa was surprised Burdette designated her as team-leader for the Utah assignment. Bags of gear, surveillance equipment, and clothing were loaded into a black Cadillac Escalade for the thirty-minute drive up to Park City.

Neesa had checked out the parking garage, the public restrooms, and the other tenants of the office building, memorizing the layout. She tied her curly black hair into a ponytail, pulling the braid through the slot of a Colorado Rockies' baseball cap and walked into the dental office.

From behind the reception desk, Cyndi Preston feigned a silent greeting.

"Hi," Nessa said. "I have an appointment today."

"Sorry, but we're running a bit late. If you haven't already filled out our online patient forms you can sit at the computer kiosk and take care of that."

"Thank you. How long will the wait be?"

Cyndi sighed. "Hopefully no more than thirty minutes, maybe less."

Neesa sat at the computer terminal and surveyed the eco-friendly waiting room. She glanced at the screen but kept the corner of her eye on Cyndi, assessing the suspect's appearance, demeanor, and disposition.

Cynthia Morgan Preston seemed to be nervous, fingering her hair into tight corkscrews. Dark folds of skin beneath her eyes made her look tired. The suspect kept busy with work, and tried to appear calm. But nervousness radiated from her.

Neesa had memorized the printouts of Cyndi Preston's life. Divorced from Jeff Morgan but with two children. Remarried to Richard Preston three years later. Employed as a dental office manager with Doug Abrams, her brother. Both audited by the IRS in 2007. It was found she had a refund of $127.40 coming.

The information was bland, innocuous.

Except for one aspect.

The marriage to Richard Preston.

$$\blacktriangle$$

Burdette wondered if the media's portrayal of the cloud was a ruse, a prank to drum up ratings. Maybe a government experiment to which the geeks at the Defense Advanced Research Projects Agency wouldn't admit to? He clicked off CNN and returned his attention to the work on his desk.

He double-checked the list of surveillance teams routed to Winnemucca, Boise, Reno and Park City. He memorized the names of the lead investigators assigned to detail the past and current whereabouts of each person bequeathed the title of *Cloud Survivor,* including work history, social media connections, and all relevant connections to Winnemucca.

The information poured in.

Preston was the standout. He once claimed to be a Truther, a diehard fringe element of the Tea Party, but rarely attended any meetings. He had stormed a Congressional candidate's political rally, shouting through a bullhorn that Arizona should provide information about his son's death in Afghanistan. Burdette read Preston's angry emails to members of the Joint Chiefs of Staff, and even the President of the United States, some that should've had Preston sent to a mental institution for an *extended evaluation.*

Did Preston have something?

Invent something?

Find something, only to lose control of it?

Burdette had decided to accompany the Winnemucca contingent, a team of eight agents to handle the seven cloud survivors that lived within a hundred mile radius of the Egg. Another agent would take a commercial flight to Boise and interview neighbors, friends or anyone who had contact with Preston.

A three-man team headed by Neesa was already onsite in Park City monitoring Cyndi Preston. Steve Cable's unit was in Reno, observing Matt Preston. Two agents from the Arizona office were assigned to observe Cyndi Preston's twin children in Phoenix.

His interest was the thing lying twenty-six miles north of Winnemucca.

Annoyed at the sloppy work of Caldwell's team, he made a mental note to review the personnel files of the three agents stationed in Reno. Intuition told him to backtrack, remove the most obvious source of the anomaly. Burdette punched a number into his cell phone, the direct line of Colonel Danny Coyle

His contact at the Pentagon.

"Big Jon." Danny said. "Ready for the slopes?"

"Before I waste my time, is this egg thing one of your fucked up special ops you don't want to admit to?"

"Well, good day to you, too."

"Is it, Danny? Is it a good day?"

"Hey, we're in the dark as much as you. You got a real live one in your ball-park, buddy."

"Give it to me."

"Hurry, hurry, hurry, always worrying about time. Anyway, a couple of intriguing items. Infrared can't penetrate the thing. Radar indicates a solid object. Heat, radio waves, lasers, nothing gets through. It's surface temperature remains at a steady 73 degrees but the heat generated doesn't dissipate in the colder air, like it's insulated. They've started calling it the Egg around here, too. And it is like an egg, stores warmth inside and radiates remarkably little. None in fact. The only thing coming out of that thing is, get this, pings of sonar.

"Sonar? You've got to be kidding."

"Frequencies all over the spectrum, random, like it's searching for its mother before it'll hatch. God help us if she happens to fly out of the sky and sit on it. DoD is shutting the site off as of 1300 hours tomorrow. Martial law imposed within a hundred mile radius. There's talk of firing a few Sidewinders at it, just to see what it does."

Typical.

The military would always shoot first and asked questions later.

⋏

Satisfied with his odd meal, and the tap water, Rich gave in to exhaustion. His memory of the previous two days was disjointed. He belched and noticed the bouquet of body odor and urine on his clothes. A shower was in order.

He sat on the couch and unlaced his boots. The smell made the need for a hot shower even more acute, but he lacked the energy to move. Hypnotized by the reds, blues, and blacks of the television screen, Rich closed his eyes and fell asleep.

Rich's brain activity quickly dropped to an acceptable level, and the Alpha probe executed its data-sharing module. The operating system was not unlike a personal computer, requiring a reboot with the installation of the new program. Rich's mind entered REM sleep, and the AI began sorting, filing, data maintenance, system diagnostics, and the translation of functions to the host species. Given time, the operating system would organize each application, create menus with data input prompts and even construct a Help file.

Given time.

The doorbell rang. And rang again. Rich's consciousness floated up from a bottomless black well. For a moment, he couldn't remember where he was. The sound of a key inserted into the door's deadbolt brought Brooke up from her bed and over to the door with her toenails clicking across the hardwood floor.

All remnants of sleep faded with the screech of the front door swinging open. Rich's shoulder ached, his leg muscles were sore, but he stood up, and glanced towards his bedroom. Then he remembered the shotgun was in his truck. In Nevada.

Through a gap in the curtains, he saw a white economy truck parked at the curb. Brooke's tail was wagging.

"Oh my, I didn't know anybody was here."

The dog-sitter, Linda. A stocky woman with a mop of short curly gray hair.

"I was just checking to make sure Brooke was okay. I didn't see your truck so I figured...."

Rich rubbed the back of his neck. "Yeah, my truck broke down but I'm back."

"Yeah, okay, Brooke had her walk last night. She was pretty stiff after, but she loved the company, I can tell"

"Thanks Linda. I appreciate you taking care of her. I'll get you paid by tomorrow when I get my truck back."

"Oh, not to worry. I just wasn't sure you were home 'cause you didn't call and I didn't know, so. Cyndi said to keep checking." Linda bent over to rub Brooke's ear. "I wasn't sure if you got held up by that stuff growing down there in Nevada."

"Yeah, a little bit. All is good. I'll put your money under the statue tomorrow."

"If you go out, stay off 55. The road is clogged with people taking their trucks and trailers into the mountains." She shook her head. "It's like they're all trying to escape. That Egg thing I guess. But I heard folks in McCall are forcing people to keep right on going. Won't let 'em gas up or even step foot inside the grocery stores. It's crazy what that thing is doing to people."

Rich shook his head. "You have no idea."

"Well… sure, no problem."

She sniffed then wrinkled her nose. She looked around the house but her eyes settled on Rich. "Brooke didn't have an accident in here, did she?"

He cringed, "Uh…no."

She went out the door, and walked with a slight limp to a rusty white Tacoma. As he shut the front door, he glimpsed an Ada County Sheriff's black and white turning into his neighborhood from the main access road. He turned the deadbolt.

The mention of his name on the television had conjured images of reporters trespassing onto the front lawn, camera lights blazing, shoving microphones in his face, and bullying him for answers. Answers he didn't have.

He walked into each room and closed the window shades.

His bedroom was dark and he undressed. The rumpled bed called to him. Two days lost inside that fog, and his tiredness confirmed that, whatever happened inside, it wasn't restful. Waiting for hot water in the shower, he stared at himself naked in the mirror, unhappy with what he saw. His workday once filled with climbing ladders, pulling wire, bending metal conduit, and carrying heavy boxes had kept him in decent shape but unemployment had his midsection getting soft. A three-day growth of salt and pepper stubble on his face, his stomach bloated from the picnic, and dark crescents beneath his eyes…he looked like a weathered old man.

The hot spray massaged his scalp, and Rich fixated on the ruffles of a purple towel hanging over the shower glass. He relaxed and his thoughts traveled back to the cloud, reliving the helplessness and terror. He concentrated on his forsaken blue truck. Andy's truck. A truck that would never let him forget the scent of his son.

He closed his eyes. A ring of gold burned on the truck's passenger door. The fire opened a gap, and his truck - still isolated in the fog - appeared. He reached out to touch it, his arm was pulled gently into the burning fluorescent image. The smell of sage. The utter quiet.

He jerked his hand away and opened his eyes.

The door of the truck faded then was gone.

Rich dried himself off, skipped the shave, and put on clean boxer briefs, blue jeans, and a white t-shirt beneath a warm camouflage hoodie. He felt like a new man.

A crazy new man.

That vision in the shower. The air had smelled just like he remembered. Unsettled, he went to the garage intending to refill Brooke's water bucket and stood staring at the bucket half-full of dirty water. A stupid bucket of water. A stupid orange bucket that managed to get him home.

"I'm losing it."

The garage was empty but reminded him of the missing truck, and his late father's shotgun. And the laptop, the iPhone charger, even the bag of dirty clothes. He couldn't even get to the grocery store for dinner. He was helpless, the truck was helpless, just as Andy had been helpless.

The amber fluorescence burned. His eyes stretched wide open, mesmerized by the sight of bug-splattered chrome and cobalt blue metal. Sage and warm ozone filled his nostrils, his outstretched hand tingled with low voltage electricity, and Rich took a step.

A single step.

And touched the truck covered in a patina of gray dust. A sensation of falling, like jumping off a short wall, a brief, insignificant sensation.

But Rich stood on grass, surrounded by the thick fog.

Touching the hood of his truck.

Chapter 9

Burdette's phone vibrated, and he listened to a technician tell him what he wanted to hear. Credit card transactions put Preston in Reno on Friday. The last swipe occurred at a gas station in Winnemucca on Sunday thirty-eight minutes before Officer Clayton Crane estimates the cloud appeared. The last transaction was about the same time he texted his wife.

Then Preston's phone issued a single data message late Monday after the cloud had captured the world's attention. The timeline meant one thing. If Preston's phone was able to transmit, then he wasn't anywhere near the Egg.

A wry smile crossed his face.

Preston was probably drunk, spouting political condemnation inside a bar, or perhaps in bed with the town tramp in a Winnemucca hotel room. Smart. Use the turmoil surrounding the cloud to cover a bender. It would fit with Preston's profile perfectly.

"What was written on the last text?" Burdette asked, dropping the smile.

"Egboj," said the tech.

"Excuse me?"

"E.G.B.O.J."

"Analysis?"

"Nothing definitive on those exact five letters, but thousands of hits on a minor permutation. An organization in Thailand that trains and tutors young people in some fashion. A massage parlor in Tokyo. But the search engine returned thousands of hits for the acronym of Everything's Going to Be Okay. Probably fat-fingered it."

Probably so. A man halfway through a bottle of Jack Daniels could easily misspell a single word. Still…

"Dig into that organization. Find a thread linking Preston to Southeast Asia."

"Yes sir."

"Location of the towers his transmission used?"

"Uh…. That's a bit unusual, sir. It originated from an undefined GPS location."

"Explain."

"We found the message by searching Mama Bear's phone. Tracing the IP address backwards, the sender's GPS location wasn't viable. The sender was Papa Bear. We checked every which way. But it wasn't sent from anywhere our tracking system recognizes."

"How's that possible?"

"Don't know. But then how is that egg-thing possible?"

A scenario of raiding a seedy motel room and dropping the curtain on the Winnemucca Man mystery theatre crossed his mind. Burdette was a firm believer of Occam's Razor -- the simplest solution was usually the correct one. Burdette pondered the Egbok acronym. Or was it code for a bigger plan? Did Preston know how to circumvent the energy pulse produced by the Egg? Preston had to realize his face was on every television screen in the country. He could get what he wanted, go on any news show anywhere, and demand answers about his dead kid.

And yet he issued only a hint of a garbled communication.

Much like Osama Bin Laden.

Right before 9/11.

⋏

The operating system analyzed the human's fixations, and although the command was crude and rudimentary, the alien parasite interpreted Richard Preston's thoughts as data input sufficient to initiate action.

The intense concentration was interpreted as a request to open a pair of wormhole terminals. The system had searched the host's memory, located the orange bucket in a room and deciphered the coordinates using an analogous antonym to Google Earth's search algorithm. With the terminal's coordinates defined, a signal was issued to the multitudes.

Invisible to Rich's naked eye, the motes floating near his body bonded, using a similar subroutine to the one that enabled his capture. Combining their self-contained wormhole generators, they opened a portal and enlarged it to allow the human to pass through.

Until a viable communication link with the host was established, the artificial intelligence would continue to operate by default programming.

▴

The last hours were too good to be true. He knew it. He'd dreamed the whole thing.

Rich collapsed onto the truck's gritty hood, overwhelmed by disappointment, dehydration and lack of sleep. The hallucinations were reliving themselves, playing a cruel joke on him. Had a jokester injected his energy drink with LSD? Or maybe in the water bottle? Or maybe sprinkled in with the pretzels?

With his cheek pressed on the hood, he stared at the white dust coating the truck. He traced a squiggle through the dust, then a Mobius strip - the infinity symbol - then he drew the symbol for Pi. He didn't know why he chose those symbols. Andy had been fascinated with mathematics, but Rich had never given the strange math symbols a second thought.

He tasted the gray dust on his fingertip, and with its blandness came a sad realization. He had never left the side of the highway. He was still stranded in the weird fog. Rich pushed himself off the hood and walked to the truck's door. Locked. He patted his pockets but didn't feel the keys. He shook his head and stared at the mountain shrouded in mist.

"Yeah. Right. You've lost it, Preston."

He spat.

Brushing dust off the rear window, he spied the black laptop case, luggage bag, and the shotgun. Just as he remembered. The air was still, eerie. He dropped the tailgate and the fog absorbed the jarring noise.

He sat and studied his shirtsleeve. He wasn't wearing camo driving home from Reno. He looked up into the corridor of fog. A foolish journey. But his knees hurt and his shoulders were tender. And the cottonwood tree, its branches dropping out of the fog, its thick, rough bark.

Rich jumped off the tailgate.

The amber light burned in the center of his vision.

Rich ignored the lure. False promises. A mind fuck. The picture of the tree in his mind burned open to reveal the cottonwood. Just as he knew it would.

Bullshit.

He'd punch the hallucination right out of existence. Rich stepped through the burning hole like a drunken cowboy, into fog thick enough to swim in. Rich inhaled deeply and released his breath slowly. His fingertips stroked the fluorescent orange lichen growing on the bark. The warm, stale air felt right with the memory. His eyes followed the dry creek bed, down to the distant truck.

The blue label of the empty Aquafina water bottle caught his eye. A spot of color in a pallid nightmare.

He'd never left.

He'd been here since…

Since he died.

The exhaustion pulled at him and he dropped to the ground. He would haunt this lonely tree, as penance for what he did to Andy. He hung his head between his knees.

"You deserve it, Buckwheat." He said, and chuckled humorlessly.

Brooke seemed real. Linda had certainly seemed genuine. But trauma could produce stunning detail. He pictured an auto wreck and his throat constricted.

Cyndi sat at his funeral. Her beautiful eyes hidden by sunglasses, her smile strained, grief aging her face like it had at Andy's wake. He pushed the thought away.

He tossed pebbles and watched them disappear in the fog. Memories surged, of joy, of pleasure and contentment, comforting him. The peaceful second honeymoon spent basking on beach loungers as ocean waves crashed on the shore, snorkeling with dolphins in the bay of Lanai, and long walks on a windswept cliff with Cyndi. An overwhelming sense of peace.

The amber light burned at the center of his vision, burning the edges, burning away the pain.

Rich stood but wobbled. His muscles cried for him to lie down and sleep. He reached out, to experience the peace of Hawaii again.

And stepped into sensory overload.

The sun was hot, the air humid, and a salty sea breeze blew in his face, the thunder of waves crashing on the beach. His boots sank in the deep sand and felt wonderfully sluggish. Rich grinned. The hallucination was perfect.

He turned in a circle, appreciating the authentic details of his surroundings. People in beach recliners read books and stared at phones. Three young girls scribbled letters in the wet sand. Palm fronds rustled in the breeze.

People pointed at him, and he waved back. He grinned foolishly. This was his mirage. He made it, he owned it, and he may as well enjoy it.

He gazed at the white-capped ocean blue for a long moment then removed his hoodie to tie around his waist. He walked up the service access road to the trailhead of a narrow path and headed to the tip of a volcanic jetty. He greeted a young couple holding hands on their way back to the beach.

Nothing short of perfect. A magnificent panoramic view of an endless ocean.

Rich sat on a rock and spotted the misty spouts of distant whales. So this was what happened when you die. Go anywhere you want, relive any memory that made you happy. Exactly like the neurosurgeon that died, came back to life and wrote *Proof of Heaven* had described. He had read the book at Cyndi's insistence. She'd finished reading it in bed one night not long after Andy's death and jostled him awake. She made him read it from start to finish, as if he was a sick child and the book was medicine. Andy's in a better place, she'd said with tears in her eyes. Death was just as the doctor described. Except you travel in an instant.

So why wasn't Andy here to greet him, as the book had promised?

Rich returned to the beach and found the shade of a large Canary palm. The hoodie rolled into a pillow, he let unending surf lull him to sleep. If people knew what dying was like, they wouldn't fear it. Only the living felt the pain of death.

He fell asleep.

"Hey, Buddy."

A meaty hand shook Rich's shoulder. "You can't sleep here, Buddy."

Rich rubbed his sweaty face and opened his eyes. His shoulder felt numb. His head felt full of cold, sluggish oil.

"When is this?" Rich asked.

"What?" The bald man said. "This is now! And you gotta go. This is a private beach."

Rich rubbed the sweat out of his eyes. "Yeah, sure." Why would heaven have security guards?

"You a little over dressed for these parts, Bro."

Snarky security guards. "Yeah, okay, I'm going." Rich sat up, blinking from the bright sun.

"Ya gotta leave now or I call the cops, man."

The man's threat slapped Rich. "I said I was going! Where do you want me to go?"

"Dude, you can go anywhere you want. Just not here."

Rich grabbed his hoodie and stood up, and continued wiping his eyes. The ocean rolled with white caps.

Deep inside his mind, a crack had opened. A revelation shined through. Whether it was intuition or part of the dream he'd been having, Rich knew the man was correct.

He could go wherever he wanted.

He figured he slept an hour, and his stiff muscles screamed for him to stay down for a week. He felt surprisingly refreshed as the cobwebs in his head receded.

The guard waited, chewing on the tip of hand-held radio antenna.

Rich's attention focused on his encounter with the mote swarm.

"Wait," he said. "Mote swarm?"

The guard pointed the wet tip of his antenna toward the access road. "Swarm on out of here, Bro."

The painful images had eased their constant intrusion. A barrier of sorts had been constructed to retain them, built by… a tiny presence lurking inside his head. Rich's shirt was soaked with sweat and his mouth was dry. He thought of dunking his head into the orange bucket again. The burning, amber and orange flared.

No!

The mote swarm? Where did this…how did he know….

He stared at the ground as he walked up a narrow path lined with flowering Hibiscus. The cloud - the mote swarm- existed. He wasn't hallucinating, either. He was hopping from place to place, the miles in-between spanned by the amber light. He was sure he would find a wet towel hanging on the shower at home, and he'd find his truck covered in a layer of motes.

Motes?

The path widened and an array of flowers and tropical shrubs greeted him as he entered the Four Seasons resort. He brushed sand from his clothes, and raked his fingers through his hair. He remembered the nightmare of being in the fog.

Not fog.

A mote swarm.

He issued a thought to the presence in his head.

"How did you get me here?"

The image of a golden burning light started to form in his mind.

"Stop!"

The images ceased.

He negotiated a path through the white chaise lounges surrounding the pool, ignoring the looks from people soaking up the sun. He sat down at a bar where the bartenders looked chopped at the knees in the sunken walkway behind the bar. Bare-chested guests, stuffed bikini's, flowered shirts busied the pub. And him in camo and a hoodie.

He folded the hoodie, sat on it, and ordered two bottled waters. He reached for the wallet in his back pocket and exhaled. No wallet, no credit cards and no cash.

"Cash or room charge?" The bartender asked, setting down two wet bottles of Evian on the bar.

"Um, room charge, but I don't have my room number yet, we just arrived."

"No problem, sir. Compliments of the house. Where you from?"

"Uh, just came in from Nevada." Well, it was true.

"Whoa! Nevada! You escaping the alien invasion, too?" He chuckled. "Hey, did you see it? That weird egg thing?"

Rich shook his head.

The bartender lost interest in Rich and hustled off to attend to a waitress waiting at the serving station. Rich stared at the Fox News program and drank one of the water bottles in large gulps.

Mote swarm.

"What are you?" Rich whispered at the television.

Images flowed like pages of a book, fast, hectic, each filled with schematics, numerical formulas, vectors, cross sections, and text written in strange symbols. The rate of the pages increased.

"Stop."

The images ceased. He took the unopened bottle and found an isolated wrought iron table close to a planter of tropical flowers. His back to the pool, he stared at the Egg displayed on the television and sipped from the second bottle.

"Let's try this again. What are you?"

The images appeared again, in the same order and speed. "Stop."

Okay, whatever was in his head, it seemed to want to communicate with him. They just had to figure out how.

Rich whispered, "What are you? Slowly."

The images cascaded through his mind's eye at a discernible pace. Slow enough to study, but too fast to understand.

"Slower," he muttered.

Every image presented itself, not unlike the photographic slide shows his father liked to show after Thanksgiving dinners. Rich recognized nothing.

"Wait."

An image of a teardrop particle floating in a three dimensional space, shaped like an almond shell. Tiny craters pitted its surface, the pointed end dotted with larger dark orifices. The object began to rotate like a gyroscope.

Continue, he thought.

The sequence of images began to flow again.

"Would you like anything from the bar, sir?"

Rich jerked his face up to see an attractive Hawaiian woman carrying a serving tray.

"Oh. Ah…, no thank you, not right now."

"Happy hour is on till seven so drinks are half priced." She cocked her head and narrowed her eyes. "You look familiar. Where have I seen you before?"

Rich shook his head. "I…I just arrived. Have you ever been to…Montana?"

"Sorry, no."

He looked down at the empty water bottle and waited for her to walk away.

"Did you bring me here?"

The answer came as a pulse of color, a shade his mind associated with a traffic light turning green. The itch in his head said *yes*.

"And how did you do that?"

A new set of images swam into his thoughts at a dizzying speed.

"Slow down." He felt as if he was reprimanding a child and glanced at the tables of tourists around him.

The pictures slowed, pausing at the 3D almond shaped object filling his head like a hologram. It rotated at a viewable speed then began spinning like a child's top, gaining speed until it became a blur, then joined by hundreds of additional blurs. The amber light burned a picture of his travels. Brooke's orange bucket, his blue truck, a lonely cottonwood tree, and a sandy beach, each shining beyond the dimension of burning amber.

"Stop. I got it." He said.

Think hard about something, or somewhere, and the bright light burns open a doorway.

He waited for the tiny pulse to respond, but it said nothing. Maybe his understanding wasn't close enough to the truth to qualify for a green light.

Fuck me, Mildred.

This was huge, unbelievable. And could only be explained to someone he trusted. Someone who wouldn't advocate for a mega dose of Thorazine. Someone who would listen to his story, and withhold judgment until he was finished.

Someone just as likely to tear him a new one after going MIA for two days.

His chair screeched as he stood up, and he focused his mind on a symbol adorning a red brick building.

An amber light burned.

A

Matt Preston wove his way through the bustle in a corridor of the Joe Crowley Student Union, his face pointed at the floor. His eyes darted to the assortment of sneakers and flops passing by. He slowed at a blockage, joining a crowd gathered around MSNBC's broadcast of events outside of Winnemucca.

His birth mother had called earlier in the morning, something she normally did only on birthdays, or Mother's day, and occasionally Christmas. She sounded incredulous that Dad's name was being broadcast all over the television. She sounded like she always did, somehow keeping the conversation about herself. She was always at the center of her own attention, even Andy's death was dismissed, like he never existed.

No familiar faces were among the students or faculty as he sorted through the conversation around him -- *Aliens,* Independence Day, the Sta-Puft marshmallow guy might hatch from the Egg at any moment. The jokes were no longer funny.

Matt worked his way in closer, to listen to the television broadcast, but could only read the crawl.

The military was mobilizing. Two drone aircraft had been downed. The Egg's outer shell was impervious to heat. One fatality. One unaccounted for. Richard Preston reported missing by his wife.

Matt dropped his backpack and resisted the urge to shout at the crowd to shut the hell up. Not that it would have mattered. The news anchor began asking questions to a guest claiming to be an expert on the military's experiments at Area 51.

Cyndi had texted that Dad was okay and he assumed the message meant Dad was home in Boise. But that would have made the news, for sure. Matt watched the screen, his attention waning.

His hands dug into his pockets. Fuck! Dad actually seemed happy a few days ago, talked about taking a float trip on the Salmon River with him and Noah next summer. Now this. He pulled out his phone and tapped the button. The battery was dead.

Brian slid up beside him trailing a heavy dose of Axe body spray.

"Hey, man, you watching the invasion?"

"Shut up." Matt said. "They're talking about my Dad."

Two men watched Matt Preston from the litter-filled condiment rack of the student union's Panda Express, both anonymous in the crowd of students. Each wore a midnight blue Wolfpack sweatshirt. Each discreetly tapped notes, or snapped pictures with their smart phones.

They abruptly separated. One squeezed ketchup packets and continued his observation of the Baby Bear. His eyes darted from the television screen to the ruffled brown hair of the subject.

The other paused to admire his two-day growth of beard in the bathroom mirror.

Junior professor type, he thought.

Steve Cable of the Department of Homeland Security closed the toilet stall door, sat down and texted a report to Burdette.

Chapter 10

A Starbuck's sign hanging from a canopy of an outdoor sitting area gave Rich an object to focus on, distinctive, often visited, allowing him to step through an inexplicable doorway. Into the parking lot of the Newpark shopping center in Park City. People outside would assume he'd just come from inside. People inside would hardly notice him in the bustle.

The sun had just disappeared behind hills burning with the stark colors of late autumn. The cold mountain air chilled his sweat, the skin on his arms puckering with goose pimples. He pulled on his hoodie.

Walking at a brisk pace, he felt underdressed and conspicuous, surrounded by people in high-dollar ski jackets. Actually, a cup of hot coffee sounded terrific. He was procrastinating, and he knew it, but the caffeine might help. Besides, the coffee shop was only a short detour from Cyndi's condominium. The brief nap seemed to have made his thoughts a tad more cohesive, and the flow of unpleasant images would now stop with just a murmur.

The din of Interstate 80 a short distance away was amplified beneath a cloudy sky. Rich walked backwards, taking a few steps until he was satisfied that the Olympic ski jumps cut into the side of the mountain were real.

Surprise her. Knock on the door and just tell Cyndi his story, as if he were a child who'd just returned from a strange Disneyland, but instead of Mickey Mouse ears he came home with the gift of instantaneous travel.

She'd believe it. Sure, she would.

A cup of coffee would zing his brain alive again. Rich ordered a small cup and licked his lips watching the young barista pour the steaming coffee. Reaching for his wallet, he groaned again. He'd forgot to go back to Boise for his wallet. His cheeks flushed when he told the barista he'd forgotten his money. He turned to walk away.

She said, "How about you just catch us tomorrow when you come in?" And handed him the hot cup.

He thanked the girl, unsure if he would return. After a quick fix of cream and Splenda, Rich held the cup up to his lips, and looked down at the tattered front page of the Salt Lake City Tribune resting on an empty table.

The headline *-Mysterious Egg Still Intact*, followed with a subheading of, *Government Stays Silent on Day Three of Mystery*.

Rich sat down and read the article. He could fill in some of the answers, and add more questions to those already being asked. Cyndi's name was in a short paragraph at the bottom, along with his as the supposed, *Winnemucca Man.*

He lifted the cup to his lips and found the sip cold and bitter. Would anyone believe him? Cyndi was only a few hundred yards away, and if she didn't, well… then he might as well find that cliff he'd been contemplating, and jump.

▲

Egboj.

The text did little to reduce the stress ailing Cyndi. She was desperate to hear Rich's voice. She hit the redial button on her phone and heard Rich's voice mail greeting.

Egboj? Was that a drunken butt dial? Had Rich finally gone off the deep end? Maybe he finally drove to Alaska like he talked about so often. Maybe the grouch should find his dream job plucking crabs from a stormy ocean. Maybe then he'd realize his life was full of blessings instead of injustice.

The phone calls, patients non-stop chattering, fighting with insurance claim representatives bent on nickel and diming every procedure Doug prescribed, Cyndi was exhausted. TV news reporters lurking downstairs in the lobby had inflamed a painful knot of muscle between her shoulder blades. Twice, reporters had barged through the front door with harsh camera lights, and firing questions about Rich's whereabouts.

"Get out!" She'd snapped.

The undeterred reporters backed out, but only after Doug threatened to call the police. They simply moved, congregating in the lobby downstairs, waiting to ambush her at the front exit.

She regretted not hiring the receptionist Doug had asked for months ago. She hated her name being associated with the mysterious Egg, but Doug thought the sudden uptick of interest in his practice was priceless. The around-the-clock cloud media coverage had morphed itself into a marketing campaign Doug could never have imagined.

The staff had trickled out, each offering condolences, leaving her and Doug in the strangely quiet office.

Cyndi texted Matt - Dad ok will call after work.

Matt returned the text message with a single letter - K.

Cyndi retreated to the break room, dampened a small towel and slumped down on the couch. She folded the cloth neatly across her eyes then heard the door open.

"You gonna be okay?" Doug asked.

"Just resting."

"Anything new from Rich?"

"Nothing, but when I see him, I'm throwing his phone in the toilet."

"If he texted you then he's gotta be okay."

The clang of dirty utensils dropped into the steel sink made her jerk, but she didn't look.

"I just want to go home and lie down," she said.

"Then go."

"And deal with those vultures? They're like leeches, suck you dry and keep coming for more." She turned the towel over and pressed the cool side down on her eyes but now her lower jaw began to ache.

"Tell you what, I'll go down there and tell them that you'll be down to talk to them in a few minutes."

Cyndi removed the towel and saw Doug staring out the window. The news vehicles were parked across the street. "What?"

"And while I'm doing that, you jump in my car and go home. Windows are tinted so black they won't have a clue."

"Until what? They figure out I'm not here and follow me home." She groaned and turned the towel again.

"It'll get you home, and tomorrow, well, we'll deal with that tomorrow," Doug said. "Anything I should say or shouldn't say? You know. Andy, Rich, and the twins. That's family but it might get out. I mean they're gonna want to know everything about Rich, and you're a big part of this now."

Her muscles resisted movement and she pondered spending the night in the office. Peaceful, secure, but no shower, or clothes. She had to go home. "I know he's all right. I think I would feel something if he was dead or… I don't know."

"Take the Tahoe to Winnemucca if it'll make you feel better. I think it's only five or six hours away."

"Maybe."

Cyndi got up and checked her purse, shut off the lights, and waited a few minutes while Doug went to greet the horde of questions. Using the emergency stairway, she ran down four flights to the parking basement, and drove into the cloudy night sky.

She carefully eased the family-sized SUV into the cramped garage. The overhead door closed, the chain rattling above her head, Cyndi relaxed, feeling as if she'd escaped with her life. Doug was right. She could pack some clothes and be in Winnemucca by midnight.

⥾

Neesa Becks expected Cyndi Preston's arrival.

Neesa straightened her back and tried again to find a comfortable way to sit on the chair inside the Rocky Mountain Power panel truck. She watched Cyndi pull into the garage. Surveillance at the office building had radioed, advising of Cyndi's approach. She checked the two cameras recording the activity around Cyndi's small alpine condominium. She'd seen media avoidance behavior from celebrities, suspects, and politicians. Cyndi was good, especially for an amateur.

Of course, that mysterious Egg blocking a highway made her something considerably more interesting than any celebrity.

⅄

Energized by the dose of caffeine, Rich walked out of the warm coffee shop and crossed a busy street, taking a direct path to Cyndi's condominium. He shoved his hands into the hoodie's pocket, and crossed the parking lot of a Whole Foods store and onto a narrow side street.

His head was buzzing. He hoped it was the caffeine. Cyndi wouldn't believe his story. She'd accuse him of abusing alcohol again, or fooling around with another woman. She knew better. That just wasn't in his nature.

Still, missing for three days without even a text, she was definitely going to be pissed. The traffic noise on Highway 224 grew louder, making him even more nervous. The condominium faced the town's main arterial, buffered only by a patch of grass and a bike path.

Rich stood on the sidewalk outside the front door. A service van parked high on the highway was spinning its yellow emergency lights, slowing traffic. He took a deep breath, walked to the front door and knocked.

Heavy footsteps thumped down the stairs, and he ran his fingers through his hair. The porch light came on, bathing him in bright white light.

The door flew open.

"Get out of here, you freaking-."

Rich stepped back, his eyes opening wide. "This a bad time?"

⅄

With the local media distracted by Cyndi Preston's brother at the office building, Neesa expected nothing significant to happen until the eager reporters arrived at the condominium, and established their version of a circus big-top.

She sat up straight. A tall, unshaven man dressed in a camo sweatshirt and blue jeans turned the corner. He was hesitant as he approached the six-unit condo building. She checked the camera zooming in on the man's face. The digital pictures instantly uploaded onto the laptop were downloaded into the DHS facial recognition software program. Within seconds, the computer screen flashed red.

Target Confirmed.

But she already knew that.

The man disappeared into the residence and shut the door. Neesa grabbed her smart phone and texted Burdette.

Poppa Bear came home.

⚊

Burdette stood above his bed and rolled a white tee shirt into a compact tube then placed the item neatly into the corner of a black travel bag. He cocked his ear and rushed to check his phone vibrating on the kitchen table.

Though furnished with durable rental furniture, the one bedroom apartment appeared vacant, except for two framed photographs perched on a mantle above the gas fireplace.

Plenty of old girlfriends had tried to decorate the place, and he had shown them gratitude. But once the relationship was over, he boxed up the artwork, or silk plant, or knick-knacks, and dropped them off at Goodwill. The feminine touch was difficult to live with.

He checked his phone.

Preston finally showed his face in Park City, with his tail tucked between his legs. The Winnemucca Man was nothing more than a drunk or a man cheating on his wife. Pity.

Burdette returned to his packing.

Except…

Burdette returned to the table, ordering the iPhone to call Neesa.

Neesa answered with a simple, "Yes, sir."

"What do you have?"

"Preston arrived on foot. They hugged, both went inside."

"Walked from where?"

"From the direction of the Redstone Plaza, a block to the north."

"*How* did he get there?"

Silence.

"Let me clarify, Neesa. How did Preston enter Park City? Did he drive, bike, drop in via hot air balloon?"

"I don't know. I can't find any rental cars or airline flights associated with his name or credit cards. It's possible he's using an alias."

"Possible. But it doesn't fit with his profile." Burdette walked to the bedroom window and looked down on a streetscape glistening with rain. "Just walked in off the street, huh?"

"That's all I have. But he is here. Facial recognition software confirmed it."

"What have they been talking about?"

"The parabolic microphone didn't make the trip, so I don't know," Neesa said.

"I understood that was standard equipment."

"Not sure how it missed the jet. Alex is down in Salt Lake getting one from the local branch."

This wasn't good, not good at all. "Neesa, do you know why you were given this opportunity?"

"I have the target's location covered. He won't be able to move without me in his shadow. Or would you like us to retrieve him now?"

"Answer my question."

Burdette absorbed the silence and checked his watch.

"Because I'm the best man for the job. That's why."

Burdette pictured the fiery woman on her knees in the elevator, dishing it back.

"That's correct, Agent Becks. Start acting like it." He let the statement sink in a moment. "Leave him. Complete the background checks?"

"All tight. Nothing's changed from the briefing yesterday. Well, that nothing is something. We haven't received Andy Preston's military records from DoD."

"Explain?"

"They're giving me the runaround -- the file is classified, need signatures authorizing release, yadda, yadda, yadda. Next time I call they'll tell me it's been misplaced."

A rebuff from the military, unusual, but not unheard of. "I'll make a call."

Burdette didn't understand why the Army didn't manufacture a cause of death for Andy Preston. It was almost certainly a case of friendly fire that a Colonel or General wanted covered up for any number of political reasons. Why they insisted on hiding the boy's cause of death was a mystery but not a surprise. Hell, just tell the family an IED exploded or he was KIA in a Taliban ambush.

Burdette felt a degree of empathy for Preston in that respect. He'd taken hours fussing over every word of every sentence in each of the seventeen letters of condolence he'd mailed to the parents of soldiers he commanded. Preston clearly never got that courtesy.

He made a mental note to speak personally to Specialist Andrew Preston's company commander.

How had Preston arrived in Park City unnoticed, slipping past the media and his own investigators? Hitchhiked the 300 miles? Possible, but not likely. He had help, maybe a girlfriend, maybe accomplices, maybe somebody with enough money and intelligence to develop that Egg blocking the highway? Preston just didn't seem like the type.

His phone dinged with a new email from Neesa. Burdette opened the attachment, a file of photographs depicting the suspect arriving home. Studying the first grainy picture, he winced from the photo's poor quality. Preston was wearing a camo shirt, jeans, boots and the scruffy beginnings of a beard.

Add a piece of cardboard written with '***Wounded vet, please help'*** and Preston could blend in with the hundreds of panhandlers working the Portland street corners.

He walked over to the dinette and opened his laptop to view the photographs in more detail. He scrolled through the sequence of poor quality photos, as if the pictures were taken with a dusty lens. Strike two for Neesa.

He furrowed his brow and leaned into the screen.

The final two pictures of the sequence, each a high-resolution crystal-clear picture of the porch and the front door.

The dust was gone as the door closed behind Richard Preston.

▲

Rich saw a loving smile, dark brown eyes capable of tearing through the armor of his soul, and the only thing in the world preventing him from putting an end to his own miserable existence.

The surreal world of murky fog, technical images, motes, and a tiny odd itch disappeared with her touch. He squeezed her, inhaling her familiar scent, stroking her beautiful hair, and dreaded what was to come.

Cyndi pushed him away. "What are you doing here? Are you all right?"

He pulled her close to his chest, wanting to spill his guts but he wasn't sure. He didn't want to hear her questions, not without having answers.

"I'm okay," he whispered.

Cyndi pulled away and checked his eyes, searching for something. She kissed him, letting her lips linger on his chafed lips. Rich's worries crumbled. She could do that to him.

She pushed him away. "What's going on with you, missing for two day, and the Egg, and the Winnemucca man and the freaking news people and …"

Rich closed the door.

"You have no idea how real this feels." Rich hugged her again but the embrace was brief.

"What do you mean real? Why didn't you call? Where have you been? Were you inside that Egg?"

He shook his head. "You're not going to believe it, and it's gonna come out slow so just be a listener for a bit." The aroma of grilled meat hung in the air, making his stomach gurgle. "Anything left to eat? I'm starving. Then I'll tell you a story, and you can tell me I'm nuts."

Cyndi's eyes narrowed, her crow's feet showed. But she didn't object. Instead, she turned and marched into the kitchen.

She performed her version of a chef's waltz, pouring a carton of egg whites to scramble with turkey meat, tearing apart a bagel for the toaster. Rich sat at the dinette table and scratched at the varnish, and began the story.

By the time he told her about the jackrabbit encased in the mote swarm, the cooktop's gas was shut off, and Rich was served the eggs and a bagel lathered with peanut butter. He didn't eat, he didn't dare. She leaned against the stove, folding her arms across her chest and listened. Entombed by dust motes.

Blacking out. Waking up, suffering from dehydration, and finding himself back home in their garage.

He pushed the food away, and put his face into his hands, rubbing his forehead. It all sounded so crazy when he said it out-loud, but he'd lived through it.

'You know I can't hear you when you do that," she said in a firm, almost angry voice.

Cyndi sat down across from him. He told her of traveling from the living room to the truck with one step, then stepping back to the big tree. He told her of his thoughts of death and hopes of seeing Andy on the other side, waiting to escort him into heaven. Of falling asleep on the beach of Lanai, and drinking cold water at a favorite hotel.

Cyndi stood up and began tossing the dirty plates, pans and utensils into the metal sink. The fury in her actions, the whistle of an approaching train wreck. It was far too familiar.

Rich finished, claiming he traveled from Hawaii to the Starbucks two blocks away by simply concentrating on the sign and stepping through a burning doorway.

"And here I am." The caffeine buzz was gone. Telling his story hadn't lifted the weight on his shoulders, it had doubled it.

"Son. Of. A. Bitch." Cyndi slammed the refrigerator door hard. "You run off to who knows where, doing God only knows what and come home with a fucking story like that?"

"Cyn, I know how it sounds but-"

"Sounds like you jumped back into the bottle again, Preston. Sounds like you had too much fun and can't remember what the hell happened." She waved her hand signaling she was done with him.

The accusation stung but didn't surprise him. "I don't think I've slept more than an hour since… I'm living that Groundhog Day movie. I can't think straight." Rich stood up.

"I don't think you were ever in that cloud. You never left Reno, did you?" She banged her chair against the table, the tip of her tongue sliced across her front teeth.

He had no energy to debate her.

"Okay, show me how you just go anywhere you want, go to Starbucks and get me a latte. No wait, poof over to Hawaii and get me a cold water. Then you can go to bed."

He could but he wasn't thinking straight. His eyes darted here and there, settled on a family picture of the three boys, and Nikki. And Brooke.

Cyndi pressed her lips tight, her hand came up, squeezing a wooden spoon as if to throw it. She shook her head then turned her back and stared at the sink.

He had to do something. He had to prove himself to her but he couldn't think right, just like when he was dying at the tree. Just like he was dying here.

Wait, there was a way

Rich disappeared.

⚔

Cyndi turned to face him, resisting the urge to throw the spoon for insulting her with such bullshit. She would order him out. Enough was enough.

Rich was gone.

A familiar scent hung in the air, moist and stuffy.

"We're not finished here, Preston!" Cyndi yelled. That fucking man had gone upstairs, to bed.

"Get back down here, now!"

She started for the stairs off the small living room, looked up to the landing and bedroom door. She growled and shook her head. He'd gone to fucking bed. The man wanted to play games. The man wanted to sleep? Let's see how much noise he can sleep through, starting with a few dirty fry pans that might happen to find the side of his head.

She made a 180 degree turn.

Cyndi gaped.

Rich… appeared in front of the table, outlined by an amber glow visible for a fraction of a second. The aroma she had dismissed as a memory returned. Her eyes stayed glued to his scruffy face, and tired raccoon eyes. Rich embraced her and kissed her lower lip still hanging from what was impossible. She wouldn't, couldn't return the kiss.

A hacking sound, a guttural discharge followed by a rhythmic thumping on the table leg.

Cyndi rubbed her nose. An unmistakable musk permeated his clothes.

Rich looked at her with droopy bloodshot eyes. Exhausted eyes.

"I love you, but I need sleep."

He placed a piece of stiff material into her hand but she couldn't remove her eyes from him. How the hell…

It was true. It was. Every word of it. True.

Rich plodded to the stair landing and trudged upstairs like a tired old man. She watched him closely until he closed the door to her bedroom.

A nudge of a familiar cold, wet nose made her turn and look down to see Brooke, slapping her tail against the chair. The dog smiled as if waiting for a biscuit. Cyndi dropped to her knees and hugged her *precious* Brookie. She unclipped the leash and stared at something that should be hanging on a nail by the garage door. In Boise. She looked back up to her bedroom door as Brooke's tail wagged faster.

Holy crap.

She shut off the lights except for a small lamp and stretched out on a soft leather couch. Brooke followed close. Cyndi's mind wobbled with what she'd seen, or hadn't seen, comforting herself by stroking Brooke's soft fur.

She texted Matt that Dad was home, adding a smiley face. Cyndi wanted to call Nikki, and Noah, and tell them everything. But how would she explain Rich's sudden appearance? Or the golden outline, the musty smell of the home in Boise, and the arrival of Brook?

But she did see Rich walk out of thin air, she did smell the house that was hundreds of miles away, and she was petting Rich's evidence. Something happened to him inside that Egg, , that fog, that was obvious. Rich said he'd felt a presence in his head since escaping the Egg. Maybe that thing had planted a seed inside Rich, an alien seed, maybe that's why she felt as if he had changed.

Brooke's tail thumped the couch as Doug rattled the lock before walking in the front door.

"Who's your friend?" Doug asked.

Not sure what else to say, she went for the truth. "It's Brooke. Rich brought her from Boise."

"So he's here?"

"He just got in. He was in…He was home the whole time."

"See. Things are never what you think. All that worry for nothing. Let's keep Rich in hiding, it'll keep the reporters hanging around? We'll be booked up for a year."

She shook her head. "Did you just really say that?"

"Hey, I got two homes to pay for and I miss my girls. He's okay and so are you, now let's milk this pig for all she's worth." Doug dropped his gym bag and walked up the stairs into his bedroom.

Cyndi shut off the light and climbed the stairs accompanied by a million questions. She coiled the leash and placed it on the bathroom vanity top, stared at it while she brushed her teeth.

She unrolled it, plucked silky hair from its buckle then placed it on the carpet outside her bedroom door. She put on cotton pajamas and climbed into bed. Rich was snoring loudly but she could endure the noise this time, glad he was home. Cyndi shimmied close to Rich, getting warm in the man's body heat.

Rich was muttering. Familiar words; *Andy, Noah,* a word she'd interpreted as *Christmas.* Words she'd heard before, over the years.

She pulled away from him and rose on her elbow. New words.

Isolation. Download. Host. Swarm.

She stayed awake, leaning in to hear the words he grunted between snorts and snores. She recognized the last few words.

The first one seeming to answer the question that kept her awake.

Wormhole.

The other causing her knees to curl up to her chest.

Fucking-Army.

Chapter 11

R ich woke and saw the small clock shining red numbers over Cyndi's shoulder. 4:33. A yellow light flashed like a strobe through gaps in the window's plastic shutters, painting the white walls with shadows.

Comfortable in the warmth, Rich felt rested for the first time in…days, a week but feeling unsure the last few days hadn't been a dream. Or a nightmare.

The insect entrenched in the back of his head stirred. He thought of it as a burrowing scorpion, razor sharp claws cutting into his brain matter, feeding its hungry mouth. It was the reason he'd been captured by the…. mote swarm.

The images returned, speedy and incomprehensible. He reminded the tiny presence to slow down and a wave of déjà vu swept over him.

"What is this?" he whispered.

Data.

He rolled over on his back. It was his inner voice, and the source of the obscure internal itch. And it was talking in words.

"What kind of data?"

Transmitted data.

"From who?"

Download incomplete.

"What download?"

Insufficient input.

Talking like a computer.

Affirmative.

"That's what you are?" Rich scratched grit from his eyes.

Operating system.

"Operating system of what?"

Operating system of data transmitted.

"What data transmitted?"

The conversation felt like Abbott and Costello's "Who's on first" skit.

Download incomplete.

Rich groaned and tried a different tack.

"Who sent the information?"

Download incomplete.

Well, it was talking now, but it wasn't saying much. He remembered the FORTRAN computer programming class he struggled to complete twenty-five years ago. Infinite loops, syntax errors, flawed logic.

"How did you get me here?" Rich asked.

The thing answered, but with burning images of an orange bucket, his blue truck, a scary cottonwood tree, an ocean and a Starbuck's sign.

"Stop."

The images ceased.

"What's that burning you're showing me?"

No response.

Little prick.

Rich thought of Spock in Star Trek, the droids in Star Wars, and Data of Star Trek – the Next Generation. Computers, or people that acted like them, and Data won - easily. If they could do it then so could he.

"Explain the image shown."

Transit wormhole portal.

"Whoa." Rich said. "I make wormholes?"

Negative

"What creates the transit wormhole portals?"

The hologram of the almond shaped object filled his mind. "Stop. What are those called?"

A long pause. Then it answered.

Beta class mote probe.

At least that's what Rich thought he heard, "What are beta class mote probes?" He regretted the question. The images he studied in Lanai started again. The images ceased with a whisper and he sat up against the headboard. "Where are the transit beta mote probes?"

Locations transitive. Locations universal.

"Everywhere?" He imagined the night sky as if viewed while lying on a sleeping bag. Immense, infinite, and humbling.

Affirmative.

"Even in here?" Rich asked. He sat higher against the headboard, and tilted his face to the ceiling.

Affirmative.

"Can they see me?"

Affirmative. Followed by. *Visual recognition program available.*

"Can I see them?"

Affirmative.

"Show me." Rich quickly rephrased the question to avoid the flood of images. "No wait, I want to see them." He swallowed and searched the room.

Beta class mote probes within visual range.

He froze when Cyndi moved her leg, but he saw nothing.

"Make the motes so I can see them."

Plumes of dust flew in from gaps of the window, sprinkled up from the blanket, and fell from the ceiling, forming a marshmallow cloud to hover above the bed. He pulled the comforter from his legs. The stuff had scared him in Nevada and scared him now.

But where could he run. Jump out the window? They were outside, too.

"You control the dust?" He quickly corrected himself. "I mean the motes. I mean you control the transit class beta motes?'

A long pause. Too long. Then the ping returned.

You are we.

"You are we? What the hell does that mean?"

Silence.

"We control the dust. I mean the beta dust motes, the transit stuff?"

Another long pause. The scorpion returned, shoving another claw-full of his brain matter into its bloody mouth.

Rich eased his legs over the edge of the bed, and stood up, checking the closed door. He pressed his body against the headboard wall. The cloud grew into a grey thunderhead spreading out against the ceiling. His heart pounded. The claustrophobia returned. The dust was going to entomb him again. And Cyndi.

Affirmative.

He repeated the question. "We control the transit mote stuff?" The identical answer was repeated and he relaxed a bit. "Why?"

Download incomplete.

Rich groaned. "How many motes are floating in this room? It's got to be a lot."

1,333,867.

Son of a bitch. That many and all in a closet of a bedroom. He thought of the cloud in Nevada and changed tacks. "The motes see me too?"

Affirmative

"Show me."

A grainy image flooded his mind as if a camera was dialing into focus and Rich sat back down. He saw himself, and Cyndi sleeping, and a nightstand illuminated by the red LED readout of 4:59. Two sets of yellow lights flashing through two sets of blinds.

Rich looked at the clock, his wife, and his eyes matched the picture. Distinct, but it was like watching himself through a sleazy hidden camera.

I can see what they see?

Affirmative.

He slipped back beneath the covers. "How do they know *where* I want to go?"

Alien mathematical formulas overlaid on the pictures of the places he'd visited replaced the overhead view of Cyndi's room. Arabic symbols for all he knew.

Stop. The quick command eliminated the vertigo producing images.

"The motes know what I'm thinking?"

Negative.

"You know what I'm thinking?" Rich watched the cloud above his head rotate like a meandering hurricane. His heart fluttered.

Operating system interfaces host.

"I'm a host?"

Affirmative

"Fuck me, Mildred. I'm a host? A host to what?"

Cyndi stirred.

Operating system.

He flinched, banging the back of his head on the headboard. He checked Cyndi then slipped his legs to the floor. This conversation needed privacy.

He eased out into the hallway. "You talk to the motes?"

Operating system interfaces with mote components.

"And the operator program is you that I hear?"

Operating System.

Yeah, yeah.

"And I tell you where I want to go and the motes make it happen?"

Make it so, little voice.

Affirmative. Data input required.

"What's the data input?"

Memory location data.

"I go to places I have memory of?" The pauses between question and answer grew longer and unnerved him. Maybe it was lying, maybe it needed time to think them up.

Affirmative.

"You are the operating system, right?" He groaned at the stupidity of his question.

Affirmative.

"Do you have a name?"

Negative.

"Can I give you a name?"

Irrelevant.

Dumb question, but definitely Data of Star Trek. Just need to think it.

Affirmative.

"You hear all my thoughts?"

Affirmative.

He needed to move, get out of the small room, away from the millions of motes floating on the ceiling.

1,333,867.

His muscles were stiff and slowed his escape to the bathroom. Maybe he strained some muscles when he was inside the mote swarm. He kept the lights off and splashed cold water on his face. Dear Lord. Don't turn on the light. And you won't see some kind of Borg monster staring back at you from the mirror. He took a long drink from the faucet. He closed his eyes and flipped the switch.

No mechanical implants, no converted pupils, only a heavy growth of black and gray stubble on his face. Homeless, a vagabond, the old man who murdered his own son, that's what he looked like.

*Get out! Leave you little prick. I'll kill you like…*The corner of his mouth twitched and he turned away from the mirror.

Rich emptied his bladder, and wondered if the motes saw him standing half-naked with his dick in his-.

Affirmative.

Great. Either he had just hit the lottery, or, unintentionally drove into the biggest pile of crap imaginable.

He brushed his teeth with a sample toothbrush courtesy of the Park City Dental Spa then eased back into the bedroom to grab his clothes.

"What are you doing?" Cyndi moaned into the pillow.

"Shhh, just gonna get a snack. Go back to sleep."

He suddenly felt excited about his odd conversation. Whatever was happening inside him was a little less scary with what he was learning, and continuing the conversation in a cramped condo with Cyndi and Doug bombarding him with questions wouldn't work. He slid back to the bathroom, put on his clothes, shut off the light and concentrated on an orange bucket in a garage.

Rich stepped into the pitch-black garage back in Boise, bopping his forehead on the tennis ball hanging from the ceiling. He roamed the dark house, room to room, having a conversation with the operating system. The answer to his questions was, *download incomplete.*

In the darkened mirrors, and picture glass, his reflection continued to grab his attention. He sure looked like himself but something was growing inside him. Would the thing take over his mind, his body, begin to have a say in his appearance, clothing, even the food he ate? Could it feel his pain?

He stripped off his clothes, jumped into the shower and allowed the hot water to scald his scalp and back.

"When will download be complete?"

The answer returned - cryptic, annoying, intriguing, and frightening –

Unknown.

The morning sun transformed the dining room's window shades from a dark plum to diluted crimson. After a breakfast of toast, oatmeal, and coffee, the pangs of guilt surfaced. He shouldn't have left Cyndi. But he didn't lie, he did go for food, just in a kitchen 350 miles away.

He placed his food near the stack of mail Linda had brought in. An envelope stamped with a red Final Notice was on top. It hadn't been on top when he'd left.

Somebody had been in his house.

With the truck's spare ignition key retrieved from a drawer, he conjured an image of his truck, intending to retrieve the items left inside. He stepped into a dark world of eerie dust. His heartbeat increased, and he remembered the squeeze of the dust coffin. The beta class transit coffin. The semi-darkness made him hurry, grabbing the laptop, carryall bag, and shotgun and stepping back to Boise.

Lying on his mattress, he let his heart rate slow, repeating questions to the voice. New ideas formulated as a melody of *download incomplete* lulled him asleep.

⋏

The lights of downtown Portland illuminated the overcast sky as hints of the coming day cracked an orange smile over the Cascades. Dressed in his standard field attire of blue denim jeans, white business shirt and a navy blue Pea Coat, Burdette hesitated before boarding the Gulfstream GIII jet charter. The co-pilot waited at the stairs, and Burdette confirmed the one-hour forty-five minute flight time to Winnemucca.

He took a deep breath and boarded, acknowledging eight team members with a slight nod, and placing his overnight case beneath his seat. As he sat down, his smart phone vibrated in his chest pocket.

The screen showed BLOCKED.

"Deputy Chief. This is Janet Evans. I understand you're en route to the Winnemucca site this morning."

The Secretary of the DHS was not asking.

"Yes, ma'am."

"There are a few things you need to be aware of."

Her abnormal intrusion into the chain of command made him sit up straight. "Go ahead."

"One. The Department of Defense has received permission from the President to quarantine the site for up to a 100-mile radius. The Army will impose martial law as of 1300 hours. Get what intell you can before that happens. I'm not fond of playing subordinate to the flat tops at the NSA. Clear?"

"Yes, ma'am."

"Second, I'm exchanging a few favors with the Vice-President. We'll allow a few Microdyne techs onto ground zero, to gather samples only. In return, Childs' associates will release a proprietary theory explaining the substance. I think he already knows, but nothing comes out of him without a price tag attached."

"Yes, ma'am."

The call ended.

Burdette shook his head, disgusted at the idea of Vice-President Henry Child's pet defense contracting company screwing around with his investigation. Even more annoyed with the thought that Microdyne knew something about all this and were keeping it to themselves.

The annoyance was brief, but Neesa Becks' equipment miscue still simmered. He had debated whether to replace her as team leader in Park City. Since the mystery of Preston's whereabouts was resolved and he decided to deal with her after the Winnemucca Egg mystery was resolved.

Burdette gripped the armrest as the twin jet engines whined, increasing in intensity. Breathe in slow through the nose. Out through the mouth. He closed his eyes and practiced his Zen ritual of imagining the placid waters of a Pacific inlet, drifting on his kayak in an easy rhythm atop a carpet of kelp.

He fondled the tiny canister in his pants pocket, but a Xanax would dull his judgment. A last resort. His sister Robyn often teased her Captain Macho Man about his weakness, and having to suffer through eleven parachute jumps in Army Ranger School. Her memory brought a thin smile to his face. He looked at the date on his watch - twelve days until the anniversary of her death. He promised himself to make the plane reservation to visit his mother when he returned. Robyn's suicide extinguished the last few sparks of life his mother held onto. Alzheimer's, dementia, the diagnosis didn't matter, his mother was in splendid physical shape, but with the mind of a one-year old.

He lowered his face and brushed away the moisture forming in his eyes.

The aircraft began to roll, making two sharp turns then gained speed.

In through the nose, out through the mouth.

⚓

Mathematics in a dream state was impossible, Rich was sure of it, so he counted the blades of the ceiling fan above his head. Five. He was awake. He rubbed at his eyes and asked the voice - the ping - the Data thing- the little prick -,

"Is the download complete?"

Negative.

The answer was deflating. His life was shit, Nikki and Noah hated him, Matt numbed his anger with pills, and a little prick bug was eating his brain. And yet he could travel anywhere, instantly.

Self-pity gets you nowhere.

He stood up and stretched his hamstrings for a count of thirty. He questioned the voice, while brushing his teeth, making coffee, and wandering the house, trying to find a question that would unlock some new information. What he got was - *download incomplete*. Reheating a cup of coffee in the microwave, Rich turned on the television to CNN and watched a picture of the sun rising over the monstrous egg shape. He grimaced at the taste of stale coffee but felt energized, his thinking stimulated, the best in days, even years. How much of that was the bug's doing?

As if he were talking to someone sitting on the couch, Rich asked, "I can see what the motes are seeing, right?"

Affirmative

"Show me what that Egg thing sees." He pointed at the television.

Pictures flowed into his mind's eye - sagebrush spiced with pumpkin lichen, clear blue skies, rust colored rocks, dew sparkling on brown blades of grass, mesquite branches, prickly pear cactus spikes, camouflaged military vehicles appearing as toys, aluminum towers, and human-beings with weird instruments, some prodding the cloud with metallic rods. All in a astonishing, painful level of detail.

He clutched his head, his eyes bulging with intense pressure. The volume of information made him scream, "Stop!"

The images stopped, the pressure subsided, but Rich matched many of the images with those on the television - only reversed.

He prepared the next question carefully, "Show me what the motes see outside the cloud. Slowly. Always slow."

Blue sky dominated his mind's eye, followed by a diorama of sagebrush, rock cliffs and sometimes the highway. "Stop! Show me that view of the highway."

Bright halogen lights beamed into his eyes, mobile satellite dishes, hundreds of vehicles, indiscriminant humans bustling like ants at a summer day picnic.

The little voice in his head interfaced with the Egg. Maybe controlled it.

He sat down and watched the CNN anchors gesturing to the Egg behind their podium. It made coffee and acid rise in his throat. The mainstream media was useless, unwilling to help in his crusade to force the Army to release Andy's military records. They were just vultures, and accomplices of the military machine. Now the media's tunnel vision had zoomed in on the motes - controlled by a voice in his head. The media didn't help him in his time of need – fuck em.

"Can we make this cloud go away?"

Affirmative. Dispersion input required.

Rich noted the instantaneous answer. The disconcerting gaps of time had disappeared.

He stared at the television and saw the American flag atop a transmission tower fluttering with intermittent puffs of wind.

The American flag.

A funeral shroud. On Andy's empty casket.

"Let it blow away in the wind."

We.

A milestone word built into the Designer's programming. A word confirming a communication link was firmly established with the host, an acknowledgment from the host of a symbiotic relationship. The operating system executed two subprograms that had required the use of this simple word.

The first subroutine issued a signal to thousands of beta motes inside the Boise home. The 128-bit binary order leapfrogged from mote to mote, room to room, city to city, spreading like a virus at light-speed, reaching motes on isolated mountaintops, finding their brethren in deep ocean trenches.

Compile Hub.

On the sundrenched sand in a remote desert of northwest Iran, motes probes nearest to the coordinates embedded in the signal initiated the program. In a landscape void of apparent life except for a few deep-rooted bushes battling heat for survival, eight mote probes chemically bonded, fusing molecules of hydrogen into unbreakable links. Forty-three seconds later, an additional sixty-four motes attached themselves at critical junction points to create a miniscule lattice-shaped object.

A table-sized sheet of motes shifted in ripples and waves, condensed inward, as if a thin linen cloth was being pulled from its center. Three minutes later the sheet collapsed inward again, ripple and shift. A pea-sized nodule formed.

Three more iterations, and from the hot sand a white knucklebone of a finger pointed skyward. Seven iterations and five fingers reached up, the thumb bone still curled around a black metal trigger-guard half-buried in sand.

A violent gust of wind blew, causing thousands of circular sheets hidden in the sand to ripple and shift, excited, waiting for their chance to join, like a school of mating jellyfish surfacing in a placid ocean of sand.

The shimmering sheet condensed, growing smaller with each iteration. Ripple and shift. The epicenter grew into a marble-sized nodule. Again, and again, the sheet condensed, exposing the crown of a human skull.

The sheet puckered. Wave and shift. The sheet condensed, exposing a human face picked clean of organic matter, its perfect teeth grinned. Wave and shift. A spinal column and the collar of a shirt. Wave and shift, and a gust of wind. A swath of beige cotton painted in colors pretending to match the desert.

Ripple and shift, the Hub sucked the sheet in.

A uniform, violated with bullet holes and stained with the black of old blood.

Wave and shift. The skull tilted in the wind, and continued to smile.

Wave and shift. A tag of black letters on the uniform - **U.S. ARMY**.

And again the Hub pulled the sheet inward, adding mass to its structure.

Exposing another tag.

PRESTON.

The second program executed – a subroutine that used a large, complex file of data written and compiled to coerce the host into completing the mission. Again, the module was untested in the field.

The program might run haywire.

Burdette's mind floated lazily on a placid mental ocean, keeping the nausea accompanying his airsickness at arm's length. The jet banked hard to the left, lining up its approach to the east-west landing designation of Winnemucca's municipal airport. Burdette's phone vibrated and displayed Alex Spring's caller ID. Alex was a parrot, practicing a never-ending Aussie accent, using the same words over, and over, "Hello, Mate. Don't get your knickers in a knocker. Shrimp on the Barbie."

But aside from the bad case of Australian Tourette's, Alex was a competent agent.

"Go ahead." Burdette said, then gripped the armrest as a sudden downdraft rattled the jet.

"The object is breaking up, just started," Alex said.

Burdette noted excited voices in the background. "Explain."

"Five knot wind blowing east, and the egg is disintegrating, into a cloud of dust."

"Hazmat teams?"

"They've broken through. The rejection factor is no longer in play."

"Capturing the residual?" The trace elements would be the key to solving the mystery.

"Ah… the dust moves away like a flock of birds, stays out of reach. I think Smiley managed to grab some in a drink cup."

"A drink cup? Dust that avoids capture? You have a few too many Fosters for breakfast, Alex?"

"I know what it sounds like, Captain, but--"

"My ETA is approximately one hour"

"It'll be gone by the time you get here."

The aircraft taxied to a crowded hanger. Jets of all sizes had overwhelmed the remote airstrip's facilities. The helipad on the west end was equally inundated, with helicopters, many with rotors warming up to capture the recent developments.

In the front seat of a white GMC Yukon, Burdette checked his watch while the others loaded the gear. Doors slammed shut and Burdette gestured with a hand slicing forward. "Let's roll."

As soon as they were underway, Burdette called the DHS shift manager in Portland.

"Travis, what's satellite imagery of the site showing?"

"The cloud has increased in size to almost ten square miles, drifting to the east and breaking up over the mountain range. Weather satellites show a seven-knot easterly flow."

Screw the military. They'd have no business militarizing the site now that the thing was disappearing. This was now a crime scene, his crime scene. He wasn't privy to the operations conducted by the NSA, CIA or Department of Defense but it didn't matter.

This was a clear case of domestic terrorism.

A

The second cup of coffee tasted primo as the television flashed a 'Breaking News' banner. The Egg had cracked, breaking into a billion pieces, drifting like a bank of coastal fog hitting the hot inland sun.

"Report that, bitches."

The helicopters circled, the cloud thinned into opaque rivers, split into rivulets, and disappeared into pine-carpeted mountain canyons. A sense of mischievous power lifted his cheeks into a wry smile. And yet an odd sense of loss as the dust disappeared.

"What's Cyndi doing?" He pictured Cyndi's bedroom. The image of Cyndi spun into focus, as if Rich floated above her bed. She was semi-awake. Her leg stroked the top sheet in a slow easy rhythm. He thought of going to her. Telling her what he just did. But would it matter? He didn't know anything more than what he told her already, except he had a bit of control over the dust. Was it his dust?

"Can I see her whenever I want?"

The short reprieve in his battle of semantics was over.

Insufficient data - no memory parameters.

He groaned, but the five-word answer was a new record. GIGO, baby. Garbage In. Garbage Out.

He shut the bedroom image off and wandered around the house again. The caffeine had made him jittery. He stopped at Cyndi's photographs hanging on the hallway walls. He looked at a photo of Noah and Nikki posing together, shining eighteenth birthday smiles, Andy at bat in little league, eight-year old Matt wearing a cheap plastic Groucho Marx mask he bought in a souvenir shop in Tombstone.

Matt.

Maybe tell him the fantastic story? Maybe redeem himself a bit for Andy's death. Tell his son about a gift that only sci-fi movies could think up. It had to get his attention.

It had to.

He put on clean blue jeans, a white undershirt, and a pressed white dress shirt starched for a possible job interview. He checked his eyes in the mirror again, fighting off an absurd thought of being assimilated into a race of human-computer operating systems.

Rich visualized the red brick and mortar of Nye Hall, then the roadside curb where Matt had quickly climbed out of the truck and walked away. Rich waited, hoping his son might turn and give him a final wave. No such luck. The sidewalk image burned, but he abandoned it, running to grab his wallet, and five one-hundred dollar bills from an envelope pinched between the mattress and bedsprings.

The memory burned again and the curb on Virginia Street burned with it. He stepped through the wormhole portal to be greeted by a cold north wind. He hunched his shoulders, dug his hands deep into his pockets, and walked to the white metal pedestrian bridge used by students to avoid the dangerous traffic on the busy street. He shivered

Why hadn't he put on a jacket?

"No response?" he sarcastically asked.

Maybe the thing ought to provide a weather report before opening any portals.

Hundreds of bicycles filled the racks separating the twin six-story dorm buildings, but the early hour kept most students inside. A sign declared admittance only with proper identification.

He didn't need to show anybody anything.

Rich saw where he wanted to go, opened a portal, and exited twenty feet from where he disappeared. The lobby was quiet, except for two Asian girls reading textbooks on a ragged couch. They didn't notice his entry.

Rich pressed the elevator up-button, to go to the sixth floor, room 617. And after everything that had happened in the last few days, he was suddenly nervous at seeing his own son.

⋏

The graveyard shift almost finished, a DHS agent nabbed a few hours of sleep, the other remained watchful. Or as watchful as he could be. The surveillance of Matt Preston was fraught with boredom. Steve Cable stubbed out his Marlboro and sat back. The entrance to the dormitory was just a few feet away, watched from inside a Cox Cable van given special parking consideration by the campus police.

Steve kicked the DHS agent dozing in a camp chair beside him.

"Hey, get up, get up! We got Preston here. Man, he was right there at the front door. He was fucking there. He's gotta be inside."

"Not possible," his partner said, but sat up anyway. "Neesa has him in PC."

"I'm telling you it was him. Roll the recording back."

A few taps on the mouse-pad and the laptop replayed Richard Preston walking into the parking area from the overpass then his sudden disappearance at the front entrance.

"Some kind of glitch," the man said, wiping sleep from his eyes. "Did he enter the building?"

"Had to. Why do you think he came all this way? Upload the tracking."

"Already did. Waiting for the visual recognition response."

Steve split his attention - from the window and back to the computer screen resting beside him. "See, it was him! Call Talley, wake him up."

"Isn't Poppa Bear supposed to be in Park City?"

Steve shook his head. "Neesa's toast."

Chapter 12

The stainless-steel elevator doors slid open and Rich stepped into a glass-enclosed lobby. A scarred sign directed him to his right, and he entered a long hallway made from cinderblock walls coated with paint so often that the mortar joints were barely visible.

Rich stood at another intersection, reading the flyers and stapled posters on a bulletin board. He began to practice different dialogues with Matt, often concluding with a sarcastic, "Oh yeah, there's a computer download going on in my head, but it lets me go anywhere I want."

Navy-blue room doors opened and students filled the hallway, headed for common area bathrooms. Just babies. Young adults by age, but they were still children - with acne, bed-head, and pajamas.

He felt old, out of date, and suddenly in the spotlight. The doors continued to open and girls in robes, and sweats, and towels crowded the hallway, carrying toothbrushes and baggies bulging with makeup. They giggled comments to boys hurrying to use morning accommodations.

Matt had said the dorm was co-ed by floors, not rooms, and he'd hoped the hallway would be deserted. He no longer looked homeless, but even so, he felt their young, suspicious eyes looking his way. He stepped back.

At the end of the hallway, a slim man in a long t-shirt and a scruffy beard looked his way. The spitting image of Shaggy of Scooby Do fame. Had to be the residence monitor.

Crap! He turned to leave. Maybe he'd call or text Matt and they could meet later for lunch, at a less hectic place. He rubbed the top of his forehead, shielding his face and turned back towards the elevator. He stopped at the intersection and looked back down the crowded hallway.

Shaggy, the hall-monitor, was blocked by a group of girls crowding the hallway.

The bug in his brain twitched. He posed a question, "Are there motes in here?"

Affirmative.

"I don't see anything, show me."

He arched his brows as dust dropped from the ceiling, lifted up from the carpet, even appearing to ooze from the slick block walls. A girl dressed in a towel swatted the air.

A voice yelled from the mix in the hall. "Wake and bake."

Answered by a chorus of, "I want some."

"Can I see what they see?" Rich asked, mouthing the words.

Affirmative.

"Show me."

A multitude of images - hustling students, bare skin, the dark stained carpet, T-bar ceiling, a dead fly, a rainbow, of dark color. The images flew at him in an incomprehensible speed. Rich grabbed his head.

The hall monitor pushed past a shirtless boy, his face intent on Rich. He yelled over the din. "Hey, you!"

"That's enough, stop." The pain subsided, and the hallway colors returned to the Wolfpack silver and blue.

He pressed the elevator call button and walked in. Shaggy the hall monitor sneered as the door closed in his face.

"Can I see Matt?"

Insufficient memory data.

Did it mean it didn't know who Matt was? Or where he was?

The elevator stopped at the third floor and opened for three girls carrying backpacks. Their chattering conversation intensified, happy with having the elevator to themselves.

The phone rang, the ringtone injecting a measure of angst into Neesa. All day she had felt as if she failed a college final exam. Neesa closed her eyes, exhaled and tapped the accept button.

"Neesa?"

She had heard Burdette's slow sit-down-while-I-rip-your-head-off tone all too often.

She cracked her neck bones with a twist. "Go ahead."

"Have you followed the events of the last few hours?"

"Yes, sir. The egg has broken up and blown away. Very weird."

"That's true. But not those events. The events transpiring in Reno. Are you monitoring the operational status log?"

Lovely. Let's start with a condescending tone and jump right to her jugular. She took another deep breath. To be fair, she'd missed something. Again.

"I really haven't had time," she said. "Switching off with Mel, watching the condo."

"Let me recap for you. Steve Cable identified Preston entering his son's dormitory less than an hour ago. Now let's see."

She heard him count in a whisper.

"If you've been losing sleep waiting for Preston to get out of bed, then what's he doing in Reno?"

"No one has entered or left this structure since the dentist arrived late last night," Neesa said. "No one."

The white Tahoe began backing out of the garage. "The Doc's truck is leaving, I need to roll. Can I call you back after reset?"

"Listen to me. Stay put. Make a visit to Preston's condo. Go inside if he doesn't answer the door and take a look around. Then, Neesa, call me at your earliest convenience."

No way could Preston have traveled the 550 miles to Reno overnight. It was at least an eight-hour drive, plus another three to get through the roadblocks and traffic jams in and around Winnemucca. A commercial flight was impossible, airline pilots refused to land in Reno because of the Egg.

Her fingers tapped icons on the laptop, initializing the Big Brother tracking program, commandeering camera's throughout the Park City area - Highway 224 traffic cameras, security cameras on the Whole Foods, TJ Maxx, retail shops, bus stops, I-80 overpass cameras, Foxpoint Homeowner's Association security cameras, all drafted into service. Neesa watched the tracking program flash innumerable vantage points as it followed the white SUV using a GPS program.

She relaxed seeing Eric's black Escalade within twenty yards of the target. Someone was on it.

She checked her sidearm, put on a light jacket to conceal it, and climbed from the van to pay a visit to the Winnemucca Man.

The portal opened and Rich stepped into a sloped loading dock behind an Albertson's grocery store in the Boise suburb of Eagle, less than a mile from his house. Gray clouds pillowed in the sky kept the air crisp, and still. He'd seen the rarely used dock during his trips for groceries or coffee. It was a good, isolated spot.

Across the street was a small strip mall and a Starbucks coffee shop, and Rich joined a line five deep. He fidgeted with his phone while listening to customers' excited talk of the Winnemucca cloud and its disappearance.

Beta transit motes, people, let's get it right.

He craned his neck at the counter and the chubby customer ordering the triple super-duper latte with shots of this and a dash of whatever.

Like you seriously need that, Buckwheat.

His eyes darted from the customers to the baristas, not allowing his eyes to linger and draw attention. A woman wearing a stained green apron swiped his credit card as Rich glanced down to the newspaper stand by his knees.

His own face stared back at him.

Boise Man Still Missing in Cloud was headlined in large black letters on the front page of the Idaho Statesman. An equally ominous headline, **Person of Interest** sat below a picture matching his driver's license. His mouth was suddenly dry. He rubbed his forehead.

The click of camera shutters, a flash of bright light over his right shoulder. A young man in a blue and orange Boise State University hoodie, aiming his smart phone at him, snapping pictures.

Rich grabbed his coffee and retreated through a growing murmur. Customers nodded towards him, others pointed. A young mother ignored her crying baby to stand and point her phone at him. A few were undoubtedly dialing 911.

Rich pushed through the front door.

Crossing the street, he glanced back over his shoulder. Customers had followed him out and gathered at the front door, most holding their camera phones at arm's length, filming him. His adrenaline surged. Now he knew what a hunted animal felt like.

He jogged back to the rear of the grocery store with the hot coffee slopping from the lid's vent, burning his thumb.

He pleaded with the voice in his head to open a wormhole portal.

▲

An agonizing hour ticked off before Burdette's Yukon reached the Egg's former nest. He had ordered Alex the Aussie to prevent the media and military from trespassing beyond the existing perimeter barricade. Alex had grumbled the task was impossible and asked permission to use the local *Mates* as backup.

They passed a mile-long convoy of military vehicles idling on the shoulder, obviously waiting for the order to seize the site. Soldiers milled around Humvees and diesel trucks that towed equipment hidden beneath camouflage tarps. Three trailered M1-A1 tanks intended as military business cards lead the convoy.

A half-mile from the site, police cars, media equipment, assorted sedans and trucks jammed the highway. A row of bright orange Porto-Potties lined the shoulder, opposite a brigade of roach-coach food vendors readying for business.

Burdette directed the driver to use a fenced-off swath of grass beyond the highway shoulder. The barbed wire was simply clipped by the driver using his Leatherman utility tool, but their off-road travel was jarring. Narrow culverts cut by rain caused the SUV's weighted rear end to slam into the ground, raising clouds of dust and taking a toll on their speed, and kidneys.

They slowed at a roadblock manned by a Nevada Highway Patrol trooper. He waved their SUV to halt. Burdette climbed out, baring his teeth at the hundreds of men, women, and hippies walking on the road, and into the expanse of sagebrush left by the Egg's disappearance.

"Damn," Burdette hissed. "What are these people doing in my crime scene?"

The trooper crossed his arms and stood back. "You can have it if you show me some identification."

The driver flashed his badge and ID. The three men in the backseat climbed out and waited for Burdette's lead.

"Scott, inventory every person out here. Get help if you need to, but I want the names of everyone."

Uniformed police officers, men and women wearing EPA and FBI jackets, women in tie-dyed tees, men talking into microphones, military officers dressed in desert camouflage, the crowd swarmed the area. Burdette shook his head.

Nothing could be done. There were too many people. Still, the area looked pristine and dwarfed the hundreds of people spreading out into a super-sized Easter egg hunt in search of clues or souvenirs.

Burdette scanned the sky, looked up and down the highway, found his bearings and headed for the blue Ford pickup.

"That would be the last vehicle to enter the egg before it became impenetrable."

Burdette looked at the trooper escorting his group and noted the nametag on the man's uniform, Clayton Crane.

"And you would know that how?" Burdette asked.

The man increased his pace to catch up.

"I was first on site. Your tech guys have my cruiser. Figure out what went wrong with it yet?"

"Nothing yet, Officer Crane. How long after the cloud appeared did the William's twins appear?"

"Pretty quick, within ten minutes."

"But you never saw the Preston man?"

"Like I told your investigators, – I would've seen him if he came out. The place wasn't so – well – so crowded."

"Interesting."

A red Ford Taurus was treated with forensic precision; photographs, fingerprints, and gathering trace materials. He walked the short distance to the truck, noting the Famous Potatoes license plate of Idaho.

What triggered a cloud of dust to solidify? Was it Preston, one of the vehicles? Or was Preston a victim here?

Burdette approached a technician working inside the truck, his coveralls stenciled with traffic yellow DHS letters. "What do you have?"

The gray-haired tech stopped dusting for fingerprints on the dashboard. "Not much. Same shape as the others. We'll have lab results as soon as we can get this back to Reno." He pointed at an assemblage of plastic bags, paperwork and small vials at Burdette's feet.

"Residual trace?" Burdette asked.

"Got a bit. The entire area hasn't been canvassed yet. But check the hood out. Kind of intriguing."

Burdette swiveled on his heel, pausing to study the granite mountain peak that was for days, the backdrop of every cable news' broadcast. He turned his attention to the mix of men and women canvassing the grass and sagebrush, recognizing some as belonging to the FBI and NSA.

Ten yards up the highway, a dark haired man with olive skin tone and white coveralls dropped to his knees and spooned a sample of sand into a glass vial then screwed the lid tight. The technician's face seemed familiar, but his slicked-back black hair and clean-shaven skin didn't fit for a technician stationed at a remote site without even basic accommodations. Maybe one of the Microdyne employees he was warned about?

The names of the people swarming the area would be inventoried and reviewed. Burdette walked to the front of the truck and squinted at the symbols outlined in the black fingerprint dust. Pi. Mobius. And, well, a squiggle, one-half of the equivalent symbol standing on end. The symbols seemed too complex for an uneducated electrician. He snapped several pictures using his phone and emailed them to Portland.

He checked his email. His text messages seemed to double with the Egg's disappearance. He dialed Neesa Becks as the black-haired technician passed by, within five feet, looked Burdette in the eye, and nodded with his chin. Neesa's phone rang five times.

"I was just getting ready to call you back. Preston's wife and the Doc are back at work. The parabolic mike has arrived and will be up within the hour, and-" Neesa said.

"Any idea how Preston got to Reno?"

"I have no idea but he-."

"And then to Boise? You know he's in Boise. Check the operational log, young lady. Make it a habit. The file containing the internet flags. Seven hits on Facebook showed Poppa Bear at a Starbucks in Eagle, Idaho less than thirty minutes ago. Instagram, Twitter, his picture is popping up on all of them. He has to have a private jet at his disposal." Burdette said. The one-sided conversation more of a sounding board for his own thoughts, "Now, go question Cyndi Preston."

"You want me to break cover?"

"This Egg and Preston are linked. Let's put this clown to bed, then we can focus our attention on this unknown substance. Approach her with all that charm you have, identify yourself, then twist her arm into producing her husband. Convey the fact he is only wanted for questioning, at the moment. Then threaten to arrest her and parade her in front of that media circus you got going there. If she isn't dialing the phone by then, promise to arrest her children in Phoenix and Reno. I want her walking on eggsh... I'll deal with her when I get there."

"You're coming here, sir?"

"When I've finished here, I'm flying in. And Neesa?"

"Yes, sir?"

"No more slip-ups."

Burdette called Steve Cable in Reno.

"Preston still inside?"

"Gotta be. Talley's still looking. Exits are covered, but it's a big building."

"Then check the log, Steve. He's home. In fucking, Boise!"

Regular people checked email, surf the internet, played silly games, and paid their bills with smart phones, but his trained agents couldn't review a critical status log. "Where's Baby Bear?"

"No way. No fucking way did he get past us."

"Then he has a twin, a clone, a doppelganger from a parallel universe. Where's the kid?"

"Still asleep in his room, doesn't have a class till 2:00. Captain, I'm telling ya, Poppa Bear didn't leave through any door. And how the hell could he get to Boise that fast?"

"Working on it." Burdette hung up.

He looked at a white puff of a cloud sitting above the mountain peak. Preston's magic act was good, but a charade. That much travel in a twelve-hour period required sophisticated travel plans, a jet, ground transportation, and a lot of money - the type of financing that left a paper trail. The kind usually out of reach for a construction worker.

Maybe the monstrous egg was a test run, for something on a larger scale, even more deadly. Preston had the key. He had to know what the dust was, and how it was able to render sophisticated electronics useless.

That made the man dangerous.

Scrolling through numbers on his smart phone, he thought about the conversation with the DHS Secretary. The Vice-President already knew what the dust was, so why hadn't that crucial information been disseminated? Burdette held his finger above the dial button. Was it coincidence Andrew Preston's military records were stonewalled by the Army and the V.P. was a former member of the Joint Chiefs of Staff?

Not likely.

He made one final call. "Prep for Salt Lake, takeoff in two hours."

⚔

Rich stumbled over a chunk of sandstone as he stepped from the portal. It wasn't like he could see exactly where he was going. The portals burned the image he concentrated on, leaving anything, or anyone, around it unseen until he passed through. The doorways might be dangerous if he wasn't careful.

The morning air was crisp and clean. The flat landscape covered in sagebrush and creosote stretched to the horizon, sliced open by the merlot-colored cliffs of a canyon dropping 1500 feet straight down to the Colorado River below. The Touweep overlook on the Grand Canyon's north rim was awe-inspiring.

Rich had brought Matt, Noah, and Andy on a men-only camping trip to this very spot, driving two hours on a washboard road - to be stunned by Mother Nature's spectacle. The sheer cliffs were interlaced by deep vertical crevices, and house-sized boulders sat precariously on narrow ledges. No tourist walkways, no fences, no signs warning of a danger due to falling, Touweep was primitive, unblemished and heart stopping.

Rich stood terrified as Andy teetered on the edge, raising his arms like wings, and swear he would jump and soar like one of the eagles circling below. In hindsight, the reason for Andy's death-defying performance was clear. Secrets, lies, and mistakes can't fly unless they're given wings. They made camp as the sun fell, and the four mountain-men wannabes sat in silence, dangling their feet over a cliff, laughing, and listening to the faint roar of Rattlesnake Rapids a quarter mile below.

Rich was not alone. Two blue nylon dome tents occupied the overlook's two campsites close to the edge, where a sleepy camper needing to empty his bladder might simply disappear in a moonless night. Disappointed by the thought of others invading his memory, he searched the far side of the canyon a half-mile away, fixed his sight on a locomotive sized chunk of sandstone and opened a portal across the canyon.

Rich shuffled to the cliff edge, his stomach fluttered from the dizzying height. No roads or trails, and access only by helicopter. And now beta transit wormholes. Here he felt secure and sat down cross-legged. The high-octane coffee began to make his bowels groan and rumble.

He began talking to the voice.

ꓥ

Cyndi stared at the computer. The cursor blinked like a hypnotic talisman. The soothing sound of the waiting room waterfall was completely wasted on her.

What Rich claimed was impossible. After a good night's sleep and in the comfort of a warm bed, she'd convinced herself Rich was delusional and his sunken cadaverous eyes proved it. Andy's death had finally sent Rich over the edge. Brooke's miraculous appearance was a trick. The dog was on the patio, tied up, and waiting for her grand entrance. This might make a great story for the kids, but no way did he just pop in from Boise.

Still, that burning outline of color when he appeared out of nowhere, and the smell of home. How did he fake that?

He wasn't a liar. He'd hide from the truth maybe, avoid it, but he wouldn't lie. What he claimed was impossible, and yet that giant egg thing in Winnemucca had been impossible.

What did he find inside?

What found him?

She curled her hair with a pencil, pulled it loose and began twisting it again. The door opened, and an unexpected patient walked in. Dressed in a black pants suit and white blouse, Neesa looked as if she was heading to a board of director's meeting.

"Good morning, Neesa." Cyndi said. "You weren't scheduled-."

"Mrs. Preston, we need to talk." Neesa brandished her DHS badge and identification.

Cyndi arched her brows and stood up. "Excuse me?"

"Read my identification. I am with the Department of Homeland Security. We need to discuss Richard Joseph Preston."

"Rich hasn't done anything, what do you want him for?"

"Should we talk here or take a drive to our office in Salt Lake? Which would be more convenient?"

Cyndi shook her head, folding her arms across her chest and narrowed her eyes, "I said Rich hasn't done anything so what's this about?"

"Here or somewhere else?" Nessa nodded sideways towards two waiting patients reading magazines. The woman's implication was clear.

"Hold on a minute." Cyndi retreated down the hallway and into Doug's empty office. Her hands trembled as she searched for ICE on her phone. She tightened her jaw, waiting for his voicemail message to finish.

"Call me now! There's a woman here who is threatening to take me to Salt Lake and she has a badge. Now, Preston."

She found Megan in the sterilization room and escorted her to the front desk, whispering instructions to the girl and assured her of a quick return.

Cyndi walked out the door with Neesa following two steps behind. Midway down the long hallway, at a water fountain separating the public restrooms, Cyndi turned.

"Now, what is this about?"

Neesa pulled her jacket back at the hip to expose a holstered handgun. "Where is your husband?"

Cyndi recoiled, "I really don't know."

"Please, Cyndi. We know he arrived home last night. He was spotted in Reno this morning and then in Boise about an hour ago. Where is he and who's helping him?"

Oh. My. God. He was telling the truth. She restrained a smile. "I don't know. He could be anywhere." How absurd the truth sounded.

Then she realized what the question meant and her cheeks started to burn. "You've been watching me?"

"Who is helping your husband, Cyndi? Park City is full of wealthy people. Is that why you live here, to stay close to the funding?"

"Helping him what? What funding? What are you talking about?"

Neesa nodded past her, and Cyndi turned to see a bulky man in chinos and blue shirt easing his way toward them. She straightened her back.

"Let me be clear," Neesa said. "Your husband is a prime suspect in a case of domestic terrorism."

They locked eyes. "Terrorism? Are you-"

Doug came out the office door and headed towards them. He was tall with muscles bulging from his lemon scrubs - a fanatic for the gym.

Neesa pointed her finger at Doug, "This does not concern you, sir. Please return to your office."

Doug stood next to Cyndi and lifted his chin. "When it comes to my family everything concerns me."

Neesa used her index finger again, this time smoothing her hair back in a needless gesture, "I won't get into this here, Mrs. Preston. You'll need to come with us. Sir, step back."

Cyndi followed Doug's glance to the man now five feet behind them, badge and weapon clearly displayed. Her stomach roiled. This was ridiculous.

Doug dialed his phone, lifted it to his ear. "Hold on, don't go anywhere, Cyndi."

"Sir, step away or you will be impeding a federal investigation." Neesa reached behind her jacket tail.

Cyndi raised her hands. "Everybody calm down. This is getting out of hand. Doug, who are you calling? What do you want with Rich? This is unbelievable. Just calm--"

Her heart soared then quickly crashed. She closed her eyes and cursed herself for calling Rich.

Her husband stormed out of the office door, his arms rigid, his hands balled, his stride long.

Fight written on his face.

⚓

The coffee had squeezed his colon into working overtime, until Rich ordered a portal directly into the bathroom at home. Sitting on the throne, Rich had listened to Cyndi's voice message. She sounded angry, but her voice cracked with fear. Adrenaline surged as he tucked his shirt in.

A portal to the Dental Spa was easy. He'd spent ten hours wiring the circuit to power the lobby's elaborate waterfall. He walked into a lobby buzzing with excited patients and employees.

Cyndi cocked her head with a 'don't make it worse' expression. Easy for her, but she wasn't the dog looking for a fight. He nodded to Doug and grinned at Cyndi – a false smile meant to soothe her.

She pressed her lips together.

The black girl was gorgeous, armed and the enemy. And, obviously the leader. "I think this young lady is finished with you guys. Go on back."

Cyndi frowned and reiterated that 'don't' face. He pulled his lips tight - a Two-Faced smile - and prodded them towards the office door.

"Don't worry, I got this." he said and waited until they paused at the Spa door.

His back to the agents, four years of pent-up anger surged like a desert flash flood - full of wild flotsam, and growing with a violence that took no prisoners.

Four years of politician's empty promises. Four years of unreturned emails and letters. Four years of being handed over to a government intern that only delivered the runaround.

He turned, baring his teeth. "Stay away from my wife." He took a step towards Neesa, as his fists closed tight. "Now, I'm someone you want to talk to? Nothing but crickets from you people so fuck you, lady. Fuck you and the horse you rode in on."

Both agents moved their hands to their weapons. The woman's partner puffed out his chest, and straightened his back. Rich pointed at him. "You're gonna need all nine bullets, Buckwheat."

"You need to come with us, Mr. Preston," the woman agent said, in a calm tone.

Rich took a step closer to the pretty woman. "Fuck you. Ignore me for years and now all of sudden I'm somebody you want to talk to."

"Preston!" Cyndi barked from the doorway and her voice sapped a degree of anger from his heart and his words.

"Got something to share about Andy now?"

Rich squinted, boring his eyes into the woman's chocolate eyes. She turned to her partner and held up her hand to keep him back.

"I didn't think so. All take and no give."

His right hand twitched. He saw the vein in her throat quiver. He saw the man's cheek burn red beneath his black beard. All targets for his fists.

"We have Andy's two-oh-one file at the office." The woman agent lifted her chin. "You come with us, answer our questions and you get what you want."

Rich flinched then calculated his first punch, picturing his knuckles kissing Buckwheat's eye socket. But hitting the woman was impossible. They probably knew karate or Israeli Kav Magra, something that would take him down to the carpet. Doug might join in, help him, and then lose his business for the effort. He couldn't do that. A no-win situation. He looked back at Cyndi pressed up against her brother's chest. She shook her head.

Rich took another step towards the woman. "Tell me what's in it. Throw me a bone so I can believe you. Or we're gonna have a serious problem."

She lifted her chin higher, cocked her head. "Are you threatening me?"

Rich smirked. "You and whatever bullshit agency you work for."

He shot a warning finger towards the man moving closer.

"Feeling froggy? Then jump."

"This is bullshit, Neesa," the man said, brandishing his cuffs.

The woman held her hand up and cleared her throat. "It's classified, but I'll allow you access to the file once you've answered our questions about the incident in Winnemucca."

Rich narrowed his eyes, "What's so hush-hush about a lowly PFC dying for his country? Tell me that?"

Neesa flinched. "Is this a test, sir? *Specialist Four* Andrew Preston was KIA in the Akbar Province of Afghanistan, but I'm sure you already knew that."

Rich licked his bottom lip. The lying bitch thought he was a dumb schmuck, a puppy begging for a biscuit. The door to the men's room was just a step away.

"Enough, Neesa." Buckwheat said. "This clown's coming now."

"Whoa, hold on there, Skipper. Sounds like you have what I want. I'll be coming along right peaceable." Rich held up his open palms. "But I gotta pee before we take that drive down the canyon." He licked his lower lip again, and nodded at the man's handcuffs. "Put those on and you'll have to hold it for me."

The female agent glared.

"Hurry the fuck up, douchebag," the man ordered.

"Bite me."

He pushed through the bathroom door with the Buckwheat three steps behind him.

He punched a wet towel hanging on the rack - in his own bathroom - 357 miles away.

⋏

Rich paced along the edge of a thousand-foot cliff fuming over Neesa's deception. Andy had requested and received a lateral promotion from Specialist to Corporal. Same rank and pay grade, but the new title sounded retro, and Andy loved anything from the decades before his birth. He had called Nikki and told her of his new title, said he was just waiting on the paperwork. Three weeks later, two uniformed men knocked on the door and sent Rich falling to his knees.

He teetered on the cliff edge, raising his arms like wings. If he jumped, would the thing inside him save him? Maybe he should turn himself in and save Cyndi and the kids from suffering from more of his embarrassing behavior.

She'd be okay. Probably give him a tongue-lashing, and maybe he deserved it. But *only* from her.

"And what do you got to say? Didn't crawl inside me expecting all this, did you?"

Download incomplete.

Words he began to loath.

Rich lowered his arms, and absorbed the spectacle of God's creation. The grand vista made him feel irrelevant - a speck of dust on a higher power's blueprint. A feeling he got gazing at infinite stars in an infinite night sky.

The sun at its zenith revealed hidden crevices and created strange new shadows. The air was cool, but Rich wished he'd brought water. The confrontation had cleared his mind and he accepted the premise that his own internal GPS was the required input the operating system needed to burn open wormholes.

"What are you downloading?' he asked.

Data.

"What kind of data?"

He regretted the question as the strange images flooded his mind.

"Stop. I don't understand the data."

Download incomplete.

"When will the download be complete?"

Unknown.

"Ya little prick." He began pacing the cliff edge again. Computer talk, just like Data. "*Why* is the download not complete?"

Insufficient memory access.

'Yours or mine?" He rephrased. "Operating system's memory or the host's memory." A long pause. A golden eagle circled high on a thermal.

The computer was broken. Return it to Best Buy.

Insufficient memory access.

"What kind of memory access is required for your download?" he yelled.

Biological shut down. External input zero. Memory receptors open.

"Say that again, slower," Rich said.

It did. The longest dialogue he'd heard yet and he tore the statement into bits, looking for a clue. Hypnosis. He'd done that to quit smoking. Become hypnotized to finish the download?

Negative.

Rich asked the same question five times, it answered identically five times and it gnawed at him. Three conditions. Not hypnotized. He pictured lying in a dark room… quiet…

"Asleep, you mean asleep."

Affirmative.

So he needed to sleep, and the download would be complete. No voice came back at him.

"If I go to sleep you'll finish the download? And you'll tell me what you're doing in my head?"

Download reinitialized.

Rich got excited. Answers for the bizarre cloud of dust motes, his ability to travel hundreds of miles with just a step, and especially the answer to why a computer program was put inside in his brain.

He turned from the canyon edge to pee and his mind filled with a vision - of Matt walking down the dorm's long hallway that he had visited earlier that morning. Wearing jeans, t-shirt and in the middle of two other boys. Matt was gesturing, mouthing something. He could hear nothing.

Rich waived the vision away, certain it was a subconscious reminder to call his son. He stepped back into his living room and called Matt. He shut his eyes, and prayed Matt wasn't in class or the library, prayed he would answer.

"Where you been, what's with you and this cloud and being wanted? How come you haven't answered my calls or texts?" Matt's words gushed out like water from a broken dam.

"Hi, son. How are you?" Rich said.

"This isn't about me. What's going on?"

"A lot's happened, and, well, it's a great story but ah…."

"I got time, tell me now."

"Is everything good? You should have enough card swipes to keep ya eating till Christmas break."

"Enough, Dad. What happened to you? People are saying the Prestons' are some kind of terrorists and shit like that."

Rich winced. Cyndi had scolded him often, *Cuss now and your sons will swear later.*

He sighed, "Yeah, I'm starting to get that. It's a long story. We should probably talk in person."

"You're driving back? The news said they found your truck in that egg thing."

"Yeah, it's kind of complicated. Let's do lunch tomorrow. I'll take ya to that Wolf Den again. I'll get the Awful-Awful this time."

"Got class till four but-"

"Skip class, this is important. I'll call you when I'm on my way. Okay?"

"Not running off to Alaska, are you? You wanted people to rise up and demand answers about Andy. Now is your chance, the whole world would listen to what you have to say."

Matt was right. But the world wasn't ready for his story, not with so many questions remaining unanswered.

Rich steered the conversation to Matt pledging SAE fraternity, cleaning the frat house each Sunday after Saturday night's chaos, and caroling profanity-laced songs to an adoring sister sorority. Rich's anger had disappeared, and he felt content with their conversation.

"Can't wait to see you tomorrow," Rich said.

"Okay, text me when you get here. You're driving all the way back down?"

"Just a hop, skip and a jump these days. I'll see you tomorrow."

"Hey, Dad, that Egg thing you were in, do you know what it was?"

Rich hesitated. "Yeah, Matt, I have an idea. Not one hundred percent sure, but I'll tell you when I see you. Love you, bye." He waited.

"K, love you bye," Matt said.

Rich smiled. Matt would never be too old to tell him 'I love you.' If a nineteen-year old could say the words…. His smile faded. The Homeland Security agent's lies surfaced again.

Rich flexed his fingers.

And like a rubber band, they curled back into fists.

∧

The aircraft's turbulent ride caused Burdette to pace the tarmac of the executive air terminal in Salt Lake City. His stomach tightened with one final spasm and began to relax. He accepted Steve Cable's incoming call and listened to a report on a conversation between Matt and Richard Preston.

DHS software determined Matt Preston's cell signal originated from the campus library, Agent Talley confirmed Matt's location visually.

"Poppa Bear's cell location returned scrambled again," Steve said. "Just like before. But they set a play date. The meeting time is undetermined, but Senior intends to enjoy a Wolf burger at the den. Bloody and greasy burger, if you ask me. Anyway, the kid said Daddy wanted people to rise up and revolt, and demand answers. But here's the kicker, Senior conceded he knew what the egg was. Sounds like we have the ingredients to make a case."

"Indeed." Burdette hung up.

Slumped in the rear seat of a black Escalade, Burdette rolled his window down halfway, letting the cool air clear the last of the airsickness from his body. Was Preston a case of faulty intelligence? As part of the team of investigators in search of Sadaam's supposed WMD's, he'd learned one thing - you can be spoon-fed bullshit until you crap out diamonds.

Threads linking Richard Preston, his dead son, the Vice President's Microdyne corporation and the strange dust were coincidence, maybe. He'd written Preston off as an opportunist, using the egg object to shield an alcoholic bender or a date with a mistress. Now it was a glaring reminder of jumping to conclusions.

Preston was either a magician or had planned everything to absolute perfection.

The driver stomped on the gas pedal to pass a tanker truck and the lurch of acceleration agitated his queasy stomach. He surmised surveillance operations conducted by the NSA, FBI and CIA would reveal nothing more than his own. DHS field reports uploaded into the server were shared with the other government entities, but the case fell under guidelines spelled out in the Patriot Act, therefore jurisdiction of the domestic terrorism would remain with him.

Burdette ignored the lateral gee's of the SUV as it sped up the curving three-lane Interstate 80 into Park City. Preston's cell phone-locator beacon returned an undetermined address, and that fact alone unnerved him. Preston was a master electrician, but being able to wire a house didn't give him the expertise needed for disabling a phone's transmitting sequence. And he had recently relocated to Idaho, a stereotypical refuge for Aryan nationalists, sovereign citizens, and isolated enclaves of anarchists. He fit the profile for membership in a disaffected group, but nothing in the man's background check pointed in that direction. If Preston's goal was anarchy, then why jet around like a globetrotting billionaire?

The unanswered questions added to Burdette's queasiness.

Burdette made his decision, one that would skirt the law, even with the latitude afforded by the all-encompassing Patriot Act. He would deal with potential repercussions later. Burdette decided to "retrieve" the family members closest to Preston.

He had no doubts the angry father would come out gunning, but he would come out.

Burdette called Steve. "Put in motion a silent retrieval of Matt Preston, no media, and minimal civilian observation. Proceed at 0400 hours. I'll direct the operation from Park City. Full head gear, I'll be riding high on your heads."

"Aye, Captain." Steve said. "We'll yank him out of bed- that's if he's even asleep yet. If anybody asks, we'll say his parents are sending him off to drug-rehab boot camp."

"Excellent cover story. Have a passion for that field, do you?" Burdette said.

He ended the called and dialed Neesa.

As his caffeine buzz crashed, Rich felt the lingering weariness of dehydration take its place. He wanted, and needed, to play catch up in the sleep department, and maybe the download would finish. He paced the wood floors of the home in Boise but was too nervous to lie down. Someone might be across the street watching him right now. A SWAT team might knock down the front door while he slept. Cyndi's house was under surveillance.

He checked the streets through a crack in the drapes. The neighboring homes appeared normal. He fingered the curtain frame as he waited for a car to drive by on Floating Feather Road, a hundred yards away. Long minutes passed. No police, no cars, people, dogs, bikes, nothing whatsoever moved. Impossible. He'd spent enough sleepless nights to know that even at three in the morning, something traveled up the busy street every few minutes.

He rushed into the garage and gathered the nylon bag containing a camping tent, a sleeping bag, and a pillow wrapped in a white garbage bag, and took it to Touweep. He made three trips, each one more hurried. The final passage included a box of Ritz-Bitz crackers and a one-gallon jug of water.

A cool wind blew from the south, but the afternoon sun was still warm. Years of working in temperatures that could exceed 120 degrees prepared him for the heat, made him savvy to its debilitating power. He removed his dress shirt, and used the long sleeves to knot it around his head like an Arab sheik.

He spread out the tent, the pressure of the last few days angering him.

"I've done nothing wrong. This is bullshit, you freaking motes turn my life upside down, and now I'm on the run."

He used a rock to pound a tent peg into a crack, "And for what? You don't tell me a frigging thing except download incomplete." The steel peg collapsed and he tossed it over the cliff.

"At least you gave me a hell of a way to run away."

He paused before hammering another peg and searched the canyon below, debating whether to move all the gear down to the river below. Maybe later. His muscles were tired, and besides, the view was amazing.

The blue and gray domed tent finally anchored with a single peg, he stored the gear inside the tent to provide ballast. He admired his accomplishment as sweat poured down his face. A nostalgic memory of camping with his boys caused him to sit and hang his head.

His children hated him. Who could blame them? He would grow to be a bitter old man, a man who caused his son's death.

He heard a tiny scream, and looked up. Another faint scream. He crawled to the cliff edge and looked down. Three inflatable river rafts negotiated the whitewater below.

Just push off and fly, all the way down. End it all.

Not yet.

Not until he learned how Andy died, if he'd suffered.

A blast of hot wind buffeted the tent, causing it to swivel on the single anchor pin. The tent settled at the cliff edge. The cliff face turned angry red as the sun began its descent into the horizon of creosote and cactus. Deep cracks and crevices stretched open, revealing secrets hidden for millennia.

Rich rolled out the sleeping bag inside the tent, grumbling over the forgotten air mattress. Intending only to test the accommodations, he sprawled atop the sleeping bag.

A trace of Cyndi's lavender shampoo scented the pillow.

He fell asleep.

The probe continued integrating data into the organic memory lattice as soon as the sensory input fell to acceptable levels. Three hours later, it executed the untested module, setting it free, to gauge its effects on the host.

The subroutine executed, rather it woke up, and slowly assessed its situation. Confused, and disoriented, the AI traveled through the host's memories, building models of its location and condition. The subroutine reached for a pillow, tongued a strange taste, nothing responded. It worked what felt like a mouth.

Dada?

END OF PART ONE

Chapter 13

The nightmare was no different from others Rich endured after Andy's death. Two men wearing military uniforms, gold service bars on their sleeves, a rainbow of medals and ribbons pinned to their chests escorted his baby-faced son to a black car idling in the street. Andy looked back over his shoulder, long black hair hiding his eyes, and cried, "Why did you say that?"

Rich couldn't move, paralyzed on his front porch, the snarl of construction machines intensified - a chain saw, maybe a wood chipper. The soldiers pulled Andy to hurry, and looked back at Rich with evil smiles, and nodded their appreciation.

Except it wasn't a dream.

His eyes jolted wide open and stared at black. The nightmare was real, and Matt was their victim. His heart jackhammered into the soft down of the sleeping bag.

But... no, it had to be a dream. Didn't it?

As if a film played in his mind, two men dressed in jeans and black windbreakers were escorting Matt – Matt, not Andy - down a hallway. The men wore helmets with mini-cameras riding high and emitting a green laser beam. The strange light brought him to full consciousness. Their faces were shadowed, but their jackets displaying a gold DHS was clear.

Matt fell to his knees, naked except black boxer shorts. The men jerked him to his feet and continued down the hallway of navy-blue doors spaced every few feet.

Rich sat up and flicked sand from his eyes. The vision wasn't a dream. It was happening at this very moment, as he sat doing nothing. He stood up, bumping his head on the tent frame. The pain exorcised all doubts of where he was. He tripped over the nylon threshold of the door flap and stepped into a moonlit night.

Son of a bitch!

Concentrating on dimples in a stainless steel elevator door, he stepped into a wormhole – falling with the portal's tug - and emerging into the dormitory's elevator lobby. He turned the corner into the long corridor, fluorescent lights buzzed. He narrowed his eyes.

He blocked the soldier's path to the elevator.

Rich pulled off the white shirt still tied tight to his head, unsure of what to do. The men exchanged words. Matt looked half-asleep, possibly drugged, maybe in shock, but he straightened his back when he recognized Rich.

"Papa San." One of the soldiers said, and released Matt's arm, dropping his hand to a holstered weapon. "Bonus points for us."

Rich narrowed his eyes at the men a few feet in front of him. "And you're taking my son, where?" His voice carried loud and clear.

The snarky soldier approached, showing empty palms. "Frat party. But we'd rather go with you."

These men were no different from those who shipped Andy off to the meat grinder in Afghanistan, fodder for Taliban ambushes and IED's. No way would he allow them to take his youngest son. A portal wouldn't help. He wasn't sure Matt would be allowed to pass through. So…. charge the men or surrender. He would never surrender, especially in front of his son.

"Show me," he whispered.

Dust fell from the ceiling, rained from the lights, lifted off the stained carpet, steamed in from beneath blue doors, and floated off the shiny brick walls. The air grew heavy with floating dust. The temperature warmed.

The men holding Matt faded from view.

He balled his fists, steeling himself for a charge while the advantage was his. Bowling pins. He'd knock them all down, then pull Matt up and lead him out the back exit and then to…, it didn't matter. They'd be safe.

Their weapons made him hesitate. He lowered his head.

A green laser pierced the fog from behind him. He turned his head and was blinded by the green beam of light. Someone seized his wrist, twisted his arm and jerked it up his back. Pain shot up his shoulder blade. Rich screamed, twisting his head around. The hall monitor he'd seen earlier. Shaggy.

"This dust seems to follow you, sir." Shaggy said. "My boss would like to know why."

Shaggy reeked of cigarette smoke and body odor.

Rich asked a portal back to his garage and saw the floating tennis ball just a step away. He tried to step forward but the snarky soldier blocked his way, pushing his face inches from Rich's eyes.

"Where ya going, Papa San?" the snarky man said. "Bathroom breaks are not allowed on my watch. Tell me how you managed that little trick."

"Let him go," Rich said.

"Or what?" Snarky said.

Rich struggled to pull his arm free, intense pain shot into his shoulder. He was powerless and he hated the feeling. He was powerless to find out about Andy, and now he was powerless to help Matt.

He closed his eyes and searched inward for help, adrenaline prodding his brain to think logically. But nothing came. Helpless. Helpless. He remembered his entombment by the mote swarm, the complete and utter helplessness.

Rich narrowed his eyes. The man in his face had breath rank with a mixture of coffee and cigarettes. Everything about him stunk of the military. Rich closed his eyes, picturing the Shaggy's gaunt face attacked by a hive of motes, his black windbreaker swarmed by trillions. The motes controlled him, now he controlled the motes. He formed the crude mental picture and asked the voice, "Can you do the same thing to them?"

Affirmative.

"Then do it!"

"Do what, Psycho?" Snarky reached for something behind his back.

Insufficient quantities for isolation.

The number of motes required to duplicate that Egg was inconceivable, but more dust was possible. "Call it, make it, I don't care. Just get it here."

"Not psycho, Steve, he's schizophrenic," Shaggy said.

Sparks began to pop in the hallway, snaps and crackles sounded as the motes self-replicating process gained momentum. The temperature kicked-up to sauna levels. Shaggy's grip on his arm loosened.

The motes swarmed.

His arm was released, and his eyes grew wide. The dust fell on helmets and jackets, conjoined into a thin film, a layer, a blanket, piling on at an inconceivable rate.

"What the…" Shaggy gagged and swatted at the fog. His face jerked wildly, his green laser cut through the muddy air like a light show at a heavy metal rock concert. Rich stepped backwards, somehow reliving his own nightmare.

Shaggy stumbled as his white arms waved wildly at the fog, then he slowed under the onslaught of motes.

Rich spit a wad of gritty saliva, remembered a wad of motes becoming a tongue of sand, snaking down his own throat. He stepped back again.

The mote swarm swirled, undulating like a flock of birds, landing on faces, clothes and weapons. Their bodies took on a grotesque shape, like drops of melted white plastic. The Shaggy thing emitted a faint green glow. Cameras. The light beams were tied to their helmet cameras. Someone, somewhere, was watching all this.

Rich turned to face the last soldier, his face knotted in a mix of anger and fear. Matt and the man stood frozen in horror. Matt suddenly pulled his wrist free and stepped back.

"Him, too," Rich said, and concentrated on a yellow DHS. The air was overrun, saturated with motes, and noise. Snap. Crackle. Pop. The dust swirled around the man and he disappeared into a dust devil of grey-white anger. He wasn't sure where they were all coming from, but he didn't care. The process took just a few seconds.

Disbelief etched on his face, Matt stepped back from the squirming blob, its final shape still in flux, changing with weak attempts to swat away the impossible.

"Hold still!" Rich yelled.

Matt's head jerked to face his father then back to the thing resembling a stunted grey mushroom. Matt's eyes wide with terror and disbelief made Rich move quick, reaching his son with a few long strides.

"Told ya it was a weird story." Rich embraced Matt in a bear hug.

Matt was trembling. "What is that stuff? Who are these guys?"

"You won't believe…."

He pushed Matt backwards and held him by the shoulders. Tears raced down his son's face. A mental picture exploded from the back of Rich's mind. A new vision. Green laser lights. Yellow DHS letters. Men dressed in the identical black clothing. The vision came into focus. A green laser light knifed into the bedroom as the door pushed open. Rich squeezed his eyes shut, separating the reality of the dorm hallway from the vision of the bedroom. The laser sliced back and forth, hitting the television, the nightstand, the white comforter,

And settled on Cyndi's terrified face.

Burdette leaned back in a chair, but the cramped interior of the utility van stuffed with gear wouldn't allow it. Though the van parked a hundred yards from Cyndi's condominium he still felt miles away

Burdette checked the real-time video transmissions of his joint operations on two screens. A time-date stamp in the bottom left corner with the agent's name in the top right of each image. He watched both Neesa and Steve's camera perspectives on the screens. He'd interrogate Cyndi Preston personally after Neesa's retrieval. A spouse was often the weak link in a conspiracy. Considered routine and low risk, the operation was proceeding like clockwork.

He checked his email, and sighed at the confirmation of his flight reservation to Denton, Texas. He'd still have to visit the storage space with his mother's belongings and Robyn's meager few items. Wasn't much inside, a few old lawn tools, a rug and two antique dressers, one drawer full of photographs protected inside zip-locked baggies - the last remaining evidence that a Burdette family tree ever existed. He'd choose a few pictures of Robyn in happier times to share with his mother, hope they might spark a memory in her addled mind.

Robyn might have been married by now, maybe a couple of kids to keep the Burdette lineage moving forward, if not in name, at least in blood. She loved kids.

Burdette shook his head seeing Matt Preston lash out at Steve after being rudely awaked. The boy threw on a T-shirt handed to him by Steve. On the other screen, Neesa's team was disembarking from the black SUV parked twenty feet south of the condominium's front door.

"Three squared plus four squared equals five squared," he whispered. "Everything's five by five." The simplicity of the sum of squares, life should be just as easy.

He ping-ponged his eyes between the two screens. Burdette sat up straight as Richard Preston appeared on the screen. He'd turned a corner dressed in a white T-shirt and a… Was that a white keffiyeh?

He leaned closer to the screen. Steve's camera focused on his target. Preston removed the headgear and tossed it to the floor, his facial expression was blank, but his lips quivered. A facial tic? Tourette's syndrome, maybe? He released his breath and sat back as Talley restrained Preston from behind. He picked up his phone to schedule a flight to Reno. He could interrogate Cyndi Preston in route.

The screen flickered with static then went white.

Tapping the escape button once, he cycled to Talley's camera. More static. Hitting the button again, hard, Burdette watched through Ryan's transmission.

What the…

The hallway was engulfed in a grey fog, smoke perhaps. The air cleared, revealing what looked like giant snowmen standing next to Preston. Seconds later, Burdette's final viewpoint turned white. He tapped the escape key, switching from white to white, only the names at the top of the screen changed. With a quick glance, he checked Neesa's viewpoint. Her team was entering the condominium.

Burdette tapped his smart phone. "Get back-up to Nye Hall, now!"

⋏

Cyndi turned on her side and groaned, the red 4:02 of the clock shined like a doomsday countdown. There would be no more sleep, but she didn't want to abandon the warmth of the down comforter.

Neesa's threat to arrest Nikki, Noah, and Matt had haunted her all day, and now kept her tossing and turning in bed. She was relieved Rich chose to flee instead of starting a fight. And it had surprised her.

She had hid a smile when neither DHS agent could find him inside the bathroom, then held Doug's arm tight as Neesa came at her, brandishing handcuffs. Doug shielded her and offered his phone, telling Neesa that his lawyer, Paul Heaton would like some questions answered before any action was taken.

She had a hard time buying Rich's incredible story, but that was before his exit from a bathroom where there was none. She wasn't surprised Rich hadn't returned to the condo.

It still bothered her, though. What was the thing in his head, the voice - what did it want? And why him? Dear Lord. The thing gave him the ability to teleport, or transport, or whatever it was called, to any place he could recall. Absolutely incredible, if it was true.

She turned over again, and stared at the flashing yellow beacon hitting the blinds.

She lifted her head from the pillow.

The stairs creaked.

Someone stepping on the loose boards. It wasn't Brooke, she refused to climb the stairs with her stiff hips.

Cyndi wiggled to the edge of the bed and her hand felt for the baseball bat beneath the bed, one of the few items she'd brought from Boise. She'd kept it twenty-six years, as protection, and as a reminder of Nikki and Noah's father. It's what she'd use on him if she ever saw that loser again. He'd bought the wooden bat as a gift for Noah on his birth, buying Nikki nothing. Typical of the man-child who simply disappeared before the twins' first birthday.

The bat now between her legs, she reached for her phone sitting on a copy of the Four Agreements she had started reading again. It wasn't Doug inside the house. He had flown home earlier than planned after his wife demanded he do something about the media carnival blockading their cul-de-sac in Phoenix.

She tapped in the wrong passcode to the iPhone, then again, and cursed Apple's latest operating system. The bedroom door cracked open, and she froze.

A thin green light beamed in, followed by a man dressed in dark clothing and goggles.

Cyndi pressed the emergency 911 button on the phone. The door widened, and she threw the phone at his goggles. Followed by the book, and the clock-radio. She threw the comforter back and slid over to the window. She came to her knees and raised the bat for a swing. The bat trembled.

"Get out of here! The police are on the way!"

"Cyndi Abrams Preston, you need to come with us."

The voice belonged to a woman. Neesa.

"How did you get in… Get out of here!"

"Get dressed, Mrs. Preston. We're taking a ride."

The door opened to its full width, and the green light probed the windows, nightstands, lingered on the bat, and settled on Cyndi's face.

"Paul said you needed a warrant." Her anger intensified in the glare of the laser. "Get out of my house. Now!"

"Get dressed and come quietly, or we'll take you just as you are. Your choice."

"Take me where? You people can't just-,"

"Tell it to my boss." Neesa's calm tone lost its patience. "Get dressed!"

Oh God, Rich, what have you done now?

Over Neesa's shoulder, more green beams sliced through the darkness. She tossed the bat at Neesa's feet and yanked a pair of blue jeans off the television. She shook them out. "May I have some privacy, please?"

"No."

Cyndi glared, then slipped off her pajama bottoms. Neesa's green light cut the air in front of her face, searching the room.

She stopped climbing into the pants, her left leg still bare

It was raining.

Thousands of tiny particles of dust falling through the emerald light.

⅄

Military medals, police badges, politician's titles, each evoked contempt inside Rich, an emotion he felt powerless to stop since Andy's death. The grieving process had stopped for Rich, leaving him stuck in the anger phase. He recognized it, Cyndi pointed it out, and yet he couldn't get past it. Down deep, he knew Cyndi was right - it didn't matter *how* Andy died, he was dead, so move on, celebrate Andy's short life rather than destroy yours. But he had to know, he had caused Andy's death, and the thought of his kind-hearted son made to suffer was unbearable.

If he hadn't said what he did, then perhaps Andy would still be alive.

The operating system in Rich's brain observed a different type of anger. Beastly, primal, the kind of rage borne from a primate seeing his mate violated.

"We gotta go, now!"

"Yeah, okay, what the hell's going on?' Matt asked. "Why did you look like that?"

"Like what?"

"Wearing that Arab thing on your head."

He shook his head and ignored the question. 'Can Matt travel with me?'

Spatial proximity required.

"Dad? Dad? Dad?" Matt waved a hand in Rich's face. "Earth to Preston, you there?"

He looked at Matt but didn't acknowledge him. Think! Spatial means space. Proximity means closeness, so then… what? He'd dragged Brooke through a portal but never even considered the possible consequences, he'd been too exhausted to think straight, Hell, he almost fell asleep with scrambled eggs and peanut-butter bagels for face pillows. Brooke had retched and gagged a little, as he had, but she was otherwise okay. Then again, he hadn't checked on her or asked Cyndi. He thought back to pulling Brooke through the portal. With a leash.

Of course. 'If I hold Matt's hand will he be able to come with me through your doorway?'

Affirmative.

"Trust me, son, we gotta go," Rich said. "Close your eyes, it'll feel a little weird." He locked Matt's wrist in a tight grip.

"Where are we going?"

Rich checked the three eggs of globular grey reaching to within inches of the nine-foot ceiling.

He whispered, "Are they all right?"

Isolation objects stable.

Doors squeaked open, sleepy faces peered suspiciously into the hallway. The encased men might be mistaken for anything - snowmen for a fraternity prank - but not human. He felt a twinge of empathy for them and the dark hell they inhabited. But they were alive. And they tried to kidnap his son, so served 'em right.

Curious young men and women began to crowd into the hallway. Rich's grip tightened on Matt's wrist with a sudden surge of paranoia. His ability to command an obscene amount of microscopic dust to do his bidding was disconcerting. Was this just the beginning? Would he slowly change into a machine, and do its bidding? Was that what the thing inside was doing?

Camera phones flashed bright lights in his eyes, mixing with green lasers in his head and he became confused by his second sight. Rich clutched his head, "Stop. I don't want to see this place."

Matt pulled his arm free. "What's wrong with you?"

The view of Cyndi continued. She was topless, and the man aimed his laser at her stomach. He grabbed a handful of Matt's shirt and bared his teeth. 'Will the motes come with me, through the portal?'

Affirmative.

He added a third perspective to his mind. The front of Cyndi's condo, viewed as if he was a pizza delivery driver looking for a street address. 5683. Black and distinct on the white wood fascia.

"Open the door. Now!"

Matt pulled back, "What's wrong with-."

Rich tightened his grip as the image burned open. Cyndi's open front door guarded by an armed soldier.

"Cover your eyes!"

⁂

Burdette couldn't believe what he saw. Steve's botched retrieval operation at the Nye Hall was beyond any rational explanation. He watched the video again, searching for a clues. Simple equipment failure just didn't fit. The safety of Steve's team in Reno was the highest priority and with any blown operation, time was of the essence. Unfortunately, the nearest assistance would have to come from the UNR campus police. His eyes bounced between the static white screen, and Steve's recording from just moments ago.

His finger paused over the escape key. Steve's real-time screen began to produce fuzzy images. Ghostly apparitions crowding the hallway. The screen shot meandered to a sharp focus. A crowd of students, excited about something.

Burdette dialed Steve several times, each terminated with a CALL FAILED. He returned his attention to the monitor, tapping the escape button to shuffle the camera images produced by other members of the team. They appeared safe, moved without any apparent injury, gesturing wildly and talking with each other. The audio had failed.

Neesa's video feed flickered with the same white static.

His hand twitched once, then he fingered the keyboard with several function strokes, switching images transmitted from the three agents inside the condo. Electronic interference. A jamming device?

He banged open the rear doors and jumped out on to the quiet highway, in time to witness the impossible. White powder sprayed from… the air? Like an invisible fire hydrant had suddenly burst open across the street. A horizontal plume of white spewed into the air, and drifted like smoke into Cyndi Preston's front door. The eruption slowed to a trickle almost as fast as it had begun. It was the same dust that formed the Egg in Nevada. He was sure of it.

Two men appeared from the same spot where the dust had shot out.

Preston! Dragging his son.

Rich held onto Matt's shirt after they emerged into the cold night air. The full moon hovered over the mountains as orange wisps heralded a new morning over the eastern hills. The black asphalt was white as the dust dissipated in a gentle breeze.

Matt broke free and fell to his knees. He vomited.

Rich reached his hand out. He'd done the same thing by the orange bucket the first time he passed through a portal. He commiserated with his son but there were men inside with Cyndi, and they had made her undress while they watched.

Standing in the middle of the street, he closed his eyes, and balled his hands. "Show me."

From the millions of tiny Beta cameras, Rich's mind filled with a million points of view then condensed into a single fuzzy picture. Cyndi was in her bedroom, lacing her running shoes. The man in black stood over her, his green laser spotlighted the back of her head.

His jaw tightened. He pictured the man swarmed by a million motes, a trillion.

The number of airborne motes inside the bedroom increased, amplifying Rich's grainy viewpoint into omnipotent clarity.

It was the woman, Neesa. The pretty little liar.

The gold DHS symbol on her jacket faded, covered by a coating of grey dust. All of them! More!

Dispersed by a breeze just seconds ago, the dust stormed back, like a swarm of angry bees returning to defend the hive, and their queen.

More!

The world turned white. Rich saw only red.

Cover it. Cover it all. And don't touch Cyndi.

And the dust obeyed. The motes replicating in the blink of an eye covered the windows, doors, railings, roof, constructing a sheet of grey to span the open front door.

More!

⅄

Burdette screamed, "Neesa, get your team out of there." His earpiece was silent.

Battlefield training made him hold, assess the situation. He'd guessed the teenager that had fallen to his knees was Matt Preston, possibly wounded. That would make Preston even more dangerous. Preston stood by, watching the condominium as the substance attacked the building.

He glanced back to Neesa's monitor displaying the identical white static recorded just minutes ago in Reno.

Not flipping possible.

The crackling of static discharge gained momentum, sparks began to fly and he pulled his weapon free of its shoulder holster. Burdette checked the clip. The headlights of an oncoming vehicle illuminated the van's interior then died. The laptops and interior bulbs died. The signage of Newpark – The Newer Side of Park City - died. The moonlight remained.

He climbed over the wood and wire fence separating the housing development from the busy highway. Burdette sidestepped black gopher holes as he jogged down an embankment then ducked beneath a pine tree thirty yards from his target. He paused.

The hair on his arms stood at attention. His jaw hung. The volume of dust growing each second accompanied by an alien light show of tiny supernovas, the pops of tiny firecrackers, the gritty sound of dust attacking the house.

Neesa and her team still inside.

⋏

The dust found its way in - from beneath door thresholds, gaps in the window frames, down through plumbing vents, air ducts, fireplace flues. The motes poured in at amazing rate and heat generated by the replicating motes warmed the cold mountain air in a wide radius.

The dust swarmed the agent on the landing of the stairwell, and another standing guard at the dining room's sliding glass door. The dust multiplied. His dust. Neesa never stood a chance.

Rich had ordered the operating system to attack the men as it had in Reno. The AI relayed the specific numbers of motes required, but Rich ignored the exponential details and asked for more. These people invaded his home, actually Doug's home, but the semantics mattered little. Cyndi was inside and by default, that made it home.

The motes' imprisonment technique confused the men, their reactions were slow and their response was weak as the dust hardened into an impenetrable shell. Rich was convinced a rampaging bull elephant stood no chance against the swarm. The elapsed time took just seconds.

Cyndi was out of danger and nothing could hurt her while his dust was inside.

His dust. He was beginning to like the sound of that.

Perhaps he had asked for a bit too much, still…

He kneeled next to Matt. The vomiting had stopped, and his abdominal spasms had eased, but Matt groaned, and spat out remnants of the bile.

"You'll be okay." Rich gently rubbed Matt's back.

Movement over his right shoulder made him turn. A dark silhouette was walking towards him. The moonlight shined on the man's smooth scalp – like a light bulb sitting on big shoulders. He was a big fucker, imposing, but his dust could overwhelm him in seconds. Rich glanced at the work van on the highway. He was the one that had been watching, he was the guy in charge, and he'd seen everything those helmet cameras recorded. He'd seen his wife forced to undress. Saw her naked.

C'mon Buckwheat - mano e mano.

He took a step towards the man, his right hand flexing and balling. Twenty yards away the glint of a gun in the man's right hand. It wasn't aimed at him – yet - but the nut-job might start firing blind in the dark. He might hit Matt. Cops were trained to shoot first and conceive a convenient cover story later, or give no explanation at all like in Andy's case.

"Get up, Matt," Rich said.

The dark figure increased his pace and raised the weapon.

"I need you to get up!" Rich said. "Now!"

Matt staggered to his feet. "Where are we?"

In the glow of the bright moon the man's round, bald, head shined and he appeared like some weird religious apostle.

A portal burned open inches from his face but Rich hesitated. He saw the man's face, his stiff jaw and square shoulders. A badge hung around his neck. A military man.

The man shouted his name, ordered him to stop.

Rich flipped him the bird with one hand and pulled Matt through a portal with the other.

Chapter 14

The wormhole terminus exited in front of a fireplace, just thirty feet away, on the other side of Cyndi's front door. The air was hot, and thick with floating motes. Rich was stunned. The dust had covered every square inch of furniture, carpeting, wallboard, ceiling light fixtures, stair railings, doors and windows, a version of hell conceived for a horror movie, in its starkness and complete silence.

Even through the haze of floating motes, the two men encased in dust were obvious. A teardrop-shaped blob on the landing of the stairs and another blocked the door of Cyndi's bedroom.

"Whoa! What happened?" Matt said.

Rich shook his head with deliberation. "I guess… I guess they did what I told them."

"You told a bunch of dust to do this?"

"Well, not exactly this but…"

"Whoa." Matt brushed past Rich, tiptoeing on a carpet of dust to the fireplace mantle to study the contours of a vase. Or at least that's what it should have been. Matt leaned his face in to inspect the dust then touched it with his finger.

Matt jerked his hand away. "Cool."

Rich smiled then heard a muffled sob upstairs.

"Oh, crap. Cyndi." He climbed the stairs two steps at a time, squeezing in-between the egg-shaped man and the stair railing.

"Preston!" Cyndi shouted. "I hear you out there!"

"Hold on." But Rich couldn't get past the second blob blocking the doorway. "I'll get you out, hold on." He wasn't quite sure how. Maybe release the motes from the blob blocking the door, and risk being shot? Or open a portal to the other side?

"Get me out of here! What is all this crap?"

Rich stepped back and rubbed his face. The lumpy structure connected to the ceiling by a stalagmite of motes was formidable. He asked the little voice to move some of the motes. But only on the right side. The gap should allow enough space for Cyndi to squeeze through, and then the dust could return.

Affirmative.

He stepped back again as motes disengaged, undulating like tendrils of smoke, floating up from the area just as he'd pictured.

"Take my hand." He reached into the mote soup, his fingers and forearm tingled from the static electricity. More motes floated free, and the gap widened. The face of the person encased inside became discernible. The pretty liar - her sharp cheekbones, and pouty lips. The skin around her exposed eye twitched, and her eyelash, white with dust, blinked. She stared at him, like a frosted Cyclops.

He flinched, then drew closer and narrowed his eyes, and whispered into her eye. "Don't fuck with me."

His attention turned back to Cyndi. "Grab my hand and squeeze through." His hand searched blindly then found her fingers. He pulled but she wouldn't budge.

"What is this stuff? What's it gonna do to me?" she said.

"It's what I told you about. Don't worry, feels kind of like a warm bath. Tingles a little."

Cyndi groaned as Rich pulled her through the gap. She buried her face in his chest and wrapped her arms around his waistline. She was trembling.

"It's all right," he said. "It's okay."

Cyndi pushed him away, slapped his chest with her open palm, "If you had just moved here last year none of this would've happened."

"You're probably right."

Cyndi pointed at Neesa's eye. "You know who that is?"

"And what choice did I have? Let 'em take you, and Matt?"

"Matt, too?"

Rich nodded.

"You guys quit fighting." Matt shouted up from the kitchen. "Hey, Dad, check this out? It's like walking on a trampoline, and it zaps you if you poke it too hard. That's sick. Hey, can you make 'em get off the fridge?"

Burdette halted in mid-stride, disbelief short-circuiting his next step. Preston had simply disappeared, and his son. No backwash of air, no sound, a brief flash of gold maybe but they simply disappeared. A computer generated special effect? Ghosts in the machine.

He searched the asphalt from where the two had disappeared and thought about Preston's sudden appearance in the dormitory hallway, hundreds of miles away. He studied a splatter of vomited chicken and strands of ramen noodles. He tilted his face up at the two-story, forest green building covered in the same substance that had formed the Egg outside of Winnemucca.

Preston had gained control of it.

He approached the building with small steps, his weapon held at his side. The building was crawling with ants, but it was the dust, swarming over ridges and valleys that defined windows, forming a sheet to shield the open front door. What looked like a dryer vent vanished as the dust sank inside like sand falling through an hourglass. He touched a spot where a doorbell had been, and received a jolt of electricity as if he'd stuck his finger into a light socket.

He backed up into the street and slid his weapon back into its shoulder holster.

Burdette ran his hands over his scalp then clasped his neck between his thumbs and began a painful massage. The dust solidified, hardening in front of his eyes. Was the stuff biological? It collected on his agents but left Preston and his boy unscathed. Was it a new form of nanotechnology – one that provided a means of teleportation. That would explain the sightings of Preston in Reno, Boise, and Park City, and his ability to travel hundreds of miles in a matter of seconds, and now protected by an impenetrable shield of dust.

A shiver washed over his arms and chest.

Unimaginable technology in the hands of an emotionally unstable man.

He checked his watch, and then checked his phone. Both had ceased functioning. He stepped back to the sidewalk across the street and stared at the blanketed condo, and for the first time in a long time, he was unsure of what to do next.

He folded his arms. An older woman in a puffy pink ski jacket approached on the trail encircling the housing development, a burly wolfhound pulling on its leash. She stopped to let the dog do its business, ignorant of the alien substance. She fidgeted with her phone, checked her headphones, and finally looked up to see the building and dropped the leash.

Know just how you feel, Ma'am.

His mind reeled, with the potential implications, and of Neesa's team trapped inside, and the dust's protection of Preston. How was he going to get them out – nothing could penetrate this...

The sunrise coaxed morning joggers, bikers and dog walkers to begin their daily routines. People passed in front of the condo, then gathered to form a small crowd, to commiserate over dead smartphones, and share opinions.

Burdette paced the narrow street in front of the building. The equipment inside the van would be useless, but the digital recordings had automatically uploaded to the Portland office before the malfunction. Someone there had to know what was happening.

The traffic signal directing vehicles into Newpark or the Utah Olympic Park in the opposite direction no longer functioned. Disabled Subaru's, Audi's and service trucks traveling into Deer Valley began to clog the four-lane highway, the first pieces of a monumental traffic jam.

He climbed up the embankment, and walked past a growing crowd of onlookers and found an idling Summit County Sheriff's SUV blocked in by disabled vehicles. He presented his credentials to the officer and explained a course of action he wanted communicated to the trooper's superiors. He requested the use of the officer's cellphone.

His first call was to Steve Cable. "Status? The others?"

"Yeah, we're fine. But we have no idea what happened. This… that stuff just started crawling all over us, we couldn't move," Steve said. "It was like being buried alive. I don't ever want to feel that again."

Burdette remained quiet, remembering what he'd seen on the laptop.

"Sorry, Boss. We should have cuffed him immediately, maybe…

"Maybe nothing. But I don't think that would have changed a thing."

Burdette stared at a rooftop covered in white dust. It sparkled with silver courtesy of the morning dew. His people were still trapped inside.

"Nessa?" Steve asked.

"Nessa's team is… like you were. Encased. Inside the Preston condo."

"Shit, it's safe…I think. But fucking uncomfortable. What do you need from me?"

Burdette shook his head. "Not sure what we do at this juncture, but to coin an old phrase, I think we're gonna need a damn bigger boat."

⚔

Rich held Cyndi's hand, helping her down the two flights of stairs. She kept her eyes on his as she squeezed by the DHS agent on the landing. She took tentative steps appraising the condition of her house. The anxiety was palpable in her voice.

"That bitch was taking me to jail. To jail for God's sake! They invade my home and I'm the one going to jail."

Rich was surprised at her reference to Neesa. It wasn't like her to curse. He nodded in agreement. She stopped and studied his face carefully.

"Is this the same stuff that got you in Nevada?" She paused on the last step, and raised her voice. "Hi, Matt."

"Yep" Rich said.

"Hey, Cyn." Matt stuck his head in from the kitchen. "Dad, I'm starving. Can you get this stuff off the fridge?"

Rich smiled inward. They acted as if they'd just seen each other in a coffee shop an hour ago. They acted as only family could.

"What are they?" Cyndi squinted as she studied a snowman made from a potted philodendron.

"I'm not sure exactly, but they're called Beta class transit motes." Rich said with a smidgen of pride.

"Dad, dad…, dad, dad."

Matt's annoying habit made Rich smile. Like Christmas was just around the corner – surrounded with family, enjoying the quirks of those he loved most. And, for a change, he would have something to offer besides sullen bitterness.

He asked the voice to lift the dust from everything inside the kitchen - except the egg-man at the door. The room began to come alive. His spirits soared when Matt and Cyndi moved to his side. He put his arms around their shoulders and held them tight.

The grey covering turned to dust again, swirling up as puffy clouds, or the heavy smoke of burning wet wood, the billions of particles rose like heaven had summoned them home. The leisurely reappearance of multi-colored granite countertops, wood grain cabinets, and a smudged, stainless steel refrigerator door enlarged the dining room and kitchen. The high ceiling dropped with the collection of countless motes.

The large egg shape remained, guarding the mote-covered sliding glass door. Inside was the pretty liar's partner, the Buckwheat with the handcuffs, Rich knew it without asking the voice.

He pulled out one of the oak dinette chairs to sit - nothing would penetrate the condo – nothing would harm them while they remained inside and he re-laxed. Matt's reaction amazed him – it was as if having control over an alien technology was something that happened every day. Youthful naiveté. Andy had been full of it, too, it was what led him to enlist in the Army. And ultimately die.

Rich felt a wave of grief crash down on his shoulders. Seemed like his own exuberance for life had died, with Andy.

Cyndi was manic with a wide range of emotions, fear, disbelief, and anger. All flowing from her voice and actions. "How are we going to explain this? Those are people inside there. Doug's gonna have a stroke. They will arrest us now for sure. I am not going to prison." She threw her remarks into the warm muggy air, unwilling to wait for a response.

Rich stayed silent, letting her run down. Then they'd be able to talk.

She ducked her head as she walked through the narrow hallway and into the mote-covered living room, released an exasperated groan, and returned. She stood opposite Rich and crossed her arms.

He began rubbing his palms together. Every question he didn't hear last night was building up steam.

"That was the truth last night, wasn't it?" she said.

Rich nodded.

Matt turned from the open fridge.

"You talk to something in your head that tells this… this stuff, what to do?"

He nodded again.

"And the traveling bit? They control that too?"

"Let's go to Vegas again." Matt said.

He ignored Matt and nodded.

"Wait, " Cyndi said. "Where's Brooke?"

Rich found the old retriever beneath the living room table, encased in a rectangular blob of motes, and he ordered the dust off her copper coat. Brooke stood and shook as if she just emerged from a river bath. Her bushy tail swept the air when Matt called to her.

Brooke's excited dance with Matt completed Rich's holiday cheer. The surroundings were a bit odd, but the gray dust was a decent substitute for white snow. For the first time in years, Rich felt at peace with the world. He wondered if that was the doing of his friend inside his head. His friend? Was it his friend?

Cyndi walked around the table and began to massage Rich's shoulders. "Your story was too out there, Preston. Sorry for doubting you."

The pain from Shaggy's arm-lock throbbed but he soaked up the warmth of her touch. "I wouldn't have believed me either."

Coming around to face him, Cyndi bored into his eyes. "What the hell happened to you out there again?"

Brooke refused to move from his hand scratching her ear, and Rich enjoyed watching Cyndi and Matt prepare breakfast together. Matt's elation for eating something other than school cafeteria food and Cyndi's joy of a mother cooking for a child again was a gift.

A ritual game of shovel and snatch ensued. Matt opened a bag of pita chips and shoveled handfuls into his mouth. Cyndi snatched the bag away and put it back in the pantry.

Matt retrieved eggs and fresh spinach from the fridge. Cyndi held up two skillets of different sizes and asked, "Are these good to cook on after that dust was on it?"

"The stuff was inside me and didn't seem to hurt."

"Uh…yeah, okay." She rinsed the utensils under the kitchen faucet.

Rich took a sip of coffee. "I think I need help."

Cyndi and Matt both faced him.

"I'm not sure exactly what to do."

Cyndi put down a carving knife, came around the kitchen table, and sat next to Rich. "Then let's come up with a plan."

With a mouthful of peanut butter, Matt mumbled, "Egbok, Dad."

They drank coffee and enjoyed omelets bulging with sautéed mushrooms, onions and bacon, and buttered sourdough bread. A real family meal, without the arguing or uncomfortable silence caused by Andy's death.

⚔

Outside the house, Summit County Sheriffs, Park City Police, and a multitude of government agencies had mobilized to contain the second appearance of the strange dust. A quarantine zone was instituted - residents within a two-mile radius were ordered to evacuate their homes. Starbucks, Whole Foods and ancillary businesses were ordered closed, with the morning shift employees sent home. Roadblocks were set up to reroute traffic on Interstate 80 in Salt Lake City and as far east as Evanston, Wyoming.

Local news stations, required to feed the appetites of their respective national affiliates, found alternate routes into Park City. Morning radio programs interrupted drive-time programming with audience-grabbing special reports, their DJ's promising further details after each lengthy commercial break. KJUL 94.3, the Jewel, advised their listeners of a possible outbreak of biological terrorism, and warned them to stay away from Park City, while Mayor Williamson declared the town safe as ever.

Speculation ran rampant. Again.

News choppers flew the short distance from Salt Lake City and hovered miles away with pilots wary of the accident at the Winnemucca Egg. Their cameras zoomed in on a white blanket covering a small section of a condominium complex with eight individually owned units, but the dust covered only a small portion.

On the air, media personalities posed a host of questions. Why was only part of the structure enclosed by the strange film? Had it harmed other residents? Who owned the property infested with the odd substance? News media catering to East Coast breakfast viewers concentrated their programming on the newest sighting.

The second appearance of the substance of unknown origin intensified the curiosity of the world. The United Kingdom and France tightened border security, scrutinizing anyone with an American passport. Israel cancelled joint military exercises with the United States Navy and called up 50,000 reservists.

Other varied interests: U.S. security agencies, scientists and defense contractors intensified their research, searching for clues, or an advantage, some salivating for the potential new technology.

An advantage some would stop at nothing to get.

⋏

The Preston family sat at the wooden table, finishing the hearty breakfast, with Brooke receiving most of Cyndi's toast. Rich asked to hear details of what transpired before he arrived. Cyndi and Matt's stories sounded similar, but their emotions and reactions were quite different.

Matt told his story with nonchalance, as if thugs dressed like *Call of Duty* soldiers pulled him from his room on a regular basis. The masculine bravado was for Cyndi, but the quiver in his voice said the episode frightened him.

Cyndi's retelling came fraught with fear and emotion -the noisy stairs warning of an unknown intruder, the baseball bat coming out from beneath the bed, and her confrontation with Neesa. Cyndi cursed like her husband, affirming her loathing of Neesa.

Feeling the moment was right, Rich threw his balled up napkin onto the table. "Let me tell you what I know or what I think I know."

His story came in fits and spurts, and Cyndi had already heard most of it. Rich paused at the part that made him feel exposed and vulnerable - the trip to Touweep, enjoying a cup of coffee and having a long, frustrating conversation with the alien computer's operating system. A voice and yet not his voice, distinct but yet part of him. A presence entrenched in his mind that was burrowing deeper. A powerful entity able to command unimaginable quantities of dust.

He tried several different ways of telling how he heard the voice, how he distinguished it from his own thoughts. He knew they couldn't understand, and wouldn't comprehend. But he tried. He talked about how often he heard *download incomplete*. How the cryptic responses kept him from understanding exactly what the thing wanted.

Rich refused to meet their gaze, embarrassed, but this was a unique situation and the sizable egg guarding the window behind him proved it.

"What does it want with you?" Matt asked.

"I don't know."

"And why you?" Cyndi added.

"I don't know." Rich saw his own version of *download incomplete* feeding the frustration on their faces.

He told them what little he knew of the Beta-class motes, how his inner voice controlled them, and how the motes could show him a picture of a place he had visited.

"How did you know I was being arrested?" Matt asked.

"I'm not sure." Rich said.

"Ask your friend."

"How did you know Matt was being arrested?" Rich asked. Aloud but directed inward.

No response, but then he expected that.

Rich scratched the stubble on his face, reconsidered the question and asked again, this time almost mumbling. "Why did you show me Matt in the dormitory hallway this morning?"

Visual request stored in command queue.

Rich thought about the response for a bit then smiled.

"What?" Matt and Cyndi said in unison.

"It just said, visual request stored in command queue. That tells you what it's like to talk to this thing." He held his hands up. "But when I was waiting by the dormitory elevator, I'd asked if I could see Matt. It couldn't do it because Matt wasn't visible in the hallway and I'd never been in his room. I've been getting a lot of images of you since then, but I just thought they were subconscious reminders to call you. So I ignored them."

"So it kept fulfilling that one request over and over, and you didn't know it." Cyndi said.

"Yeah. We were lucky." Rich said. "I don't know a fraction of what I want to. But it told me in so many words that I had to sleep, to finish the download, something about no distractions, mental stimulation being zilch."

Matt shrugged. "Sure, download a new version of the iPhone operating system, and it makes you turn it off before you can use it. Maybe that's what you're doing. Rebooting."

Made sense. Rich raised his eyebrows. "Looks like somebody's coming after you guys to get to me."

"She's Homeland Security," Cyndi said. "The bit-, the girl you got into it with, the thing upstairs."

"What?" Matt said. "Did you punch her out?"

He shook his head. Homeland Security. A patriotic title for Big Brother, another name for the Gestapo, or the Russian KGB? But now wasn't the time to vent his political opinions.

"No. I don't know why they're coming after me. I'm no threat to anyone."

Matt lifted his eyebrows and gestured to the snowman behind Rich, his body language screaming, "HELLO!"

Cyndi sat back. "I can only imagine what's going on outside right now. I mean, that cloud in Nevada worried people. Now it's here. And under your control. Of course the government is terrified." Cyndi began to twirl a strand of her hair into a corkscrew. "You don't think they'll try to get Nikki and Noah?"

Matt chuckled. "Good luck with Nik. She'll have them regretting that move."

"I don't know, but I need to sleep. Maybe get some answers. Re-up."

"Reboot, Pops. It's called reboot."

"We can't stay here, this place is horrendous." Cyndi began to slather peanut butter on the last piece of toast.

"If we're gonna go somewhere," Matt said. "I wouldn't eat that."

"Why?"

Rich ignored them. "Listen, if we're being watched then our phones, credit cards and all that other stuff you read about them doing is in play. We need a place -- some place we can regroup. And it has to be a place I've been to, that I have memory of."

Matt got up to search the cabinets for something else to eat.

The room was quiet. Rich had an idea. "Cyndi, go pack a bag, your laptop, and whatever cash you have. Can you steal us some clothes from Doug?"

Chapter 15

The Blackberry he borrowed from a Utah Highway officer vibrated non-stop after Burdette forwarded his Portland phone number to the new phone. He let most calls go to Officer Natt's voicemail but Burdette took calls from his Section Chief, the undersecretary of DHS, and finally the Secretary herself. He'd relayed the same facts all the way up the chain of command - that Preston was still inside the protected condo, and Neesa and her team were almost certainly encased in the dust, just as Steve's team had been. Since the three agents in Reno were released unharmed, and he believed Neesa's team would receive the same treatment.

The DHS Secretary came quickly to the point. "What's your threat assessment?"

"It's hard to say. The situation is too fluid to warrant a definitive answer. But I think Preston somehow controls the dust. And it gives him the ability to travel considerable distances almost instantaneously."

He knew the statement sounded absurd, but it was the truth.

"You know what you're implying, Deputy? We have an unstable man controlling a weapon that could wreak havoc on this country's infrastructure and…, and let's be clear here, he can teleport hundreds of miles?"

Burdette swallowed. His silence was his answer.

"Very well, then. Get yourself on a plane and you can explain this to the President. A National Security briefing has been scheduled and you'll be the keynote speaker."

"Yes ma'am. But I'm not leaving my team."

"I sympathize, Mr. Burdette. But this is not a request."

"Ma'am, I-."

"Not a request." The phone call ended.

He considered what he would say. EMP's and teleportation. They would laugh him out of the room. Maybe he would only add his insights to the meeting. After all, the Vice-President seemed to know more about the dust than he did.

Summit County police officers, Park City firefighters and four delegations of reporters from Salt Lake City surrounded the white van he had used for the surveillance operation. He heard excited voices coming from the large group. He set the phone down on the hood and ran to the vehicle.

The limestone facade and timber gables of the condo began to express colors as the dust floated up in gentle spirals, seemingly helpless against a light breeze, dissipating downwind. Like a black beetle escaping a spider's web, a man dressed in a DHS windbreaker emerged from the condominium's front door and waved to the crowd.

Neesa's team was safe.

And Preston was gone.

⮝

A memory is nothing but tiny bits of information collected through experience. Pictures, films, and books lacked dimension required for a true experience. Local aromas, air temperatures, cacophonies of sounds and tastes unique to the local cuisine, vibrant colors of indigenous plant life or people's clothing, all combined to create a new dimension, of information. A memory.

Rich was no different.

He thought he had traveled quite a bit over his lifetime, but vacations and weekend jaunts had remained in the West, having never set foot east of the Mississippi River. He had visited Mexico on occasion, before the drug cartels put a damper on tourism. Romantic weekend getaways with Cyndi remained close to home with so many children, but they'd visit resort hotels near California beaches, or Southwestern cities large enough to include Cyndi's favorite haunts -- shopping malls. Rich's favorite destinations were remote sections of southern Utah or Nevada near their Arizona home. And a single trip to Hawaii.

Hiding out in a hotel or motel required a credit card, something easily traced by government computer geeks. Their home in Boise had to be under surveillance, and his campsite in the Touweep. Well, Cyndi would put the kibosh on that location before he could even unzip the tent flap.

So Rich had opened a portal to a gravel parking area and walked into the cold drizzle of a mountain rain. The clouds hovered low in a valley surrounded by hills dense in Douglas Fir or Ponderosa pine. The cottonwood and willows had shed their leaves with the approach of winter and the grassy meadow had already turned golden. Set back five hundred yards from the main access road and shielded by heavy brush lining Wilsons Creek, the log cabin made an ideal hideaway.

For a single week in July and still employed, he was able to afford the hefty rent of an A-frame log cabin on the banks of Rock Creek, thirty-one miles east of Missoula, Montana. Getting there was easy - Allegiant Airlines made Missoula a bi-weekly destination and charged a measly $149.00 for the round trip airfare. The small town atmosphere, mountain air, and the abundant rivers and lakes provided a peaceful respite from the heat of Phoenix. Every year they returned home with a copy of the local real estate booklet offering waterfront homes for sale, a few pages dog-eared as potential summer homes, but the dream was soon lost and forgotten in life's daily grind.

Rich climbed three wooden steps onto a covered rear porch and peered through the windows searching for signs of tenants. The rear door was locked so he opened a portal three feet from where he stood and walked into a cherished memory. The house was just how he remembered it, clean, warm, smelling of pepper and pine, and more importantly, the kitchen countertops were void of any renter's personal items. There would be disposable paper towels and plates, and toilet paper. Pots, pans, utensils, and items required for cooking were stored where he expected.

Satisfied with the inspection, Rich returned to the condo.

Cyndi had Rich remove the dust from her bedroom and bathroom in order to pack some clothes and toiletries. As she fussed about what clothes to pack, he warned her of the possible side effects of passing through a portal for the first time. When he asked the voice for a gateway he realized his requests had become irrelevant - the jump to Rock Creek and back was made by remembering the location and simply stepping through. No request, no wait, no body scan, no blue-shirt idiots of the TSA, no boarding pass, just go.

Each toting a bag of clothes, Rich took Matt's hand and squeezed Cyndi's hand, her anxious eyes calling for reassurance. He leaned down and gave her a peck on the lips. Matt used baby talk to encourage Brooke, who was leashed and eager to follow.

He glanced back at the men covered in dust. His dust.

Follow us, he thought to the voice. *Release the stuff outside into the wind after we leave.*

Hearing no response from the voice, Rich stepped out of Utah.

The motes disengaged from the ceilings, furniture and three DHS agents, gathering in mass near the portal opening and followed the family to Montana.

Cyndi dropped to her knees and spilled her breakfast on the gravel driveway. Rich kneeled and pulled her hair back from her face, noting the portals had the same effect on everyone the first time.

Why?

Download incomplete.

Right.

Cyndi washed her face and rinsed out her mouth in the kitchen sink then walked through the cabin opening the windows. She climbed the stairs to the loft and shouted a few, "Hey remember when's" down at Rich. The downstairs master bedroom ignored, Cyndi chose to sleep upstairs in the open loft with the windows cranked open to catch a refreshing breeze. The peaceful gurgle of the creek's rushing water below offered its welcome.

They held hands again as they walked through a portal and into the parking lot of an Albertsons supermarket in Newport Beach, California. The store looked as it always had, busy but manageable. Matt had warned Rich about the riots at some grocery stores, courtesy of the Egg, but the laid-back California beach people were mostly interested in the ocean.

Rich dutifully pushed the cart, keeping his face lowered. He looked over his shoulder often, searching for someone hiding in the bustle of shoppers and beach goers. But they were mostly tourists, like them, and the faces changed as often as the weekly rental agreements.

Cyndi meandered in the produce section, inspecting tomatoes and squeezing avocados. Rich became irritated that she was taking too long, and he reminded them to use cash before walking outside to wait in the parking lot.

Long minutes passed before they exited, pushing a cart full of white plastic bags - soup, chips, microwavable pizza, salad fixings, bagels, peanut butter, and diet soda, the diet of the middle class. His paranoia made him take control of the cart, ordering them to latch onto his belt loops to maintain spatial proximity, and they returned to the cabin.

Cyndi had purchased a cheap, disposable cell phone to call Nikki and Noah but cell service was limited in the valley rimmed by two steep mountain ranges.

Rich accompanied Cyndi onto the wet sand of Gold Beach, Oregon. A cold wind blew off the ocean. They squatted behind a hefty garble of driftwood and called Nikki - she'd worry the most and her penchant for uttering 'oh no' and 'uh oh' was taken directly from Cyndi's genetic playbook. Rich listened to the phone conversation and topics like wormholes, dust motes, and an early morning raid by the Department of Homeland Security were never mentioned. She handed the phone to Rich.

He hesitated. He wasn't Nikki's favorite person.

Cyndi frowned and pushed the phone closer.

He took it. "Hey Nik,"

"Couldn't you have just driven to Alaska and had Mom meet you up there if you wanted an adventure?" Nikki said.

"It's pretty weird." Rich felt a sudden urge to apologize.

"Trouble finds you pretty easy these days."

"Seems to. Not sure what we should do."

"Tell somebody your story. You wanted to be news and now you are. You gotta capture the moment, take it for a ride."

"I don't know, for now we'll lay low until I figure something out. I think you and Noah should fly under the radar too, for a while."

"What do you mean?"

"Just be careful, okay? We'll check in with you every day until this blows over."

"Rich?" Nikki said. "You take care of Mom. She hasn't been dealing with this lone wolf crusade you've been on, I mean, she's-."

"I know."

The twins were two years younger than Andy was but they'd bonded into a tight knit unit, tighter than even genetic siblings might be. During their high school years, Nikki and Andy became particularly close. After Cyndi told her children the truth of why Andy joined the Army, their relationship with Rich went straight downhill. Their conversations became strained and awkward. He didn't blame them. Kill one child and lose the love of three others. Over the last four years, the distance between them grew into a chasm, as wide as Touweep, but not so wide that the sound of their voices would let him forget what he'd said to Andy.

Nikki's jabs were subtle and sharp. Noah's blunt and bulldozing. Both were livid when Cyndi announced their move to Boise. Nikki helped Cyndi pack, Noah went missing. Cyndi seemed to age overnight with the stress of trying to keep her family intact.

That was when it began, Rich's thoughts of suicide. That maybe Cyndi, maybe all of them would be better off without him.

Especially now.

The call to Noah was much different. The young man offered to broker a deal with the authorities. Rich was only a person of interest for now. Rich made this mess. Now Rich could climb into an orange jumpsuit and clean it up.

"Send Mom down here. I'll pay for the ticket. You and Matt can do some fishing while we negotiate a deal. They'll give you what you want, Rich, I'm sure of it. Just get Mom out of it."

Noah meant no insult, but Rich heard the undertones. You can't take care of yourself, let alone Cyndi - let a real man take over, one with a job, one with a future, one who doesn't open his mouth and say shit that killed his own son.

"Maybe," Rich said. "Just give me a couple of days to figure something out."

"I'll start making some calls. See who might be interested in helping out. Uncle Doug has called a few times wondering about Mom."

"A couple of days then I'll do what you asked. I'll send Matt, too."

They returned to the cabin. It had most modern conveniences; gas fireplace, satellite TV, phone and even internet access was possible through a painfully slow dial-up connection pirated from an analog telephone line.

Matt and Brooke were waiting for a frozen pizza to emerge from the oven when they returned. The laptop was open on the countertop, inches from the phone jack Matt had plugged into. An ancient Sony television sat atop a cheap plastic stereo stand in the corner of the living room. The voice of CNN's Wolf Blitzer blared, the screen showed aerial footage of Cyndi's residence blanketed in white dust.

A picture of Rich's angry face, complete with bloodshot eyes, was in the upper right hand corner. A mug shot courtesy of the Scottsdale Police Department. The picture changed, became Cyndi's DMV photo, and changed again into Matt's face taken from a student ID.

The blood-red breaking news banner flashed.

A Family of Terrorists?

"Hey, Dad, I think we're famous." Matt said.

$$\blacktriangle$$

Burdette exhaled a slow controlled breath when the pilot notified the passengers of the delay. Their holding pattern above Andrews Air Force Base was as enjoyable as an Interstate pileup. He sighed and looked out the window, down at the sprawl of homes and commercial buildings far below. It reminded him of Dallas.

A pang of guilt injected itself into his already acidic stomach. A few more days and he'd sit with his mother and relive the painful memories of his sister. Robyn had followed him into the Army two years after he'd enlisted. Her aptitude scores exceeded his and allowed her admission into Officer Candidate School. They talked often, supporting each other and giving up hometown gossip the other hadn't heard.

They grew up fatherless in rural Denton, Texas and Burdette took on the role of big brother. A role he took seriously and uncompromised - a protective relationship that made their conversations easy.

Burdette had received his promotion to Captain while assigned to the Pentagon, modifying field reports concerning the fruitless search for WMD's in Iraq. He had called Robyn to tell her the happy news. Stationed in Baghdad, she sounded sullen, depressed, and quick-tempered when he pressed her for the reason why. Two weeks and three subsequent calls later, she finally admitted being sexually assaulted by a superior officer. Burdette was livid. He wanted to fly to Iraq and choke the life from the Major responsible. His request for a leave of absence was denied.

At his insistence, Robyn filed charges, and a stink was raised. Her accusations were dumped into an Iraqi potty pit, and buried - the good ole' boy military justice system functioned perfectly. Robyn self-medicated and overdosed on a plethora of pain pills. Burdette immediately resigned his commission.

The jet's wheels touched down, and Burdette readied himself for the politicians waiting at the White House. He never cared for the egocentric, greedy species. DHS Secretary Evans seemed to be an exception.

Two Secret Service agents escorted him to a black Lincoln Navigator, where he reviewed Preston's file on his laptop during the short drive to the White House. There, the two agents ushered him into a large meeting room filled to capacity. All eyes turned in his direction, and none of them seemed friendly.

He felt conspicuous among the fancy grey suits and red ties. The only suitable clothing he'd packed was a pair of khaki dress pants and a wrinkled blue business shirt. He swallowed a lump when he recognized the President, Vice President, Secretaries of Defense, State and his own boss Homeland Security. He recalled the names of three members of the Joint Chiefs of Staff, Directors of the FBI, CIA and the National Security agency. The oblong conference room was rimmed with assistants and aides who sat or stood behind their respective employers.

With a nod from Janet Evans, the Secretary of Homeland Security, he sat at the last empty seat next to her. Unpacking his laptop, Burdette listened to a whispered conversation between two Cabinet officials to his left.

"Appreciate you coming to help, Deputy," the President said.

The room silenced, aides scrambled back to their seats, and the shuffling of papers ceased.

"Mr. Burdette has joined us to give some insight on the purpose of this meeting," the President said. "His input comes from the front line, so to speak. Please proceed, Deputy."

Burdette's face flushed. He ran his finger over the laptop's mouse pad and the screen lit up. He inhaled through his nostrils, stood up and cleared his throat.

"Yes, sir. Thank you."

He began by presenting a brief synopsis of the seven known cloud survivors and their elimination as suspects with regard to the Egg's origin. Then he turned his presentation to the person they all wanted to hear about.

"Richard Joseph Preston came onto our radar after being reported missing by his wife, Cyndi Preston. Observation teams were dispatched to Boise, Reno, and Park City, to locate and observe Preston, Preston's wife, and his youngest son, Matt. After confronting Mrs. Preston about the whereabouts of her husband, a heated confrontation with Mr. Preston ensued, followed by his inexplicable escape."

"What do you mean inexplicable escape, Deputy?" The Director of the F.B.I asked.

"Yes, sir. If you'll be patient I'll get to that."

Burdette read the transcripts of the telephone conversation between Matt and Richard Preston, emphasizing the statement that elder Preston admitted to knowing what the Winnemucca Egg was comprised of. With the help of Secretary Evans' assistant and a wide screen HD monitor at his back, Burdette replayed the video recording of Steve's encounter with Preston in the dormitory hallway.

"I personally witnessed Preston appear in Park City. He was helping his son." He paused. "Helping his son escape this same dormitory in Reno. He literally appeared from nowhere. As I approached the suspects, that same substance attacked the building, and my men. Preston simply disappeared, just as he appeared, from nowhere."

"Impossible," the NSA Director said as others murmured to each other.

The President held up his hand for silence then prompted other agency representatives to debrief the group. Burdette gleaned new details but learned little. The disabling of vehicles and aircraft in close proximity to the Egg was indeed caused by a precise low-level short-range electromagnetic pulse, prompting an outburst from Joint Chief General William Reynolds.

"Do you know what an EMP weapon like that could do to our military? It could incapacitate 95% of our assets. Two of our drones were downed in Winnemucca. The second one was hardened to withstand a pulse from a twenty megaton nuclear strike."

"Do you know what a weapon like that could do *for* our military?" said Vice-President Henry Childs as he pushed his frameless glasses up higher on his nose. "How would you like to shut down an entire army, all at once?"

The balding bureaucrat was a notorious advocate for the acquisition of new weapon systems and a battlefield EMP would get no argument from the military contingent.

"Mr. Burdette," the Director of National Science said. "How do you explain the disappearance of Preston when you approached?"

"I have no rational explanation, sir," Burdette said. "But whatever mechanism he controls would explain how he escaped from my agents. He didn't just walk into a bathroom with my agent two feet behind him. He walked out of Park City. It would also explain how he was able to travel hundreds of miles in an impossible time span."

Looking around the room, the President asked, "Do we know what the dust is? Its composition, nature or origin? How has this Preston fellow learned what our people can't seem to figure out?"

Burdette lifted his chin. There it was. They've known about the dust. They've been studying it. He looked over to Secretary Evans, but she leaned forward in her chair, avoiding his eyes.

The rare moment of silence was interrupted by the Vice-President. "Mr. President, I received an email just a short time ago from my associates at the Microdyne Corporation. The specimens of dust secured at one of their facilities have activated. He likened them to miniature fireflies. They have hypothesized the particles are an advanced form of nanotechnology. Possibly even extrater-restrial in origin."

"Bullshit." General Reynolds said.

The President was unfazed. "Explain."

"MC attached a report defining their proprietary interest in the material. They've examined individual nodules using cameras with unique microscopic capabilities and spectral imaging analysis. As you know, examination has been difficult due to their unusual configuration and the small size of the specimens. The little buggers activated around the same time the Egg formed in Nevada. And most disappeared when the Egg disintegrated. I'm sorry sir, but I'm afraid the research raises more questions than answers."

"We appreciate you being able to share that information with us, Henry." The President's veiled sarcasm brought a thin smile to Childs' face.

Childs' affiliation with the Microdyne Corporation was common knowl-edge, even after publicly divesting himself from the weapons contracting com-pany as a condition to accepting the nomination as the President's running mate. The former Chairman of the Board, Childs' and his beltway connections had given the young company a political footing in order to grow into a research and weapons development behemoth. His company's staunch support of Israel had made him wealthy, selling weapons and technology to the Israelis, paid for with the same money the U.S. government donated as foreign aid.

"Deputy Burdette," the President said. "Your assessment of Richard Preston? Will he play ball?"

"Sir, he is emotionally unstable, and should be considered a wild card. I have no clear evidence of any terrorist activities, but Preston and the dust seem to move hand in hand. So far, the dust has been benign, except for its capacity to swarm. None of my people came out any worse for wearing it. Sir, I have not yet received Andrew..."

The room erupted with heated debate. "Benign? A pulse that fries circuit boards is not harmless?"

"No injuries have been reported from its presence."

"Tell that to the family of the reporter killed in that helicopter crash."

"Gentlemen!" Henry Childs held up his hand.

The room fell back into silence.

"I, for one, disagree completely with the Deputy Chief's assessment." Childs said. "The dust is not harmless. I also disagree with his dismissal of possible terrorist links. Look at the man's clothing on that recording. White keffiyeh headgear. He looks like he's been training in an Al Qaeda desert camp. Deputy Burdette, your past accomplishments are duly noted, but this time you are wrong."

Burdette bristled with the accusation and the politician's twisting of his words. He lowered his eyes. A soft hand offered her grandmother's touch on his forearm, but the Secretary of Homeland Security remained silent.

"This *Winnemucca Man* is dangerous, unpredictable and needs to be caged at the very least and by whatever means necessary." Childs said. "And that includes…"

The President raised his hand for silence and turned to the National Science Advisor. "Neil, any thoughts on how he's getting around?"

The bearded man cleared his throat. "I would suggest that Preston might be traveling via short wormholes. After all, if the dust could generate the intense energy required to issue a controlled EMP then why not a Lorentzian traversable wormhole? They are mathematically possible. Physicists, including Einstein, have agreed on the possibility of their existence. But, Mr. President, I would strongly recommend against alienating a man controlling this kind of technology. It's sheer folly."

The President continued to listen to speculation, hypothesis, and possible courses of action. He stood up. "First, a statement that the administration is working diligently on solving the mystery of the dust is to be issued, emphasizing that it has formed no threat to the general population as yet, and reiterate that biological terrorism is not in play."

The President folded his arms across his chest. "Richard Preston cannot be allowed to leave the U.S. He cannot be subjugated by any foreign government." The President glared at Childs. "Regardless of its friendliness towards the U.S. All options in achieving this goal are on the table, lethal force included. The integrity of the U.S. military is paramount."

He leaned forward on the table and looked Directors and Cabinet members squarely in the eye. "Mr. Burdette will spearhead the effort to apprehend Richard Preston. All of you, I repeat – all of you will give him whatever he needs." The President's tone and body language left little doubt who was in charge.

Burdette nodded slowly. He felt vindicated by the President's continued confidence, but Child's accusations still simmered.

"Thank you, Mr. President. I do, uh, have one request that has, ah… up to now, been denied."

The President sat down and took of sip of water, then leaned back and intertwined his fingers but didn't look at him. The President knew what was coming.

"Sir, I've been requesting Andrew Preston's military 201 file, and it seems to have been misplaced. I think we might offer this in trade, to Preston, and maybe he might play ball as you say. His son's death, and the apparent cover-up, have made him suspicious of government."

General Reynolds cleared his throat. "Deputy, I've reviewed that request, and there is nothing in that file that might help in your investigation. There is no cover-up. That information is simply classified and cannot be released."

Out of habit, Burdette stood up to address the officer. "With all due respect, sir, you're freaking kidding me. Have you read my report? Finding out what happened to his son is what drives the man. It's his purpose in life. Its torn apart his marriage and alienated his children. And you say it can't help my investigation? I… respectfully disagree." He offered an upraised palm. "I maintain a top secret clearance if that is-"

"I'm well aware of your clearance, Captain." Reynolds locked eyes with the President.

Two stone-cold poker faces.

General Reynolds shifted his glare back to Burdette. "Corporal Preston died in the line of duty. Unfortunate. But he was a soldier."

"How, where, why, that's what Preston wants to know. Give him that and maybe we-."

"He's irrelevant to this matter, Captain." Reynold's face flushed crimson. "He was nobody. A communication tech doing his job."

Burdette heard the good ole boy attitude in the sanctimonious sack of shit's voice. The same callousness that drove his sister to suicide, the same arrogance that drove him to his words. "You're wrong, General. He's the key to finding Preston, and goddamn it, whether you like it or not, that boy, that nobody, is somebody now!"

Burdette placed his folded dirty shirt into the plastic bag meant for the Sheridan Hotel's dry cleaning service. He thought of how the briefing ended and shoved the rest of his clothes into the bag. They were hiding something about Andrew Preston. And he didn't fucking like it.

He felt worn down, kept busy with interdepartmental meetings, intelligence briefings, Senate subcommittee hearings. Each meeting took its toll, and to top it all off he'd been ordered to attend a private briefing with the Vice President. The smug politician's comments still stung.

The jet was fueled and ready.

A couple of hours and he would pick up Andrew Preston's military file and bid good riddance to a city that had rubbed him raw. He had no doubts the file would be heavily redacted and missing key components but at least the President had shown good faith. He relaxed with a few breaths. In a few short days he could put this behind him and let the lights of Dallas and his mother welcome him home.

Burdette was wary as he was escorted into a large office and greeted by a menacing Kodiak brown bear standing seven-feet tall. The room was decorated like a Sportsman's Warehouse - mounted billfish and salmon, a bull elk, a bald eagle, assorted exotic animals from across the world.

Appearing relaxed in a cardigan sweater and jeans, Vice-President Childs introduced him to the CEO of the Microdyne Corporation, Jessup Grey and the company's head of security, David Gurion. He recognized the security chief as the same man he'd dismissed as a technician collecting soil samples at the Winnemucca Egg. There was something odd about the group of men. Too diverse, like they didn't belong together.

"Mr. Burdette, I'm glad you could attend this meeting on such short notice." Childs pointed Burdette to an carved oak table by a picture window with an impressive view of the Capitol building. "I hope you didn't take what I said personally, but I…we… all have duties to perform. And I have to admit your engagement with General Reynolds was quite refreshing."

Childs' attempt at reconciliation was snake-oiled to political perfection.

"No sir, and thank you, sir."

Childs sat down and waved Burdette to a seat. "Have you learned anything new since the security briefing?"

Burdette remained standing with his posture at a military at-ease. "I stand by my earlier assessment. The threat posed by Preston is still unclear. I have amended two items to the report, of which I am sure you are aware. The visual analysis team concluded the Jihadi headscarf worn by Preston in the dormitory was an ordinary white business shirt. We found it in the trash dumpster."

Childs tilted his head and arched an eyebrow.

"Second, he and his wife have been in contact with her biological children in Phoenix. The Morgan twins are under surveillance, their cell phones are monitored, but Preston's incoming calls originate from a Nokia disposable phone. Origin undetermined. Either way, Preston has not left the country."

"Interesting. He seems to be hiding very efficiently for an amateur. What are you proposing? To bring him in, that is?"

Burdette checked the two men watching him intently. Gurion openly stared at him, chewing gum as if it was cud. Jessup was antsy, glassy eyes beneath long bushy eyebrows screaming for a pair of scissors. His thumb tapped a file folder in a nervous tic.

He recited a similar briefing he'd delivered three hours earlier to the Secretary and top Homeland Security officials. "That is the plan, sir."

Given assurances that the Microdyne Corporation was at his disposal, Burdette was dismissed. He checked his watch but ignored the time. Childs' could've gotten the same information with a few phone calls. Childs had ordered him here to put him on display, like a lab specimen.

What the hell was that all about?

On the cab ride back to the hotel, he replayed the short meeting over in his mind. He swiped the card key three times before his rooms' lock flashed green, still concentrating on finding a reason for the meeting. The hotel room was cluttered with snack wrappers, empty cans of Red Bull, empty water containers. The hotel's housekeeping service declined for three straight days. He sighed and began to close the door then noticed the Do Not Disturb sign off the handle. He snatched it off and threw it on the bed.

Too freaking late. The story of your life. Don't let anyone in until it was too freaking late.

His feet hurt, and a headache was pounding its way in. He talked himself out of using the hotel's fitness facility, and instead showered and dressed. He turned the television on to a cable news program and listened to the vilification of the Preston family. As terrorists, as un-American, as a danger to millions of people. The court of opinion had tried and convicted them without any evidence being presented. He shut the noise off.

He began typing on his laptop, issuing orders to execute his plan to capture the Winnemucca Man.

⋏

The Preston's lived like any normal family on vacation, almost. Rich would take Matt and Cyndi grocery shopping each morning, in a new town or city. The irony didn't escape Rich, knowing he could go anywhere within the limits of his memory, only to emerge into towns close to the cabin -- Clinton eight miles west of the Rock Creek exit on I-90, or the Albertson's in Missoula, a scant thirty mile jump.

Rich refused to enter the grocery stores, the paranoia too overwhelming. He'd hide in a secluded side alley, or walk behind the store or mill around the trash dumpsters like a vagrant. Anywhere to avoid the watchful eyes of people. As much as he enjoyed spending quality time with his wife and son, he knew his life was in shambles. Their secluded hideaway wouldn't last forever - a dreaded maintenance man, utility worker, perhaps even the property owner might pay a visit, intent on winterizing the house for the cold months ahead.

Matt seemed to be enjoying the adventure, whooping it up whenever his name was mentioned on the television, concocting schemes to visit exotic faraway locations, and frustrating Rich when he proposed bizarre and very possible futures for the Preston clan. Rich was adamant about Matt going back to school, and graduating.

Cyndi was coping with the situation, but she was preoccupied with Nikki and Noah and their safety.

The simple life back in Boise seemed so far away. Gone forever. He cursed himself every morning for driving into that damn mote swarm.

He weighed the possibility of turning himself in to the local authorities. What could they charge him with? He hadn't broken any laws. When he put that option on the dinner table, Matt reminded him of the assaults on the egg-shaped Homeland Security agents. The government detaining him on trumped up terrorist charges worried him more.

As hard as it was not to act, he wanted the download finished before he made any crucial decisions. The purpose of the operating system implanted in his head, and the reason for the countless numbers of Beta class transit motes were critical in his strategy for the future.

The creek's soothing gurgles lulled him to sleep each night, but Rich woke up alone. Cyndi moved to the bunkroom adjacent to the loft, citing his loud snoring or his muttering gibberish as the reason. Each morning, as the sun transformed the misty meadow outside the window into a Nebraska wheat field, he heard the crying of a child, more of a whimper, as if it wanted its mother. The first time he heard it he flew down the stairs, convinced the sound originated from the front porch. The sound disappeared before he opened the door. Each morning, after the subtle crying faded, he would ask if the download was complete?

The answer was always the same. *Negative.*

The images that once overwhelmed his mind began to flow evenly, like a slideshow, and only when he asked to review them. But he understood little, and just solving the mathematical equations alone would require a team of mathematicians, led by Hawking himself.

Each day a vote was taken on a place to visit for the afternoon. They were bound by his memories, and it was one of the few times Matt asked, and listened to his father's experiences.

They spent the afternoon in Seaside, Oregon, and walked up and down the cold, windy beach before exploring the colorful shops lining the main boardwalk. Most of the shops were closed, sheets of paper taped to their doors blaming the dust. At a t-shirt shop still open for business, Rich bought a lime-green University of Oregon hoodie. He followed his family with the hood pulled over his plain white baseball cap. They found a Chinese restaurant that served clam chowder and fried shrimp, and ate in silence.

The following afternoon was spent at Fisherman's Wharf in San Francisco. The tourist trap was deserted. Harbor tour boats floated unattended, chains across their gangplanks. The tour boat to Alcatraz was cancelled until further notice. The outdoor mall on Pier 29 felt quiet and eerie. A man dressed as a cowboy, his skin and clothes painted silver, entertained a small gathering of people with his robotic moves. The street performer startled his audience by suddenly blowing white powder from his hand – then miming his escape from the cloud of dust hanging in the air. The Apple store in Ghirardelli Square was open and empty, attended by only two employees, each focused on a wide screen monitor streaming a news program. Behind the employee countertop a big screen monitor warned that Apple's warranty does not cover electronics damaged by the dust.

Matt shook his head and walked away.

Adventures that should have created joyful times, and memories to be cherished were instead, reminders of what the dust had done to the world. They returned to the cabin in silence.

"Dad, we gotta do something. It's like people are freaking paralyzed, hiding at home or something, waiting to see what happens." Matt switched the television to CNN for his daily monitoring of the Preston name.

CNN interrupted a reporter covering a fifth consecutive day of the wildly fluctuating financial markets for a special report. Black and white photographs appeared of Rich standing in a darkened dormitory hallway with a white cloth wrapped around his head. Rich ignored the grim analysis of the commentators as he read the captioning.

Preston Linked to Muslim Extremist Group.

The media manipulating the truth. Again.

Rich's mood sank, down into a familiar dark hole, an altered state, born from the death of Andy. Black and depressed, a state of being he had hoped he buried back in Phoenix.

He knew what was coming.

He was helpless to stop it.

And now, it was infinitely more powerful.

Chapter 16

Inside a bland modular construction trailer, bright warm sunlight encouraged flies to congregate at the open door. One landed and marched across the top edge of Burdette's laptop. He swatted it away and returned his attention to the email, and waited for the attachment to download.

A pop-up screen asked what he wanted to do and he tapped the mouse pad to open the file. Pictures of bruised and bloodied Iraqi women glared back at him.

He slapped the desktop. "I knew it!"

The email from a friend working at the Secret Service contained David Gurion's DHS background check. Born in Tel Aviv, the thirty-five-year old had retired as a Major from the Israeli Defense Force before recruited into the Mossad. He had obtained a legal work visa, and was currently employed as Security Director for the Microdyne Corporation at an annual salary of fifty-two thousand dollars.

Since he'd been offered upwards of 150k for a similar position, Burdette knew the salary and the position was bogus.

He skipped to Gurion's Mossad record. His whereabouts were unknown for large gaps of time but that wasn't any surprise. Last known assignment was in Iraq, around the same time Burdette was accompanying civilian contractor's snipe hunting for Sadaam's weapons of mass destruction. He was assigned to the Sixth Corps Criminal Investigation Division in charge of the infamous Abu Ghraib prison outside Bagdad, but CID Command expelled Gurion after substantiating charges of torture and abuse. Pictures of the military's humiliating treatment of Iraqi prisoners disseminated to the media were mild compared to the photos of Gurion's treatment of young Iraqi women.

Burdette clicked the file closed. The guy was a piece of work.

No doubt, Childs was aware of Gurion's military record, and his penchant for sadism. He had to assume Childs approved, maybe found it useful on occasion. There were hundreds of ex-military officers qualified to manage security details for the Microdyne research and development division. Why hire a sadistic head-case?

Another development concerning Burdette was the leaked photographs of Preston in the dormitory hallway, the white shirt tied on his head. The grainy black and white images had been expertly photo-shopped to make Preston look like a Muslim. The headdress was wrapped around his head instead of knotted, and eyebrows and skin were darkened on his already tanned face. Burdette didn't have to guess who released it, only why. Having the media misrepresent Preston as an Al Qaeda sympathizer served one of two possible purposes - push him deep underground, or more likely, infuriate him and force him into the open to defend himself in the court of public opinion. Neesa had described Preston as a sundried rubber band - one stretch short of a snap – and the pictures just might do the trick.

Burdette's trap was ready - a specialized cabin provided by Microdyne and installed in an unfinished 10,000 square foot warehouse. Situated in an abandoned industrial development on the outskirts of Phoenix, the warehouse was uniquely secluded and satisfied all requirements for the operation. Loading docks and large door openings allowed equipment to be wheeled into the building's epicenter. Electrical switchgear and transformers anticipating heavy power loads were shielded from the dust's EMP discharges with a Faraday-cage made from one-inch thick copper plates.

FBI snipers stationed on building rooftops a quarter of a mile away had an excellent vantage point and a clean line of fire.

But the trap was inside the warehouse, a mobile clean room, manufactured with specifications usually required for remote locations - a medical lab for first responders to confront possible viral outbreaks in Africa or biological terrorism in third world countries. The warehouse was refitted to accommodate air handlers using high efficiency particulate air filters to scrub outside air, and ultra-low particulate air filters, ULPA, to remove internally generated contaminants. The clean room's entrance was outfitted with a positive pressure regulator that prevented particulates over five microns from entering the room when the doors opened. An aluminum table and four chairs bolted to the polished concrete were sealed with a polyurethane finish to prevent particulates from finding a handhold.

MC specifications required all authorized personnel to enter and leave through the airlocks, including the air-shower stage. Additional agents from the local DHS, FBI and a SWAT team from the Phoenix police department waited on standby.

Burdette went inside the warehouse, still troubled by Gurion's presence in his investigation. He talked to the MC project manager in charge of construction.

Satisfied with the new interrogation facility, Burdette made a phone call.

⚔

Cyndi squatted with her back against a stucco wall, her denim jeans inches from the filthy asphalt and talked to Nikki on the disposable cell phone. Rich's attention was divided between Matt waiting at the corner, ready to explore the Las Vegas Strip, and Cyndi's conversation.

They arrived expecting to blend into the torrents of people filtering in and out of the resorts and casinos. Instead, if San Francisco was a ghost town then Las Vegas looked like a Middle East war-zone. Hundreds of abandoned automobiles clogged the six-lane street, rental cars, cabs and delivery trucks, a smorgasbord for tow-truck drivers coming and going like ants. Black and white police cars held positions at the major intersections as drunken teenagers shouted taunts at the officers. Street vendors argued with each other, and screamed for the attention of the few tourists passing by.

Wearing the green Oregon hoodie, a black baseball cap and sporting a week's worth of stubble on his face, Rich felt trouble was lurking in every doorway and around every street corner. The tourists and street vendors seemed oblivious to him and the only recognition he had received was a "Go Ducks" from a dark skinned homeless man sitting on the curb, who then continued a mumbling conversation with himself.

He'd gone to bed early, fuming over the television reports of him being an Americanized virgin-seeking Jihadist. After breakfast, he resisted the urge to visit Touweep and blow off some steam.

"Vegas, baby," Matt said.

Cyndi had hunched her shoulders and said, "Why not? And you should call your mom, Matt."

Rich shook his head with exasperation. The former Mrs. Preston had refused to talk to Rich since learning of his culpability in Andy's death. It didn't matter. They rarely spoke while Andy was still alive. The old wound of infidelity ran deep, and Rich wasn't the forgiving type.

The public exposure nitpicked at his psyche. His anxiety spiked if he became separated from Matt or Cyndi by anything more than a few feet. His mood was heavy - a dark thunderhead gaining mass each hour. His jaw ached from the constant grinding of his teeth. He kept his distance from Cyndi, or rather her phone.

He imagined Nikki and Noah pleading with Cyndi, telling her to get the hell out of Dodge. Without him. They might be right, but he wasn't going to hear it from them. Love and family was give and take, but all they wanted was Mommy. And they had no right to blame him, as if Andy had been more important to them than to him. Screw 'em.

Don't go down that black hole. Not again.

Hidden in the hoodies' pocket, his hands began to knead themselves until the joints in his fingers hurt and the skin burned from the friction. He looked up at the apex of the New York-New York Hotel roller coaster across the street. A train of cars dropped with three riders, their faces gleeful. Their screams false. He hated them. Hated how easily they laughed at death.

Rich pictured the yellow railings, the greasy tracks, the service platform at the top and a golden light burned. He saw the view from the top. He reached into the warm backwash of air, felt the vibrations of clinking metal. He would stand at the top of the world and scream his rage at the fucking insects below. Then dive and fly right at them. Let them see true death, make them feel just as helpless as he did.

"Dad. Dad, Dad." Matt waved a hand in Rich's face.

He stared at his son. His eyes refused to blink. The garish hotels and the signs of the Strip faded.

Dear God.

He took a deep breath and swallowed a knot stuck in his throat. *Don't go there, Preston, don't go back there.* He wiggled his fingers to relax his tense arm muscles.

"Where the hell do you go?" Matt asked. "It's like you check out, like you smoked some sketchy shit."

Rich shook his head and stared at the asphalt. If he told them, they'd run. He'd have no one left. Not one. They'd all band together and agree that the funny farm was the best place for him to sip Thorazine and paint wormholes on canvas.

What is funny? What is farm?

The voice! It had changed, sounding vaguely familiar.

"Son of a bitch." Rich turned around. "You talk, I mean, you asked a question. I mean you're learning, huh?"

"Dad, dad, dad." Matt waved Cyndi over. "You're talking to the thingy, right?"

"Yeah. Funny is ha-ha. Farm is where you grow shit." Rich said to the little voice, and lifted a smile. The grin of a parent hearing his child ask his first question. "You might want to start with an easier one."

Rich smiled and he held up his hands to stave off the questions. "It asked a question, damn, it asked *me* a question."

Embarrassed by his dark, miserable secret, Rich's gloom passed with the anticipation of more questions. And some possible answers. The voice still sounded computer-generated but yet had acquired some softening human qualities.

The remaining afternoon was uneventful, apart from Matt breaking ranks to wager a borrowed five dollars on video poker in the Excalibur Hotel. Rich stood over his son, reminding him if he hit a jackpot he wasn't old enough to collect it - never mind the fact that Rich would jerk him back to Montana before the jackpot lights could even begin to flash for help. The illicit thrill faded, and Matt hit the cash-out button.

Late in the afternoon, the Prestons' found an empty side street between two maintenance buildings of the Luxor Hotel and disappeared.

The new voice lifted Rich's spirits. He didn't know why. Maybe because future conversations wouldn't be so damn one-sided. Maybe because the voice had taken on a tone that was soothing, like an innocent child. He regretted his angry thoughts towards Nikki and Noah and vowed never to let them surface again.

Rich decided to travel to Los Angeles, locate a reputable television station with a major national affiliate, and give an interview. Noah was right. The media would lose interest in him, but the government wouldn't. Unless he turned the tables. He'd accuse the government of withholding information about Andy, lying about the Preston family being terrorists, and, maybe, threaten to blanket Washington D.C. with dust if they didn't back off.

He'd allow the television cameras to film the dust collecting on a random object, rejecting Matt's offer to be a guinea pig, and to prove the dust was not a weapon. They'd return to the cabin and watch the fallout on the television. Cyndi could forewarn Nikki and Noah, and offer to come get them if they wanted. The twins might have to deal with the media hounds hungry for an interview, but since they didn't know anything of value, their appeal would fade fast.

Picking flakes of tuna from his spinach salad, Rich's heart fluttered, as if it missed every fifth beat. He anticipated the attention his claims would generate. He felt like a man on death row, eating a last meal of canned fish. He could see no other way to end the running and hiding.

Rich took Brooke for a walk as the sun dropped below the ridgeline. He strolled a hundred yards down a trail worn flat by anglers and wildlife. Rich waited on a steep embankment above the gurgling water as Brooke crossed the stream.

"Seven nights and you still aren't done?" Rich said to the thingy. "You've turned my life into crap." He picked up a stone and threw it across the water. "Hell, you just added the fiber."

Astronomical mapping complete. Would you like to review it?

"Oh, yeah, show me a bunch of frigging stars again. Like that's gonna help? Show me what you want, ya little prick. Why you're in my head. Show me how to change water into wine, why don't ya?"

Rich was certain the thing in his head had changed. And it learned quickly, having developed a small vocabulary in just hours. Still talked like Einstein with complicated words, as good as riddles. But with the voice of a child.

Almost like Andy's.

The images he could flip through mentally were like an encyclopedia, one that would require brilliant science geeks to actually understand. Astrologists and physicists. Biologists and zookeepers, too. Definitely biologists, every animal or insect he could think of seemed to be catalogued, including those scary, toothy things swimming in the darkness of deep oceans. He was sure the motes had used their swarming technique on the animals, deciphering their DNA coding, indexing their eyes, hooves, genitals with strange symbols. Each creature had a page attached that looked like a sheet of weird music, weird numbers instead of notes, like a song had been written for each one.

"Remembering that fish you caught, the one Brooke wanted to help you with?" Cyndi said.

He hadn't heard her coming.

"Or are you talking to your little buddy?"

"Thinking about going down to the Pentagon and having a little powwow, bringing my friends, all of them, you know." And in his best Scarface voice, he said. "Say hello to my little friends."

"You wouldn't."

"Bet me? Lucky for them I've never been there. If I can figure out a way…"

"I was thinking about that, Rich. Are you sure it's…"

A pair of tawny mule deer with their white tails erect came splashing across the stream, running right at them. Cyndi moved closer to Rich, but the deer veered left and disappeared ten yards downstream. He searched upstream for the source of their terror. Brooke stood on the opposite bank, her dark bronze coat dripping with water, her tail stiff, her face searching for her quarry.

"Just when you think she's getting too old." Rich said.

Cyndi hugged his arm.

"Nikki and Noah hate me now, huh?"

"They don't hate anybody. This wasn't your fault. Could've been anybody driving on that road."

"You know that's not what I'm talking about."

Cyndi squeezed. "Forgive yourself and I think they will too. You shut everybody out, and they feel it. Open up, let it out. They'll come around."

"Easy for you to say. You didn't..."

"Bull. It's not easy for me to say, nothing's easy with you." Cyndi tugged on his arm, demanding that he look at her. "I loved Andy, he had a gentle soul and what you said cut him deep, and he was going to prove you wrong, and he did. He did, dammit." Tears were in her eyes. "But he wouldn't want you to torment yourself either. Or this family."

Her words were honest, and true, and still hurt. Andy's kindness and compassion pitted against the horrors of war and destruction. And he was the catalyst that had combined the two. That's why nothing else mattered until he learned how Andy died. Was he blown to bits by a bomb, shredded by bullets, fucking run over by his own Humvee? Did he see it coming, feel it when it hit him? Why wouldn't they just tell him?

Rich looked away, at Brooke crossing the creek's slick rock bottom with cautious steps.

"Remember when Nikki started going out with you on your evening walks with Brooke?" Cyndi said. "Feeling you out about her being gay? You coming home and whispering to me that she might be a lesbian, and what we would say if she comes out? We had it all planned. You said you'd accept only cute lesbian friends into the family but you would love her anyway. God, you are so dense sometimes."

He sighed, and stared at the gin-clear water. He remembered Andy switching off the Sunday Night Football game he was watching. The Cardinals needing a win to make the playoffs. Andy flipped his long hair off his forehead and heaved a nervous breath, then blurted out, "I'm gay, Dad."

Rich suddenly felt nauseous.

If he only he had a second chance, he'd embrace his son and tell him, to each his own, and it didn't matter and he would always love him.

Halfway up the embankment Brooke halted, smiled, wagged her tail twice and persevered.

"You can't take it back," Cyndi said as if able to read his mind. "Move on. Don't alienate Nikki and Noah. It doesn't help. And for God's sake, watch what you say around Matt. There's a grain of truth in your humor, Preston, and sometimes it hurts like hell."

Cyndi was right, and she spoke the truth, it was his duty to listen. After he got Andy's records.

"Maybe I can sell this stuff in my head. You know, get rich and live happily ever after." Rich said. "It's amazing stuff. The world's going to change, and in a big way. And I'm gonna be right where I don't wanna be, right smack in the middle of it." Rich looked to the sky. "Are we doing the right thing or just being naive?"

Cyndi shook her head. He could tell she was thinking about something else. Probably the twins, maybe Andy.

The evening light waned. Rich interlaced his fingers into hers and they began a slow walk back to the cabin.

"Egbok, Preston," Cyndi whispered. "Egbok."

"Maybe Matt will crash early, and we can have a little, you know, alone time. We're overdue."

"Uh, huh, maybe." Cyndi said.

She didn't sound optimistic.

⋀

Noah froze when he glanced up from the soapy washbasin. The wine glass he'd been washing dripped suds on clean glasses drying in the rack. An exotic woman bypassed Jenny, the dining room hostess, and sat down at the end of the polished sandstone bar of the GrapeStreet restaurant he co-owned with Nikki and Eric. Her dark skin was flawless and coiled locks of black hair glistened. She checked the bar's small seating area as if searching for a friend. Her white top matched her white denim jeans and the top three buttons of the silky form-fitting blouse were left undone, obviously to show off her assets. The contrast between her ebony skin and her white clothes only seemed to enhance her ample cleavage.

Noah dried his hands. Women of this caliber rarely entered the restaurant alone. After two years working behind the bar, he had become accustomed to serving female beauties, but a posse of chattering distractions always surrounded them.

Noah checked for stains on his black polo shirt and pants, and scratched a smudge of ranch dressing off his crotch. GrapeStreet's grape and wineglass logo proudly embroidered over his heart, he rubbed the stubble below his ear and wished he'd used a razor that morning. Four days' growth was cool, but two days looked sloppy. Noah spiked his dark brown hair with wet fingers and approached the goddess.

Experience taught Noah to listen, and react appropriately to the moods and demeanor of his patrons, but this dark beauty wrote her own playbook.

"Hi, I'm Noah. I'll be your server tonight. What can I get you?"

"Hi, Noah, how about a white wine spritzer."

The woman's smile was flawless.

"Coming right up. Expecting company this evening?" Noah pulled a bottle of Chardonnay from the ice and poured a generous portion. He waited for the answer before mixing in club soda from the dispensing gun.

"Nope, just hanging with myself tonight."

Noah flashed a smile. "Well, you've come to the right place for that."

"Excuse me," The woman said and answered her vibrating iPhone. "Okay. I'll get right on that." She tapped a button and dropped the phone into her white leather handbag.

"Work, huh? I haven't seen you in here before. What's your name?"

"Yeah, work. They always want something." She smiled and offered her hand. "I'm Lisa."

⋏

Nikki checked her hair in the rearview mirror. The sun-bleached chestnut hair barely reached her shoulders, and she brushed away the bangs clipped at a jagged angle. She checked her smoky hazel eyes.

She checked the time and sat back in the car seat. She had hated lying to her mother - there were more than just a few reporters hanging around the small house she shared with Noah - but she didn't want Mom worrying about her and Noah.. The street was practically a block party for reporters of every sort - newspapers, local television channels and even a satellite truck for CNN. It was the people with the bright cameras lights, and the paparazzi, that bothered her ever since the strange dust had landed on Mom's house in Park City. Seemed like her and Noah's private lives had been pried open for public consumption.

The evening after the Park City dust disappeared into the air, a shrewd reporter from KPHX Channel Six had knocked on their front door, loaded with questions about their Uncle Doug, the person responsible for the lease on the condo in Park City. Noah denied the existence of an uncle, any uncle period, and shut the door in the man's face.

From that day on, Nikki and Noah agreed to stay separated except at work, spending the last few nights with close, trusted friends, trading vehicles, rarely venturing out into the public except for the gym or work.

The restaurant remained a bastion of normalcy but it wouldn't stay that way. They had watched Uncle Doug on the television, manhandled by reporters attempting to goad any response from a suspected terrorist's brother in-law. Eventually a co-worker or friend seeking a few minutes of fame would disclose the twin's ownership of the GrapeStreet restaurant.

Nikki turned the air conditioner fan on low, her thumb began tapping the wheel. She made up her mind to book a flight to wherever Mom was hiding, and bring her back home. Why she stayed with Rich was a mystery. No, not really. She knew exactly why. Loyalty, vows, even love. Nikki admired her mother for working hard at her marriage, and since Andy's death, Rich was impossible to like, let alone love. He had changed, always hiding inside that man-cave he'd built inside his head. He was quick-tempered, like a freeway road rage monster, whether he was driving or not.

And he was the only father she'd ever known.

But a terrorist? No freaking way.

Their blended family may be dysfunctional but they certainly weren't the crazies the media was portraying. Mom was sticking by his side, again, but she was hiding something too. Nikki could hear it in her goodie-two-shoes phone conversations.

It had to be Rich. Again.

But he wasn't abusive, and besides, Mom wielded a 'Belle' effect over the Beast. A snap of her fingers could chill the man out, like a bucket of ice water.

Her future husband, when she met him, wouldn't be a beast, but she'd still be a Belle.

She applied a quick smear of clear lip-gloss and climbed out of the car. She checked her reflection in the Volkswagen's dark-tinted windows and adjusted the black bra straps beneath her sleeveless cotton top. The challenge of creating cleavage failed, and she flashed an ugly face at her own reflection. She brushed dust and lint from her tight black yoga pants, and walked towards Ferraro's restaurant.

Greeted by the grandeur of an architectural rock waterfall and its cool mist, she vowed to get something like that for GrapeStreet someday. She dismissed the thought and smiled. David waited by the window. The man's mixture of cologne and deodorant was intoxicating as he kissed her cheek. He looked even better than yesterday when he'd asked to speak to the Grapestreet manager, only to compliment her on the efficiency of the staff's service. A chiseled chin, dark skin, and exotic eyes seasoned the man's pheromones.

She walked ahead of David to their table. Nikki knew he was giving her skin-tight pants a careful look. Nothing much she could do about her do-nothing top half, but strenuous workouts on the elliptical trainer had her bottom portion ready for any inspection. She hoped David had a brain to match his athletic body. If he played his cards right, she might sample what he had on the menu.

The conversation flowed, improved by a bottle of Ferrari-Carano merlot. David said he managed a small bistro in the downtown Phoenix area. She wasn't familiar with the name or the location but downtown Phoenix was full of new restaurants still looking to make a name. Common business interests, vendors, contractors, and health department hassles kept their conversation rolling.

They finally ordered a plate of bruschetta with another bottle of wine.

During dinner, David asked the right questions, and better yet, gave the right answers to her questions. Nikki's phone vibrated in her purse in the empty chair.

"Go ahead and get that if you need to." David said.

She shook her head. "Probably just business. It can wait."

"These are crazy times, yes?"

It was the first time she detected an accent in his voice. Something a little stiff. German, maybe? "You have no idea."

He laughed.

She felt content. The waterfall's moist, cool air was romantic, and David's wit and charm disarmed her defensive nature. The languid meal ended with the sharing of a chocolate mousse dessert.

Expectations coursed through her mind. Was it the wine? Should she or not? She couldn't look like an easy lay - a sure way of never seeing a second date. She decided to play it cool and exchange email addresses.

Maybe a kiss.

It was so hard to do the right thing.

Nikki hoped David didn't turn out to be a flake like so many others, and he might even pass one of Noah's brotherly, overprotective interrogations. They walked out of the busy restaurant and into the warm desert night. David excused himself to make a phone call, pulled out his cell, and muttered a few words. Definitely a foreign language. Middle Eastern? She was impressed.

David asked her to follow him to his car, so he could retrieve the business card of the wine distributor they had discussed over dinner. Approaching the white Navigator, Nikki heard the engine start. She was impressed again. Oh how she would love to have a remote start for her car, to cool off the oven waiting inside before sitting on hot vinyl.

Opening the passenger side door, David searched the console lit by dim dome lights. Nikki craned her neck inspecting the vehicles immaculate black interior.

He did have a nice butt.

David turned to her and said, "Sorry, baby."

What? All her good feelings about him slipped away. She hated to be called baby, hated any woman being called baby. She found the term ancient, chauvinistic and condescending.

She folded her arms across her chest. "Why'd you…"

Her right hand flew to her hip, just above her right buttocks. She felt what might be a cactus needle. But how did…her muscles turned to wet spaghetti, her thoughts became jumbled, incoherent. She wondered what color the needle was.

David Gurion twisted a grin, feigned to catch Nikki in his arms and let her fall hard to the hot black pavement.

⅄

Noah held the door open for Lisa as they walked out of the restaurant. The night was alive with flying ants and moths fluttering in the lights shining off the building. They paused as Lisa searched her purse for her car keys. Noah looked around, unsure of what to do with his hands. He counted the digital cameras of the GrapeStreet security system. He might have to replay what the cameras recorded, make sure he didn't look like a fool. Make sure Lisa was real.

His hand spiked his hair and he ran his tongue over his teeth. He had offered to escort Lisa to her car and she accepted with a smile that buckled his legs.

That was just a small victory, he still needed to get the gorgeous woman's phone number, or at the very least, her email address. He would definitely Google her, see what kind of pictures she posted on Facebook.

"I'm over here." Lisa pointed towards a white mini-van.

Noah walked alongside her, distracted with editing his all-important dialogue that flew around inside his head.

"I really enjoyed meeting you," she said. "Can we meet again?"

"I'd love to."

That was easy. Maybe he underestimated his own charm. Probably not.

Lisa stopped at a grey Toyota SUV.

"This is me. Don't worry. There's no baby seats hiding inside."

Noah smiled and nodded. "How come? I mean girls like you, I mean women--

Lisa lunged at him, her hands embracing him behind his neck. Her hands were strong. She smashed her lips into his. Her sweaty lilac scent. Sweet Chardonnay on her breath.

Holy mother of God!

Noah relaxed and returned the kiss. Blood flooded into his groin.

Down boy. Not now!

Lisa broke the embrace and gently pushed him back. Noah was stunned and his eyes darted from her cleavage back to her eyes. She cocked her head and smirked catching his divided attention.

Her smile dropped as her right eyebrow rose.

Noah frowned. Why the change? What had he done?

He glanced over his shoulder to see a man wearing a blue polo shirt stitched with a yellow DHS. He pointed a weird looking thing at the small of Noah's back and fired.

Fifty thousand volts of electricity coursed through Noah's body. Streetlights became UFO's, the dark pavement melted into the grey SUV. Lisa's white clothing and her face melted together into a bizarre Picasso caricature.

Noah slumped to the pavement.

Neesa wiped the sweat forming on her brow as her partner handcuffed Noah. How could anybody stand to live in the desert and the heat? A fall evening, for God's sake, and the air was still stifling hot.

Neesa buttoned her blouse. She might've forgotten a piece of equipment in Park City, but the tools that worked on men always traveled with her.

Chapter 17

Cyndi was somber as she took her time showering. She fussed over what to wear. Most of her clothes, shoes and jewelry were back in Boise but she finally settled on a pair of jeans and a white blouse. She'd planned a detour to a Target or Wal-Mart to go shopping for Rich's interview – for all of them. With millions, perhaps billions, of people watching, they needed to look credible.

While shopping, she intended to call Nikki and Noah and finally tell them the truth, the extraordinary truth, of what happened to Rich – the thing in his head and its ability to order up wormholes and control the dust.

Eating a breakfast of sliced fruit, oatmeal, and toast, Matt remarked how tired he was of the same dull breakfast every morning and why couldn't they make a simple trip to get an Egg McMuffin or a Krispy Krème donut? After all, what was the use of wormholes if they lived like hermits in a cave?

Cyndi opened the blinds in the upstairs windows to allow the sun to warm the cabin. Her mind wandered as she stared out the window. Brooke was making her morning rounds, sniffing bushes and marking trees. She hugged herself, ambivalent about returning to the cabin. The house was warm and safe, but it was isolated, and she missed the subtle comforts of a home with neighbors. A house for family to visit.

Cyndi held back the tears. This wasn't the time for self-pity. She had, at times, shut the door of her bedroom in Park City and cried over her nomadic and unsettled life, disconnected from those that truly mattered. And now they were on the run from the federal government. She yearned for normalcy to return, to move back to Phoenix, to her old home, near her children. Be able to drive a short distance to Smith's Food King and push the shopping cart down the aisles worried only about food prices. To hear Rich drop his keys on the kitchen counter after work, see him twist the cap off a cold bottle of beer, tired from his labor but satisfied. To enjoy the triumphs of her children, anticipate the joys of becoming a grandmother, and laugh at the innocence of grandchildren.

She closed her eyes and soaked up Rich's warmth as he put his arms around her waist. She leaned back and settled into his chest. She smiled wondering if he used the portal trick to get close without her hearing him.

"I was wondering if we'd ever have a home again," Cyndi said.

"We will, I promise."

The comfortable moment lingered in silence, but she knew he made a pledge he couldn't keep. He needed to work on himself first - he needed to talk to a professional grief counselor about Andy. She had found one in Park City that suggested Rich was subconsciously alienating himself, distancing himself from the people he thought he betrayed. Rich needed to reconnect with her, then family, then friends, then, maybe with society. Doc Thomas told Cyndi that she was the key to Rich's recovery, perhaps the only person preventing him from falling into a suicidal depression. Shelling out $375.00 for three sessions with Dr. T. was invaluable, and she took his words to heart, but Rich's black fugues were occurring more and more frequently. His temper simmered on a hair trigger.

Now a voice in his head. Was it a gift from God? Someone for him to talk to? Or was it something that might finally push him over the edge?

"Let's go!" Matt shouted from downstairs.

Cindy broke Rich's hold and rushed into the bathroom to dry her eyes.

She dabbed on makeup thinking about Matt. Poor Matt - caged up with dull parents for the past week, no available friends, no college girls, no Facebook account, no smartphone to maintain a social life. But the time alone with his father had been good, and necessary, for both of them.

Cyndi was the last to gather in the living room.

"Open sesame." Matt said and chuckled.

Rich grabbed their hands. "Hope we know what we're doing."

Los Angeles supported plenty of twenty-four hour news stations, any of which would he happy to invite him to sit down in front of their cameras. Getting there wouldn't be a problem. Rich had lived in Riverside for six long months, an absentee new father, and an apprentice electrician learning the trade at the construction site of the Four Winn's boat-manufacturing facility. If he didn't drive home on the weekend, he headed to Huntington or Newport Beach, a six-pack of Miller Genuine Draft in the cooler and the endless surf replacing a television.

CNN, ABC, CBS, or NBC, exactly which one was irrelevant. If one televised the story, they'd all have it within minutes. His favorite Fox News and their 'fair and balanced news' was withdrawn from consideration. All the other major news programs had dropped the 'Richard Preston, Muslim Terrorist' angle after it became clear the photographs were unreliable. But Fox News continued their vilification of the Preston family with an onslaught of so-called experts claiming to understand what rattled around in the head of a disaffected American citizen who'd lost his son in an unpopular war.

Rich wanted his story broadcast nationwide, wanted it dropped on the world like Hiroshima, ending the speculation, wiping out the hysterics and the widespread belief that his dust was a threat to people or national security. He wanted to end the assertions that the Prestons were homegrown terrorists with sinister intentions.

Revisiting the Albertsons' grocery store in Missoula, they emerged into a crowded parking lot bustling with big trucks towing fifth wheel trailers, motor homes, and cars packed full of personal belongings. Dark, billowy thunderheads gathered over the Bitterroot Mountains and people were literally running for the hills.

From the parking lot, he planned a series of jumps to reach the department store. In the grassy meadow downstream of the cabin, he had practiced opening another portal as soon as he emerged from one, like an Olympian leaping over hurdles, though his pace was usually slow and tentative. The closest less than six feet from another.

Rich kept his distance as Cyndi pulled out the phone.

Cyndi sat on the curb beneath the overhang of a leafless Maple and dialed Nikki again. Voice mail. Cyndi finally left a message.

"No worries, call me. We'll come get you." She giggled. "You have to hear this in person."

Rich took a deep breath watching her dial Noah. He crossed his arms and turned his back.

"Who's this?" she said.

Rich turned and frowned.

"Where is Noah? Why are you answering his phone?"

Covering the phone with her hand, Cyndi whispered. "They have Noah."

He snatched the phone from her. "Where is he?"

"Right in front of me, Mr. Preston. You want him, you come get him. Are we clear?" It was the pretty liar, Neesa.

"And where is here?"

The woman gave him an address in Phoenix.

"You don't get it, do you, lady?" Rich said. "I'll bury you."

He hit the end button and stared at the phone. He couldn't look at Cyndi. He didn't need to see her face. Her skin would be drained of blood, her eyes would be blinking fast as if irritated, her shoulders slumped in an odd angle. He'd seen it before, he caused it, he woke with it every day and ate breakfast with it after Andy's funeral. He had vowed never to see it again.

Query?

Shut up.

"Dear God. They're not going to stop. Now they have Noah!" Cyndi grabbed the phone and dialed Nikki again. "She's not answering. They have her, too."

Where would it stop? Cyndi's brother, sister, cousins, who would be next? Killing random strangers until he gave himself up? He should have found a way to the Pentagon. Found a way to Andy's military file.

Motherfuckers!

Surrender. With the condition that Cyndi and the children receive immunity for any bullshit charges they could invent. Neesa's smug, condescending tone echoed. It was a taunt. A challenge, to a duel.

One he would gladly attend – seconded with an army of trillions.

"Let's go!" he shouted.

His teeth began to grind. He couldn't meet Cyndi's eyes. She pulled on his arm, firing off questions but he ignored her.

Shaggy. Skippy. Neesa. Light Bulb Head. All the Buckwheat's would be there. He balled his fist, imagined his fist pummeling their faces, helpless in tombs of dust.

His dust.

⅄

Behind one-inch thick panes of tempered glass, Burdette listened to Neesa's conversation on the opposite side, baiting Preston. He raised his right arm toward the ceiling and twirled his hand to indicate the operation was now active. He checked the warehouse for Preston. The man could appear at any second.

Technicians and agents on assignment from the FBI, NSA, and Army CID scrambled to their positions. Loudspeakers inside the warehouse, on the roof and nearby buildings sounded an intermittent three-beep signal. Four FBI agents climbed into hazmat suits to patrol the perimeter of the warehouse. No way could the dust penetrate the guard's self-contained air systems, but Burdette wasn't convinced the agents could retain mobility beneath the weight of so much dust.

Noah sat in a chair bolted to the slick sub-floor. He yanked on the handcuffs on both wrists. "Where's my sister?"

Burdette checked his khaki trousers and a light blue business shirt specifically laundered for the capture operation. He adjusted his weapon's shoulder harness and ignored Noah's question. The kid's skin had to be itching beneath the synthetic fiber pajamas he wore. Burdette had tested the dust-free clothing and Noah would soon begin to chafe around the groin and armpits.

"Where. Is. My. Sister?" Noah said. "What did that guy mean by, we lost the Morgan woman?" Noah yanked on the cuffs again. "Tell me, you fuck!"

Burdette stiffened. Steve Cable was discovered in the crapper of the restaurant with a broken neck. Talley was found in his vehicle with a dart sticking in his neck. Assigned to maintain surveillance of Nikki Morgan, his two-man team had been upstaged. The tiny darts bagged and sent to the FBI for analysis, but

Burdette knew who had shot them. It had all fallen into place as soon as he heard about it. And he had to admit, Nikki's abduction was a smart move, but one that didn't bode well for the girl.

He ignored Noah's tirade but still felt a bit of empathy for a brother's protective instincts. In his place, Burdette would've reacted no differently. Bare hands, knives, razor blades, a shoelace, he would've killed anyone to protect his sister.

His plan assumed the strange dust would either precede Preston or at least be nearby. The controlling vector was unknown, but if Preston couldn't use his dust inside the clean room, then only two alternatives were left for him. Run away or surrender and Preston wouldn't run. His Glock 9 mm. aimed at Noah's head should make the angry father hesitate, think twice and second-guess himself, persuade him to finally surrender.

Unless he was a complete lunatic.

Surrounded by high-powered assault rifles, Taser stun guns, even tranquilizer guns loaded with fast acting paralytic agents, Preston would then be handcuffed, stripped and sanitized, and escorted into the clean room for interrogation. The plan wasn't foolproof, there were too many variables and the capabilities of the strange dust topped the list.

Burdette turned and stared at Noah. He thought of Microdyne and their chief of security David Gurion's violent past, and the photographs of abused Iraqi women. He thought of Vice President Henry Childs, who pretended to employ the sadist.

Power, money and sex.

In the end, it was always about power.

⨩

Cyndi held Matt's hand as they watched Rich from inside the cabin. Rivulets of rain ran down the picture window framing the front yard. Cyndi shivered with an involuntary spasm.

Rich stood sideways to them, his head hanging and his black hair wet and shiny. His green sweatshirt was soaked and his jaw muscles beneath a salt and pepper beard were grinding like a flourmill. His fingers flexed, then balled into fists. His lips moved. He was talking to the thingy.

The thingy. Matt's nickname for a voice inside his father's head. A voice she couldn't hear but one that had always concerned her. Would it eventually take over his mind, then his body? Would it finally drive him insane…she closed her eyes not wanting to think about it.

Rich had told them he was familiar with the address Neesa had given him. He had installed electrical outlets and light switches for an office remodel for Creed Mechanical less than a mile away. He said finding the exact address wouldn't take long after he arrived. When she said she was going with him, his face knotted and he growled. "No."

He sighed and apologized for his abruptness, then ordered them to wait inside the cabin.

Cyndi turned her face as a faint, translucent mist rose in the field where Brooke often roamed. The mist floated, impervious to the rain, rising to the tops of the withered stems of field grass. The dust turned opaque. The mass appeared to multiply, compress, then expand again, as if it was living and breathing. The grass disappeared. The kitchen lights flickered.

Cyndi shimmied tighter to Matt then squeezed his hand into hers. Spidery willows, leafless raspberry shrubs and tall Lodge-pole pines faded into grey shadows. The sunlight already muted from the rain clouds disappeared in dark shadows.

Rich stood motionless, staring at the ground.

Static electricity crackled. The dust swarm expanded to consume the wood porch railing three feet from her face. She resisted the urge to run out the back door and into the forest. Matt's muscles twitched. The lights flickered again with a boom of thunder.

"My God, what's he doing?" Cyndi said.

Matt wiped at his face. Cyndi glanced up and saw the smear of a tear, then saw another trickle down his cheek.

Matt's voice quivered. "Wished he would've just went to Alaska."

Alaska. Rich's ill-conceived Nirvana. A place to run and hide but Andy's ghost would follow him there, too. He couldn't escape his guilt, his words, in the vastness of the last frontier.

Brilliant flashes of dry lightning, the splintering dry wood. Cyndi stepped back, pulling Matt. The static charge of the swarm invaded the cabin. The hair on her arms stood up straight. Rich was lost inside the whiteout of alien dust. An equal amount of desert dust would suffocate the life from anything caught inside. The dust began to move as if it turned liquid, swirling in currents and eddies. Picking up speed and momentum.

Like a school of mackerel avoiding a predator, it gathered and condensed behind the shadow of a solitary man. The windows and floorboards vibrated as the flying dust sanded the house. Gritty and powerful.

The lights failed. The inside of the house sparkled with thousands of tiny bolts of lightning. The rumble of the shifting motes was deafening.

Matt wiped his face again.

"Don't hold it in!" Cyndi yelled over the roar. "Don't be like him, spit it out!"

They watched Rich take a step forward and disappear through a splash of gold.

Matt swallowed. "He finally has somebody else to blame, somebody to fight other than himself."

Torrents of dust spun counterclockwise then streamed into the golden outline of Rich's wormhole. Cyndi covered her ears. The whirlwind milky grey spun at a dizzying speed, a horizontal cyclone, funneling itself down into the burning maw of an alien storm drain.

Chapter 18

Rich flinched at the suddenness of a bright sun as he stepped back home, into the dry warmth of the Arizona desert. His wet sweatshirt was heavy and he wiped the rain from his face. He glanced up at a beige building he'd labored in less than two years ago.

The dust storm followed, its wake of hot air stinging his back and neck, whipping his wet hair, his scalp tingling from the static charge of the passing swarm. The spread of dust flew up and dissipated into the desert.

The buildings signage was gone, the missing letters outlined in desert silt, a reminder of the area's economic meltdown. Miserable tumbleweeds had overwhelmed the neighboring acreage, gobbling up the for sale signs of Simpson Real Estate. The wandering weeds had spread like an infection into the rocky foothills, mixing with Joshua and Mesquite trees. The address provided by the pretty liar was a half mile away, on the opposite side of the street.

Searching. The voice acknowledged.

He'd conceived the search while waiting for the dust to multiply in the yard. He'd forgotten he was able to see what the dust recorded. Sagebrush and soil, dormitory doors and dark hallways, the mundane pictures the motes transmitted held no significance.

Until now.

Rich pictured Noah's face, his spiked brown hair, soft nose with dark eyes pinched in a worried frown, identical to Cyndi's, and a bright unending smile. He waited, concentrating on Noah's face. Less than a minute passed.

Search complete.

A grainy black and white image presented itself. Noah dressed in strange blue pajamas, both his wrists handcuffed to a stainless steel chair.

"Pan back," he said. The image zoomed out. "Hold."

Noah sat in a room enclosed with thick glass, one that reminded Rich of detention cells depicted in the movies, imprisoning Hannibal Lechter or a James Bond super-villain. The room was isolated, centered in an empty warehouse.

The big man with the shaved head guarded Noah. Light Bulb Head, no yellow halo this time, but his shoulder holster, and weapon hadn't changed. The pretty liar, Neesa, stood guard at what looked like a maze of glass and metal doors. Men in hazmat suits walked the perimeter carrying military style assault rifles, canisters of air riding on their backs. A room that had been built for him.

Freaking idiots.

Like he'd just walk in, and ask to be shot. Suicide by police. The irony didn't escape him. He'd considered the idea, going out with the shotgun's double-barrels blazing. But he wouldn't spread his own misery. Even the Napoleon paramilitary pukes had children.

Rich remembered what the dust had done to Cyndi's condo then remembered the Egg and how it all began.

"Do it!"

Insufficient quantity to achieve visual projections.

When you're asked to jump, don't ask how high, just do it. Call it down from the hills. Just do it!

Through the eyes of the motes, he watched the Buckwheat approach the pretty liar and mouth a conversation. He saw Shaggy standing near the open loading dock door checking his handgun. He saw the big man put his hand on Noah's neck. Rich's face became a snarl. *Get your hands off my son.* His impatience made his jaw throb.

Let his motes have their say first.

His motes.

He turned his head as a dust storm rolled down from the foothills, an avalanche of grey and sand, picking up size and volume, churning like an Australian desert blizzard racing towards the warehouse. Rich made a short jump, emerging three hundred yards from the building.

The dust enveloped the warehouse.

"I'm a survivor, I'm a winner, things are gonna change. I can see it."

⚐

Burdette winced as his earpiece erupted in static. A sniper's voice stuttered through the audio mayhem. "Subject in…. Permission to take the shot?"

"Negative!" Burdette said. "No go. No go."

Noah's face was a knot of confusion. Even though he had heard Neesa taunt Preston, he still had no clue why.

But his plan had worked and Preston was here. Burdette's mouth was suddenly dry and his uneasiness grew. Burdette checked his old wind-up sports watch, making sure the mechanical second hand still worked. Beyond the glass, his team was ready and waiting throughout the building. He blinked as the bright sunlight coming in from the open loading dock doors faded, a haze of grey mist entered. Technicians monitoring the fresh air system at the far end of the building disappeared from view. The words of the President's Science Advisor returned. If it was sheer folly to alienate the man then, perhaps, it was outright madness to provoke him?

Stationed at the room's entrance, Neesa stood ready to escort Preston through the rigid entry protocols before entering. She became a ghostly shadow. Burdette wiped small beads of sweat off his forehead. The fluorescent lights flickered and died. Cool, clear air continued to blow from the ceiling vents. Three lights fired up, and his room returned to white brilliance. He felt confident the lights would stay on after shielding the backup generator in twelve inches of concrete. The strange dust flew in with astounding speed.

"Neesa?" Burdette said into his headset. "Neesa. Anyone copy?"

The air outside his enclosure became muddy. Light shining down from the roof's large sun-domes faded. Burdette thought he was prepared for the dust. His apprehension grew as he checked the heat-sealed joints between the panes of glass and the fluttering white ribbons tied to the egg crate air vents. The dust collected on the outside of the glass in a light patina, like a sprinkling of pow-dered sugar. He inhaled through his nose with slow deliberate breaths.

He was trapped, in his own trap.

Noah's face was frozen, his eyes wide as plates. Then his eyes narrowed as if he'd just completed a sudden realization. Burdette waited behind Noah and grabbed his neck.

Noah wrangled his cuffs again. "Don't fucking piss him off. He's not…"

"A little late for that," Burdette whispered.

Burdette was still convinced he'd planned the trap correctly. The clean room technology did prevent the swarm of particles from entering. The warehouse walls disappeared into the mist. The primer-red steel columns and roof trusses faded into grey. His team, all top men and women in their fields became nothing more than shadows, fleeing, melding into the fog.

He glimpsed Neesa. At least he thought the marble sculpture of grey was her. The men with the protection of the Hazmat suits ran towards the room then disappeared in the blizzard. The interior of the building was nothing but grey dust. His protective glass dimmed as the motes stuck to the slick surface.

Burdette swallowed hard. In the starkness of snow white, he prayed his for-tress would hold.

"Let's make this easy, Preston," Burdette said. "You can't get in here."

A plate-sized spot of dust melted off the glass in front of Noah. Burdette eased his arms up into a two-handed firing stance. A maniacal face looked in from the porthole. Preston's eye's looked white and crazed. His black hair wild and stiff.

All chance to reason with him was lost, maybe there never was one to begin with. A long moment passed but Preston didn't move. He just stared into the room, his eyes darting to every corner of the clean room. His lips twitched in a silent mumble. Burdette was sure Preston would be diagnosed as schizophrenic, and that the diagnosis would be wrong. He was psychotic.

Burdette tightened his grip on his weapon as Preston disappeared and the oval window returned to grey.

The dust suddenly dropped off the glass like a magician's trick. The ware-house beyond was surreal, a moonscape of white.

He couldn't shoot, that might puncture the glass… and allow the dust to come pouring in. He lowered the weapon, his trigger finger tapping the trigger guard. Stay with the plan. He clicked the safety off and raised the barrel to Noah's temple.

Noah yanked at his shackles again. "You're as crazy as he is."

"And necessary. Your stepfather will surrender."

"My father, asshole, that's my father."

Burdette pinched a nerve in Noah's neck. "Stay quiet."

Outside the enclosure, Preston appeared in a flash of amber light, just as he had in Park City, his pea green Oregon sweatshirt and its golden O an odd contrast to the bleakness of grey. The lunatic stared with a blank expression then began to pace the length of the glass, back and forth like a nervous caged animal.

Burdette locked his eyes onto Rich's distant stare.

"Stalemate, Preston." Burdette said. "You want him? Then put your hands on the glass and…"

Preston increased the distance of his pacing, stretching it to some unseen demarcation until he turned, and marched like a soldier to the far corner, faced the dust-covered wall and stood frozen. Preston had lost it. He stood motionless, staring at nothing but grey dust. He suddenly turned 180 degrees, and lifted the corner of his mouth in a half-smile.

Burdette tightened his grip on Noah's nerve.

The man would be found incompetent to stand trial…

Preston began to sprint, shouting incomprehensible words, yelling for some 'little prick' to do something.

He ran past Burdette with the craziest set of eyes he had ever seen.

And disappeared.

⋏

David Gurion's thirty-minute commute to the Phoenix International Executive Air Terminal was like most of the others. Different city, different landscape, but the ride was always the same. Quiet. With a hint of anticipation.

Nikki Morgan remained silent, hidden in the cargo area with enough Midazolam and Seconal in her system to keep her unconscious. Gurion's two associates looked to be playing with their iPhones, but their eyes were scanning the freeway on-ramps and medians for police cruisers and unmarked surveillance vehicles. U.S. Homeland Security's central computer and its access to hundreds of traffic cameras made them nervous.

"America the Sly," Gurion said in Hebrew. "They watch their own people, like Hitler did, only with cameras and computers instead of the S.S."

The men grunted but said nothing.

The executive air terminal was deserted and the gate guard was missing. They drove inside the hanger, and one of the men ran to close the big door as another carried Nikki's body up the stairs of a Microdyne executive cargo jet. He dropped Nikki in the leather seat furthest from the cockpit.

He squatted and brushed the sweaty bangs from her eyes. She was so lovely for an American. He shut the window screen, covered her with a blue blanket, and pulled out a thin insulin syringe from his shirt pocket. He stabbed Nikki through her stretch pants then ran his hand along the backside of her leg, enjoying the tactile sensation.

Yoga pants. America's delightful gift to the world.

"Give her much more of that and she might not be any use to us." An associate said over his shoulder.

"Au contraire, my friend. Dead or alive she will be useful. Preston only needs to think she's alive. If the Americans are successful getting to Preston, then she will disappear into the desert. Perhaps she may be used for bargaining power, it is not for us to say."

"Do we still get a sample? He said none of that this time."

Gurion leered at Nikki. "Let's get airborne."

⚔

The arch in his left foot screamed and his right knee felt like sandpaper rubbing rough lumber but Rich ran hard. He visualized the exit point and his legs gave everything they had. The motes burned open a portal just as he ordered.

The terminus was eighteen inches off Burdette's right shoulder.

And it felt like hitting a three hundred pound professional wrestler who didn't follow the script. The man's muscled body was tense, rigid, and caught off guard by Rich's sudden emergence into his blind spot. The man pivoted to face him, raising the Glock to fire, but Rich clutched his wrist with both hands and pulled the weapon down.

A gunshot. An explosion of sound. The bullet ricocheted into a pane of tempered glass, shattering it into a spider web of cracks.

The man used his backpedaling momentum to twist and slam Rich with a hard elbow above his left ear. Rich screamed but held on. The man's sudden move changed their trajectory as they spun in a pirouette of dance.

Another gunshot and shards of sharp concrete exploded, stinging his calves. His legs churned, and burned, as he pushed the man like a football dummy, moving him away from Noah. He would drive the man down to the floor.

"Now. Now!" Rich screamed.

He smelled the sage and felt the atmospheric pressure change as they fell backwards, down towards hard concrete, and through a wormhole.

And onto the hard, angry, red rock of Touweep.

Seeing Noah through the porthole had made Rich consider surrendering. How long had it been? At least a year, probably more, but Noah was still the six-year old mop-head Rich had adopted into his heart. The man's trap had worked. It had kept his dust from helping him.

Then the man standing over Noah put his hand on Noah's shoulder.

Fuck him.

The tiny voice confirmed a small number of motes remained inside the room, hidden in the corners of the floor and ceilings, the heaviest concentration in the seams of Burdette's leather holster and between the bullets inside the gun's ammo clip. A measly ninety-one motes.

But enough to start the replication process.

Three hundred and sixty-seven seconds until the few motes could clone sufficient numbers to isolate Burdette. Six minutes but it was too long.

The Light-Bulb-Head was unpredictable. He might use the time to put a bullet in Noah's head. And then blame Rich for the tragedy. People that owned handguns or assault weapons were on a power trip, had some imaginary superiority bequeathed to them by a manufactured piece of metal. The worst of them walked elementary schools, or crowded movie theatres, or office buildings, killing anybody that moved. Cops were the worst.

He could take his lumps, a fat lip, maybe a broken tooth or two, but he wanted that weapon out of the mix. Burdette outweighed him by at least thirty pounds, all muscle, and probably learned some self-defense shit. But Rich had surprise on his side and he could move him, push him, and force him in a direction of his choosing.

Through another wormhole.

Rich had paced along the glass partition talking to the thing in his head. The voice rattled him by suddenly asking for the purpose of the transit portals.

Why?

Because he wanted to get inside.

Why?

The thing asked its questions using Andy's voice, as a young child. Why this, why that? The questions were relentless. Especially about what he ordered it to do.

"Enough. Just do it, ya little prick!"

The thing in his head seemed to flinch, then shrink and almost hide, then it said, *Okay.*

Rich released his grip on the man's wrist and rolled twice on the hard sandstone, shards of rock stabbing into his back and arms. He crawled to his hands and knees, and saw the man's gun aimed at his face.

Rich stood up, a half smile lifting his lips. "Go ahead, Buckwheat. Do it." He took a step towards the man. "It doesn't matter. Do it!"

The man jerked as the spasms tore through him. He retched and dropped the weapon, clutching at his stomach as if he'd been gut shot. He vomited dark brown liquid, chunks of something meaty, and crawled into a creosote bush rooted in a crack at the edge of the cliff. His hands squeezed the branches in a death grip, stripping the poisonous leaves to flutter into the canyon.

Rich grabbed the gun by its barrel and tossed it over the edge of the canyon. A sudden hot gust of wind sent the tent flap whipping wildly. He bent over the man and began searching his slacks, and shirt pockets, slapping away his feeble attempts to stop him. Rich paused to read a badge, Jonathan Burdette, DHS. Finding what he wanted, Rich backed up two steps and glared.

A step forward and he returned to the glass room. Noah trembled, his wrists blotched with purple welts.

They locked eyes.

"What have you done?" Noah said.

Rich shook his head then used the key he'd taken from Burdette to unlock the handcuffs. Noah waited and Rich felt his eyes boring into him. Accusing eyes. Eyes that had shamed him four years ago. Eyes that still held their power.

Noah stood up rubbing his wrists then flicked his chin towards the dust exterior. "How'd you do that?"

"It's a long story. Where's Nikki?" Rich asked.

"I don't know. They were talking about losing her, or she's missing, or something like that."

Rich stared at him. "What?"

"What have you done now? Is this why they came after us?"

"Let's go."

"Where? We gotta find Nik."

"To see your mother," Rich said.

Fuck me, Mildred.

Query: What is Mildred?

"Shut up!"

"You shut up," Noah said. "You're fucking certified, Rich."

Rich resisted the urge to latch onto Noah's earlobe as if he was a four-year- old, and instead, grabbed Noah's wrist. He ignored the screams as he pulled Noah into Montana.

⚔

Burdette climbed to his hands and knees as his nausea and unsteadiness eased. He wiped the spittle from his chin. His hand reeked of creosote, like the wood railing of a horse corral. Turning his head, his stomach dropped like a rock, a tiny twelve inches away from falling off a cliff. He coughed up soft chunks stuck in his throat but his unsettled stomach still churned.

"What now, Preston?"

He backed away from the cliff edge and stood up. Sagebrush and creosote. A different continent, another planet? The maniac had somehow teleported him to the middle of nowhere.

"Preston!"

The sound of his voice died in the lonely, hot breeze.

Burdette dropped to his knees, seized by a painful spasm in his abdominal muscles. His thigh and calf muscles cramped. His vision blurred as vertigo washed over him, and he curled into a fetal position as the spasms shot up his neck and into his head. He vomited again. Dry heaves of mucus and spit.

And Death.

⅄

Cyndi knelt beside Noah, rubbing his back as the spasms started to subside. Their clothes were soaked and a light drizzle tinkled on the metal roof.

Rich put his arm around Matt.

"Nikki?" Matt said in a whisper.

Rich sighed and shook his head. He wouldn't be able to handle Cyndi's emotionally charged questions when the time came. The fear of failing her again was unbearable. He was responsible for the chaos engulfing his family, again. Just like with Andy.

Rich stepped off the stairs and back to the clean room. He sat on the chair still dangling Noah's shackles.

Spread out and search for Nikki. He pictured Nikki's face, her angled haircut, a quarter inch crescent shaped scar below her right eye, a small mole below her left nostril, small imperfections cloaked by her toothy smile. He waited, ripping off the tips of his fingernails, hoping for an image of Nikki to rush into his mind just as Noah's had.

An ungodly amount of motes covered every square inch of the building. Doing nothing.

He asked the voice, the operating system using Andy's voice, to release the dust to help in the search.

Rich stood up and stepped through a portal, back to the vacant industrial building. The sky was hazy as a hot wind blew in from the Phoenix skyline, laden with silt and now joined with the dust streaming out of the warehouse.

"Find her!"

Searching. The voice said. Then the Andy voice spoke. *Who is Mildred? What is Buckwheat?*

It was Andy as a three-year old. Questions upon questions. His answers only beckoning even more questions. What's that? What are they *dune-ing?* His stick-tight son had been full of curiosity, and Rich relished every inane question that often tested his patience.

Why was the thing using his memories of Andy? Why not Matt's or Noah's? He heaved a breath and stepped back to Touweep.

Burdette looked dead, slumped against the tent in a meager dollop of shade. His blue shirt was stiff with dried brown bile. He looked like an alcoholic suffering from a weekend bender - pale, lethargic, nothing tasty left to drink. Been there, done that.

But it could be a ploy. Maybe he was waiting to pounce if Rich came within striking distance. Squatting down five yards away, Rich studied Burdette.

He began to toss small shards of sandstone at Burdette, each with more force until one hit him in the forehead and his eyes fluttered open.

"You look pretty bad for just coming through a hole," Rich said. "You should have lost a little lunch, but you…"

"A hole?" Burdette wheezed and paused for another breath. "What hole?"

"Wormhole. Pretty sure that's what I use. Where's Nikki?"

"Don't know." He spit. "You're under arrest."

"Really?" Rich said with a snicker. He stood up and put his hands out as if asking to be handcuffed. "Guess you forgot the cuffs, Buckwheat. Maybe my son has a pair he can loan you."

Burdette wasn't faking, he was sick. Rich walked up to Burdette and kicked him hard in the thigh. "Where's Nikki?"

"What'd you do to me? How'd you-"

Rich kicked him hard in the legs again. "Where's Nikki!"

"Fuck you." Burdette said and spat again.

Rich tightened his jaw and turned away. The tracks Burdette had created crawling to the tent looked like those of a lizard. Or a snake. The man's physical condition confused Rich. The portals had never caused such a severe reaction. Matt, Cyndi, even Brooke seemed normal a few minutes after first emerging, then downright hungry.

"Why's Buckwheat so sick?" he asked.

Unknown. Isolation required for analysis.

He thought of ordering Burdette entombed in the dust, discover the reason, but his weak condition might work in Rich's favor. Or he could drag him to a hospital and tell the doctor he's suffering from what? Wormhole sickness?

Rich straddled Burdette's chest. The man reeked of sweat and vomit. "Nikki? And I'll get you to a hospital."

"You're under arrest." The words were a rasp.

Rich slapped him hard across the ear then stood up. Maybe he thought he had more cards to play. Rich groaned and walked to the cliff edge. He wiped sweat running down his forehead, fanned his hoodie, cooling his t-shirt soaked in sweat.

Sweat. Burdette wasn't sweating. He was dehydrated.

Rich marched to the tent and pulled the plastic container of water from the inside.

He stood over Burdette and shook the half-empty water jug.

"Last chance. Where's Nik?"

Burdette just blinked, expressionless.

"Then bake."

Rich stepped back to Montana.

⅄

Cyndi stood behind Noah, rubbing his shoulders and neck as he scarfed down a turkey sandwich, potato chips, and pasta salad. Matt was rambling, bombarding him with incredible stories, of dorm room battles and narrow escapes, maggot-man monsters and living on the run. Noah listened and nodded.

"Freaking walking down the beach one minute, then gambling in Vegas the next." Matt said. "It's sketchy but cool."

Noah mumbled with a mouthful, "And you're a wanted criminal, too."

"You're just jealous that your name isn't Preston."

Cyndi smiled while listening to their banter. The purple welts on Noah's wrists steered her thoughts back to Nikki. She took Noah's empty plate to the sink and spied Rich through the kitchen window. She knew he wouldn't join the reunion.

She saw a despondent man standing in a dreary rain. His head hung, like Brooke who had been caught sampling something from the counter. He walked down the game trail paralleling the creek. He halted, as if to ponder the water and pulled the sweatshirt's hood over his head.

She turned when Noah called.

"Mom, is that true?"

"What?"

"Rich controls that dust?"

She nodded and thought of Rich's ability to manipulate the strange dust. She folded her arms, wondering if Rich's shame kept him from coming inside the cabin.

Rich had been tough on Andy growing up. Like most fathers, he pointed out the imperfections of his firstborn son. Andy's sloppy handwriting at age seven, awkward running style at twelve, the lack of a prom date at sixteen. Lots of love and attention in between, but criticisms nevertheless. With Noah, Rich had taken a more hands-off approach, supportive, but delicately distant, as if Noah's lack of common DNA had hung a Do Not Disturb sign around his neck. Rich treated Nikki as if she was a princess, the daughter he'd never sire, a girl incapable of mistakes. Noah felt the slight as he grew up and his secret resentment of Rich surfaced after Andy's enlistment, then amplified into contempt after his death.

Cyndi turned to look for Rich by the river's edge. He was gone. A sudden tiredness diluted her jubilance with Noah's arrival, and she gripped the countertop as her legs turned soft. She stroked the flat edge of the granite with her thumb and attempted to steady herself. Rich would bear the responsibility for Nikki - bear a weight equal to what Andy's death had strapped on his back.

And Noah would push him, with as much in-your-face guilt as he could muster.

And her precious baby girl was missing.

Cyndi closed her eyes and absorbed the laughter of the boys. She tried to swallow, but the sudden fear of losing Nikki became a knot of rope. One stuck in her throat.

⚔

Rich abandoned Phoenix, frustrated and dejected. No images had flooded his mind, and the childlike voice was quiet, but he had no place to go. Noah was at the cabin and he wasn't ready to listen to him. He stepped onto the massive chunk of blood-red sandstone at Touweep. A strong wind greeted him, threatening to push him off the cliff edge. The air was already twenty degrees hotter. In the late afternoon Touweep was a brick oven dialed up to maximum.

Burdette looked defeated, beaten down by the sun. His eyes were swollen shut, his scalp was roasted, and the hot sun continued to pummel his crotch and legs. He had managed to stay in the shade of the tent, keeping critical areas of his body out of the blazing sunlight.

Rich looked away, sickened.

No animal deserved to suffer.

Rich made a quick jump to a Flying J truck stop near Twin Falls and braved the long line of people to purchase a gallon of distilled water. Returning, he fed Burdette the water, trickling the cold liquid onto his parched lips, then pouring the water over his head.

Burdette opened his eyes and snatched Rich's wrist. His grip was weak, and Rich freed himself with a quick twist. Pouring half the jug over Burdette's head, Rich stood up and waited. Burdette blinked into a semi-conscious state.

"You look like shit." Rich backed up.

"Feel like it, too." Burdette rasped.

"You gonna make it?"

"Depends on you, I guess." Burdette raised a crooked finger to point at the jug of water Rich was holding.

"No, depends on you. Where's Nikki?"

Burdette attempted to sit up but slumped back. "Don't know."

"You lie. You'll broil until you tell me."

Burdette licked his lower lip with a white tongue that resembled sandpaper. He eyed the water. Rich took a small sip as an enticement.

"Want this? Just tell me where my daughter is."

He held out the half-full container.

"Don't know."

Rich turned his back and walked along the cliff edge, considering his options. Give him the water and possibly lose an advantage. Don't and the man would surely die.

Rich shook his head and returned to hand over the jug of water. The plastic jug dropped from Burdette's weak grip and spilled, transforming the red sandstone into a pool of crimson. Rich groaned, picked it up and poured the water into Burdette's mouth, most spilling down his chin and onto the front on his stained shirt. Burdette grabbed the plastic handle like an addict needing a fix and swallowed a large part of what remained.

"I helped you, now you help me. Where's Nikki?"

But Burdette had passed out.

Fuck me, Mildred.

Query

It's just a saying. It means…please not now.

Rich loitered around the campsite, cursing himself, and Mildred, and Buckwheat. He hopped back and forth between different areas of Phoenix and back to the tent, hoping the motes had found Nikki or Burdette had regained consciousness. He didn't want to face Cyndi, and he didn't have the energy to deal with Noah. He stole a jug of water from the Flying J in Winnemucca, disappearing by the row of video poker machines.

Back at Touweep, he stared down at a thousand feet of open air below. How easy it would be. To see his son again. Close his eyes and just leap, freefall for a couple of seconds and Andy would greet him in heaven.

Andy's voice. *Fuck me, Mildred.*

Nikki regained consciousness, her eyes blinking at the silver sunbursts of two halogen lights blazing above her. She wiggled her toes then held her breath as she listened. Men were talking, joking about a Palestinian whore, not worth five euros. She didn't recognize their voices. She attempted to wipe away the crust irritating her eyes but found her arms restrained with bands of thick synthetic material. The skin on her thighs and buttocks was chilled. She realized she was naked and strapped to a cold stainless steel platform. She pulled at the wrist straps, and tried to move her legs. They were bound in a similar fashion.

Raising her head, she saw her torso covered in a white sheet of impermeable plastic. A dress made from a garbage bag? The neon-orange toenail polish on her bare feet was the only color in the stark white room. She remembered the twenty-five dollar pedicure. Preparation for a dinner date with….

She'd kill the bastard. Take a butcher knife from Grapestreet's kitchen, and slice and dice David's genitals. Her helplessness stoked her rage. She thrashed and let loose a scream. Her dry throat burned for the effort.

"Calm down." David said bending over her face. "No one is going to hurt you."

"What did you do to me?" He was wearing white scrubs, like a hospital technician.

"You had a seizure and passed out. I had to take you to a hospital."

Nikki hesitated. The bourbon and cigar on his breath said he was lying. "Untie me. Now!"

"Calm down, young lady. You need to settle your ass down." David's tone was stern.

"Screw you. Let me go!" She screamed again. The sound seemed to bounce of the glass walls, unable to escape.

"I warned you, bitch." He waved over a man dressed in a white hazmat suit. The man's face was covered, and he approached on her right side and jabbed a thin syringe into her thigh muscle.

"This will be over before you wake." David smiled. "Then the real fun can begin."

He was sick. Fun - the last word Nikki Morgan heard before she faded into unconsciousness again.

⅄

Shifting Burdette's considerable bulk into the shade was like lifting three bags of Portland cement all at once, and it caused Rich's sciatic nerve to shoot pain down his left leg. Burdette had muttered a few incoherent words and slapped feebly at Rich's hands but hadn't really regained consciousness. After several attempts, he managed to drag Burdette into the shadow stretching off the tent and into the canyon.

He groaned with exasperation. Start off wanting to kill the man and now he had to play nursemaid. Rich poured more water over Burdette's head, but it only aroused his tongue to lick his lips. He checked Burdette's pulse - healthy and fast.

Rich rubbed his forehead and sighed. Reluctantly he returned to Cyndi and the cold drizzle of Rock Creek. His sweaty clothes chilled his skin as he paced outside the cabin on the gravel driveway. The aroma of meat frying on the gas stove wafted from the back door and called him inside. Easing the back door open, he sat down at the dinette. Cyndi, Noah, and Matt sat with him, quiet, and patient. He told them about Burdette, and the unsuccessful search of Phoenix.

He picked at a spot of dried ketchup on the wood table. "I don't know what else to do."

Noah spoke first. "He's telling the truth, he doesn't know where she is. But he knows something. I saw it on his face when some guy came in and said somebody was dead and they lost her. As much as I'd like to forget him, you can't let him die. "

"Agreed." Cyndi gave Noah a thin smile for his act of forgiveness and compassion. "He has to know. But he's not telling you." Cyndi stood and went to the stove. "He's our best chance to find Nik."

He listened to their council, and there was no blame or accusations aimed at him. Just a sense of working together to get past this. Rich should have come home sooner. He glanced at Cyndi as she served him a generous portion of ground turkey meat and potato salad. She'd been crying. The skin around her eyes was still flush from a cold compress she would've used to hide it. He'd seen the puffy redness before, and it hurt.

He shoveled the goulash into his mouth as fast as he could swallow, hurrying to return to the stricken man. Not for Burdette's sake, but Nikki's. And Cyndi's. He refused her request to accompany him. Her presence, her compassion, her fear, would only confuse the situation.

Cyndi shook open a plastic grocery bag and placed a sleeve of saltine crackers and can of Coke inside, and tied the handles shut. Picking up an empty plastic two-gallon water container sitting by the recycle bin, she asked Matt to fill it from the kitchen sink.

Rich ran upstairs, used the bathroom, put on a black baseball cap and tucked another into the back of his pants. Cyndi had followed him upstairs. She grabbed the hoodie at his chest and bored her bloodshot eyes into him. Shrinking him and empowering him at the same time.

"Find her, Rich. You bring her home. I can't lose another…" She buried her face in his chest.

"I will. I might use the dust to see if it can force him to…"

Negative. No way, Jose. Andy's voice again, when he was six-years old.

In kindergarten Andy often hesitated before he spoke, carefully choosing the right words. They had to rhyme, and mimic the rap music he'd discovered while scanning the truck's radio stations.

Maybe he could disburse the dust world-wide? Search every square inch of the whole planet?

Affirmative. Time is Prime. One hundred thirty-three years to do that.

"Beat it out of him if you have to." Cyndi said with tears falling from the corners of her eyes.

Her words stunned him. But they explained the emotions that had to be churning inside her.

"He'll tell me. Even if it's from my own jail cell, he'll tell me."

Cyndi squeezed him. His resolve and doggedness ignited with her touch.

Rich took the stairs two at a time, grabbed the plastic bag, grunted with the heavy water container and stepped back to Arizona.

It was possible Burdette was telling the truth and didn't know *where* Nikki was. So far, he was only aware of the cast of DHS idiots involved in this screwed up mess. Was another competing government entity trying to trap him? The CIA, the NSA, the 'Shop'? Kidnap Nikki and use her as bait as Burdette had. One course of action was clear - he'd keep returning to Phoenix with the hope the motes search routine would return an image of Nikki.

The logic dawned on him, and made him feel stupid and foolish. Then afraid. His physical location was irrelevant. If the motes found Nikki, the Andy voice would tell him.

Burdette was still his best hope, his only human hope, and he decided to leave the Homeland Security man where no help could find him. At least until he got answers. Burdette's physical appearance disturbed him though. Hunting rabbits in the lush desert of Arizona, he never allowed an animal to suffer or go to waste.

And Burdette was suffering.

Maybe Nikki's location could be coaxed from Burdette, especially if he thought his own life was about to fall off a cliff?

Chapter 19

Burdette was watching as he stepped out of a portal five feet away. Dangling the Albertson's grocery bag in one hand and the oblong container of water in the other, he felt at a sudden disadvantage and took a quick step backwards, stumbling over a chunk of sandstone. The brisk wind had died to an occasional whisper, and the sun laid on the flat horizon.

Burdette's skin was blotched red from heat and sweat. Setting down his luggage, Rich pulled the empty gallon container from Burdette's grip and began to refill it.

"Almost died in that cloud," he said. "Came out dehydrated worse than you are. Guess the little prick wanted to save himself."

He winced breaking the promise to himself to stop cursing the computer, the entity, the Andy voice that seemed to be maturing inside his head.

"Little prick?" Burdette said in hoarse, raspy voice.

"Long story. You must've had some kind of bad reaction to the portal. Maybe some kind of beta transit airsickness?"

He ignored Burdette's wary squint, and placed the man's hand into the jug handle.

"Drink. It's better than dog water."

Burdette gulped the water down as fast as it flowed. His neck muscles strained as his throat accepted the liquid.

"Cyndi sends a care package." He placed the saltines and the can of Coke by Burdette's other hand. "She thinks the salt on the crackers might help. The Coke's from Noah."

"You're still under arrest."

"Yeah, so you keep saying."

Rich walked over to the canyon's sharp edge and suddenly felt small, like a flea on a sandy beach. Rich wondered if Karma had come around, or maybe the irony of blind Justice handing down her punishment - saddling him with two pricks, one tiny, a passenger to whatever he thought or did, and imitating Andy. The other prick five paces away, too heavy to carry, too weak to hate, and holding the key to finding Nikki.

The river below was barely visible. Just soar for a few seconds. End it now.

Actually, that would not end it. You'll have to keep playing.

Rich froze.

At eight-years old, Andy was on an *'actually'* kick, prompting debate and speculation, starting every conversation with the word actually. It was cute in the beginning but quickly came to border on obsessiveness. Pointing out a weakness in Andy's quest for world domination in a Saturday night game of Risk, Rich was rebuffed by his son, "Actually, that won't end it. You'll have to play on."

"Why are you doing this?"

It's me, Dad. Andy said.

"Quit acting like my son, you little prick."

He felt it shrink then hide.

Just as the real Andy must have felt. Dear God.

He closed his eyes and swayed in an imaginary breeze. His feet shuffled towards the edge, inches felt like miles. He raised his arms like wings.

Not yet.

Nothing to lose, Rich turned and marched over to the prone man. He squatted on his haunches and refilled his jug. "You're not going anywhere. Neither am I. So why don't I tell you what you probably want to hear."

His thighs ached as he told Burdette his disjointed story, of driving into the dust cloud, being herded like a cow up to a cottonwood tree, discovering the wormholes in his own dehydrated delirium. How he fell asleep in the very tent Burdette sat against, his shirt still tied around his head, and then the encounter with the three idiots in the dormitory hallway.

Burdette coughed. "One of those idiots is dead."

Rich flinched. "Me?"

"No. Someone else." Burdette had the saltines in his hands, trying to tear the plastic open, but he was too weak. Rich drew close, snatched the crackers and ripped them open with his teeth.

He handed the crackers to the pathetic man in front of him. He had once hated this guy, and the others like him. He still hated the people who held his daughter. But they were scared of the dust. Hell, sometimes he was scared of the dust. So he told his side of the confrontation with Neesa, her trickery and deceit. Burdette nibbled at the crackers and washed each bite down with a sip of water, never taking his eyes off him.

Rich couldn't sit still. He paced the cliff edge, pausing to stare at a fiery copper sunset burning behind Burdette.

He told how he learned about the dust's ability to help him, first at the dormitory, then at Cyndi's condo, and in their own encounter inside the clean room. Finally, he knelt down next to helpless man, feeling strangely lighter for having shared his story.

"Totally. Fucking. Bizzaro, huh?" he said. "And every word is the freaking truth."

Burdette was expressionless and silent. Rich waited. There had to be at least a chance that his admission, the truth, would pry the location of Nikki out of him.

Hope, like the last bit of daylight, slowly faded with Burdette's silence.

"Look around." Rich gestured with his arms. "You're here, Buckwheat. And I can disappear in the blink of your eye."

Burdette didn't flinch.

Rich arched his aching back. "You ain't gonna die, Buckwheat. I won't let that happen. You got water and a bit of food. There's a sleeping bag inside, and the night will get cold."

Still no response.

His story told, his emotions spent, his hopes gone, Rich teetered on the edge of the cliff. The last shadows of the sunset turned black and disappeared.

"I've done nothing wrong. Maybe I was in the wrong place at the wrong time. Hell, maybe it was the right place, right time, I don't know. I'm just trying to keep my head above water and deal with what's happening, that's all. I'm not a threat to anyone. I just want my little girl back."

"You are a threat. You've got to know that." The man's voice was so husky and low that Rich could hardly make out the words.

"How?"

Burdette took a sip of water, swallowed, and breathed deep. "How do you know what that thing wants with you? How do you know what it's doing to you? How do you know I'm not on the right side of this?"

"You kidnapped Noah. You kidnapped my daughter. Does that sound like the right side?"

"Don't know…"

There was nothing in the man's blank expression. Rich closed his eyes and gave up. He was tired of hating, and the anger. It had caused nothing but heartbreak.

"All right," he said. "I'll call your girl, your pretty liar. Tell her where to come get you. I'd drag your ass out of here, but you don't seem to travel too well my way."

Burdette tried to speak, took a sip of water.

"You can find my body down there." Rich pointed into the black canyon. "Then you can let my girl go. Leave my family alone."

Actually, fuck me, Mildred.

"Wouldn't-" Burdette coughed. "Won't matter. She'll disappear."

Rich turned at his words, optimism and fear jittered through his surrendered soul. He hustled to the tent and squatted next to Burdette, but his face and expressions were lost in the night. Rich scrambled into the tent and unpacked the Coleman lantern. He pumped air into the fuel tank, his hands shaky and unreliable, and lit the mantles with matches stored in the tent pockets. A bright white light hissed, casting lonely silhouettes into the desolate desert.

He returned to Burdette's side. "My daughter. Where is she?"

Burdette finally met Rich's eyes. "I honestly don't know. I wish I did."

"What do you know?"

Rich listened as the beleaguered man told him about his actions during the Egg investigation, and his suspicions regarding a second investigation shadowing his own.

Burdette mentioned the manipulated photos with Rich wearing terrorist rags, words that brought Rich to his feet.

With deliberate words, Burdette told him of his strange meeting with Vice President Henry Childs and David Gurion. "Nikki's disappearance coinciding with Noah's apprehension was my confirmation that the Phoenix operation was a test, a trial run."

He warned of Gurion's checkered past and his penchant for abuse, and his employer's reputation for retaining political power.

"It's all a chess game." Burdette took a sip. "You're the black king."

"And you've just changed sides?"

"I don't know what the sides are." Burdette's eyes grew weary, but he gave Rich a final tidbit.

"Andy's file is locked away, even from me. You'll need a Presidential order to get it, or…"

Burdette passed out.

Rich called 911 from a Chevron in St. George, Utah. He told the operator a stranded hiker was dying on the south rim of Touweep. He milled about the campsite hoping Burdette would regain consciousness, and abandoned him only after waving the lantern to assist the Search and Rescue helicopter locate the remote camp.

He returned to a sleeping house. The microwave's green digital readout said 2:34 AM. Noah was asleep on the small couch in front of the television. CNN's Sanjay Gupta was explaining the health ramifications of Israel's shutting down a critical water pipeline to the Palestinian enclave in the Gaza Strip.

Rather than risk the squeaky stairs, he used a portal up to the double bed in the loft. He sat down on the edge of the bed and rubbed Cyndi's hot backside. She sat up with a jolt. He whispered the information Burdette had divulged. Stripping his clothes off, he answered her questions coming at him hot and heavy. Lying next to her as the busy day dragged him down, he repeated what Burdette had told him, and then again.

"This ends tomorrow. We'll get Nikki back."

He fell asleep.

⋏

No way could Cyndi fall asleep, again. Hours of tossing and turning finally allowed her to enter a semi-dream state, but she was never fully asleep. She was awake in an instant at Rich's hand. The first time Rich told her what Burdette had said, she felt confused and overwhelmed. A chess game? What the hell did a game have to do with her daughter? Vice-Presidents, Gurion, the Mossad, the black king? It was madness.

She sat up against the headboard, and asked Rich to repeat his story. She mentally assembled a chessboard, putting human faces to the kings and pawns. Except this game seemed to have more than two kings. She assembled the pieces as Rich repeated Burdette's story yet again. The chess game analogy nagged at her. Why would Rich be the black king?

Rich's control of the dust was the catalyst. Any government would kill to control the amazing technology. It could make any small country an instant superpower. Her loathing of men and their quest for power simmered, kept on a low flame by her inability to act. For now.

Cyndi knew chess. Her father taught her on his visits home between tours of duty in Vietnam. She loved the game. She loved the quiet, uninterrupted time with her Air Force Major father she got to know for just a few weeks at a time. When he was gone, she'd practice, playing her mother, playing her friends, playing herself mostly. Sitting across the board, her Poppy often reminded her to consider the possibilities, two, five, ten moves ahead.

Cyndi imagined the unspeakable horrors and unimaginable terror Gurion might inflict on Nikki. The flame of her anger clicked up a notch.

Rich was right, this was going to stop.

She got up and stared out the window as starlight rippled on the creek. The air was cold and she hugged herself. The cold kept her thoughts flying in hundreds of directions, each one a possible move in a game she was a part of, whether she liked it or not.

She'd lost her passion for chess to hormones and puberty. Almost a half-century had passed since she played, but time couldn't change the basic structure of the game, its myriad of possibilities and geometries given to each piece. One guiding principal of the game held true regardless of the opponent.

Unleashed from the shadow of the black King, the black Queen was the most powerful piece on the board.

⚑

The house awoke to the aroma of turkey sausage, and Cyndi banging the backsides of frying pans like a psychotic cymbal player. Rich rushed downstairs. The crazy woman clanged pots, rattled ceramic plates, and slammed bread into a toaster, inciting a riot of noise.

Rich furrowed his brow, and approached with cautious steps. "You all right?"

"All right? I'm fucking great! I haven't slept a wink, and this stops now, Preston."

Noah sat up from the couch, rubbing sleep from his eyes. "Mom, what's up? What's wrong?"

"Cyndi, what are you thinking?"

"I'm not thinking. I'm knowing." She pointed a polished steel spatula like a knife. "We come out. Those people who have Nikki will surface." She got in his face and tapped the utensil on his chest. "Then you go get her."

"What are you talking about?"

"Never-mind. Can you go where you want? Ask that little prick if it sees the place, can they open a gateway to it. Go on, ask."

Stunned by the simplicity of Cyndi's request, he asked.

Parameters of the destination are required.

"It needs parameters," he said. "Just like I said."

"Mom, what's up?" Noah said again.

She crashed an empty steel pot atop the stovetop. "What's a freaking parameter?"

"It's something I've seen in a place I've been to. Jeez, Cyndi."

"Jeez? Is that all you got, Preston? Not a 'fuck', or a 'hell', or a 'bitch.' Just a golly gee whiz?"

"A parameter," Noah interrupted. "It's a set of requirements or variables. If it's for a computer then it's data input."

"Something you've seen? How about if you've seen the parameters in a book, or a picture or movie? Would that do, huh?" Cyndi asked.

The woman was frenzied, and yet she asked an intriguing question, one that had never occurred to Rich. Cyndi knew something. Something she had been hiding.

Can you find places in books?

Actually, Dad, transit doors can be opened using any visual input. But exiting coordinates need to be confirmed by local Beta's.

"Maybe?" Rich said. The answer was confusing, but hearing the voice of his son scared the hell out of him.

Cyndi lowered the spatula and handed Noah a piece of paper. "This is a list of things I want you to Google. Lots of pictures. As many as you can find, minimize them and keep them ready. Google has maps, too, right? I want some of those." Cyndi wielded the spatula like a baton. "Go get dressed. We're going to town."

Rich arched his brows and looked at Noah.

He shrugged.

"Now!" Cyndi bared her teeth. "I want to call my daughter."

The parking lot of the Albertson's grocery store in Newport Beach was cloaked in a thick coastal fog. Cyndi pulled her hand out of his, but she seemed confused as she checked the shops and bungalows lining the half-hidden street. Getting her bearings, Cyndi led the procession, marching at the front of the line as if she was late for an important appointment.

Rich hurried to keep up. Cyndi's ponytail pulled through her black ball-cap was swinging in rhythm with her quick stride, brushing the back of her purple windbreaker. The stainless steel spatula still gripped in her right hand.

Cyndi wanted Wi-Fi, a strong signal for the laptop, and they found it two short blocks away, at a Human Bean Café squeezed between Tobacco Road and Chronic Taco at the end of strip mall. Frumpy in borrowed jeans and white t-shirt, Noah followed Cyndi to a small oval table meant for two people. Matt and Noah jockeyed for control of the Mac's mouse-pad with Cyndi settling the matter by tapping the spatula on the table.

Rich leaned against the wall behind them and crossed his arms.

Why was the voice talking like Andy? He could almost picture his son's face speaking the words, a goofy grin waiting to laugh.

Noah tapped the keyboard and Googled what Cyndi had listed on the piece of paper. She stood over his shoulder, pointing and approving internet pages of faces and buildings. She wanted the most recent photos, tapped the spatula for Noah to minimize a page and again to open a new tab, like a General commanding an intelligence gathering.

"Rich, you're going to call Nikki. And the voice on the other end is going to tell you to go somewhere."

Rich arched his brows. Did she have a clairvoyant dream that foretold the future or something? Was the thing in his head spreading? Cyndi grabbed his hand and pulled him close to the table. She angled the laptop's screen so he could see.

"Look at these pictures. Visualize them like you were behind the camera. Start shuffling them, Noah."

Rich squinted at the screen, then moved in closer to put his hands on Noah's shoulders. He squeezed gently. Rich recognized the man's face from the television news - an arrogant politician and an uncompromising douchebag.

"Look at him, Preston. Remember him like you have a few beers with him every Friday after work. Remember him. Noah, go to Google Earth. The satellite one. Start zooming in. No, go back, zoom in slow."

Cyndi made him repeat the process twice more.

"Tell your little buddy to find that man, in that place," she said. "Can the thingy get you there?"

Piece of cake, Andy said. *Search parameters complete.*

"Yeah. But why?"

Her kick-ass-and-take-names body language was frightening. He saw an ugly side of himself in her demeanor, her speech, and he didn't like it. "What are you doing?'

"Was that a yes? Good," Cyndi said. "Then let's make a call."

Cyndi dialed Nikki's number and shoved the phone at him. "It's you they want."

He swallowed. "Yeah." He put the phone to his ear.

"Good morning, Mr. Preston. Very simple. If you want Nikki back, do exactly as I say"

"I'm listening." Rich said.

"The dust follows you like a plague, so if I see it, Nikki dies. If I see a cloud move with the wind, your daughter dies. If I see the smoke from an automobile, she dies. Clear?"

He detected a slight accent. The voice had to be Gurion's. "Where, Buckwheat?"

The voice paused.

"Northwest corner of Riley and Oquendo. Kirkland Washington, ten minutes," Gurion said. "Pity if this fog drops much lower. I might make a mistake."

The call ended and Rich's stomach dropped. Gurion's voice was measured, and his tone was convincing and left no doubt he would carry out what he threatened. Rich felt like a fish out of water, flopping around, no way back to the water.

"They want you somewhere, huh?" Cyndi said. "Of course. Noah get a street view of the meeting place. Hurry."

Rich wouldn't repeat what Gurion had said. Cyndi would freak the fuck out. He gave Noah the address.

Cyndi folded her arms across her chest. "Minimize that screen. Our king is checked. Concentrate on your new drinking buddy, Preston, and picture his face. Now the city we zoomed into, concentrate." Her voice was calm. "Put them together and ask your little friend. Can you see him?"

He closed his eyes and replayed the laptop screen zooming down from space, into the city, down onto the building's rooftop. He pictured the man, his silver beard and bushy eyebrows, just as she asked.

"Show me," he whispered.

The images were grainy, not much dust for imaging. A man sat at an oblong conference table thumbing through a pile of white paper, his white button down shirt open at the chest. A cigar smoldered in a simple glass ashtray at his right hand. Layers of smoke hung in the air. Six other middle-aged men sat at the table talking or reading newspapers.

"Yeah, he's with six other guys. What are you planning?"

"Of course he is. They're waiting to see if their knight can finish the game." Cyndi reached up and grabbed his face in her hot hands, boring her eyes deep into his soul. "Because I'm going to pay him a visit, and you're going to send me. Send me with as much dust as you can, but get me there. It'll give you an advantage. To bring Nikki home."

Fuck me, Mildred.

Actually, a smooth move, Buckwheat.

He couldn't swallow.

"So be it," he said. "You can have all of him you want. Nothing's gonna happen to you."

He closed his eyes, pictured the dust cloud rolling down from the foothills of Phoenix, pictured the swarm rolling down from the mountain in Nevada. He hissed his intentions to the Andy child in his head. Make it, find it, but bring it.

Dust particles began to drop like rain from the open black ceiling, turning to thick rivulets.

Time is ticking. Outside might be better.

Rich looked at his sons. "Stay here."

He led Cyndi out the glass front door and into the middle of the parking lot drive aisle. A black Mercedes braked, and blared its horn. Rich gave the yuppie driver a middle finger and faced his wife.

"I can't come get you until I've got Nikki." Rich said.

Nature's fog disappeared, replaced by dust and its lightning and the crackle of alien static.

More!

"You better not." She kissed his stubbly cheek. Her lips were soft and dry. "Bring Nikki home, you hear me."

She whispered a request into his ear.

"If that's what you want," Rich said. "You ready?"

Nothing, absolutely nothing nor anyone would hurt her.

More!

"You go through last." Rich shouted. The light show of lightning and static made them watch.

The quirky colorful building signage disappeared as if Merlin conjured the Dragon's breath. The gloom and static of the dust crossed the Pacific Coast Highway. Automobiles died, girls pedaling bicycles disappeared, morning commuters ran to escape a dust storm rolling in from the silvery ocean. Noah and Matt stared from behind the storefront with eyes wide and white, their palms pressed on the vibrating glass.

Gathered for miles off the California coast, the dust continued to replicate on the placid water. Waiting.

Rich clasped the back of Cyndi's head and pulled her close, and he still needed to yell over the roar of a growing maelstrom. "Remember when we first met, and took the kids to Tombstone?" He stroked her hair, and felt her nod. "Remember Noah getting in trouble for running around the stores, shooting his finger like a gun, screaming that same thing over and over. You had to paddle his butt and sit him down in the car until he cooled off. Remember what he was yelling?"

She shook her head.

"That line. From the movie I rented the night before, trying to get em all fired up about the trip. You know the Wyatt Earp movie. Not the Costner one, the other one. Remember what Noah was yelling?"

She nodded and looked up to give him a weak smile.

Rich kissed Cyndi but he saw in her eyes that she was already elsewhere.

The dust swirled in the patterns of Jupiter, combining, transforming into a condensed cyclone, a writhing snake with a pointed head. One poised to strike just yards off his right shoulder. The static charge levitated the hair on her head.

More!

The hot backdraft whipped cigarette butts, bits of paper and beach sand into the fray. He shielded her body as dry lightning lashed out of the phenomenon. It stormed into the wormhole, angry, and unstoppable. Rich gritted his teeth as the dust burned his cheeks and neck, and he squeezed the one who kept him alive in this world.

The world went silent, still.

He sighed and gently pushed her through the portal, and released his grip.

Rich wanted to scream, at the Buckwheat's, at the pretty liars, and the cruelty of his world. His face felt raw from the dust brushing his skin like sandpaper. His dust. Fuck his dust. Let someone else have the heartache it brought.

Actually, we need to go, Daddy-o.

"You see her too, huh, Andy? She's holding that spatula like she did when she was gonna paddle some butts."

Nature called her fog back, in fearful, easy wisps. He wiped away a tear and tightened his jaw. "Pity that fool."

Chapter 20

Rich rarely initiated a *'remember when'* but when he did it usually made Cyndi smile. She thought of their weekend trip to Tombstone, and the first time they had traveled with all four children. Two single parents, each blessed with two healthy children, each considering themselves as damaged goods. It was also the weekend she decided Rich was her soul mate.

He was always a quiet man, except around the children, when his personality changed as if somebody toggled a switch. He was animated, laughed and played, a child himself who enjoyed four young children vying for his attention. She felt as if each child had brought specialness to his lonely world. Rich had displayed infinite patience with the rambunctious Noah running up and down the old western town's boardwalk, screaming the movie line and garnering scornful looks from the other parents. She knew Rich was the one when he bought ice cream cones and sent the kids to play in the dusty street while they laughed about Noah's antics.

Cyndi's smile faded when she stepped into the room, an alternate universe, a dimension of pure grey, void of light and sound. The portal closed behind her, cutting off the scent of sea salt and home. Moments ago, she had felt the violent cyclone roar past them like a runaway train at breakneck speed. There would've been no chance for anyone inside the room to escape.

Inside the cavernous room, sparkles of moats floated, illuminated by the faint light of small windows sheeted in grey. The storm had spread its wrath into every corner of the room, covering furniture, people, walls and ceilings and the carpet. She felt the tingle of electricity through the rubber of her sneakers. She fanned the spatula at dust hovering in her face, and wished she had brought a flashlight instead.

Cyndi took a step toward what appeared to have been an oblong table. Six blobs melded onto the edges. She imagined the six men before the dust attacked. Each would've worn expensive designer suits, ties and shoes, the standard costumes of the unscrupulous politicians. They would've had a few seconds to raise their hands and shield their faces from the dust, but not much else.

She wiped away a bead of sweat running down her temple and took another step. Rich was right, but she never expected to see it. Hell had come with her. She took another step and looked up to see the last twinkles of light fade from the windows, never considering that halfway across the world the sun was setting.

As her pupils adjusted to the darkness, she spied the white King through the rain of floating particles. Another time or place she might have laughed at his appearance, but all humor was lost in the hellish landscape. Captured by the dust where he sat, the man turned his head in her direction. His head and neck jutted above a mound of dust, and it was all he could move, except a bare finger protruding like a phallic symbol from the table of grey.

Just as she asked, Rich had left the maggot alive, its head exposed and squirming.

They locked eyes. The muted sound of air raid sirens began to blare in the distance.

Cyndi approached the man-thing.

She raised the spatula, cocking it like a flyswatter.

"Check, Mr. Prime Minister."

⅄

Police sirens grew loud and hurried Rich back into the coffee store to find Noah and Matt. They stared at him like he was…"Show me those pictures again."

"Yeah." Matt said. "About that…"

The laptop's screen was black.

Noah tapped the mouse pad then began pushing the power button. Nothing.

"My fault. I should have thought of that." Rich said.

The store lights and menu boards were dark. Anything electronic would be fried, and he had only minutes to find a meeting spot over a thousand miles away. He rubbed his face.

"Dad, dad, dad." Matt said.

Noah grabbed his wrist. "Take us to my house."

Rich paced the floor of the apartment as Noah powered up his laptop at the dinette. He and Nikki kept the place decorated - or rather undecorated. Minimalist they called it. Three stainless steel picture frames sat on the granite bar top. Rich stared at the center one – Nikki, Noah, and Andy squeezed together for an overhead selfie.

I remember that! Andy said.

What else do you remember?

Just bits and pieces, but its coming back. Get some more sleep, Daddy-o.

Got it, Rich." Noah said. "What were the street names again?"

"Riley and Oquendo in Kirkland Washington." His words, his voice, but it felt as if the words were forced out of his mouth. By Andy, or the thing that pretended to be him.

He stood behind Noah and looked at a satellite view of the planet Earth on the screen. The camera began to zoom in with short jumps until it landed on the residential intersection specified by Gurion. Noah changed the screen's perspective, clicking on the street view feature to see all four corners of the intersection.

"Okay, he's got it. We need to get out of here." Rich said.

"Leave us." Noah said. "We're safe here and we have a few things we want to work on."

"Work on? What are you…"

"You wanted to go public, right?" Matt said. "We got an idea on how to do it. But we need internet access."

"I don't know what's gonna happen, but if I'm not back by dark…, run and hide. I'll find you."

"Is Mom gonna' be okay?" Noah asked.

He asked for an image of Cyndi, waited a second, then said. "She's fine."

He met Noah's eyes. "I'll get Nik home."

Said as a promise but he wasn't sure if the words were for their comfort or his own. He wasn't convinced he could bring her home. Something about Gurion's voice, his violent history, his connection to the infamous Mossad, all of it worried him. Rich's anger had ruled for years, dictated his actions and reactions, but it was an emotional blind spot. If it was triggered, it could only help Gurion achieve his goal. And he would bet Gurion knew what that trigger was.

"Matt told me everything," Noah said. "Wish you would have clued us in."

"Yeah. Probably. But I've tried to keep you out of my..."

"This is *our* mess, Rich. Bring her home. And why don't you forget about Alaska and come home, too?"

Rich gave him a weak smile. "Think I might when this is done. Had enough adventure for a while."

Rich patted Matt's shoulder. "Stay here. We clear?"

Rich stepped onto the sidewalk at a street corner in Kirkland. The sky looked undecided, spots of blue overrun with fast moving rain clouds. He paced the edge of the curb, and listened to Andy count fifty-three steps between two lampposts. He tried to extrapolate scenarios of how the encounter might play out. Burdette's warnings of the sadistic nature of Gurion had Rich flexing his fingers until they hurt. He tried to shut off his apprehension and steel himself against whatever Gurion might have planned.

It wasn't working. He wasn't weaponless, but he felt like it.

Burdette's attempts at abducting his family seemed almost comical compared to Gurion's threats on the phone. Getting a fat lip or a bloody nose, or even sitting in a stinking jail cell were the only repercussions he had considered until now. The stakes of the game had risen to a lethal level.

"Think we can get your sister out of this, Andy?" Rich mumbled.

Actually, Father, that parameter is in your hands. Why do we hurt each other so much?

The Andy voice was comforting, not because of its power over the motes or its intelligence, but because Andy was alive again, at least through his memories. The thing was a computer and could never duplicate Andy, would never even come close. But still, the childlike intelligence was growing up, and gaining momentum. And it was his, and only his, and he'd nurture the computer program just as he did Andy. He was proud of Andy, of his accomplishments, his gentle spirit, and even his honorable service to his country. Now he was just as proud of an alien entity that had chosen his dead son as a role model.

"We've done it since the beginning of time," Rich answered.

I want to go home.

The silver Chevrolet Suburban made a third pass, each time arriving from a different direction. The vehicle's tires screeched as the driver navigated a sudden U-turn and pulled alongside Rich. The passenger side window slid down.

"Get in, Mr. Preston."

Rich opened the rear door and climbed in. The black vinyl interior smelled of cigar smoke. A burly man with the jowls of a French bulldog grabbed his wrists and tightened a thick plastic zip-tie as handcuffs, straps that would need wire-cutters or a sharp knife to cut. The Bulldog man pulled a strange looking weapon from a gym bag at his feet and pointed it at Rich's chest.

Sitting in the shotgun seat, a handsome, olive-skinned Clooney type turned around to face Rich. His dark deep-set eyes darted over Rich's jeans and hooded sweatshirt. He grinned as the barrel of a chrome revolver came up to rest on the seatback, also aimed at his chest.

"Mr. Preston. This may be difficult for you to understand, but we are on the same team. To a degree. If we see the dust, you get tased. If a gust of wind finds a pile of sand, you get tased. The moment you get tased, your daughter dies, because you didn't follow the rules. Are we clear? And I promise you." Gurion flicked his chin at the Taser. "That Taser will knock the snot out of a charging bull."

"So you know what my little friends can do then?" Rich said. "Happens pretty fast. You might not see it coming, Buckwheat."

Gurion dropped his smile and narrowed his eyes. "That's up to you, but you now know the rules. You actually might be more valuable dead than alive, but who's to say until you're actually dead."

Actually, fuck you Mildred, ya little prick.

Settle down, Andy.

"And, yes, we will allow you to see Nikki. This needs to be a mutually satis-factory relationship if it is to work. Yes?"

The ride was short and silent. Rich stared out the window, checking on Cyndi via the motes, and calming Andy's anxiousness. The vehicle circled a two-story office building with a glass dome above the front entrance and ornamental steel canopies cantilevered off the parapets. They drove beneath the building into a parking garage, the antenna twanged as it brushed a yellow sign warning of low clearance. The garage was dark, vacant except for a late model white van and green Mini-Cooper. They parked in a designated handicap zone.

Bulldog jabbed him with the Taser. "If you sneeze, 50,000 volts flies up your ass."

Escorted down a white corridor decorated with pieces of abstract artwork, he waited as Gurion swiped a card through a reader device at a heavy metal door. It clicked open. The restraints had rubbed the hair from his wrists and were already working deep into the first layer of skin. Rich scratched his nose, testing the straps again.

Walking through a small reception area, they turned left into another hallway. Instead of artwork, picture glass windows were spaced evenly on the left, the drywall was white, polished and sterile. Halfway down the corridor, the group surrounding Rich stopped.

"There's your girl, Preston." Gurion pointed into a window.

Through a glass vestibule, on the other side of what Rich figured was some kind of sealed room, was another, more compact, clean room. Nikki was strapped to a stainless steel gurney, her wrists and legs bound by heavy white straps. She was motionless. A man in a Hazmat suit hovered above her, displaying an uncapped syringe in his right hand.

Rich swallowed, hard and slow, then his teeth began a methodical grind.

How long to isolate her?

Actually, one-hundred-ninety- nine seconds to complete isolation subroutine. Poor Nikki.

That's your sister in there, Andy. How about five seconds?

No way, Jose.

Gurion thumped Rich's head with the butt of the gun. "Pay attention. This is how it's going to work."

Rich sneered. The man was already trying to provoke him but Nikki was all that mattered. "Let her go." Rich looked for a twitch of Nikki's fingers or toes.

Bulldog jabbed the Taser into his chest. "You come into our nice, clean office. You undress and shower, and then we have a question and answer session. We don't like what we hear, well, we have lots of pharmaceuticals to help you talk."

"Fuck you."

Gurion crowded him. "We expected that attitude, Preston. One quite common among Palestinian fathers. We will show you several battlefield techniques designed to induce your cooperation."

These men seemed to be enjoying the game.

"My book hasn't been written on the subject yet, Preston, but let me give you a brief synopsis." Gurion smiled. "Now, picture Big Ben here." Gurion motioned to the driver behind him. "He won the lottery to go first, but he tends to spoil the fun for the rest of us with his size. Hence the name. Picture Ben penetrating Nikki while you are forced to watch. The record is five, Preston. Five times before an Iraqi father broke down and told us what we wanted to know. And that is just my opening chapter. The book gets better as we get deeper into it."

Rich's fingers began to flex. His heartbeat accelerated as adrenaline flooded his bloodstream. He fought the urge to lash out. With his wrists bound he wouldn't stand a chance.

A cellphone rang and Bulldog answered, saying something in Hebrew. He watched Gurion's facial expression change from pleasure to betrayal.

Cyndi's gambit.

"You were warned." Gurion pointed the gun at his face. "No dust!"

"Fuck you, Buckwheat."

Gurion nodded to Ben. "Not me, but Nikki. Your removal of the dust at home will be the first thing you do."

Isolate Nikki. Now!

Can't. Insufficient Betas.

"Remove the dust, Preston, and I will spare Nikki chapter two."

"And I'll suffocate every one of them."

"And they will gladly die for their country." Gurion lowered the pistol. "And Nikki will get to experience my novel. Some of it which may be written here today."

Rich screamed and lunged for Gurion's throat. He drove Gurion back into the glass, his hands tight around the bone and muscle of the man's unshaved neck. A jolt of electricity hit his spine and shot down his legs. Rich screamed as the Taser blast buckled his knees.

Andy screamed in his head.

Gurion slapped Rich's arms away with little effort and laughed. A second shockwave hit his back. His body seized up in one incapacitating cramp, and he fell hard to the cold vinyl floor. Another Taser was jammed into his ribs and Big Ben shot another charge of high-voltage into his body. Rich lost all muscle control, and his crotch warmed as his bladder released.

Laughing, all he could hear before he fell into a black void, joined by the agonizing scream of Andy, dying again.

Cyndi circled behind the silver-haired head. She bared her teeth and slapped the spatula hard against the man's ear. "The Lion of Zion. You look more like fish bait."

She stepped to his side and patted his cheek with the cold steel. Prime Minister Uzi Dayan turned his head and stared at her with defiant, angry eyes.

"Do you know who I am?" Cyndi asked.

"Very impressive, Mrs. Preston."

"Of course you do. You know all about my family."

Dayan swallowed, his Adams apple bobbed, restricted by the collar of dust. "What are your intentions, Cyndi? May I call you Cyndi?"

"Your Gestapo has taken my daughter." She slapped his ear again, harder. "And this will stop."

The man bristled at her reference to the brutal Nazi Germany police force. Just the reaction she had predicted from the Prime Minister of Israel.

"I won't ask you to sit down," he said. "As you can see."

"I am quite comfortable, sir. Have you considered all the consequences of your sick plan? You conspire to kidnap American citizens, and intimidate them to do your bidding. Your dogs are breaking all kinds of laws."

"My dogs-" He spoke with a thick guttural accent. "-as you call them, are doing their job."

"I see. They're just following orders, are they?'

"My duty is to protect Israel, and I will do what I deem necessary to fulfill that responsibility. I will continue on the path I have chosen until I am sure your husband poses no threat to this nation."

"What you are is a paranoid maniac. My husband has done nothing wrong. My kids have done nothing wrong, and you talk as if we are the enemy. Well, if we weren't before, we are now."

"And I suppose you have fully embraced what this computer is doing to your husband. Will he lead an invasion of this planet? Your husband scares the hell out of me, this nation, the world."

"Oh, please. You want what he has, what he knows, simple as that. Don't give me a speech. " She tightened her hand on the spatula's warm steel.

"Your husband moves through space with the snap of his fingers. He controls a substance that can accomplish this. And you don't question the reasoning? Please, you have proven to be smarter than that."

Of course she had questioned the reasons. Every morning and every night lying in bed. And the answer was always the same. God had answered her prayers. Maybe in the most bizarre possible way, but God had answered. And He gave Rich what he needed.

Two things," she said. "First, remember you're talking to the mother of the young woman you handed over to your pet sadist. Do you really think you can persuade me? Second, you'll need reasons - why Rich covered your government building in dust, why you kidnapped an American citizen on American soil to use against America. Did you think no one would notice?"

"Now you truly sound like the wife of a disgruntled terrorist. Emotional and distraught. Our countries are the best of allies, we help each other, did you forget?"

Cyndi bared her teeth and raised the utensil. He stared at her with a smug face, one accustomed to getting what he wanted. She smacked his ear hard. He winced and bared his tobacco stained fangs.

"You think the American government will forgive this? Sweep it under the rug? Oh, I'm sure the Vice-President would help you sell what Rich knows, back to us probably, but I think the American people will learn who the real terrorist is here."

"Regardless. The technology belongs to Israel. We discovered it, and we will take possession of it."

"Rich will have a say in that."

"Then it would appear we are at a stalemate," The Prime Minister said.

"Stalemate? Are you kidding me? You've made an enemy of a powerful man, the man that controls what may be the greatest gift to the world. Probably made enemies with America, and you call that a stalemate? Even if you kill us all, you've already lost, Buckwheat."

The Lion of Zion's jaw quivered.

Designed to protect the probe's integrity from the host planet's natural electrical disturbances such as lightning or the electromagnetic bursts from its sun, the probe executed a simple preservation program. The integration of human and alien operating systems ceased.

The burst of electricity from the Taser was unnatural, manufactured, and triggered a response. A second Taser blast caused a total system shutdown as the probe retracted the thin monofilament tendrils used to access the lobes of Rich's brain, leaving the maturing artificial intelligence unprotected.

The Andy entity screamed, its pain real, a malignant sensation causing the Alpha to issue a sudden burst of radio waves. The transmission was weak, traveling less than two meters and found only twenty-three active motes – mostly specks of dandruff on Gurion's scalp. In turn, 763 dormant motes trapped in the fabric of Rich's sweatshirt and boots activated, and called to 8,437 motes floating randomly in the air of the hallway.

Hard-coded into every probe was a sixteen-byte root command. An instruction duplicated during the replication process.

Andy's scream caused a single word command to be issued by the system.

ISOLATE.

What happened next occurred in the same amount of time that David Gurion used to kick Rich in the ribs twice, and once in the face.

Tiny particles within a five-mile radius of the Alpha's signal executed their response. Buried in beach sand, confined beneath grass, leaves, and bark, or floating in water, the Beta's fired thrusters, lifting themselves free to execute its transit program. Floating in the inlets of the Washington coast, embedded in the mulch of old growth forests, trapped in the patio carpet of nearby homes, each mote began to spin, ingesting the molecules of hydrogen required for instantaneous travel.

Thousands of trillions of tiny wormholes opened, each ejecting a single mote into the space from which the signal originated. Less than seven seconds passed and the hallway containing Richard Preston's twitching body filled with dust.

Gurion and his associates, along with two cockroaches hiding in the wall, drowned in dust. Any Beta-class mote probes emerging into space already stuffed to capacity quickly retreated, calculated new vectors, and reemerged into a space determined by a growing consensus of motes.

The new system, an entity in of itself, directed the assault.

Motes coated the office building's exterior, the parking lot, and overwhelmed automobiles, nearby homes, and a twenty-seven year old jogger wondering why her iTunes had failed.

With the order to isolate and preserve the Andy entity, the growing accumulation of Beta-class probes would quickly dwarf the giant Egg seen in Nevada. And continued to grow with an incalculable quantity of motes converging on the Alpha's signal. The swarm instantly neutralized equipment, electrical systems, and machines. The system was indiscriminant, overwhelming all biological life forms caught within its rapidly expanding borders.

Jacobsen Elementary School with 867 children, teachers, and parents, three hamsters and Tantalus the tarantula, were isolated in cocoons. A spirited pep rally inside the gymnasium of Brinkley Middle School was silenced as cheerleaders, student-athletes, and the Bruin mascot were overwhelmed by dust.

Homes, businesses, and streetscapes, the dust consumed everything in its path. The alien blizzard of biblical proportions continued to expand.

Query.

Inside his coffin of dust, Rich heard the mechanical voice. The air was hot, and his ribs hurt with each breath. He could taste blood coating his mouth. His skin tingled as he tried to wiggle his fingers. There was no room to move. He thought of Nevada, and the scent of sagebrush. But that was just a memory.

Query.

What happened, Andy?

System reinitializing. Standby.

He swallowed grit.

Andy, talk to me son. Get this stuff off.

Rich struggled and felt his wrists still bound. He remembered Gurion.

Standby.

The weight of dust eased, but the process was erratic and agonizingly slow. Nikki was just a few yards away. Rich's effort to find wiggle room intensified. Twisting his arms, bending his knees, shaking his face, he pushed the dust away from his body inches at a time. It felt like breaking free of beach sand his children had playfully buried him in. He was soaked in sweat before he was able to stand up.

"Nikki!" His shout was absorbed by the system.

His thinking was muddled by the Taser jolts, and he was unable to remember which of the large lumps was Gurion.

"Andy? C'mon son, I need you more than ever."

Unable to pry even a hand-sized portion of motes off the window's vague outline, he yelled. "Move this shit off. Now!"

Standby.

The voice sounded mechanical, identical to what he'd first heard in Lanai.

Rich spat blood. "Andy! Where are you?"

Thin layers of dust began to float up and disappear. The mechanical voice heightened his strange foreboding that Nikki would be missing. No visions or second sight, no grainy pictures of his daughter. Rich tried a different approach, and imagined the dust rising off her body. At least an hour passed before enough dust lifted off the glass for him to see the outline of his daughter.

He ordered the voice to open a wormhole to her bedside a few yards away. He stepped forward, blocked by a dirty window.

A

Cyndi felt Dayan's eyes study her each time she walked within his limited range of sight, like a nighttime predator watching its prey.

He spoke abruptly, in a jovial way. "What now, Mrs. Preston? It would seem we are both in the same boat as you say."

"We wait. Rich will come." But she had come to Israel assuming Rich would fail. Israel's highly trained Mossad, men who probably thrived in high-stakes games of cloak and dagger would be too much for him. Guns and guile would trump portals and dust. Waiting at the cabin would have driven her nuts, and she would have berated herself for doing nothing. Instead, she planned her strategy based on sacrificing the black king. Her black king. If Rich returned, then the game was over, for now. If the dust lifted from the room without Rich, then her opponent had won control of the computerized dust.

And she would be expendable.

But she had already won the game. She had no doubt the media was converging on Tel Aviv, and even surrounded the Israeli Knesset building that Noah had Googled. The alien dust was a lightning rod for television coverage. Maybe the commentators were already asking the questions that could save Nikki's life. Undoubtedly, Burdette had informed his Homeland Security superiors of his conversation with Rich. The American government wouldn't stand for it.

Even if Rich was dead, or under their control, there was no way the Israelis could keep Nikki imprisoned, not with the eyes of the world watching.

Dayan offered a condescending grin. "And if Mr. Preston fails to appear. What then?"

She'd thought about his question. The answer now was no different from when she stood in the dark at the cabin window.

"Then we'll be entombed here, just like Pharaohs."

She squeezed the spatula and swallowed grit and dust. She put the edge of the utensil below his left ear and ran it along his throat. "Of course I'll live a bit longer than you."

The PM chuckled humorlessly and continued his study of Cyndi. "Even if the dust has no malicious intent, a man like Richard Preston cannot be allowed to exist. What he knows, what he is capable of, he cannot fall into the wrong hands. We were just the first. Your family will be pursued by governments, hounded by the greedy, chased by those craving his power. No Cyndi, your husband cannot exist as a free man in this world."

Cyndi circled behind him. She was sick of his words, his tone, and his smug arrogance. She raised the spatula to slap him.

His words, the truth, prevented her arm from falling.

Chapter 21

CNN Breaking News displayed an ominous headline - Israeli Knesset Attacked, followed by Dust Seals War Cabinet. A long-range aerial view of the building flashed onto the screen. Floodlights, red and white strobes, emergency vehicles, military personnel, and civilians surrounded the parliament building at the center of lightless amoeba.

Noah raised his fist and Matt followed with his own. They expected the headline. Cyndi was inside that building. She had explained her intentions, to maybe bargain for the release of Nikki, or at the least provide Rich with some leverage against Gurion.

CNN's flashing red banner changed.

Matt's smile dropped as his eyebrows rose.

Noah whispered, "Shit."

Alien invasion begins - U.S. Homeland Attacked.

Wolf Blitzer began his story. "A suburb of Seattle is at this moment…"

Matt looked at his older brother.

Noah heaved a breath. "We might need to get out of here."

⅄

The smell of urine soured the air inside Rich's confined space, and time slowly passed in a steady haze of grey, he couldn't tell if a minute or an hour had passed since he had last attempted to enter a portal. The edges of the gates burned open, but their corresponding exits failed to materialize.

"Andy, c'mon son, I need to get in there."

Standby.

He hadn't heard Andy's voice since he'd been tasered, though his agonizing scream was still fresh in his mind. He refused to believe the electricity might have harmed the gentle, intelligent creature existing inside his head, but the possibility lingered.

Nikki hadn't moved, still covered in a veneer of motes and strapped to what he guessed was a mote-encrusted hospital gurney.

Gurion and the other blobs crowded his small space, and the claustrophobia was making him antsy. Rich slapped the outline of Gurion's head and received a sting of low voltage electricity for the effort. If only the dust would expose Gurion's crotch or drift from Bulldog's face as it had Neesa's, and allow his knuckles to give them a kiss. All three dirt-bags were protected by his dust.

His fucking, no good, wouldn't listen to him, dust.

Looking through the window, he considered all that had gone wrong or right. His temper had failed him again, or had it provided his salvation? But did it cost Andy his life again?

Re-initialization complete.

Finally! Rich straightened up.

"I want in there."

The light burned and he stepped through the wall and into the room with Nikki. The man in the Hazmat suit stood as a snowman, his arm still hovering over Nikki. Rich couldn't help but kick a spot where the Buckwheat's shinbone should have been.

Rich leaned over Nikki's face still caked with dust and prayed for a muscle twitch, a rush of color, a sign of life.

"Nikki, Nikki," he whispered as his fingers stroked her forehead. She moaned, then startled him by dropping an incoherent F bomb.

Like father, like daughter. He grumbled with the challenge of unbuckling the straps on her wrists, and feet, but sighed as he lifted the girl's easy weight into his arms, disregarding the painful strain on his strapped wrists.

"Let's go home," he said in a gentle whisper and stepped through a portal.

⋏

Cyndi picked herself up off the carpet of dust, the tingling in her butt too much to handle. The passage of time in the dark was confusing, and the world outside their cavern seemed angry. Bright spotlights flittered over the shielded windows, air raid warnings still whined. The noise suddenly angered her, again. Faint light filtered through the windows, enough to keep her from tripping on the humps and lumps of whatever was buried beneath the dust.

She marched up to Dayan, and backhanding the spatula, she slapped the man's ear.

"Well, Mr. Lion." Cyndi said. "How did you get that stupid name anyway? Kick some people out of their homes so you could build some of your own?" She tapped his bulbous nose with the corner of spatula. "If Rich doesn't come pretty soon I will assume he is dead, and maybe Nikki, too. Which means we'll both die, locked in here forever. And I'll take my grief out on you and beat your head like a drum."

She walked behind the man before he could see her smirk. "And besides, I may need something to eat later."

She paced the short length of the office where he couldn't see her, considering her options. The dust cushioned her footfalls, weak bursts of electricity tingling into her feet.

Becoming entombed with Dayan was a real possibility if Gurion couldn't persuade Rich to release the dust. And considering Rich's quick temper and stubbornness in the face of direct orders, he was more likely to have been killed, and then Nikki would become useless. But how could she know, how much time did she give Rich, or Gurion? She decided to give the Prime Minister of Israel until the next night, then he would die, she would murder him. The last act of an angry mother and widow.

Dayan cleared his throat. "Mrs. Preston, regardless of our little game, regardless of the outcome, what kind of life could you hope to lead with a man such as your husband? Famous musicians, politicians, even the wealthy are targets for those who hunger for power. You would be the target of religious zealots or the mentally disturbed, anyone desiring notoriety in this world. I say again, Richard Preston cannot survive in this world."

Dayan's only weapon was rhetoric, polished to perfection. And she almost had to admire the way he wielded it.

"Imagine, your husband helping a Seal team rescue hostages, deposing an oppressive dictator, or even assisting our own armed forces to end a conflict without bloodshed. The possibilities are endless. Backed by the righteousness of God, your husband could find a way to live out his years safely, helping His chosen people. "

Cyndi heaved a breath and removed the sweat soaked cap from her head. She came over to face him. "Those are your objectives, not ours. Our God believes in forgiveness. Our God believes in tolerance. Our God created this world for everyone, and it's politicians like you who've screwed it up. Now you beg for our help to clean up your mess. Screw you. People like you have always looked down on people like Rich and me, and the working class, people who work with their hands, build things, anyone who doesn't fit into your nine dots. You won't even make peace with your neighbors. You're no different from the Romans, or the Nazis. Rich will never help you build your little empire."

She pointed the rounded tip of the spatula inches from his eye. "The chosen? Bah. The chosen are cleaning up the environment. The chosen are helping to feed the starving, helping people rebuild from natural disasters. Those are God's chosen."

"Making this world a better place for our children, that's what God chooses. No way will Rich help you with your shortsighted bullshit. You're an ego-centric asshole looking for more power."

Cyndi raised the utensil and clenched her teeth, and resisted an overwhelming urge to lash out.

"The dust is ours, Mrs. Preston. That will not change."

"The dust is everywhere. You can't lay claim to something God created."

"We can. We found it, and we own it. You cannot contradict the law."

She narrowed her eyes as her hand wavered. "How so?"

"Our scientists discovered it six years ago, after opening a sealed cave that was supposed to hold cargo of the great Ark, near Mt. Ararat. The substance was inside, and in such high concentrations that randomness in the natural world was not possible. Archeologists and historians were clueless, but one of our perceptive computer scientist students wrote a thesis on its existence, hypothesizing its design as memory storage for an ancient computer that had disintegrated eons ago. Moshe Taalen was laughed out of his doctorate program. But the boy's supposition remained. Moshe's hypothesis even intrigued your CIA, and your former President, enough for the simpleton to order soldiers into Iran, to follow the trail of dust leading away from Mt. Ararat."

Dayan fixed his eyes on Cyndi.

"If memory serves me, your son died on that fateful mission." Dayan twitched his lips. "Irony, Mrs. Preston? Coincidence? I think not. It is God's will. His covenant for my people to possess the dust, and all the honor it can bestow on the person who controls it."

Cyndi closed her eyes. Could what he said be true? After all the emails, phone calls, and angry confrontations Rich had put himself through, and this was why Andy died? She had no doubt Dayan would lie, cheat or steal to gain what he believed was his. But she didn't think he was lying about Andy. Sending soldiers illegally into Iran, a sworn enemy, to chase silly dust? Getting American soldiers killed for a pretense?

Oh Lord.

No wonder they hid the truth. The thought sickened her.

"What you did, to Nikki, to my family," she said. "Pray your God protects you when Rich gets here"

Dayan closed his eyes. "Richard Preston is already ours to control."

⋏

Rich's arms ached and his back muscles screamed with Nikki's weight as he stepped into the cabin. He placed her down gently on the leather couch. She mumbled.

"Nikki, Nikki, wake up. You're home, wake up."

He rummaged through kitchen drawers, found a pair of scissors and tossed them to the floor. Cutting his own wrists free of the strap would be impossible. Moistening a dishtowel hanging on the sink, he patted the cold, wet cloth on her cheeks, leaving it to rest on her forehead.

"Come on, Nikki, please wake up."

Her eyelids flickered. She groaned. "Rich."

"You're okay, don't move, don't move."

"Those men, David…." She groaned again as her right hand pressed down on the wet cloth.

"Shhh… Lie still. I'll be right back"

Rich stepped into Noah's living room. They were gone. The television was on and he frowned at CNN's report of a possible alien invasion, and the ensuing panic in downtown Seattle. He shook his head. The world had gone mad. He asked for a portal back to the cabin then paused. He heard whispering coming from down the hallway.

"Noah? Matt?"

Matt stuck his head out of the bedroom.

"Your sister would like to see you boys so let's get moving."

They seemed to take forever but finally joined him, each toting a white garbage bags with clothes.

Noah looked at Rich's strapped wrists then flicked his chin to the television. "The world's going crazy. And we did it." He unplugged the laptop's power cord and shoved it into a bag. "Let's go."

The boys fawned over Nikki as Rich retreated from the quiet reunion, and basked in the family he thought he'd lost. Through the picture glass window, he saw giant snowflakes begin to fall in the front yard. Christmas was coming. It would be the best one in years.

"Noah?" He offered his bound wrists. "A little help?"

He stood at the kitchen sink with his eyes closed, letting the water cool the red welts on his wrists. He asked the voice to "show me" and within seconds a clear color picture of Cyndi came into his mind's eye. She was engaged in a heated argument with the man buried in dust, but she was in no immediate danger.

Andy? Are you there?

The silence was frightening, and sickening at the same time. The operating system obeyed his commands but answered him with a mechanical voice. It didn't matter. It was just a computer and his family was safe.

Yeah, it did matter. Rich gripped the faucet hard, and mentally called for Andy. And again, and again.

What had that son-of-bitch Gurion done to his baby boy?

Replay visual recording? the voice asked.

He didn't answer. Cyndi would repeat what the politician said.

Replay audio recording?

Audio? Now? That might have been nice to have a little sooner. How about letting him smell which cologne the bastard wore?

Download incomplete.

An answer without saying it. Rich splashed water on his face, contemplating what he had just heard. The thingy was integrating mote-data into his five senses. Did the operating system want him to taste, touch, feel, hear and see the pictures catalogued in his head? For what purpose? He couldn't use a fraction of the information stored in his head.

"Dad, dad, dad." Matt was pointing at the television. "You gotta get that dust off. People are panicking, and they're already blaming us."

Rich looked at the television screen, and the aerial view showing a blotch of grey blanketing a residential neighborhood, stretching out for miles.

Oh, Jeez. Stop. Make it go away. Blow away, all of it.

Affirmative.

He stared at the television then exhaled when the commentator's voice became excited at the dust breaking up and floating into the sky.

Play it back, everything the politician said.

Rich watched and listened, skipping through the silent parts, replaying sections where the talking head of Israel was preaching to Cyndi.

Son. Of. A. Bitch!

Rich went to the loft, walked outside and paced on the wood deck overlooking the creek. The wood handrail was covered in an inch of fresh snow, and he absentmindedly scraped it off as he replayed the mote's recording again. Cyndi had figured out their game, but what was to stop the Prime Minister from starting a new one? The politician said he wouldn't survive on this world, wouldn't be allowed a life, or a home. Maybe Dayan was right. And maybe Dayan needed a dose of his own tactics.

Tit for tat, Buckwheat.

Rich stepped through a portal and emerged into the dark War Cabinet room. He faced the Prime Minister but he looked for Cyndi, allowing his eyes to adjust to the sudden lack of light. Cyndi dropped her utensil and rushed to him, her face beaded with perspiration, her ponytail loose and wild. His need for revenge subsided as she ran into his outstretched arms.

Rich embraced her, grasping her hand in his. "I got her. She's fine."

Her set of beautiful brown eyes closed, deepening the crevices of her crow's feet. She heaved a breath that must have been held for hours, and her body relaxed. Rich pulled her close and pecked her forehead with a kiss, smelling sweat and a faint reminder of her shampoo. He peered over her head at Dayan, and his jaw tightened.

"He said Andy died…" Cyndi said.

"I know. I heard him, every word of it." He hugged her again. "Go home, look after Nik."

The room stunk of sweat and cigar, and ozone. His sense of smell was fine-tuned, sharpened inside the chamber of motes. Now he was sure the operating system was incorporating his senses into whatever was being downloaded.

He opened a portal back to the cabin's living room and he saw his children gathered at the couch. Cyndi couldn't see the homecoming, or she'd have bolted. He held out his hand to keep the doorway open. Nodding in the portal's direction, he gently pushed her.

Dayan's chin lifted. "It would appear your understanding of the computer system continues to evolve, Mr. Preston."

Cyndi paused. "What are you going to do, Rich?"

"Just gonna have a little talk with Fishbait." He smirked. "That was a good one, by the way."

She smiled thinly. "Don't do anything you, or our children will regret. Please."

Cyndi disappeared.

Rich approached and pushed his face to within inches of Dayan's. The man's nostrils flared and his jaw tightened as he swallowed.

Rich smelled fear on his breath. "You have no idea what I can do." Rich debated whether to give him a good slapping. For Nikki. For Cyndi. Then he noticed the Prime Minister's finger protruding out of the dust and gave it a quick bend backwards. A satisfying snap.

Dayan winced but made no sound.

"You figured it out, the dust is a computer. Then you know computers take orders, and I've instructed my computer to rain hell down on your country if anything else happens to my family. Cyndi stubs her toe, Tel Aviv gets isolated. Nikki gets the flu, Jerusalem gets isolated. My sons get hurt, and the state of Israel goes back to the Stone Age. We're allies now, Buckwheat. The health of my family *is* the health of your country."

Rich pulled the man's finger back into an impossible angle again. "Get me?"

Dayan closed his eyes and absorbed the pain. "You…you can't be serious, Mr. Preston. Millions of lives-"

"Depend on our health. Call it Jewish Karma. Life's a bitch ain't it?"

Dayan said nothing, and looked down at his finger on the table.

Rich opened a portal and disappeared, knowing his inexplicable new ally watched helplessly.

CHAPTER 22

Two days passed before Nikki fully recovered from the tranquilizers. Cyndi had ordered Nikki's brothers to carry the girl upstairs to the bunkroom, away from the distractions and noises of the crowded living room. Cyndi doted on Nikki, serving her meals in bed, drawing hot baths, ordering rest, and whispering about things only women seem to share. Each passing hour Nikki had become more alert, regained motor control and even some short-term memory. They knew she was back when she returned from an afternoon walk with Brooke and shouted at them to quit treating her as if she was a cancer patient.

Only two days, and Nikki's spunk began to dominate the household.

Surrounded by her family, and spending considerable amount of time with each of her children, Cyndi seemed to thrive, always with a smile, and even laughed at Rich's stupid jokes. The joy of her being a mom again was impossible to miss.

Noah surprised Rich with his acceptance of the old family hierarchy shattered by Andy's meaningless death. He spoke plainly when accompanying Rich on trips to grocery stores and Wi-Fi hotspots. He pointed out things Rich hadn't thought about – like lawsuits, and responsibility for what he did with the dust. And the things that would forever change the world they lived in.

Holding Rich's hand for a quick trip to the Wonder Lake Campground in Alaska's Denali National Park, Noah asked, "But why you, Rich?"

They shivered and stomped their feet for ten minutes, watching a winter blizzard descend off a massive mountain range.

Maybe Alaska wasn't such a good idea.

He quizzed Rich about everything that had happened since he drove into the Egg, learning all he could. Rich felt a weight lift from his chest after Noah agreed to allow the computer's download to finish before they would go public.

Noah nitpicked for details on what information the download was accomplishing, and his eyebrows shot up after Rich admitted to acquiring a sense of taste that corresponded with the pages of symbols, or musical notes. The taste was especially pungent for those pages he associated with plants or animals. Rich laughed and said his new talent usually tasted like fish slime, oily hair, or bitter mulberry bark – but the unpleasantness would disappear as soon as the page was turned.

Sharing a quiet moment on the back porch, sipping on bottles of cold Steelhead Pale Ale, Matt, Noah and Rich agreed the operating system was downloading a program to integrate Rich's five senses with data that the motes had collected. Noah was adamant - when the Preston family finally emerged into the media spotlight, earth-shattering revelations would accompany them.

Andy's voice hadn't returned.

It was a detail Rich shared with no one, including Cyndi. Nothing he could say would coax the childlike entity to talk. A giggle he thought he heard days ago while standing at the sink resonated like a wave of Deja vu. Did the electric shock send the thing into hiding, beneath a blanket, like Matt had during scary bedtime stories? Rich convinced himself the Andy voice was too afraid to show itself. It needed time to recover and gain confidence again.

The alternative was too painful to consider.

Matt stayed connected to the television, flipping through news channels dominated by the Preston name. The breakfast table fell silent as Matt announced his new college major - political science. He explained that Noah and Nikki were the business management *dudes*, but his future required strategy, and political shrewdness to handle the ramifications of the shockwave about to hit society.

Rich was about to say a useless degree that wouldn't help anyone find a job, but he locked eyes with Cyndi, a warning look that he could never mistake. A look that said, 'You're paying for your mistake every day, don't make it again.'

Rich expressed his enthusiasm, telling Matt his assistance in any political matters would be welcome. His response garnered a smile from Cyndi, a reward quietly expanded upon later that night, during a quick trip to watch a beautiful orange sunset on an isolated beach in French Polynesia.

Matt and Noah stayed busy, traveling via Rich's transportation system to locations containing Wi-Fi access and cellular signal.

Eighteen months ago, Noah had introduced himself to a dignified and personable network anchor, and his cadre, as they dined at the Grapestreet restaurant while in Phoenix to cover the tragedy of an Iraqi war veteran killing eight people at a political rally, and wounding a U.S. Congresswoman. He made hundreds of phone calls to cut through the six degrees of separation. Noah finally reached the newscaster's voicemail, introduced himself and offered the man the interview of a lifetime. The call was returned in three minutes.

Noah requested a panoramic video depicting the studio, and a list of personnel who were to be present. He stipulated the interview was to be live, unedited and limited to no more than one hour at Rich's request. Noah also requested a list of questions the reporter would like to pose. The reporter eagerly accepted every conditions.

Over the next week, Noah made repeated calls to the news outlet, emphasizing the additional security required to prevent another Seattle mistake. The network was eager to conduct the interview as soon as possible, but Noah only teased the newscaster by telling him the interview would alter the future of the human race.

Bored with home confinement, Nikki demanded her release. Her usual tanned skin remained pale, but she expressed an eager interest in experiencing the wormhole transport system. Rich held her hand as they passed through a portal, exiting onto the gravel driveway on the other side of the bedroom wall. She hadn't become nauseous when he brought her home, possibly the drugs in her system, but he made the short jump just as a precaution. Nikki looked at Rich with an incredulous face, laughed and hugged him as if he'd just given her a brand new BMW. The sounds of her laugh kept a smile on Rich's face most of the day.

Activities included the acquisition of new clothes for the upcoming inter-view. Rich grumbled good-naturedly over the prospect of dressing up and look-ing like a fool on TV. Cyndi hugged him, told him if he got nervous, just look at her, and she'd stick out her tongue as a playful reminder to 'don't give a fuck', using his vernacular.

He agreed to a quick trip to the twin's home in Phoenix, popping in alone first to confirm its safety, then returning to retrieve the others. Rich sat outside on the back porch stoop, picking at dead marigolds in a pot and tormenting red ants with the stems. Millions of motes were hidden in the rock landscape, on neighboring rooftops as if standing guard, enough to give him a picture of the surrounding area.

Noah outfitted Matt with jeans and shirts that looked respectable, and the twins packed two suitcases full of clothes, toiletries, and personal wants. Nikki and Cyndi's *remember when's* made the time stretch more than Rich was comfort-able with.

Dropping off the bags at the cabin, they proceeded wherever Cyndi directed. Target, Ross Dress For Less, boutique stores, Men's Warehouse, shops she had become familiar with in Salt Lake City. Frustrated with shopping in Utah, Cyndi pushed Rich to The District, a favorite outdoor mall in Scottsdale.

The wide walkways were landscaped with barrel cactus and Birds of Paradise, and the mall was busy with Christmas shoppers. They checked out the second floor shops, and Matt bought some Skullcandy headphones to use with the lap-top. Noah, Matt and Rich sat on a sandstone bench as the women shopped inside an air-conditioned Ann Taylor clothing store on the ground floor.

Rich had been growing wary all morning. He was receiving too many quiz-zical looks from people passing by. He hoped Cyndi would hurry. An emergency siren in the distance died with an abruptness he didn't like. He looked over his shoulder. A mother was pulling her children in an unnecessarily hurried pace.

"Show me," he said, then stood up.

An aerial view of the mall appeared, the hexagonal layout was surrounded by flashing emergency lights. The picture zoomed in to six SWAT team members checking their gear at the mall's south entrance escalator.

"Get inside," he said.

Nikki was talking to a dowdy saleswoman, and considering whether to return for a size-two canary yellow blouse she was holding, if it could be delivered from another shop across town. Rich didn't like the woman and her beady dark eyes darting to him and away again. But it wasn't her eyes that disturbed him, it was her mouth.

Nikki asked Cyndi what she thought of the blouse, again, and the saleswoman's lips dropped as if she was angry, then lifted as if she was trying to smile, then dropped again. Her lips couldn't sit still.

Nikki handed over her Visa card and smiled anxiously as she waited for the charge slip.

Rich whispered. "Show me."

Swat teams were guarding service exits, stairwells, and the entrances. The main entrance had over twenty officers ready to be sent in.

"We gotta go, girls."

The saleswoman looked at him and narrowed her eyes. Her mouth puckered as if she'd bitten into a lemon. Was that a sneer she was holding back?

The woman said, "The blouse should be here in three business days. Thank you for shopping with Ann."

Rich took the women's hands, waited until they connected to the boy's, and pulled them back to Missoula, Montana. They ordered five large 'Take N Bake' pizzas customized to individual tastes at a Pappa Murphy's on Front Street, then added three bottles of Chianti from the Albertson's across the road and they went home.

The kitchen bustled as Rich and Noah set the table. Matt kneeled next to the television to check the news channels. The kitchen work paused. A HLN pundit ranted that Cyndi Preston was no better than uncouth trailer trash - a rude and a disrespectful criminal who needed to be prosecuted. Her assault and battery on a trusted ally and revered Head of State was shameful.

"Turn it off!" Rich said.

But Cyndi seemed unfazed by the disparaging remarks and asked Noah to set out the ceramic plates instead of paper for the meal. With a buffet of pizza decorated with a smorgasbord of toppings laid out, Noah twisted the caps off the wine.

But the mood inside the cabin had changed.

Matt tried to lighten it, telling Noah, "You're gonna be a Preston now, like it or not."

They ate pizza in silence but the air was thick, and smelled of unspoken words, not unlike the Sunday night dinner when Cyndi announced their move to Boise.

Rich sat back in his chair, squeezing his paper towel napkin into a ball. His appetite was suddenly gone.

Nikki dropped her slice of pizza and raised her hands. "No way am I letting that freaking scumbag P.M. make you look like an uneducated tramp, Mom. We need to set things straight. That sleaze deserves more than a spatula upside his cheek."

"Let it be," Cyndi said. "I know the truth and that's all that matters."

"Gotta go with Nik on this one, Mom," Noah said.

"People are quick to judge, and slow to forgive." Nikki said. "By the time the download is done, you, all of us will be made out to be some freaking lunatic alien pod people. You're already married to a terrorist, remember? No offense, Rich. We need the truth of what really happened to come out."

"What is important to me is sitting at this table and the pizza is getting cold." Cyndi said. "Now drop it."

Noah kept the snowball rolling, "We'll make a video, tell what Homeland Security did to me, and Israel did to you. We'll send it to my guy at NBC and the rest of them and-"

"No way, man." Matt said. "We put it on YouTube, put links on our Facebook pages, Instagram, and Twitter. It'll go viral in hours. The news people can pick it up from there."

Cyndi slapped the table. "I don't care what they say about me. It doesn't matter." She gave each child a stern look, drawing a line in the sand.

Rich swallowed a lump in his throat. He would cross the line - to defend her honor. "It does matter, Cyndi. It matters to me, to all of us. Those fucking

-- those commentators don't have a clue. That Prime Minister is still playing his games, protecting his ass and throwing you under the bus."

"Don't cross me, Preston. Only three people know what happened inside that War room, and nothing you or I or anyone can say will disprove what a Prime Minister says."

Rich pulled another slice of pizza onto his plate and gave her an impish grin. "You're probably right. But let's say I could figure out a way for the motes to transfer their recording of what happened inside that room onto the laptop. You okay with these social media fiends setting it loose?"

Cyndi took a sip of wine. She nodded. "If it's the truth, have at it."

Rich would remember this night. Remember his intentions of defending her honor. He would remember the pepperoni pizza dinner and the Ernest and Julio Chianti. Just as vividly as he remembered the night Andy switched off the television with his Cardinals finally beating the hated 49er's on Sunday Night Football.

And telling Rich he was gay.

He remembered opening his half-drunk mouth, telling his baby-faced son that gay boys didn't like football cause they weren't real men. Real men liked football, and women, and turn the fucking television back on.

Andy winced, his face turned beet red as if Rich had just slapped both cheeks, tears collected at the corners of eyes but never fell. Rich remembered sitting in the dark for hours, wondering where his cruel, hurtful words had come from, remembered every day of unreturned phone calls, voice mails, texts, misery, impotence and self-loathing, until Andy finally returned home eight days later, with enlistment papers.

Rich would remember this night's words just as vividly. He would replay the innocuous statement over, and over again.

Rich would regret them as much as he did his inexcusable words to Andy.

The mote's recording of Cyndi's time inside the War Cabinet room had been simple to download, at least on the motes' side of things. A marble of motes sat atop Noah's laptop and released a thread weaving its way inside a USB port. The laptop crashed twice - converting the enormous file required more memory than was available from the Windows operating system. Matt and Noah worked unsuccessfully for days, until giving up and transporting the laptop and seven - fifteen-gigabyte USB flash drives to the computing center at the University of Nevada in Reno. With the help of eager senior computer science students, the files were uploaded onto the schools Unix servers and opened to any student who wanted to take a shot at unlocking the huge quantity of data that was locked away. Computer geeks, bloggers, hackers all attempted to find the solution.

Two days later, Justin Patal, a systems analyst with Google hypothesized the recordings used a fractal-generating algorithm, and the key was simple – find the code for an object inside the room – something that stood out against the backdrop of code used by the dust. An anomaly - Prime Minister Dayan's finger - was discovered in the maze of programming and Patal's access to Google's armory of sorting algorithms opened the door.

The video sorted and compiled into Jpeg format, then compressed and uploaded to a Cloud-based server accessed by the Grapestreet restaurant in Phoenix. Public links were enabled, and the first five minutes of video was posted on YouTube. The Israeli Prime Minister appeared as a giant maggot, Cyndi Preston wielding a stainless steel flyswatter over his head. Six additional grainy, low-quality videos followed.

The Prime Minister of Israel disavowed the validity of the YouTube recordings that quickly exceeded fifty million hits. The sixty-five year old Prime Minister could only remember the angry Cyndi Preston beating him while he was helpless and trapped inside the dust cocoon. He was baffled by the sudden attack. But he stood by his version.

The U.S. President declined to comment, reserving judgment until further analysis of the video had concluded. Depending on the media program's political point of view, Cyndi was either applauded or vilified for what she did.

Conspiracy theories reserved for the National Enquirer played out in the mainstream media - of a terrorist now controlling alien technology for nefarious gains, or possibly an alien pre-invasion intelligence gathering. The 9/11 Truther Movement speculated an elaborate conspiracy was headed by the United States government as an excuse for the U.S. military to consolidate power.

The UN Secretary General emphasized to the television cameras that all alien technological information sent to the planet Earth was meant to benefit all people, not just Richard Preston, and certainly not exclusive to the United States. He demanded the U.S. government produce Richard Preston for the General Assembly to see and the Security Council to question.

Rich, for his part, was an abomination of God, or the antichrist, or the second coming of Christ, depending on which theologian or prophet you asked. Learning of Cyndi's Catholic roots, Pope Francis publicly offered safe shelter for the Preston family at the Vatican.

Speculation thrived in coffee houses, around office break-rooms, grocery store checkout lines, and family dinner tables.

Internet bloggers and pundits put forth questions, such as why Richard Preston would allow Cyndi to take such an aggressive action against the Prime Minister of Israel. And what was preventing an attack on the White House, or the Capitol Building? Preston was a subversive, claimed the House minority whip. Media outlets used, abused, extrapolated, dissected, and analyzed the claims of extraterrestrial nanotechnology, and whether it could exist in harmony with the human race.

World financial markets swooned in the uncertainty, losing a third of their value in just days, only to shrug off the loss and subsequently gain over fifteen percent at the prospect of wondrous new technology allowing tech companies to forecast unequaled growth.

Noah threw fuel onto the fire, calling the NBC anchor and telling him that Rich had almost completed his work with the alien computer. That night, the lead story of the network's nightly news show confirmed the extraterrestrial nature of the grey dust.

But where was Preston?

The question became a punning slogan of the Daily Show and Saturday Night Live.

⚔

Indicted on a grocery list of federal offenses, assault and battery of federal officers, and over 2000 counts of kidnapping stemming from the incident in Seattle alone, Rich was charged with crimes that would total over 25,000 years of prison time if given maximum concurrent sentences.

"Give me a freaking break." Rich said during a CNN Special Report about the post-traumatic syndrome experienced by a large number of residents isolated by the Seattle swarm. Americans were spoiled. Instead of returning to their daily lives, they claimed abuse and mental anguish for an incident that injured three people, a total of two broken legs, and a dislocated shoulder. Hundreds now claimed mental trauma - bullshit claims laying the groundwork for a personal injury lawyers to file a plethora of lawsuits.

Rich walked out the back door of the cabin into the frosty night and disappeared. What's one more crime with so many lawsuits already coming? A measure of justice was required. On Gurion, and Bulldog, and Big Ben. No way would Cyndi condone what he planned. But he might tell Noah, and Matt later, they would understand.

It was a shot in the dark, but with so much dust still dissipating in the sky over Seattle Rich had ordered a search of the entire area. Eleven days of nothing then the motes found David Gurion sleeping in room 6224 of the Olympic Fairmont in downtown Seattle. Biding his time, Rich used the dust like a hi-tech surveillance system, letting a small inconspicuous swarm track Gurion's movements. Bulldog and Big Ben had disappeared. Maybe he'd run a search for them in Israel.

Rich emerged into the stuffy hotel room carrying a baggie bulging with edamame pods – one of Cyndi's healthy snacks. He sat down in one of the suite's soft meeting chairs, a portal open and ready on his left. He put a salted soybean pod into his mouth and gnawed the beans out, and threw the empty casing at Gurion, asleep on the bed. Seven attempts to hit his face before a slick wet seed-pod found the man's cheek and stuck beneath his right eye.

Gurion moved quick, reaching for a chromed revolver hidden beneath his pillow. He rolled off the mattress and stood up, pointing the weapon at Rich's face. Gurion blinked the sleep from his eyes. The gun barrel turned white, capped with a white snowball of dust.

"I've always wondered what would happen if you shot a bullet into that stuff." Rich gnawed on another soybean pod. "Wanna give it a try." He threw the empty shell at Gurion. He suddenly disliked his own game.

Gurion's hairy chest was scarred by whip-like slashes. His black boxer briefs were slanted on his hips. He looked around the room but he kept the weapon aimed at Rich.

"Now, see, I always liked books that had endings with a twist." Rich gnawed another soybean. "You know, the kind you never saw coming? That's what makes a good book. Not that bullshit *you* think people want to read."

"Doing my job, Preston." Gurion's eyes were considering his options.

"Check your feet before you get froggy, Buckwheat," Rich said.

Gurion glanced down, and his eyes widened. A swarm of grey encapsulated his ankles and feet.

"Where would you like to write your final chapter?" Rich mumbled with a seedpod hanging from his lips. He stood up and wrapped the sandwich bag into itself.

Rich hesitated, all too aware that Cyndi would light into him if she knew. On the other hand, this was a man who threatened to gang rape her daughter. And besides, she had gleefully threatened to kill and eat the Prime Minister of Israel, herself.

He swallowed the last of the snack and ordered a thick layer of motes waiting on the white ceiling to cover Gurion. The substance wrapped Gurion's shoulders and arms, and Rich pushed the man backwards to fall into a wormhole exiting exactly where a National Geographic photographer had captured a head-hunters camp deep in the Amazon rainforest.

Rich stayed in the hotel room. Too hot, too muggy down there. Too many bugs.

The man had a chance to survive. Small chance but a chance nonetheless.

Rich returned quietly to the cabin, burdened by a secret only two men would ever know, one was probably fleeing blood-sucking insects that NatGeo had declared as intolerable.

⚔

Rich sat down after opening a portal and helping Nikki, Matt and Cyndi enter a quiet alley near the Eiffel Tower. He would monitor their every move, and be ready to jump at the slightest hint of danger. It was his face that summoned the sirens, it was his face that drew the suspicious eyes, and they were better off without his face calling attention to their visit.

Besides, foo-foo France was not on his bucket list.

Noah was busy on the laptop so Rich researched a file containing the schematics of a device larger than an aircraft carrier. Shaped like a long canister, the thing had hundreds of vertical and horizontal tubes crisscrossing like honeycomb. Viewed from a three dimensional perspective, the hollow tubes were cubicles, each divided again by solid partitions into smaller cubicles. The contraption didn't exist on this planet, but then neither did the motes until recently. He mentally licked his thumb and flipped through pages of incomprehensible diagrams, equations, chemical formulas, all written in unrecognizable mathematics. Sophisticated information the human race hadn't yet attained on its own.

Why so many dust probes? Why were they here? Why was this information stored in his head? Why did he control it?

A faint giggle. Like a child hiding in a game of Hide and Seek.

Andy! That you son?

Maybe he only imagined the giggle.

Noah raised his hands, flustered with the keyboard. "These symbols have no corresponding keystrokes."

Rich rose from the couch and moved to peer over Noah's shoulder. "That's what the song says."

"We gotta have something that'll prove what we're going to say."

"Just print out that song about the mammoth. That ought a keep 'em busy."

"No, you don't understand-"

"And I won't until the download is finished." Rich squeezed Noah's shoulders and returned to the couch.

Noah groaned and returned to typing on the laptop.

A muddy white Ford F-250 turned onto the rutted road leading to the cabin, and Rich watched through the picture window as the truck bounced and swayed on the puddled double-track, and onto the gravel driveway. Through the motes' perspective, he saw a big man wearing rawhide Carhart overalls and a wide-brimmed straw-hat meander up the stairs of the back porch.

Rich opened the door, surprising the man as he searched for the right key in a ring of many.

"Yeah?" It was all Rich could think to say.

"Well, hello there." The man scratched his grey stubble. "Deb said ain't nobody supposed to be here."

"We just rented the place, but we're leaving tomorrow."

"Well, okay. I'll come back tomorrow and put the place into hibernation. Sorry for disturbing, ya." He waved and turned to walk back down the porch stairs.

Rich closed the door and looked at Noah. "Gig's up"

Chapter 23

"I'm not sure I'll ever understand it," Rich said.

Musty dampness permeated the air of the doublewide mobile home. The brown shag carpet was splotched with dark matted stains and the armrests of the couch were tattered where Rich placed the yellow legal size notepad. He slumped back into the stiff cushions and put the tablet on his lap.

"I told you we need help." Noah turned around in his rickety kitchen chair and looked at Rich. "Let Matt find a math or physics professor at UNR who can decipher these symbols. At least get us started on the right path."

"And then what, the freaking Russians kidnap him, hold him hostage? We've been over this, everything I touch turns to…"

"Get real, Rich. There are people out there we can trust. Hell, let's go to the Vatican. This living like escaped convicts shit is getting old. And if you hadn't noticed, Mom doesn't want to spend a minute in this dump, and you're starting to look worse than when Andy died. Jeez."

Rich winced at the mention of Andy and pushed the tip of a ballpoint pen into the yellow foam of the armrest. "They're going back into that store again, the Ann Taylor one. Must be having a Christmas sale."

"Enough of the play-by-play. You're worse than Mom was when we were kids." Noah stood up. "Everyone's tired of waiting for the download to finish. Coming and going is great, but we have no life. I want my phone. I wanna meet some girls, have some fun, live a little. So does Nikki and Matt. We're living like hillbillies."

Rich looked around the room unable to disagree. "Go on."

Noah stood over Rich as if he was lecturing a child. "Maybe we shouldn't have gone public with that recording. The crap on the internet is unbelievable. You're a god, you're the Devil, you're helping aliens take over the world. It'll never stop. And Mom's included in every bullshit thread out there. Screw the download, waiting for you to feel what the motes feel doesn't matter anymore."

"Schedule the interview then. Because the first question he's going to ask is what's the dust doing here? And why me? Then I say 'I don't know, but maybe I'll figure it out after a good night's sleep. After that...'"

Noah flinched. "C'mon. That's not what I meant. Let's look at this like a business model. You know, the ones I'd tell you about when I was in college. The Preston family becomes a corporation, with you as the asset, the product. We sell and market your information to the highest bidder. Take the wormholes for example, you said it was a mass transit system. It'll replace cars, planes, even bicycles. We'd be rich beyond belief."

Rich started to say something, but Noah raised his hand wanting to finish.

"It's not about the money, it's about the power that money brings. Every company guards its secrets, and you're the secret. We hire security for you and Mom, everybody. We live like CEO's, or heads of state. Those guys are always targets, but they don't get assassinated, their security is too tight. And besides, we have the best escape plan imaginable."

Noah spread his arms wide with his palms up, eyebrows arched. "What do you think?"

Rich pulled the pen from the armrest's yellowed foam and considered Noah's proposition.

"And how do we get all this money?"

Moving closer, Noah said, "Like every other start-up. We find investors to inject capital for what we want to accomplish. Of course, we'll need to come up with a business plan, and projections, five-year growth plan of profits, all that stuff. And I can do that. And there's got to be thousands of guys who'd fund building some of this stuff. We talk to Bill Gates to get started."

Rich colored a drop of ketchup on his pants with the pen. "We'd make a lot of enemies too. Let's talk it over at dinner, when everyone gets back."

Rich was intrigued by Noah's latest proposal. And they did live like the poorest of the poor. Cyndi knew why, they all knew why, but it didn't help. But he didn't know what else to do either.

A smile widened on Noah's face as he stepped back to his computer screen. Noah turned to add one more point to his argument as Rich's notepad crashed onto the scarred vinyl floor.

His doodles on the yellow paper faded into the horrific vision of a dead woman lying on the ground. He could smell the copper tang of her blood.

Cyndi!

A rivulet of blood flowed along a grout joint of the tile beneath her still body. Her left hand was balled into a weak fist, her diamond wedding ring sparkling in the bright sunlight.

Without thought, Rich jumped into Arizona.

His portal exited into a group of people gathered around Cyndi's body lying outside the front door of the Ann Taylor shop. A sales-lady stood at the entrance, sobbing, biting her thumb.

Wake up! Wake up! This is fucking not happening.

Nikki was kneeling beside her mother. Sounds of pandemonium echoed in the open-air mall. Adults shoved children into the protection of a Pac-Sun store next door. Three chunky women shoppers ran with shopping bags.

Rich rubbed his forehead, and stared at two women cowering behind a concrete planter with Bird of Paradise and fiery orange flowers. The smell of cordite hovered in the air.

A hefty man in a black Jake's Crane and Rigging tee straddled the trunk of a woman, keeping her from reaching a revolver two feet from her outstretched hand.

"Get out of here!" Rich shoved through the growing crown of gawkers and rubberneckers. He fell to his knees. She would be fine, she just fainted. Brushing the hair from her eyes, Rich's lips stretched into a cadaverous grimace as he searched her face for life.

Her lifeless brown eyes stared back.

He closed his eyes. Not real. Wake up. Wake the fuck up.

"Stay with us, Mom." Nikki said in a hiccupping voice. Her right hand pressed on Cyndi's wounds, dark blood oozing through her white blouse. Nikki's canary yellow blouse smudged with blood still dangled a price tag from the cuff of her left hand. "It's okay Mom. Rich is here. Stay with us, Mom."

Nikki's tears were black with mascara.

He'd wake up soon. Even in dreams you still had to do something.

Rich slid his hands beneath Cyndi, his fingers sliding easily atop the smooth bloody tile. He lifted his wife's petite body with little effort and stood up. He was lost. And yet desperate to go somewhere, anywhere for help. A landmark, a sign, a red cross, anything. All his memories had disappeared.

Rich stared into Cyndi's unblinking eyes, powerless to act.

"We called 911. An ambulance is coming," said a female voice in the crowd.

The simple statement slapped Rich. An emergency vehicle. With help. And a hospital. It clicked. The memory of a brick porte-cochere shot into his head. A place he visited for a physical examination after being notified of Andy's death.

"Grab on!" Rich shifted Cyndi's weight in his arms and screamed, "Where's Matt? Where's Matt?"

He felt a tug on his shirt. "Go!" Matt said.

With the pull of Nikki and Matt on his t-shirt, Rich stepped through a portal and into a stinging funnel of hot wind. Cyndi's blood dripped off his arms and the wind splattered it as he ran into the shade of a red brick overhang. He ran past two senior citizens escorting a wheelchair-bound octogenarian into the waiting room of the Mayo Clinic in Scottsdale. A pleasant melody of Mozart or Chopin played from a baby grand piano in the center foyer. He slowed as two front desk attendants in black blazers scrambled around the quiet lobby desk and approached him. Neither offered help. They weren't what he wanted, or expected.

A tanned attendant blurted to Rich what he didn't want to hear.

"This is the clinic. You need the hospital. We'll call an ambulance."

"The hospital?" Rich said. "Fucking help her. Please."

The man stepped back. "You just missed it. It's a quarter-mile down the main entrance."

He had no memory of a Mayo Hospital, only the Clinic. Rich turned to leave the lobby, "Where? Show me!"

He followed the man out the glass doors and back into the wind.

"The next building. You can see it from here." The man pointed at a five-story brick building towering above the tall Joshua's and thick Mesquites.

Rich squinted at the building, shouted for a portal to open to what he prayed would be the emergency entrance. They emerged into an almost identical replica of the previous porte-cochere, startling a young couple pulling a reluctant four-year old boy inside. Nikki and Matt released his shirt as Rich charged into the building. He was beginning to struggle with the weight of Cyndi's body. He felt each drop of her blood fall from his forearms, like a tickle of death. Through sliding glass doors and into a lobby painted in soothing baby blues and beige. A Latino girl sat behind the admission desk, staring at her computer screen. Three rows of chairs held smatterings of waiting patients and family.

"I need a doctor!" Rich yelled. "I want a fucking doctor now!"

The receptionist raised her finger for him to wait and picked up the phone. Two female nurses wearing flowery scrubs poked their heads from behind rain-glass dividing the reception desk.

"Code blue, main entrance!" A heavy-set dark-skinned nurse yelled into a handset mounted beneath the granite countertop. She repeated the call. The three women disappeared. Seconds later, a nurse punched the button for stainless steel doors to open as another kicked the locks free from an idle gurney in an alcove. She rolled the bed over to Rich.

"Put her down."

Rich held her tight. She was his responsibility. He wouldn't let her go.

The nurse shouted at him. "Put her down!"

As he did, two men bolted from the double doors and pushed Rich aside. They were no older than Noah. The lobby's cold air-dried and tightened Cyndi's blood on his arms. The nurse pushed the gurney as the men ripped Cyndi's blouse open, exposing two gaping wounds above her right breast.

"GSW. Get an exam room ready. Call Bujols, we need him stat!" The clean-shaven intern yelled.

Rich watched helplessly as the interns raced Cyndi's gurney towards the open doors. He watched the intern feel Cyndi's neck for a pulse. The intern placed his stethoscope's chest piece on Cyndi's bloody breast.

Nikki squeezed his arm, placing her wet face on Rich's shoulder.

The automated doors began closing.

"I have no pulse. Get Bujols."

Chapter 24

Nikki dropped to the linoleum floor. Rich reached with a bloody hand, as if to soften her fall, touching her yellow blouse stiff with dried blood. He turned to Matt. "What the hell happened?" He instantly regretted his accusing tone, but he did not apologize.

Matt shook his head. "The psycho saleslady pulled a gun, saying some shit about Cyndi being an enemy of Zion, some kinda religious crap. Then she shot her. I think she was going to shoot Nikki, too, but her gun didn't fire …"

Nikki wailed.

Rich's chest tightened as he dropped to his knees. His sticky arms hurt and he wrapped her up. He motioned for Matt to join them and they huddled on the cold plastic floor. The sounds of children, and phones, and intercoms were lost in the surreal. He had no thoughts, no mechanical voices. Time stood still.

Until he heard the inevitable.

"It was because of you, Rich." Nikki said. "She wanted revenge and took it out on Mom."

Rich squeezed his children, and closed his eyes. It was the truth. His guilt, a demon spawned by Andy's death had been given a rebirth, rearmed with fresh pain and grief.

What the fuck was he thinking? Letting them out in public, after all that had happened. He was a fool. He bit his lip hard, tasted the copper tang of his own blood. His anger surged and tightened his throat. But there was no target for his rage but himself.

Why was he waiting for some doctor to return, like he was some stupid actor in a television drama. Cyndi was fine. They were fooling the fool. They were taking her away. To get at him again. Rich got up, balling his fists, and aimed for the emergency room's double-doors.

The doors spread open as if he willed it.

He pushed past a lanky man in sky blue scrubs coming out. Picturing Cyndi's brown eyes, he screamed. "Show me!"

Nothing.

He screamed again. "Show me, ya little prick!"

"Mr. Preston? I'm Dr. Adam Bujols." The nervous doctor offered his hand.

"Where is she? Take me to her or so help me God I'll rip this fucking place apart."

"She was dead on arrival. There was nothing we could do. We tried-"

"Bullshit. Show me where she is or…"

Nikki wailed an ungodly heart-wrenching moan.

"Take me now or…" His eyes blurred with tears.

The olive-skinned doctor wiped his hand through his short sweaty black hair and took a step backwards. Rich made up the distance with a sudden move and grabbed Bujols' collar.

The lobby's air grew hazy.

"Sir, the police have the building surrounded."

Rich grabbed Bujols by his upper arm and squeezed, then began escorting him into the hallway. "Where is she?"

The man motioned with an almost imperceptible nod. Rich motioned to Matt - to bring Nikki - and they followed him into the telescoping corridor of teal and turquoise. Rich caught a glimpse of blue uniformed security men peering around the corner of a four-way junction a few feet ahead.

This never fucking ends.

"Show me, dammit!"

He waited and the operating system showed him an image of Cyndi's face, just seconds before a man covered it with a baby blue sheet. He shoved Bujols aside and ordered a portal to open.

"Hang on!"

Matt grabbed his outstretched hand and Rich pulled them into an exam room. He narrowed his eyes and bared his teeth at the Hispanic technician attending to Cyndi. The chubby man raised his palms as if to surrender and backed out through the open half of a glass wall partition.

Rich shook free of Matt's grip and lifted the blue sheet. He swallowed hard. Dear Lord. The bullet's entry points on her right breast looked ugly, cratered, and stained in a golden yellow antiseptic. Bloody gauze and linens still tucked beneath her ribs and buttocks. Rich backed up a step as his hand reached out to touch Cyndi's cheek. It fell short.

Nikki came to her mother's side, wiping snot and black tears. "Oh, Mom." She began stroking matted hair off Cyndi's forehead. "It's okay, Mom."

Matt slumped down onto a hard vinyl chair and put his face into his hands.

Rich continued to back up, hitting the slick white wall and sliding down to the floor. It should've been him.

Make her come alive, God, please make her come alive.

Andy, make her come alive.

Rich put his face into his bloody hands then raked his nails across his forehead and cheeks. His chest heaved, his nose dripped snot and he heard a tiny voice call out, as if light years away.

She can play on, Andy said.

Incomplete data request. Download incomplete. The mechanical voice said.

He'd engrave a baseball bat with 'download incomplete' and shove it up the computer's imaginary...

She can play on, Andy said again, louder.

Talk like a machine. Speak its language.

"Query, how do I get Cyndi back? Andy says she can play on!"

Insufficient data upload. Isolation required.

Rich ignored a Homer Simpson security man watching him through the glass partition.

"Isolate her. Now!"

He stood up and pulled Nikki away from her mother.

The cop disappeared as the air turned foggy with motes emerging from tiny portals, to begin the self-replicating process. The air warmed.

Isolation incompatible. Biological construct expired.

"This biological construct needs life. Andy says she plays on?"

"Dad?" Matt said. "Andy says? What are you…"

"Hurry up, dammit."

Nikki flinched at his tone and frowned. Then her eyes widened. "Rich, if you can do this…"

Data input incomplete.

"Define data input required?" Rich said.

A long minute passed. The alien voice was mute but through the motes sensory input, he smelled Cyndi's lavender shampoo, tasted her blood, saw her white blood cells sitting idle. A faint thump, but he felt nothing more. The motes continued their scan of Cyndi. The sensation of touching her skin, stroking her silky hair, kissing her moist lips was lost with the incomplete download.

Transcendent isolation subroutine required.

"Trans-, isolate her, do it now!"

Though unseen by the naked eye, Rich sensed the pinpricks, billions of miniscule wormholes opening to eject a tiny mote instructed to isolate a deceased biological form. Rich heard the operating system's programming, sensing it through his ears or at least that's how he would describe the motes communication system. The motes hovered above their target and emitted scanning waves of light, each emission set to the smallest of definitions as the new system began mapping Cyndi's DNA. Each determination, trillions of bytes of data was transmitted to the growing consensus for compilation.

The cloud of motes hovering above Cyndi dropped like a blanket, and encapsulated her body.

Data compiled. Data currently stored within biological construct.

"What? What data?"

Data defining biological construct.

"You mean the information making Cyndi who she is?"

Yes! Andy said.

"The biological construct, reanimate it."

Biological constructs reanimation requirements complete. Isolation complete. Biological fluids required. Energy transference required.

"Specify requirements."

Construct requires fluid. Construct requires elimination of structures incompatible with animation. Construct requires transcendent energy.

"The construct's name is Cyndi, fucking remember that, Buckwheat." Rich said, then asked the system to repeat its requirements several times.

"I need a doctor in here, now!" Rich said to Matt. "Get any doc or nurse that can get an IV into Cyndi. Hurry, there might be a chance."

Matt jumped up and ran into the foggy hallway, then yelled. "I can't see out here. There's too much dust in the air."

A quick command and the air cleared, Rich sending the motes to attach themselves to the walls and ceilings. From the motes' point of view, Rich watched and heard Matt run down the corridor to what looked like a nurse's station, to be greeted by the wrong end of an assault rifle.

Two S.W.A.T. officers outfitted in black assault gear had fronted a gathering of nurses, technicians and interns waiting to attend patients in other rooms. Matt was grabbed by one of the cops, and shoved back into the crowd of hospital workers.

"I need a doctor or nurse," Matt whispered to a young nursing student.

"So do a lot of others but they won't let us pass." She said flicking her chin at the cops.

"Please we have to go. My mom needs an IV."

Dr. Bujols parted the crowd, unwinding a stethoscope off his neck, "Son, your mother is dead. An IV won't save her."

"Dr. Bujols," Matt said, mispronouncing his name. "You know who he is, don't you? If the computer says there's a chance then what the fuck do you have to lose?"

Dr. Bujols grabbed Matt by his upper arm and turned him away from the SWAT team. "Is it true? The wormholes, computerized nanotechnology, all of it?"

"I've seen it in action."

"And it can save the patient I just saw?"

"My mother. And yeah, it says it can."

"My God." Bujols leaned close to whisper into Matt's ear. "Follow me."

Both police officers guarding the hallway had their backs turned to the tightly packed group. Matt stayed on Bujols' heels as they bolted between the police and ran down the hallway, disregarding the shouts of the police officers to stop. Rich let a command to isolate the two officers die on his lips.

Bujols eyes widened as he stared at Cyndi's mote covered body. "How… what… how may I help?"

"Start an IV on her." Rich said. "Get some fluids in her."

"Why? And where?" Bujols asked. "She has no heartbeat… she can't… There's nowhere to insert a needle."

"There, Doc." Rich pointed at a funnel-shaped cavity forming above Cyndi's left elbow.

"Without her heart beating the fluids can't…"

"Let me give the orders."

Bujols shook his head but grabbed a needle, adjusted the drip on a clear plastic bag full of saline solution and started an IV drip into a dead body.

"Can you remove the bullets?" Rich asked.

"Holy Mother of God, this is madness. There is no…"

"He's not talking to you," Nikki replied to Bujols.

Affirmative. Energy transference required in conjunction with object rejection routines.

"Define energy transference." Rich watched Nikki wipe away a final tear.

Inert biological construct- A quick pause. *Cyndi requires cellular reanimation. Compatible transcendent energy data required. Active energy.*

"Where do I get the active energy?"

Biological clone.

"She doesn't have a clone, ya little…"

Compatible DNA required.

Rich locked eyes with Nikki. "Will her child's DNA work? It's the best I can do."

DNA compatibility unknown.

Rich understood the response but ignored it. "How do we transfer the energy?"

Donor requires isolation. Donor requires release of DNA energy.

"Define release of energy"

Blood.

"A transfusion of blood?"

Affirmative.

Rich looked at Nikki. "You have to give Cyndi a blood transfusion but the system needs to isolate you, too. You'll be covered like Cyndi and it's kinda…"

"Where do you want me?"

"Doc, start a transfusion from Nikki into Cyndi."

"It's too risky. Their blood type may be incompatible. Contaminated blood might back up into her system. She might-"

Nikki shot him a glare. "It's my choice. Now please start. Where do you want me?"

Bujols pulled the chair Matt had sat in and placed it next to Cyndi's gurney. He flew around the room gathering needles, tubes, and a metering gauge required for a blood transfusion. He pricked Nikki's hand with a needle and began a saline drip, then inserted another needle into the crook of her arm. Bujols hesitated as the dust funneled inwards to reveal another dime-sized spot of skin on Cyndi's right arm. He asked for more space for the connection, finding a vein would be difficult and Rich complied.

Bujols looked at Rich for confirmation then made the connection.

"Go ahead," Rich said.

The doctor turned the chrome valve allowing the red liquid to flow through a clear plastic tube.

"Stand back, Doc." Rich commanded the motes to isolate Nikki. "Don't worry, Nikki."

Bujols' stepped back, his mouth agape. The air fogged with dust, seemingly spewing from an unseen Genie's bottle. The dust gathered into a miniature thunderhead above Nikki and dropped, spreading like melted wax, coating her, thickening until only the red tube was visible.

"Now what?" Bujols asked.

"We wait." Rich wiped at tears clouding his eyes. "And pray."

ᛉ

Burdette shuffled the file of laboratory reports, field interviews, and agent summaries of the Winnemucca Man investigation destined for the archives. He couldn't concentrate, and instead glanced at the picture of Lt. Robyn Burdette receiving the gold bars of her commission. At his mother's bedside, he'd watched in amazement and his heart soared as she tapped the picture with her finger during a rare lucid moment. She recalled how proud she was attending the ceremony, and even remembered their celebration at a Chili's restaurant afterwards. His mother's brief return to the world was more than he'd expected but less than he hoped. He glanced at the quarter inch stack of papers authorizing an experimental new drug for the treatment of her Alzheimer's. He would sign them and mail them off, and with them a renewed sense of hope.

What else was there, but hope?

Scrolling through a list of unopened emails on his laptop, Burdette looked over the screen as Neesa walked into his office and grabbed the television remote sitting on the bureau. Burdette raised his eyebrows at the uninvited intrusion. The flat screen monitor on the wall opposite his desk turned sky blue and Neesa tapped in a change of channels. The screen showed the rooftop of a large building filmed from a helicopter at least a mile distant. A 'Special Report' label was flashing at the bottom of Fox News. A female reporter was talking quickly.

"Again, our source inside the Mayo Hospital has confirmed that Cyndi Preston arrived dead on arrival. Richard Preston carried the bloody body of his wife into the front entrance of the hospital approximately fifty-five minutes ago. Phoenix police have cordoned off the area and are evacuating all non-essential personnel. Cyndi Preston is reported to have suffered massive blood loss from multiple gunshot wounds. The shooting took place less than an hour ago at The District shopping mall in Scottsdale. Richard Preston has reportedly taken hostages inside the emergency wing."

Burdette looked up at Neesa, who was staring at him. "Find out who is in charge of the op at the hospital and get him on the phone for me." Burdette said. "And Neesa? Priority one."

He'd never met Cyndi Preston, but his chest still tightened. He recalled her gift, a simple sleeve of saltine crackers. A care package from Cyndi was what Preston had said. He was suffering from dehydration after being forced through a wormhole, and his emergency room physician said the water-retaining properties of the salt had possibly saved his life.

But it was Cyndi's boldness confronting the Prime Minister of Israel that had earned his admiration and respect.

Burdette closed the screen on his laptop and began to read the scroll at the bottom of the television monitor. He thought back to being stranded and sunbaked in the remote Arizona desert. With every opportunity to flee and leave him helpless with no means of communication or escape, Richard Preston had instead returned many times, with water, and finally Cyndi's care package.

Preston's happenstance story of wormholes and computer voices was incredible but Burdette believed it, believed the sincerity of Preston's words and believed Preston would have committed suicide to get his daughter back. Preston was a simple man, a lot of bluster, but he was no threat, unless he was backed into a corner. He was a little off kilter, and for good reason, but it was clear what the man valued. His family.

In return, Burdette followed the President's orders. He couldn't arrest or kill Preston but he could help him avoid capture by the Mossad. So he told Preston of his suspicions regarding Gurion. Lying helpless at the edge of a cliff, he only had two options - let Preston stroll into Gurion's trap like a naïve dope, or warn him, and hope the electrician could use the dust to outwit the Mossad. Cyndi's subsequent assault on the Prime Minister of Israel was unexpected.

And absolutely brilliant.

He had felt a rare and odd kinship to Preston during the helicopter ride out of the desert. One anomalous night in the middle of nowhere provided a rare insight. Burdette couldn't remember his own father, killed in an auto accident just after Robyn was conceived. He believed his father would've had the same loyal, strong sense of family that Preston displayed. His father would have laid down his life for Robyn, he just knew it, and it comforted Burdette in a strange sort of way.

Neesa came back into Burdette's office pointing at his desk phone. "Captain Alvarez on two."

Burdette tapped the speaker button. "Captain Alvarez, thank you for taking my call."

"I know who you are. I'm a little busy at the moment. What can I do for you?"

"Can you brief me on your operation?"

"Very quickly. No injuries to civilians, no hostages, but the dust is in play, a huge quantity in the corridor outside an exam room occupied by Preston and two of his children. At this time my officers have only taken up observation points. However, a doctor did return to the room containing Cyndi Preston's body and hasn't been seen since."

"Captain, I have a couple of suggestions if you would like to hear them?"

"Go ahead."

"If Cyndi Preston is dead you will be dealing with a distraught individual capable of commanding a substance I have encountered personally, and I'm sure you've seen on the news. That experience tells me you do not want to provoke him. Second, let the situation play out. I don't think he intends to hurt anyone. You will not be able to capture him and your only course of action would be to terminate him, and I do not think the charges pending against him warrant that course of action at this time. Would you agree?"

"Go on." Alvarez said.

"Captain, my final suggestion is simple. Do something he's not expecting. Give him the same consideration any grieving husband deserves. Offer him help."

Burdette thanked the man and hung up the phone. Cyndi's death could finally push Preston over the edge, but why was he still in the hospital?

He looked up at the television and sat up. A CNN reporter standing in front of the Israeli Knesset building in Tel Aviv was reporting the Prime Minister had reactivated over 350,000 military reservists. They were ordered to report within twelve hours. The Israeli Defense Force was on the highest state of alert.

⋏

Bujols returned with two clear plastic bags of saline solution. Swapping out the nearly empty containers dripping fluids into both Cyndi and Nikki, Bujols finished the chore and looked at Rich.

"Maybe you could tell me what is happening inside those… those cocoons?"

"I guess I owe you that much, Doc. And before I forget. Thank you. For helping me." Rich walked around Cyndi's body, touching her shell with his fingertips.

"As for what's going on inside there, I can only guess. The probes are moving through Cyndi's bloodstream with their engines burning, warming and pushing her blood, circulating it for her. That's why we needed the saline. It's keeping the blood from drying out. Right?"

Bujols nodded his head in a noncommittal slant and waited for Rich to continue.

"I think her blood is being oxygenated through a form of osmosis the probes are using inside her lungs. Nikki's blood is providing living cells for the motes to copy onto Cyndi's dead cells, reanimating them. That's why the DNA needed to be compatible."

Rich stopped, surprised by his own intuitive analysis. Or was it his? "That's not quite right. I mean, the motes copy the energy signature of each living cell and transfer it to the dead ones. They can't create a signature but they can… mediate the transfer of an existing one. I think Nikki needed to be isolated in order for the motes to copy every facet of every cell in her body. Doc, if your educated brain had the stuff knocking around inside mine you might find a cure for cancer."

"Sounds impossible, Mr. Preston, and she's been dead for almost an hour now. The brain deprived of oxygen will degrade, memory functions will be lost, synapses lost, she cannot be the same person she once was."

Matt rose from his chair and stood next to Rich, his eyes trained on him, waiting for the answer.

Rich shrugged. "What are we, Doc? What is anything, everything? Information. Information stored in cells, tissue, plants, rocks…, anything…, alive or dead. What are you? A collection of cells containing information unique to you. The cells themselves may not be unique but what they contain, small variations of DNA, well, that's what makes each of us… different. That information is never lost. It might be burned, or destroyed, but the information only changes form, it's never lost. The motes scanned Cyndi's body for that unique information and the system told me it was still intact."

Rich put his arm around his son. "I'm not a religious man, but what I think the computer was talking about was our soul. Cyndi's hadn't left yet. The energy signature of her soul had degraded, but was still intact, and it is now being reanimated with a similar one. Nikki's. That's why the DNA had to be a close match."

"That sounds incredible, but how does it occur at the cellular level?"

"The blood, Doc. The body is nourished by the stuff. Every cell in Cyndi's body is being scanned for damage, then the cells are reanimated by some kind of copy and paste routine the motes use, and then they let 'em back into the bloodstream. They copy the energy signatures of Nikki's cells and paste them into Cyndi's cells. Just the unique energy signature though, not the actual DNA. It's the spark of life."

"That's a fascinating concept, Mr. Preston. But how do these motes know to do this? What are these motes?"

"Computers, Doc, very, very small computers. Think of them this way. Thirty years ago the first computer was the size of two of these rooms, and could do only basic math. Your cell phone is a computer, and has a million times more memory and processing power than that one. Where do you think computers will be in another fifty years? One tiny mote is just like one of our PC's, times a thousand. Together, like what you see in front of you, it's fucking awesome. Put billions of motes together and, well…, whoever sent these things here have taken computers to a whole new level."

"So what's…" Bujols gestured to Cyndi. "Where are we?"

"Status?" Rich asked.

Compiling.

A slim Hispanic nurse walked into the room carrying four plastic bottles of water, then dropped them to crossed herself. "The police thought you could use some…" The nurse took a tentative step closer to Nikki's shape. "Dr. Bujols, what in God's name are you doing?"

"Nurse Martinez, you are witnessing a miracle." Dr. Bujols said with pride. "A miracle of technology."

The sun began to fade outside two small windows but the artificial light never changed. Rich stood watch over two bulbous white shapes, joined by a crowd of maintenance personnel, patients, interns and nurses in the hallway, intent on witnessing the conclusion of a miraculous unfolding.

Two male interns had donated clean scrubs tops from their lockers for Matt and Rich to change into. Rich refused. His arms folded across his chest, he remained wary of the audience gathered outside the room, pressing up against the room's glass partition. Many held cell phones above their heads to capture the event on video and pictures. Police officers remained at the rear of the assembly, conversing amongst themselves, appearing content with just observing. Rich was unconcerned. Three point one seconds to isolate the room from the hallway.

Compilation complete.

Rich swallowed. "Remove isolation."

The murmur of the crowd hushed at hearing Rich's words. The motes covering Nikki and Cyndi began to disband and float, rising at a languid pace. The crowd gasped. The enigmatic coating rose in tendrils up to the ceiling, spreading like the smoke of a fire. Rich moved to Cyndi's side, swatting the dust away as if it was a pest.

Nikki appeared and began to stretch her neck, then her legs as if she was waking from an awkward nap.

Rich hovered over Cyndi. He looked at the bullet entry wounds, pink and cauterized, and each crowned with a tiny pile of copper bullet fragments. Rich pinched the pile of metal and tossed it all to the floor. He heard the shutter clicks of camera phones and quickly covered Cyndi's torso with a clean sheet handed to him by Bujols. Brushing the matted hair from her forehead, he leaned close and studied her eyelids, her crows-feet. Tiny, lingering streams of motes floated out of her nostrils.

Was that movement behind Cyndi's eyelids? He wiped her eyelashes free of dust with his still bloody finger.

Cyndi gasped, sucking air in with three quick breaths. Her hand grabbed Rich's wrist and held tight, then relaxed. She blinked, and showed him big brown eyes full of life.

"Preston," she whispered in a raspy voice.

The sound was too much and he laid his head gently on her chest and cried. He felt her hand console the back of his head. Cyndi's hand. He melted into the sensation of her fingers stroking his hair.

The tender moment was interrupted by raucous applause from the crowd. He couldn't fault them. They had witnessed a miracle. Rich picked his head up and gazed into Cyndi's eyes then kissed her chafed lips. He wiped away the tears streaming down his face, and whispered, "Egbok."

Her arm still attached to the transfusion tubing, Nikki reached over to hold her mother's hand. Bujols began methodically disassembling the blood connection. Nikki looked pale, drained of blood, her face clownish with the black streaks of dried tears. She raised her face to the mote-covered ceiling, and smiled, and thanked God.

Rich stepped back to allow Dr. Bujols to examine Cyndi. Matt put his arm around his shoulder and squeezed. Tears fell from Rich again as Bujols listened with a stethoscope to Cyndi's throbbing heartbeat. Rich didn't need a stethoscope. He heard her heart drumming via the motes that remained in her blood.

Nikki rose from her seat and embraced her mother.

Rich felt an overwhelming sense of satisfaction, of peace. Deeper than any he'd felt since before Andy died.

The hallway was bustling with camera shutters clicking, and congratulatory voices rising with excitement. The din brought him back to reality and he eyed the police at the rear of the crowd, but they too had joined the celebration, high-fiving each other and radioing information with broad smiles on their faces.

"Thanks for all your help, Doc," Rich said loud enough to be heard by the crowd. "But we need to leave. Going home."

"Cyndi needs to be under a doctor's care for a while. Just to make sure all is well. You should leave her here for a few days while we run some tests."

"You've seen what's going on outside. The government still wants me and it's probably a zoo outside the front door. Sorry, but that's our lives now, Doc."

"I understand, sir. Then may I suggest that I go with you... to monitor Cyndi's recovery? If that's okay?"

Taken aback, Rich studied the man's eyes blinking rapidly behind his black Harry Potter reading glasses. Bujols lifted his chin as if to allow Rich to judge his intentions, then he offered his hand. "Mr. Preston, do you know what you have done… I mean, what these motes have done but Cyndi still needs a physician's care and I am offering that care."

Having a physician present as Cyndi recovered would be the smart thing to do. And Nikki might need him as well. The doctor had never questioned him, well, not with any pushback. His intuition was that Bujols was a man thirsty for new knowledge, maybe a bit of adventure. Rich didn't refuse his handshake a second time.

"Do you need to bring anything?"

Bujols beamed like a child going to Disneyland. "I had Nurse Martinez prepare everything. I mean, assuming you would grant my request that is."

Rich gathered the IV stand with the drip line still inserted into Cyndi's arm and asked Matt to help Nikki. Cyndi's gurney would maintain the physical contact needed for the wormhole transit.

"Matt, help the good doctor with the side effects."

"Side-effects? What… oh yes, I read something about that…"

Matt grabbed the man's hand and led him through the invisible doorway.

Chapter 25

The chrome IV stand tipped, its wheels catching on the threadbare carpet. Cyndi lay quiet with a blank stare on her face, the thin hospital sheet was too flimsy for the cold damp air. Nikki followed, using the gurney for support. Matt came through and pulled Dr. Bujols to the kitchen sink.

Noah jumped out of his chair to his mother's side. Bujols retched and vomited onto dirty plates and utensils piled in the sink.

"They said you were dead." Noah stroked his mother's face.

"Noah," Cyndi whispered.

Rich was unsure if her acknowledgement was a greeting or a question.

"Noah, this is Dr. Bujols." Rich pointed at the man gripping the sink. Bujols hand rose in acknowledgment, but hovered over the sink, the tap water splashing onto the scarred countertops and yellowed linoleum.

"We need to get your Mom into bed and let her rest," Rich said. "I think Nikki should sleep in there, too. We can talk after."

Four men fussed over two women, helping them into the master bedroom usually shared by Noah and Matt. Rich felt embarrassed, by the small bed, the peeling vinyl wallpaper, dirty clothes stacked on a dresser and piled up in a dark corner. He stayed with Bujols for an hour as the doctor fussed over his patients, checking IV lines, and body functions, receiving answers to his questions from Nikki, but nothing from Cyndi.

Following Bujols out of the room, he turned the light off and pulled the door closed behind him. Bujols surveyed the dark living room, decrepit kitchen, dinette set and small television. A distilled water dispenser gurgled. The room was cave-like, lit by two fluorescent light fixtures, both buzzing with a single greyish bulb. Matt switched on the lights of a tiny Charley Brown Christmas tree shedding needles on top of the television.

Bujols joined Rich at a small dinette table, and Noah closed the laptop.

"My patients are both sleeping and seem to be doing fine, considering," he said. "Mr. Preston, exactly where are we?"

Rich scratched his eyelids and looked at his two boys. "We're just outside Sisters, Oregon. Pretty close to Bend."

Bujols placed his stethoscope on the plywood table gently, as if the surface was dirty or contaminated. "This is how you live?"

"We do what we have to, Doc. Couple of things need to play out then, well..."

"Then let me be blunt, Mr. Preston. As Cyndi's physician, this place..., this home as you call it is not conducive to her recovery. Or Nikki's, as well. It's dark, damp, and I can smell the mold in the air. I'd rather you take them back to the Mayo for proper monitoring and recovery. Both will need post-traumatic stress evaluations and counseling. Cyndi may require physical rehabilitation as well."

Rich chuckled humorlessly. "I'd love to, Doc, but Cyndi would be taken into custody before you could change her IV. And that ain't gonna happen."

"Before I forget. I changed IV's but we will need to resupply tomorrow, no later than noon. Is there somewhere else we might take her? Somewhere infection or even pneumonia won't be a concern. A little sunnier, warmer, someplace she can have room to move about?"

The elation of Cyndi's revival faded, and Rich studied his hands still stained red with Cyndi's blood. He rubbed his eyes and slid his hands up to rub his forehead. "How about Bora Bora, maybe Hawaii? I can take you wherever you want to go, but it won't last. We have no credit cards, no cell phones and we're about out of money for food. I'm sure your bill will send me into bankruptcy so what do you suggest? I check us all into the Maui Hilton?"

Bujols looked to Noah and Matt but they kept their eyes down, as if they were studying one of Rich's doodles inked on the wood.

Bujols shook his head. "Then let me stay the course I have set upon, to be bold. I have plenty of suggestions. Let me start with this one. I have access to a decent-sized beach house in Carlsbad, California and I would like to offer it to you and your family while Cyndi recuperates. It is large enough for the five of you with excellent views of the ocean. Cyndi will benefit enormously from the new location."

"Kind of you, Doc, but I think they'd find us pretty quick since they know you're with us. We'd just have to move again in a few days, and that wouldn't benefit Cyndi, now would it?" Rich straightened his shoulders. He had this same debate with every member of his family. But mostly with himself.

"Rich, may I call you, Rich? I just witnessed a medical miracle. You have, within you, the ability to provide knowledge to the world that will change the future of mankind. Running solves nothing but to prolong an inevitable conclusion. You have more power than you realize. Use your knowledge as a bargaining chip, make the government drop any charges. What you have is unimaginable, unprecedented. Wield it!" Bujols' excitement intensified, and he stabbed the table with his finger. "At some point you have to make a stand."

Noah chimed in. "He's right, Rich. Mom told me what you had said in Newport before she went gunning for that Prime Minister. Rich, we gotta keep going with that attitude. You know the words. Say em. Just like I did twenty years ago."

Rich sighed and picked at a divot in the table's particleboard with his bloody fingertip, remembering the scene. Kurt Russell sporting a classic handlebar mustache in the role of Marshall Wyatt Earp in the movie Tombstone. Earp's face twisted in a snarl, angry from the murder of his family, screaming at Ike Clanton, screaming that he was coming for vengeance.

Trancelike and without emotion, Rich said the words. "And Hell's coming with me."

Noah slapped the table hard and stood up. "And Hell's coming with us, dammit. Hell's coming with us. We make a stand. For Mom."

"Hell, yeah. This running sucks, Dad," Matt said.

Rich looked at each of them, reading the eyes like he was a poker player gambling for a life-changing pot, and he was. Their lives were at stake.

With another heavy sigh and a slight nod, Rich asked Bujols. "Let's hear some of these other suggestions."

⚔

Rich walked out onto the redwood veranda carrying two tumblers of iced tea. The sky was blue and streaked in a checkerboard of wispy contrails. He paused and waited. Noah and Bujols were sitting at the patio's oblong wrought iron table having a lively conversation. He cleared his throat and said. "Call your anchorman, we do the interview."

Noah stood up. "It's complete?"

Rich smiled. "We do it when I get back. Immediately. Or I'll chicken out." He turned and continued with the drinks. His short nap had ended with the two words from the computer he longed for.

"Don't forget," Noah said behind him. "You have to announce the IPO of the Preston Companies, we need the publicity."

Yeah. Yeah. Yeah. Rich groaned. He was sick of his own name, sick of seeing it on the television, sick of hearing it in Noah's business plans. His own last name seemed to knot his stomach. In a sunny corner guarded by shrubs and a wrought iron fence, he placed one glass on a small table next to Cyndi and handed the other to Nikki. The girls relaxed on redwood chaise lounges, enjoying a magnificent view of a sedated Pacific Ocean, sea breezes drifting leisurely into their faces. They looked serene in the new surroundings.

"Hamburgers tonight, Rich?" Nikki said.

He nodded, and smiled, accepting their smiles as soft feminine gratitude. He would let Noah tell them the download was finished.

Rich stared out to the horizon. He felt oddly isolated from his family, each with a different purpose, each with goals he didn't share. Since her miraculous resurrection, Cyndi had been different, in ways that gnawed at him. She'd taken charge as they packed their meager belongings for the move to California. But she also seemed irritated, as if she blamed him for bringing her back into the world of the living. Maybe Andy had found her, to escort her on the journey to heaven, and maybe she didn't want to return. Then again, being murdered might make anyone resentful.

When he asked her about it, she placed her hands on his cheeks and assured him that she treasured every waking moment with her children. He wanted to dismiss the nagging perception of indifference to him as a side effect of Valium prescribed to mitigate any possible post-traumatic stress. She was animated, involved, and dominating in regards to the children's activities. Just as she'd always been. With him, she seemed distant and detached, like she was punishing him for something.

Her behavior had prompted his return to Touweep, to delve into the mechanics of her resurrection with the operating system. Nothing of the primitive campsite remained except one steel tent peg wedged in sandstone. He sat on his perch and pondered the power of the motes to revive a life force. Bringing a dead woman back to life went against all laws of the natural world, and he was certainly no Christ. But if the computer could resurrect Cyndi then why not Andy?

His cryptic conversation with the robotic voice finally revealed the price Cyndi paid to break the sacred covenant with death. *Unrecovered transcendent energy - 16.84.* Almost seventeen percent of her soul was lost, replaced by motes swimming in her bloodstream and emitting a generic spark of life. Thinking of her as some sort of cyborg was distasteful and revolting, but it was up to him to determine how much she would continue to pay to deceive the ferryman.

Regardless of his ungodly act, Rich refused to debate his decision to bring her back to life. A woman who loved the unlovable, a woman whose loyalty was beyond reproach, a woman who found goodness in a man where there seemed to be none. He shelved any misgivings.

Holding onto the railing, Rich watched Matt on the beach forty feet below, talking to two girls. Brooke quickly joined them, carrying a piece of driftwood. Matt kicked sand and twirled in a pirouette, his hands harmless in his pockets. The three laughed and began a leisurely stroll down the serene beach. Rich nodded.

Billions of motes hidden inside the house, outside in the lush landscaping, hovering overhead would combine with the trillions camouflaged in the beach's sand at a moment's notice. For protection. A surveillance system. A weapon system if needed.

His security needs satisfied, Rich opened a portal and disappeared.

He left the beach house and stepped onto a dirt path leading to a rocky point overlooking the Pacific Ocean on the island of Lanai. His sudden appearance startled a young couple returning to the resort. He apologized and leaned into a stiff headwind, aiming for lava outcropping that caused the angry surf to rise and spray sheets of water into the wind.

He stared at turquoise tidal pools fifty feet below and wondered if he would survive the fall. Would the motes resurrect him as they did Cyndi?

The voice said nothing.

Following a trail worn smooth on the lava rock, he found a clearing nestled in dense island brush, sat down like a shaman and started a conversation with the operating system.

"Download complete." Rich whispered, and added a caveat. "Book form. Table of Contents."

Ready.

Rich scrolled through an assortment of file markers in his head, pausing at a chapter containing the almond shape of a single mote, its exterior pitted in intricate designs. Even its heat-resistant coating contained code. The image only confirmed what he'd suspected for months. The diminutive motes were computerized probes sent to collect data, digitally recording anything, everything they encountered. The world was a big place, and he understood why so many motes were required.

He replayed a recording of a mote swarm capturing a woolly mammoth and he was suddenly immersed in sensory data as they cocooned the behemoth, penetrating the beast through its orifices to analyze blood, organs and brain. Rich shuddered, living the mammoth's terror, as the swarm examined hair, ivory tusks, saliva and the bacteria it contained, and even the tiny ticks infesting the skin. The scent of urine and musk was overpowering, and he stroked the animal's coarse, oily hair. The strange symbols he thought were the musical notes of a song were actually the culmination of the data collected about the animal. The song played in his mind like radio static. His vision faded as the trillions of motes released the creature and drifted off with the wind. Rich asked the operating system for answers to the questions intuition had already answered.

"Why are the motes so small?"

Exploration requirement. 96.2 percent of biological ecosystem contained within mote exploration parameters.

"You mean the motes explore everything? Big, but mostly the small stuff, because that's where most of the ecology is? You need small computers?"

Affirmative.

"After just feeling and smelling a woolly mammoth, I'm gonna guess that's the purpose of the isolation command."

Affirmative.

"Explain the isolation routine." Rich asked.

Isolation subroutine executed by unfulfilled search parameter.

He wished Andy would return and talk to him. Help him understand the operating systems technical crappola.

"So if the system wants to study or analyze a large creature, the motes isolate it and store information. Correct?"

Affirmative.

"Every time I had you isolate someone you were also analyzing them?' Rich said considering the future possibilities. "That's how you knew so much about human anatomy, huh? You've studied us for thousands of years? Down to the subatomic level?"

Affirmative.

"One little mote's memory can't store everything. What happens when the mote's storage is full?"

Replication subroutine executed. Alpha N plus one continued.

"You make a new one and continue? What happens to the original?"

Dormant stasis.

"So you gather all this data and send it back to your home world?"

"No, Dad, this is the most totally cool part. The most awesome thing ever."

"Andy!" Rich jumped up. "Where have you been? I've missed you."

"I… I was afraid. I was unsure of who, even what I was. But after I got access to Nikki's and Mom's memories I understood and… well, here I am."

Rich was beaming. "You mean you're a more complete program?"

"No, Dad. It's really me."

Rich didn't like the computer's trickery. His smile faded.

"I know what you think. But before you go all ape-shit, will you take a walk with me?"

An amber light burned in front of his face, and he saw the total darkness beyond. This wasn't a wormhole of his asking.

Without hesitation, Rich stepped through.

The desert night was cold and utterly silent as they stepped from the portal. Sand dunes and scrub brush for as far as the tiny amount of moonlight allowed him to see. Just ahead sat a sparkling dome, alive, crawling with geometric symbols and letters - a machine resembling a camping tent.

"Billions of motes constructed the device, with millions of trillions more waiting in the sand." Andy said.

Rich felt Andy put his arm out and point. Felt it as if he did it himself. They walked up to the device.

"We were ambushed just over this dune. Olly and Wick didn't know what hit them. I went down with one in the leg and another in my chest. There was a firefight, and I don't think my platoon could reach us until the perimeter was secure. I crawled to this spot. That's when the motes came out of the sand and isolated me. They couldn't save me, they wouldn't have anyway unless they were programmed or ordered to."

Rich looked around. Sand and scrub, and an alien machine. He started to ask him a question.

"Just hold on for now. But they did the next best thing, I guess. They copied me. My DNA, my memories, my personality. But it had no context. No basis. And it wasn't complete, so it was sent back for analysis."

"Sent back where, son."

"The Designer's home planet. It's not far." Andy giggled. *"In galactic terms. That's when they got the idea to use me, to get to you. Or, rather, persuade you. They haven't had much success. Seems the Alpha implant drives most people crazy."*

Rich nodded. "And drives the insane back to life."

Andy chuckled again. *"It's just what you needed."*

"Why, Andy? Why all this stuff in my head? Why you?"

Rich felt Andy smile.

"Not sure. Maybe because I died here. They're fascinated with us, Dad. And the stuff they sent are gifts. A trade offering. I'm a gift. Everything you'll need is downloaded. And the best part is they'll clone me a new body when we return."

Rich looked up at the cloudless night and infinite stars, and he felt tiny and insignificant. But no, he wasn't insignificant. He might be the most significant person on the planet. And then he felt determined. To accomplish what Andy and the Designers required. He spotted the Big Dipper and followed the cup's edge to locate Polaris, the North Star. He felt Andy help direct his eyes to the star he was searching for.

He would need all the help he could get. He would extend his hand to the President of the United States, and ask for his help. If the man refused his invitation to meet like gentlemen then, well, screw him. Presidents could be treated just like Prime Ministers.

Rich walked back to watch the Hub grow fractionally larger as it added a sheet of motes rising up off the sand.

"This is where they need to come, to learn, and complete the final stage of the Designer's mission." Andy said.

"Where exactly are we?"

"Bum-fuck, Iran. At least that's what my squad had called it."

"Andy, what I said…I want…need…"

"I heard ya, Dad. Remember I grew up again, in your head." Andy giggled again. *"I know you love me."*

Rich wiped at his eyes then dug his hands into his pockets from the cold air. He had his son back, and there was no reason to pursue the manner of his physical death. Quite the opposite. This barren plot of sand would be his new Touweep.

"Did I hear Nik say she was making hagamer's?"

And they went home.

Rich emerged onto the deck of Bujols' beach house. Andy chattered nervously as if he was juiced by some kind of alien Red Bull. Just nerves, probably, and there really wasn't anything for Andy to be nervous about. The smell of grilled turkey burgers wafted to his nostrils and his mouth watered. The sun had dipped to the horizon, calming the sea breezes, and painting an impressive backdrop of orange and gold spikes shining from a distant thunderhead.

Rich admired Nikki and Cyndi looking sun-soaked and renewed at the patio table, half-eaten burgers on their plates. Their shoulders were bit too red but they were smiling. Bowls of potato chips, macaroni salad and baked beans waited on the table. Noah, Matt and Bujols were discussing something as Rich walked over to Cyndi and kissed her on the cheek.

"Good trip?" she asked.

"The best." The simple question made him smile. Her eyes sparkled with flecks of green, but the furrows of her crow's feet had disappeared.

"A benefit of Nikki's blood, Dad." Andy answered his question.

Famished, Rich walked into the kitchen.

"I eat and then we go!" Rich yelled back to the crowded table. He grabbed a bun and began to create a masterpiece.

Cyndi slid up behind Rich and whispered, "You want me to make you a plate?"

He turned and faced her. "You mean, while I clean up and shave?"

She shrugged then put her face onto his chest.

His Cyndi would've said yes. His Cyndi would've scoffed and said, 'Of course you'll shave.'

Tell her, Dad. Andy yelled in his head. *Tell her.*

"Go sit down and enjoy." Rich said. "I'll be there in a sec."

Noah shouted a reminder to announce the formation of the Preston group of companies. Rich made his meal and came to the table.

Noah ended a call. "It's all set. Thirty minutes and we go live. Adam thinks he'll have to beat investors off with a stick."

Rich pulled out the last remaining chair and sat. "Adam?"

His face flushed, and he suddenly felt like an idiot, as Matt and Noah nodded towards Adam Bujols. He never asked what Bujols' first name was.

Rich eyed Noah. "So when does this company start making money? I got something I want to build."

Rich spooned a generous helping of beans on a plate dominated by the large burger. He eyed Cyndi, waiting for her warning glance about speaking with his mouth full of food. She picked at her food with a placid expression. He puffed out his cheeks and exhaled, setting the burger back on the plate.

"I have something I need to share before this interview. And I would like it kept private." He eyed Bujols' then each of his children. He cleared his throat.

"Andy's… alive." He waited, watching their reactions. "The thing in my… part of the thing in my head is Andy, his personality, his memories." He expected to be interrupted, but they sat in stunned silence and wouldn't meet his eyes. Rich smirked. They thought he had finally gone over the edge.

"What did Andy say about me dating Joey in high school?" Nikki asked.

Andy giggled. Like he always did when he'd beaten you in a game of anything. *Tell her Joey was looking to get lucky and she was wasting her time. And tell her to forget the boob job.*

Rich repeated Andy's words.

Nikki inhaled. "He was in my head, wasn't he? When I was inside that stuff, I felt him, but I just thought…" She looked to Cyndi.

"And you're not going to believe the rest of it." Rich leaned back in his chair. "And it's why we need to put this company on the fast track."

He never raised a hand to halt anyone's questions as he described his trip to Hawaii, and then the desert of Iran. Telling them Andy was alive in his head was enough to make them sit back in their chairs. He told them how Andy had evolved using his memories, and how he had matured almost overnight by using Nikki and Cyndi's memories he'd stolen just days before.

He leaned back, wiped his chin, and told them what the motes and the operating system wanted with him. He told them what he would do but not why. No one would know of Cyndi's incomplete resurrection, not her, and especially not her children. No one would know she was half the reason he would complete the Designers' mission.

He told them to hurry up and get dressed. The interview would begin in just minutes. And he would stun the world - just as he had his family.

▲

At 9:07 Eastern Standard Time on Thursday, the National Broadcasting Company interrupted the two-hour season premiere of Donald Trump's All Star Celebrity Apprentice in order to broadcast a live interview with Richard Joseph Preston. Given a thirty-minute heads-up, the BBC, Al-Jazeera, and almost every mainstream cable news programs agreed to NBC's stipulation of displaying its colorful peacock logo in the lower left corner in order to broadcast the live interview.

The interview, replayed over three million times in the first week, turned modern civilization into a mosh pit of religious, political, and financial posturing - picked apart word by word, by pundits, by scientists, by politicians, and translated into twenty-seven different languages.

Noah was spot-on in his prediction, Rich did like the television reporter almost instantly. He was greeted with a firm handshake and genuine smile. But it was the attention Brian Williams showered on Cyndi that solidified his opinion, asking about her health, offering her a bottled water or perhaps a chair to sit in. Years ago, Rich might have been jealous, maybe have taken the handsome Buckwheat aside and asked him if there was someone else he might want to fuss over. He couldn't blame the anchorman for focusing his attention where it ought to be - on a beautiful woman.

Rich tugged on the stiff collar of his business shirt, and swatted at the jabbering of make-up artists and technicians to watch Cyndi's face light up as if she had been voted homecoming prom queen. She giggled, and beamed her beautiful smile to the assistants and producers surrounding her. Rich swallowed a lump.

He was the center of her attention, once. He had been the focus of her beautiful brown eyes, once. Rich suddenly realized what Cyndi had lost when she died. And what he had lost.

The missing seventeen percent of her soul was…. him. The worst part of Cyndi had always been him. Floating in heaven and then suddenly called back, she chose to shuck the cancer in her life.

His mouth went dry and…

Dear Lord.

It's not like that, Dad.

He watched Cyndi glowing in the attention, watched her laugh, then watched her blush. He saw a woman who'd given her life to him, and he vowed to make her whole again. Noah's company would provide all the money he needed, would provide the means to hire the engineers, computer programmers, and the ship-builders. Hell, maybe he would buy NASA. They would definitely be required, and he should be able to afford it.

He would do what the Designers wanted. All of it. To find Cyndi's love again.

The lights were bright and hot, the goofy foam microphones floating above his head seemed stupid, but Rich told Brian the truth. He left little out of his story. The truth was the easiest to retell.

"People are nervous about this dust, *your* dust according to you." Brian said. "Tell me something to ease the public fears."

Rich shook his head. "The dust is like our Apollo missions or Voyager, or the Mar's Rover, machines sent to explore other planets. The alien Designers have been exploring our world for a long, long time, and they're finished. And they want the data they've collected returned in a…. a special way."

"Returned how?"

Tell him, Dad. This so freaking cool. Tell him!

Rich wiggled in his seat. "I'm just the first. Another eight thousand or so will get downloaded with data and make the first crossing, to their home-world. It's a trade. Their technology for our experiences."

"I'm not following you. Why?"

"Think about it. We take only pictures with the probes we send out. The Designers acquire it all, every little microbe, every little sight, sound, taste and smell. They want the data returned in the five dimensions we can give it, they want to experience it through our five senses."

Rich glanced at his family. "I have the design of a ship, a spaceship, an ark actually. It's floating around inside my thick skull. I'm gonna find the money and I'm gonna build it. And I'm gonna go. Finding eight thousand volunteers to go with me will be easy."

Rich told his only lie. "Why? Because they picked me. Plain and simple."

Brian Williams put his finger to his ear. "Rich, I have to warn you-"

"I know. SWAT has entered the lobby. Guess it's time to go. Another reason why I'll do what they want, huh?" Rich stood and took out the earpiece. He waved to his family to join him.

Noah pushed through the crowd and confronted Rich. "You're supposed to announce the IPO of the Preston Companies. Jeez, Rich."

Rich grabbed Noah's upper arm and squeezed. "I got it. Chill." They locked eyes and Noah's face softened. It may be Noah's company but he would know who the real boss would be.

Rich yelled over the growing chatter of the crowd. "Mr. Williams?"

The studio noise died.

"How would you like to be the first reporter to travel to the West Coast using the Morgan Company's first venture?"

Rich slanted a questioning look at his son.

Noah beamed.

"The Andrew Preston Memorial Transit System would like to welcome you as its first customer. Complimentary, of course."

Andy whooped it up. Rich took Cyndi's hand and squeezed it. He smiled and looked at each of their faces. He saw twin-grins, and eye's glistening with tears, and his own forgiveness.

Seven weeks late, but Christmas had finally arrived.

The End